REJECT

ACADEMY OF MISFITS BOOK 2

BEA PAIGE

Reject Academy of Misfits – book two

First Published: 28th October 2019
Publisher: Kelly Stock
Cover by: Everly Yours Cover Designs

For the ones who spent their lives trying to fit in.
You were never a reject. Those people just weren't the right fit for you.

Find your family, Bea xxx

"Some people are nobody's enemies but their own."

~ **Charles Dickens, *Oliver Twist.***

PLAYLIST

It is no secret that I listen to music whilst I write. Some authors like to write in utter silence, I'm not one of them. Music is my muse. I have been known to write, listen to music and sing all at the same time! Oftentimes music will inspire an idea and it's no different for this series. Delinquent (book one of Academy of Misfits) was inspired by Billie Eilish's Bad Guy. This playlist has grown somewhat since Delinquent to include songs for Reject!

Below are my favourite songs from the playlist that were perfect for Reject..

Listen to the full playlist on Spotify HERE

"Slow up," by Jacob Banks
"Let Me Down," by Jorja Smith and Stormzy
"Two Punks in Love," by bulow
"Sex on Fire," cover by Blame Jones

“Normal,” by Sasha Sloan
“Both,” by Headie One
“I hate u, I love you,” Gnash featuring Olivia O’Brien

PROLOGUE

My mum once told me that the bravest sailors weren't the ones who sailed through the storm, but the ones who remained in port whilst it raged out at sea. I never really understood what she meant by that, until now.

For seventeen years I succeeded in standing back and watching that storm wreak havoc, never once venturing into the expanse of the ocean like a large proportion of kids on my estate had done. Unlike me, they were drawn into the glamour and the notoriety of joining a gang. Some did it for the promise of a family unit that they didn't have at home. Some did it because they were too weak or too vulnerable to say no, while others did it because they were bored. And some, like Eastern, joined out of sheer desperation.

I chose to stay away.

It's true, I might've been the delinquent kid that everyone saw when they looked at me. I might've gotten into trouble with the law, but I refused to set sail into a storm that wasn't of my own making. I refused to join a gang. The way I saw it, whatever trouble I got into was on *my* terms and not for some self-proclaimed gang leader with a skewed view of the world and their own set of rules. I never wanted to be beholden to anyone but myself, and above all else, I always wanted *more* out of life than the hand I've been dealt.

Maybe it was my mother's fault for filling my head with far-fetched stories, but I wanted what was on the other side of the storm. I wanted what lay far, far beyond the horizon. Deep down I'd *craved* the life my mum used to tell me about in her stories. It gave me something to focus on, to dream about, even if it wasn't real. Ironic then, that I'm now a part of the life I worked so hard to avoid, trying to protect the people I love from falling victim to it.

And all because my love for a makeshift family meant I couldn't stand back and watch the storm anymore. I must set sail right into the heart of it because I love Eastern, Tracy and Braydon enough to do something about their situation. They might not be my blood, but they are my family and I won't abandon them in a time of need.

Pity the same couldn't be said for my own parents.

In my lowest moments over the years, I've daydreamed about my dad returning to rescue me. Mum had always claimed he never knew of my existence, that he was just a stranger, a one-night stand. But she'd spun a tale about that too. Over the years, when she didn't think I was awake, I'd hear her crying for the man who'd left her when she was eight months pregnant. I'd overheard her telling a friend once how he'd promised to return, to take care of us both. He never did and my mum refused to speak of him to me. That was one story she'd refused to tell no matter how often I'd begged her to. I think, in part, her addiction began in earnest with him, though I suspect it also had a lot to do with her running from her terrible upbringing. Maybe my father was the straw that broke the camel's back. Maybe she would've become an addict regardless. There's no way of knowing.

But her refusal to talk about him led to an unhealthy obsession of my own. I've spent many lonely nights awake and wondering who my dad is. The absence of my dad's name on my birth certificate led to many dead ends over the years, leaving me frustrated and angry. Not even Tracy knows the identity of this mysterious man who'd fathered me. Maybe he was the drug dealer who supplied my mum with heroin and kept her addiction alive even when pregnant with me. Maybe he *was* just a regular guy she'd picked up for a one-night stand, who entertained the idea of being in our lives then ran when he realised my mum was nothing more than a junkie. Maybe he really was a Chinese emperor.

I've often imagined my dad returning to find me. In my fantasies he's a handsome, though faceless man driving into my estate in a flashy sports car, promising me the life I'd always dreamed of and apologising for abandoning us both. He would grovel and beg my forgiveness and I would make it hard for him in the beginning, but eventually I *would* forgive him. In every fantasy I've ever had, I'd climb into his car and we'd drive off into the sunset to a new life where gangs weren't terrorising the neighbourhood and my only chance of survival was to join them or commit a crime ending up in prison so I wouldn't have to.

But life just doesn't work like that.

Not for me.

Not for the girl who's always carried the storm inside her.

You see, my mum had failed to understand one important fact: you can't observe the storm from a safe distance when the storm is already a part of you. We all have our roles to fill. I'd just been avoiding mine for a lot longer.

ONE

“Asia, are you listening to me?” Tracy asks, her forehead creasing in a frown.

“Sure, I am,” I say, placing my fork and knife back down on my plate. This is our last meal together before Eastern and I must return to Oceanside. She’d made my favourite: macaroni cheese. Warm, delicious and filling. It reminds me of a gentle hug and stability. It reminds me of *home*.

“You’ve been quiet all day. Are you thinking about your mum?” she asks gently.

If only she knew. I’m not thinking about my mum. I’m not even thinking about the fact that last week I turned seventeen. I’m thinking about the fact that in a few minutes I’m jumping on a train with Eastern and heading back to Oceanside. I know what I’ve got to go back to do and why, but that doesn’t make it any easier.

“Yeah,” I lie.

She frowns, her eyes welling with tears. “She wouldn’t want you to be sad, Asia.”

It’s a statement I’ve heard Tracy say several times over the years and as much as I love her, it pisses me off. “*Really*? She never seemed to care much about anything other than her next fix when she was alive. What makes you think she'd give a shit about how I feel now she's dead?"

"She loved you… she loved your brothers," Tracy whispers, her hand reaching for mine. Her eyes sad, so fucking sad. I can't look into the face of it. I can't deal with pity even if it is from someone I adore.

"No, she loved *heroin*. She didn't love us." I stand abruptly just as Eastern walks into the kitchen.

"Lissy…"

"How are my favourite ladies?" he asks, looking between us both with a frown. "Everything okay?"

I sigh. "Everything's fine." And it is. I've long since gotten over my mum's abandonment. She overdosed. I found her cold, dead body. I'm over it.

Except, of course, I'm not.

I remember that day so clearly. It's etched into my soul and carved into my heart. A bloody tattoo that beats every time my heart does. A permanent reminder of what I've lost, of what I never really had in the first place. Mum had been lying glassy eyed on our threadbare sofa clutching hold of the teddy bear she'd bought me for my birthday, a needle still embedded in her arm. The second I'd found her I knew she was dead. The room had been cold, so cold in fact that ice crept up the windowpane on the inside. It's funny how I remember that part so clearly, the tiny ice crystals making a pretty pattern on the glass. I think I thought them beautiful, as though Jack Frost had found his way into our home and dusted the windows with his touch. I'd whispered her name, and whilst warm air had huffed out of my mouth, nothing had left hers. Gone. Just like that. She was thirty-four.

"I shouldn't have brought it up." Tracy stands, pulling me into her arms and enveloping me in her warmth.

"The cold, I can still feel it now," I mutter, somehow caught between that moment and this.

"Oh, love." Tracy rubs my back and I cling onto her, fully aware that this has suddenly become an emotionally intense moment with Eastern looking on. It's rare for him to see me quite so vulnerable. But things have changed, and somehow I'm not so afraid of Eastern seeing this side of me.

"I'm always here to talk," Tracy says.

I nod my head, muttering my thanks. In some ways she's the only mother I've ever known. Some days I wish she really was my own flesh and blood, but then that would make Eastern my brother and I couldn't have that. I love him in a way you shouldn't love a brother.

"You smell good," I say after a while. A random statement, but the truth, nonetheless.

"Not like bleach you mean?" She laughs, drawing a smile from me.

"No, not like bleach," I agree with a laugh of my own.

I clutch her tighter, breathing her in, not ready to let go just yet. Not ready to leave the comfort of this kitchen that is warm and welcoming and so much like home. Since moving to Eastbourne, Tracy no longer smells of all the cleaning products she'd had to use in her poorly paid cash-in-hand job. Now she smells of fresh soap and lemons. That alone makes me happy. I'm thankful at least that Chief Inspector Crown made good on his side of the deal and got Tracy a new house and enough financial support to take care of Braydon who's currently taking a nap in the front room in his brand new, made-to-measure wheelchair. They're happy here and that's all that matters.

"Well, whatever perfume you're wearing, I'd sure like to bottle it," I mutter.

"Stop, you'll make this old woman blush."

"You're hardly old, mum," Eastern says. "You're only forty-three."

"Soon I'll be forty-four and then I've got no hope." She laughs, shrugging off her low self-confidence with a wave of her hand. She totally deserves to find someone to love her. Maybe while living here, she will. Tracy is still a good-looking woman with dark hair and eyes like Eastern but with a heart-shaped face and cupid's bow mouth. She looks her age, has fine wrinkles and slightly greying hair, but she's still attractive. Very much so.

"We've really got to get going soon," I say, pulling free from her arms. "I'm sorry I couldn't come earlier than today, but I needed to make sure Sebastian and George settled okay in their new home in Hull."

"They're good?" she asks me, her eyes welling with tears. I know she misses them too.

"Yeah, they're good." I bite on my lip, my head dropping as tears well. I miss them so much.

"You are loved, Lissy. You do know that, right?" she blurts out, clutching me by the shoulders.

I nod tightly. "I do."

"Good, then that's what matters the most." She grins, her face lighting up with happiness as she looks at Eastern over my shoulder. He traverses the table and pulls Tracy into his arms, holding her against the broad expanse of his chest. He's a whole head taller than her now and because she's so slim, she kind of disappears into his hold. "Love you, mum."

"Love you too," she replies, her voice choking. "Oh, did you get it?" she says after a beat.

"Get what?" I respond, looking between them both.

Eastern nods. "Of course I did. Let me grab it." He leaves the room briefly, returning with a bright red gift bag. "Matches your new hair colour," he observes.

He's right, it does. I dyed my hair the day after leaving Oceanside for the Christmas break. New hair, new me, or some shit like that. Maybe I just like the colour.

"Take it," he insists, offering the giftbag to me.

"You didn't have to get me anything…"

"Yes we did. You turned seventeen last week; now you're as old as I am. We can get into clubs legitimately now…"

My eyebrows pull together in a frown. "You generally need to be *eighteen* to get into most clubs, Eastern."

"What I meant was we can get into the clubs because we actually look eighteen. Hell, I even look twenty-one," he says, flexing his arm muscles. Embarrassingly, my mouth goes dry and my skin flushes at the sight of his toned arms. Though I hide my appreciation well.

"Bighead." I roll my eyes and curse him out, as is customary when his ego inflates enough to fill the room. *Of course* he looks incredible. I know that, and he most definitely knows that. Eastern is handsome with his swathe of perfectly styled dark hair, cut short at the sides and long on top. His brown eyes are so rich you'd happily pay to stare into them. Eastern's growing into himself, if you know what I mean. That short time in juvie made him grow up fast both physically and emotionally. He's still the same Eastern I've always known, but there's a weariness within him that just wasn't there before and quite a few bulging muscles too. Pretty sure he spent most days away working out.

"There'll be no clubbing, or doing anything *illegal*," Tracy says sternly. "Keep out of trouble, okay?"

"Promise," we agree simultaneously, both knowing that we're going to break that promise sooner or later. Trouble isn't something either of us can avoid. It seeks us out then grapples us to the ground until we admit defeat or fight until we can't anymore. I catch Eastern's eye and he shuts down the emotions I know he's feeling.

"Good, because I really can't face either of you going to prison."

Her eyes well up with tears and she shakes her head, sniffling a little as she wipes them away. "I'm sorry…"

"Don't, Mum. It's okay," Eastern says as they exchange looks. Hers is filled with shame and love, his with fierce loyalty and forgiveness. But I know Eastern better than he knows himself. He might have already forgiven his mum for everything she'd ignored, but that doesn't mean to say it didn't hurt that she did, that it still doesn't hurt. There's no denying the fact that Tracy turned a blind eye to his drug running. It might have only been Mary-J in the beginning, but it soon escalated into the harder stuff. She knew what he did and pretended she didn't so that the money he earned could be used to take care of Braydon's needs. It's quite a cross to bear, for the both of them. Don't get me wrong. I love Tracy unconditionally. So too does Eastern. But that doesn't detract from the fact that she should've steered him in another direction before now. She should've stopped him. Circumstance had given them both an impossible choice.

"I'm sorry, love," she repeats, more quietly this time.

Eastern shakes his head roughly, though his voice is gentle. "No apologies, Mum."

He gives Tracy an easy smile, papering over the cracks with his grin. There is a conversation they need to have, but I'm guessing now's not the time. He turns back to face me, giving me all his attention.

"I'm sorry it's a bit late," he says, finally handing me the gift bag, which he's been clutching tightly in his hand, before pressing a kiss against my cheek. It's just a quick peck, but it makes my skin flush anyway. If Tracy notices my reaction, she doesn't let on.

"You've been busy helping Tracy with the move and I've been busy with Sebastian and George over Christmas break. It's no big deal."

"So the little rugrats are good then, yeah?" Eastern asks, fondly.

"Yeah, they're happy," I say. I'm glad they're being looked after so well by their foster family, but it kills me that their happiness is a direct result of someone else's care. It should be *me* looking after them. I'm their big sister. I'm more than capable at seventeen than my mum ever was during her 'sober' periods when the authorities returned us to her care. It's complete bullshit social services won't let me look after my brothers now just because I'm still classified as a 'minor'. I'd bet my soul that most people haven't lived through half the things I have in my life and yet I'm still deemed incapable of looking after my own flesh and blood because of my age.

"They had a great Christmas. The move to Hull has been good for them. They're doing well, they're *safe*," I say, emphasising the fact. Eastern captures my gaze and nods in understanding. After we made the deal with Crown, I'd made sure that my brothers were protected too. Spending all my time with them over the break has been amazing, but I can't deny how much I missed Eastern. Being around him now makes my heart swell with both love and fear. There's so much I need to tell him.

"Yeah? That's good, Alicia. I'm glad they're okay."

I smirk. "Asia, arsehole."

"Asia," he repeats with a roll of his eyes, "Open the damn present."

"Yes, open it!" Tracy says excitedly. She's practically hopping on her feet now.

"Thank you," I say automatically, clutching the gift bag to my chest. I don't even know what I'm thanking them both for, but whatever it is, I know I'll love it. Presents aren't something I get very often so no matter what I receive, I always appreciate it.

Tracy claps her hands together and grins. I've never seen her look happier, or as stress free. Living here has done her and Braydon a world of good. The fresher air, a home that accommodates Braydon's needs, and most importantly, somewhere far away from trouble, makes for a happy home. It makes my heart fill with joy and confirms that

Eastern and I made the right decision back in Mr Carmichael's office two weeks ago.

"Stop stalling, Lissy! Open it!" she insists.

Moving aside the tissue paper, I see the long edge of a photo album. "What's this?" I ask, pulling it out and placing the empty gift bag on the kitchen table.

"Why don't you take a look," Eastern urges me. He's gnawing on a fingernail, a sign he's nervous about my reaction to their gift. It's a cute look on him. I open the front cover, my heart skipping several beats as my brain finally catches up with what my heart instantly reacted to.

"You didn't?" I whisper.

"I thought you might like it, you know, after everything…" Eastern starts, his voice trailing off as he remembers we haven't given Tracy the full story about what happened to my sketchpad. I don't even like thinking about it honestly.

"I can't believe all that work was destroyed because you left your sketchpad in the rain. *Silly, Lissy,*" Tracy gently ribs, bringing a smile to my face with her cute name for me. She's the only one who can get away with calling me Silly Lissy. Eastern smirks at the nickname, but I ignore him.

"You should be more careful with your artwork. It's precious."

If only she knew the half of it. That arsehole Monk had known how precious those sketches were to me and destroyed them anyway. I'd considered telling Tracy, but Eastern and I both agreed that her knowing the truth would only cause her worry and anxiety and she needed that shit like a hole in the head. So, we made up a story about how I left my sketchpad in the rain.

"This is amazing. I totally forgot about this," I whisper, genuinely taken aback as I trace my finger over the rough sketch of my first attempt at my tag. It's gone through many changes over the past three years but this one is special, given I drew it the day after my mum passed away. That was the day I decided not to be bound to my past. That was the day I became Asia. I flip through the album, my throat constricting with every turn of the page.

"You kept them all?" My voice is choked with emotion.

"Of course, I did. *You* drew them," Eastern answers solemnly.

I'm enraptured by this gift. Overwhelmed, actually. Every single page is filled with drawings I've done over the years for Tracy and Eastern. From funny little doodles on scrappy bits of paper to more detailed sketches that I'd given them and forgotten about until now. I can't even begin to express how much this means to me after all the sketches Monk destroyed. I look up, catching Eastern's eye. He holds my gaze, and for a beat it's just him and me alone in the kitchen. The world stops as my tattooed heart beats with hope of better things to come. Then my shoulders drop when I remember what I'm returning to Oceanside to do.

"What is it? Don't you like it?" Eastern asks, self-doubt leaking into his voice.

"Do I like it? I *love* it!" I exclaim, tucking the album under my arm and hugging Eastern for a second time. We hold onto each other a beat too long, and I can't help but press my lips lightly against the curve of his neck. Eastern shudders beneath me, his fingers gripping hold of my hips as he reacts to my closeness and show of affection. We haven't had a chance to broach the subject of 'us' these past couple weeks given we've both been so busy. The few hours left before needing to be at Oceanside might be the only chance we get to talk.

"Well, that's just perfect then," Tracy says, snapping us both out of the little bubble we've found ourselves in. "One last group hug, then you need to get to the train station. I don't want you late for your first day at school, Eastern. You need to make a good impression."

Eastern chuckles. "Mum, I love your enthusiasm and all that, but the new term doesn't officially start until tomorrow. We're not going to be late."

She waves her hand in the air. "Still, this is your chance to do things over. This is our chance to make a new life. I'm proud of you, Eastern. Now that we're out of the estate, things will be better. I *know* it." She beams at us both, throwing her arms around our shoulders.

"It will be better," I promise her, knowing in my heart that for Tracy, Braydon and Eastern it has to be. But for me…? I'm not so certain.

TWO

Three weeks earlier

"So you're really going to do this? You're going to join Camden's crew?" Eastern asks me as we leave Mr Carmichael's office and head out of the main building's front entrance.

"Are you kidding me? Of course I'm going to do this. When have I ever backed out of a promise?"

"I know… *shit*, Asia. This is fucked up." Eastern stops on the top step, his shoulders slumping as we wait for Chief Inspector Crown to finish talking with Mr Carmichael. It's well into dinnertime, and the rest of the students are eating. I can hear the usual cacophony of sound coming from the dining hall. When I look at him he's wearing a pained expression on his face, one that I immediately want to soothe.

"I can handle Camden."

"Maybe so, but can you handle gang life, Asia? Can you handle the expectations? It isn't just Camden you need to deal with, it's the rest of the crew too."

"You're not wrong there," I confirm with a wry grin. My hands go automatically to the spot on my chin that's still coloured with the now yellowing bruise. The second I press my fingers against my skin, I regret it. Eastern frowns as his gaze narrows in on that point.

"What the fuck happened?" he grunts, grabbing my hand and pulling it away. He brushes the pad of his thumb against the still sore spot. I wince.

"I dealt with it…"

His eyes become slits. "Camden?"

"No, a kid called Monk. The arsehole's still in the hospital. He won't mess with me again."

"Motherfucker!" Eastern shouts, looking at me with regret, anger, guilt. I reach for him, squeezing his arm.

"No, don't do that. It isn't your fault."

"You joining Camden's crew is my fault. I'm not sure I can live with it, Asia. We should go back in, tell them the deal's off the fucking table…" Eastern moves to return inside, but I grab his arm, shaking my head.

"Hush," I say, stepping forward and glancing around me before leaning in to whisper in his ear. "I'm okay with this, and you'll have to be too. It's the only way we can protect everyone, ourselves included."

"That makes no sense, Asia. You're not protecting yourself by joining Camden's crew."

"I can deal with a little short-term pain for long-term gain, Eastern. I *can* do this."

"Here you are protecting me again," he continues. "You kept your mouth shut about the fact I was with you at Mr Patel's shop and now you're going to join Hackney's Hackers for me. I can't let you do it… Mum and Bray will be okay now that I've talked. You could've said no to the rest of it. Fuck that, I should've made you say no."

I squeeze his arm, lowering my voice. "I'm not backing out,

Eastern. This is the end of the conversation. We can't discuss this here. Camden can't know about the deal we made. No one can. *Not ever*."

Eastern sighs heavily, pressing his cheek against mine. "I'm sorry for all of this bullshit, Asia. If I could turn back time I would change what I did in a heartbeat."

I pull back, clutching his face in my palms. "And leave your mum to support Braydon on her own? No, you did what you thought was right, there's nothing wrong with that. Even if I might not have agreed with your choice, I understood it."

Eastern places his palm over my hand and presses his eyes shut. A familiar gesture that tells me he's barely holding on to the emotions he's feeling. "It was still a stupid thing to do," he admits. "Now look where we are."

"Maybe so, but we don't have the luxury of going about things the legal way. You were desperate. I *get* it."

Eastern sits down on the top step and pulls out a packet of cigarettes, lighting one up. He draws in a deep lungful before expelling the air on one long breath. I take a seat next to him.

"You're not allowed to smoke on the premises," I say evenly, knowing full well I do the same, just not so obviously. I hang out of my bedroom window like a badass. "Do you want to get in trouble before you've even started?"

He nudges me with his shoulder. "Seriously, Asia. I don't think one cig is going to get me expelled and sent back to juvie, especially not after all the information I've just given Crown."

"Good point." Shuffling a little closer, I lean my head on his shoulder and rest my hand on his thigh. He kind of stiffens, then relaxes. He's not really used to me being so touchy-feely. Honestly, I'm not used to it either, but it doesn't make me move away. I've missed him way too much to be self-conscious now. Besides, we'd shared a pretty hot kiss not more than a few minutes ago and he's my best friend, and I hate that he's leaving me again so soon. All of that counts towards me not giving a shit about what anyone thinks if they happen across us right now.

"I've missed you," I murmur, my fingers tightening around his thigh.

"I've missed you too, so fucking much."

I shiver a little. Maybe from the cold, maybe because I'm just so fucking overwhelmed.

"You want my jacket?" he asks me.

"Nah, I'm fine." And I am now that he's here, now that he's *safe*. Kind of. I'm more than aware just how precarious his position is given all that he told Crown about the King. Eastern never met the King in person, but he heard about him enough. Whoever the fucker is, he's bad news. Ruthless. The latest *King* in a long line of them apparently.

Honestly, I want to ask him more questions about this faceless criminal, about what the fuck went wrong that day Eastern was delivering drugs. But right now, I don't want to spoil this moment together. I know, just as well as he does, that time is precious. He's going to be leaving soon with Crown, returning to Oceanside in the new term. That horrible thought is only tempered by the fact that in another week I'll be out of here too and able to see him, Tracy, Braydon, and my brothers again when we finish for Christmas.

At least I've survived the first term… just about.

I'll be able to tell him all about my time here when we've got more than a few minutes together. For now, sitting with him in companionable silence will have to be enough.

"This place is pretty fucking impressive. It's a goddamn palace. You sure Queenie doesn't live here?" Eastern asks eventually, stubbing out his cigarette beneath his boot.

"That was my exact thought when I first arrived, but unless you count the couple of marble statues with a crown of ivy and tiny dicks in the gardens out back, then no, she doesn't."

He chuckles, that ease I feel around him always, returning.

It doesn't last long.

"That fucking shit will kill you," a voice I know so well says.

We both turn to face Ford who's currently leaning against the wall behind us. I wonder how long he's been standing there.

"Who the fuck are you?" Eastern growls, standing.

I stand too, twining my fingers with his.

"Ford," he retorts, zeroing in on our clasped hands. "I'm a friend of Asia's, and you are?"

"Not someone you want to fuck with."

Ford glances between us both. Eastern grips my hand tighter, refusing to let go.

"Ford, this is my best friend, Eastern. He's one of the good ones, okay?"

Ford narrows his gaze on me, and for the briefest of moments I find it hard to breathe. I really, really don't need a pissing contest right now.

"I'll be the judge of that," Ford remarks, pushing off the wall and taking a step towards us both.

"Yo, Ford, what the fuck are you doing out here?"

We all turn to watch Sonny step outside, Pink and Kate following him.

Oh, fuck. This wasn't how I wanted Eastern's first introduction to my new friends to go down. Sonny stills when he sees Eastern, then gapes a little.

"*You're* the brick shithouse Asia drew," he blurts out. Kate and Pink eye Eastern with interest.

"No, Sonny. This is Eastern. My *best friend*," I repeat, ignoring the fact that Eastern is glaring at me. I know we're more than that now. But I can't very well tell them he's my… what? Boyfriend? That doesn't sound right, not when I've kissed both Sonny and Ford. I wanted more time to figure this shit out. I'm not ready to explain myself, not now. Not like this.

"Ignore dumb nuts here," Pink says, smiling generously as she shoves Sonny aside. She holds out her hand for Eastern to shake. "We aren't all Neanderthals carrying around clubs ready to knock out the nearest female and drag her back to his cave."

Eastern mutters something along the lines of '*let him fucking try*,' which makes this whole situation even more awkward. I glare at Pink for bringing up my precarious situation, but she just shrugs her shoulders.

"What *both* Sonny and Ford meant to say was; *it's nice to meet you*."

Sonny grunts and Ford makes a weird growly noise. I ignore them both and grimace as Eastern takes her hand and shakes it. Thank God for a little oestrogen to temper the testosterone going crazy right now.

"I'm Pink, and that's Kate," she explains, pointing to a rather bemused Kate.

"I can introduce myself, you know," Kate snaps, crossing her arms and scowling. She's doing that thing she does when she isn't sure of someone. Her resting bitchface is on hyper alert. Eastern clocks it and scowls.

"We're friends of Asia's," Pink rambles on, trying to fill the tension with light-heartedness. "I didn't know they let in visitors. Aren't you the popular one?" She winks at me and I know *exactly* what she's thinking, because I'm thinking it too. I have three boys interested in me, four if you count Camden, and I'm definitely *not* doing that.

"He's not visiting. He's joining," another voice says.

For fuck sake, could this get any worse? Think of the devil and the devil will appear.

"Camden," Eastern says tightly.

"Eastern," he retorts just as tightly.

"Prick," Sonny mutters. That draws a scowl from Camden, a smirk from Eastern and a heart stutter from me. Ford just grits his jaw tighter.

Jesus, now all I need is for Monk to suddenly turn up and this shitshow is going to turn into a shitstorm of the likes none of us have seen before. Eastern must sense my anxiety because he releases my hand and scrapes it through his hair.

"Well as much as I'd like to stand here and play getting to know you all, I'm needed elsewhere." He turns to me and pulls me into a hug. A hug that lasts a lot longer than it should given the circumstances. I daren't look any of them in the eye, I'm not sure what reaction it's going to trigger.

"Speak soon, okay?" Eastern asks when he eventually pulls back. He brushes the lightest of kisses against my mouth, presses his forehead against mine then walks away.

"Soon," I agree before he disappears into the building, presumably to find Crown who I hope is hiding given Camden is right here.

Sonny and Ford have apparently lost the ability to speak, but scowling? They seem to be doing a very good job of that. Camden just nods as though confirming some thought inside his head.

"Catch you later, Asia," he mutters, before turning on his heel and heading inside.

I literally have no words. None.

"Well, that went well." Pink grins, looking between us all. Then realising I'm about to have a coronary, she slides her arm through mine and steers me towards the annex. Kate catches up with us both and nudges me with her shoulder.

"Bloody hell, Asia," she says. "What are you going to do about that?"

I look over my shoulder at Sonny and Ford who seem to be having a hard time moving, let alone chasing after me and demanding an explanation.

"By *that*, I'm assuming you mean Sonny, Ford, Eastern and…"

"And Camden?" she finishes for me with a scowl that I choose to ignore.

"… I've no fucking idea."

"Oh man, you're in deep shit now," Pink retorts.

Deep shit? You don't know the half of it.

THREE

Present day

"Fuck, that was close!" Eastern says as he flops down onto his seat. I chuck my bag in the overhead rack and sit down next to him.

"I told you it was platform five. Why don't you ever listen to me?"

"Because I'm a plum…"

"With a capital P," I finish for him.

"With a capital P indeed," he retorts with a broad smile. "I've fucking missed this. Do you know that?"

"What, me taking the piss out of you, and you just… taking it?" I bump him with my shoulder, winking.

"Ha, ha. You know what I mean. You're the only one who can make me smile, Asia. The only one who makes everything okay," he admits.

"Yeah, I know," I reply gently, suddenly finding the big, fat, balding man occupying the seat two rows down very interesting. I know we're overdue for a very important conversation but knowing that and going through with it are two very different things. This is the first time we've been alone together since all the shit went down at Oceanside. It's the perfect time to get everything out in the open. I'd promised myself that I'd tell him everything today. Now that today is here, I've become a chicken-shit.

"So, we get to hang out for the rest of the afternoon before heading to Oceanside, yeah?" Eastern asks, clocking me biting on my lip ring nervously. He raises an eyebrow.

"Yep. We've got until 6pm before we need to show our faces," I say, plastering on a smile and hoping I'm covering up my nerves well enough.

"What are we gonna do with the few hours we've got?"

"I thought maybe we should head to the beach?" I suggest. Truth be known, I've been both dreading and looking forward to this time alone together. It'd be good to kick back with my bestie and blow off a little steam on the beachfront, but I really need to tell him about Ford and Sonny, about what happened between us… though I'm not sure whether I can say anything about Camden just yet. That's a complication I'm just not ready to face.

"Sounds good. Not sure how I'm gonna face that fucker Camden now I know what he allowed Monk to do to you."

Okay, so I can't bring up Camden yet. Not that I even know what to say about him and me, because there is no him and me. Just a weird kind of tension that I'm hoping Camden's alleviated himself of over the Christmas break. God knows I've tried to.

"It's complicated," I find myself saying.

"You're defending him?" Eastern snaps.

"No, I'm not." *Yes, yes you are.* The question is why? I search inside myself trying to find the answers and coming up even more confused. Am I defending the person he once was; Bling? Or am I defending the person he is now: Camden? Can I even separate the two?

"Good. He doesn't deserve your forgiveness, or your loyalty. You join his crew to get what Crown wants, what we need to secure our future, and that's it."

"That's it," I agree, a little too quickly. For once, Eastern doesn't seem to notice the tremor in my voice hiding the truths I've yet to tell him.

"So, fill me in on the downlow with Oceanside and the rest of the inmates," Eastern says as he removes his jacket and rests his feet on the seats opposite, effectively blocking anyone else from sitting with us.

"Apart from the obvious, what fuckers do I need to kick the shit out of, and who are the ones that I can trust? Actually, let me rephrase that. Who are the ones you trust because we all know you're a way better judge of character than I am."

He grasps my hand, not in the least bit afraid to do so now that we've stepped out of the friendzone and into the… what? Kiss zone? Almost-boyfriend zone? Maybe best-friends-that-kiss zone? Friends-with-benefits zone? Fuck, I don't know.

My head is all over the place, whilst my heart is finding it hard to cope with just how hard it's beating now, especially after that gift Eastern gave me today. Which, incidentally, is safe at Tracy's house. There's no way I'm making *that* mistake again.

"Spit it out," he says, rubbing his thumb gently over my knuckles. His touch is warm, sure, familiar and *right*. Just like Sonny's kiss was, just like Ford's too.

I'm in so much trouble…

"Let's start with Pink and Kate," I begin, knowing that I can't broach the subject of Ford and Sonny until I've plucked up enough courage. I never considered myself a coward. I've always dealt with any issues I've had head on, but those were the kind of issues that fists can sort out. This kind of issue, the kind where I'm lusting after three… four. No, three guys! Is not so easy to resolve.

"The girls I met at Oceanside? Yeah, that Pink seems like a chick I could get on with. Clothes are even crazier than yours. Until I met her, I thought you were the only one on the planet who liked to dress like a rainbow. You ain't got nothing on her." He grins, tugging on my newly dyed red hair with his free hand.

"Pink is pretty cool. She's funny, loyal, a little odd, and also *gay*," I add, you know just in case he's getting any funny ideas.

Eastern arches an eyebrow at me, then shakes his head. "Totally not interested. I'm pretty happy with my own, slightly less colourful rainbow."

"Pretty happy?" I pout.

He gently fingers my lip ring. "Very happy."

"That's alright then," I respond, internally cursing myself for being a hypocrite. Here's me warning him off my gay friend, and I'm entertaining the idea of not one but three boy… *friends*.

"I'm not sure about that Kate though, seemed a little stuck up to me," he continues, oblivious to my inner turmoil.

"She's not what you think. She might act differently to what you're used to, but I'm telling you she's straight up one of the nicest people I've met. Clever too. She rinsed her previous school's accounts by breaking into their computer system and had a good old splurge. Pretty sure she's the kind of criminal that'll end up working for MI5 or something."

"She did that? Mind… blown," he says making that brain exploding gesture with his hands.

"I know, right? Trouble is, I think she's had her fair share of shit at that posh school she went to before Oceanside. We've yet to have that conversation, but I'm betting that there's more to her story than she's letting on. Pretty sure she's been to hell and back."

"I'm guessing you're going to help her out somehow."

"Maybe? Though I'm not sure I can do much but teach her to fight."

"I never imagined you to be the type to help the waifs and strays of this world." Eastern grins to let me know he's only joking. "But somehow you're doing just that."

"Hey, I'm not a complete fucking bitch. Besides, they had my back. I *owe* them."

"I get it. I'm grateful to them, but you don't *owe* friends anything. That isn't how it works, Asia. True friends give without expecting anything in return. Are they your true friends?"

I consider his question. Can I say that they are? I've only known them a few months and aside from a few chats, it's never really got that deep. I mean I don't know much about their lives, and they know very little about mine. Still, they befriended me when they could've easily turned me away, and they looked out for me with all the Monk shit. So, yeah, I'd say we're true friends, albeit new ones. "Yeah, they are," I eventually say.

"Well, that's all I need to know. Any friend of yours is a friend of mine."

Knowing that makes my heart sing. Let's just hope he takes news of Ford and Sonny the same way. Yeah… that might be pushing it a bit.

"So, wanna spill about those jackarses I met too? What were their names Sunny and Fort?" he asks, knowing full well they're names are Sonny and Ford. My cheeks heat, my heart stutters, and my palms turn clammy. I'm so not ready for this. Not just because they kissed me, and I kissed them back, but for everything I know to be true about them both.

"Well, they're…"

"Oh, young man. Would you mind moving your feet so I can sit down? I'm feeling a bit wobbly on these tired old legs of mine," an old lady says, cutting me off and effectively saving my bacon.

"Sure," Eastern grumbles giving me a 'for fuck sake' look. I can only grimace in response, trying to hide the relief I feel. He's not normally an arse to the older generation, but he wants every second of the time we've got today to ourselves. This lady looks like she'd like a good natter.

"Thank you," she responds, easing into the seat opposite mine. "You two make a mighty fine couple, anyone ever tell you that? When I was your age I met my husband, Bertie…"

And that's how, for the rest of the train ride, we're forced to listen to Mabel ramble on about her late husband Bertie, her latest great-grandchild and how she's spent the last two weeks knitting her a cardigan with little bees on it. She even gets it out to show me. It's pretty cute. I've always liked bees. Right now, I like Mabel even more.

AN HOUR LATER, we find ourselves on the seafront at Hastings right by the funfair. It's a Sunday so despite it only being just after 1pm, it's already full of thrill-seekers, harassed parents and obnoxious teenagers. It's a pretty overcast day, so the lights on the rides have been switched on, illuminating the place and making it look magical. It's kind of depressing seeing as we can't go inside. Lack of money is a real arsehole. I can smell popcorn, candyfloss and sizzling burgers, all of it making my stomach growl and my heart yearn to step through the wrought iron gates and join in on the fun.

"Asia…." Eastern is staring at me with a devious look on his face. I know that look. It means trouble.

"What?" I ask him, adjusting my backpack into a more comfortable position on my shoulder. There's not much in it. Apart from a few new clothes, a swimsuit my foster parent Libby brought for me for Christmas and a sweet little teddy bear from my brothers, it doesn't weigh much. I'm literally carrying all my worldly goods on my back like some tortoise whose home is his shell.

"You know you want to…" he says, wiggling his eyebrows.

"You know I want to *what*? Stop giving me that look, you heard what Tracy said. No trouble."

"This isn't trouble, this is fun! Besides, I have money." He shoves his hand into his pockets and pulls out a wad of notes. There must be at least one hundred quid in his hand.

"Woah, where did that come from?" I eye him and the money suspiciously. I'm not sure how I feel about him using his drug running money to pay for anything, even if I really, really want to go into the funfair.

His face drops when he sees my reaction. "It's not like that. Mum had a little extra for the first time in forever and she wanted me to have some. I didn't want to take it, but she insisted. She felt good giving it to me, even when I felt sick pocketing it. This was a stupid idea. I'll give it back to her next time I see her."

Eastern shoves the money back into his pocket and turns to look longingly at the funfair behind us. The rollercoaster zooms by in a flash of colour and noise, and I realise that he too has never been on one either.

"Hey," I say, gently touching his arm. "If you want to spend your money stuffing your face with junk food and then puking it up, who am I to stop you? Besides, I could use the entertainment."

"You really want to?"

"I *really* want to," I admit, looking past Eastern and at a group of kids with their parents. All of them are smiling, all of them are having fun. I've spent my entire life watching, being on the outside looking in. For once, I want to be the one everyone is envious of and not the one everyone warns their children about.

Eastern beams and pulls me in for a hug. "Girl, you're gonna wish you said no! Rollercoaster first, baby!"

"*Baby*?!" I mutter, feeling equal amounts pleased and disgusted by his choice of endearment. I never thought I was a feminist… Pretty sure I'm a non-conformist, actually. But *baby*?

"What?" he turns to me, totally missing my disgust. "You don't wanna go on the rollercoaster?"

"Hell, yes I do, *darling*," I retort with a smirk.

If he hears my sarcasm, he doesn't respond. Instead, he drags me to the entrance happily handing over the ten-pound fee to get in and another thirty quid buying up tickets for each of the rides. His smile as we're locked into the seats of the rollercoaster is something I'll never forget for as long as I live. He may have made a mistake joining Camden's crew. He may have done something stupid, *irresponsible*, but Eastern has always been there for me. One mistake isn't enough to break our bond. I refuse to let it.

When he leans over and presses a haphazard kiss against my smiling mouth, my heart soars.

This, this right here is what happiness is.

Twenty-four hours later, that happiness is well and truly fucked up.

FOUR

Three weeks earlier

"Spit it out, Asia. What's the deal?" Pink asks me the second we're safely inside her bedroom.

"Give her a second to calm down, Pink. Can't you see she's about to have a minor heart attack," Kate exclaims, perching on the bed whilst I flop down next to her, groaning.

"Hell, no. She needs to spill. Right. This. Second," Pink says, stabbing my arm with her finger.

She's lucky I like her so much; anyone else would've got a punch in the face for the trouble. I peer at Pink from between slit eyelids. The girl won't give up. Kate, on the other hand, would happily let me wallow a little longer before prying the truth from my lips. She'd at least give me a few minutes to get my head straight. But even though my head is spinning, and my heart is protesting at the sudden pounding, I'm grateful to them both for being… well, them. I've never had girlfriends before. I like it.

Blowing out a long breath, I ease myself up into a seated position. "Cigarette?" I ask, looking between them both. Kate shakes her head.

She doesn't smoke and vocalises her concern for my bad habit as often as she can. Pink, however, jumps up and pulls open her desk drawer, digging around for a moment until she finds what she's looking for. She hands me one of those skinny cigarettes that will burn out with one toke. I give her a look, and she shrugs. They're a complete waste of time in my opinion. If you're going to have a cigarette, have a proper cigarette, not some pathetic skinny one like this.

"Do you want one or not?" she says, cocking a brow.

"I suppose…" I grumble.

Kate sighs.

"What? They're good for you…" Pink lights up her cigarette, smiling around the smoke that she blows out of her mouth.

"Erm, in which universe are *any* cigarettes good for you?" Kate asks, giving us both a disappointed glare.

"Oh, shush. Live a little," she retorts, chucking the lighter to me so I can join her in her bad habit.

"Actually, I'll live a lot *longer* by not filling my lungs with toxins, but sure, puff away on that cancer stick."

Pink pokes her tongue out at Kate who rolls her eyes before turning her gaze onto me. "Well, do you want to tell us what the hell you're going to do now?"

"Short of running away, no idea."

I mean, I don't think I've really thought this through. Of course there's no way I would've let Eastern go back to prison. In the moment, it was the *only* thing I could do. I'm glad he's safe. I'm glad Tracy and Braydon will be too, but in reality I've no idea how it's all going to work out, and I don't even mean my own feelings for the boys. Sonny and Ford hate Camden, and whilst Eastern respects him (at least I think he still does) he's not exactly his best buddy. Plus, as soon as I tell Eastern about Monk and Camden's role in all that bullshit, he's going to hit the roof. Camden thinks he owns the damn place, including me it would seem, judging by his recent behaviour and his stupid attempt at getting my attention by spray painting my tag. Then there's the tiny matter that soon I'll be joining his gang after telling everyone that I'd never join *anyone's* gang, least of all his. Ford and Sonny aren't going to take it well.

"Oh, god." I groan inwardly.

"Man, I don't envy you. I'm glad I'm gay because choosing between those hotties is about as difficult as it can get."

"I hope you're not including Camden in that group of *hotties*," Kate adds frowning.

I wince, finding a tiny piece of lint on my jeans very interesting all of a sudden.

"Please tell me you're not considering Camden… *are you*?" she persists.

"That arsehole? No. No, I'm not," I say adamantly.

"Good. He reminds me too much of someone else I know, and he's just as infuriating."

"Oh, yeah?" Pink says, glancing at me with wide eyes. "Want to elaborate?"

Kate waves her hand about. "This isn't about me. This is about Asia. Seriously, what the fuck are you going to do? Even I could see that your best friend, Eastern, wants to be way more than friends given how he was with you just now. And we all know Sonny and Ford are into you…"

"We do, do we?"

Kate pulls a face. "Seriously? It's pretty clear to the whole of Oceanside, actually. Those two have got it bad."

"Yeah, they're not the only ones," Pink says, widening her eyes at me and pulling some weird face that looks as though she's constipated.

"You don't mean…" I ask, pointing at my chest.

"Shit, Asia. You're fucking cool and all, but you're not really my type." Pink laughs. "I'm talking about Camden. The guy's fucking losing his shit over you."

"Hmm… Well, we won't talk about *him*." Kate scowls. I wince. Knowing that she dislikes Camden so much makes me feel worse given what I've got to do.

"Oh, I don't know. There's something about Camden, right Asia?" Pink muses. Kate gives her a shove, and I just lower my head avoiding their probing stares.

"This is a nightmare…" I mumble, and frankly so much worse than even they understand. If it was just me having to choose between the lads, then I think I could handle that.

Probably.

Maybe.

But it isn't just that. It's so much more. Why the fuck is my life always so complicated?

"Well whatever you decide you're going to need to make a decision sooner rather than later. This place is tough enough to deal with, let alone this love shape you've got yourself into," Pink remarks, blowing out a stream of bluish smoke.

"Love shape?" Kate frowns, giving Pink a confused look.

"Well, it's not a love triangle is it? It's not even a love square…" she muses, tapping her chin. "I know, a love pentagon!"

"Fuck off, Pink," I groan, dragging on the skinny cigarette and watching the ash form in one long line. I catch it before it falls. See, one toke and it's gone. Total waste of time.

"Do you want my advice?" Pink asks before proceeding to give it anyway. "You need to make a list of all the reasons why you like each of them. Whoever's got the most is the one you choose. Simple."

Kate snorts, clearly unimpressed.

"What? It's all I've got," Pink grouses.

"How about you don't choose just yet… figure out how you really feel. No one said you have to make any of them your boyfriend. If they really like you like they seem to do, then they'll wait whilst you decide," Kate adds, always the voice of reason.

"Why choose at all?" I mutter, remembering how it felt to lay between Sonny and Ford the night of the fight. They didn't seem to mind then, perhaps they'll be open to accepting Eastern too? Oh, Jesus, now what am I thinking?

"Did you just say *why choose*? As in have them all?" Pink's mouth drops open in shock. "Why you greedy little cow," she adds with an amused laugh.

"It's not a bad idea…" Kate remarks quietly. Both Pink and I snap our heads around to look at her. Now her cheeks are blushing furiously. Glad I'm not the only one who's finding this conversation beyond awkward.

"You sound like you have some experience in the 'not choosing' department," Pink says, her eyes sparkling with the gossip she's desperate to draw out of Kate.

"Fuck no. I don't have any experience at all. Managing one guy was hard enough," she mutters, her voice cracking a little.

"Wanna talk about it?" Pink ask, ever perceptive.

"No. No, I don't." Kate shuts down like she always does, clamming up, pushing us away.

"It doesn't matter anyway. I'm not here to get a boyfriend. I really don't need the complication." And I really, really don't. I'm only just getting my head around my true feelings for Eastern, let alone how I feel about the rest of them. "This term has been difficult enough."

"It's too late for that," Pink says, as she flicks her cigarette butt out of the open window. "Looks like two of your complications are on their way here now."

"What?" Kate stands, peering over Pink's shoulder. She glances at me, pulling a face. "Afraid she's right, Asia. Maybe honesty's the best policy?"

Hell no, I think. In this case, honesty is not the best policy. Honesty would get me and Eastern into a whole heap of shit. If I tell Sonny and Ford what I've agreed to do then I could risk everyone's safety. I don't know either of them well enough to know whether they'd sell me out. I don't think they would. But regardless, I can't allow my heart to rule my head. What happened in that office and the agreement I made stays between Eastern, me and the adults in the room. Protecting my family is my priority now.

Chewing on my lip ring, I look between Pink and Kate. "I'll do what you suggested, Pink, and make a list. Then I'll wait. Figure out how I feel."

"Sounds like a good plan," Kate says, giving me a reassuring smile. "You'll make the right choice, Asia."

I nod, biting down on the truth that I so want to share with them both but can't. I wonder how Kate and Pink will feel after I join Camden's crew. I hope they'll still be my friends…

Fuck, who am I trying to kid? They'll hate me just as much as Ford and Sonny will.

In my heart I know that none of them will forgive me for selling out. Not only will I lose Pink and Kate's friendship, I won't have to worry about choosing between any of the boys because Sonny and Ford will make the choice for me. What had Ford told me before? That's right, loyalty means *everything* to him, and I'm about to show him that loyalty is something I can't give him no matter how much I want to. Heaving out a sigh, I flick my cigarette butt out of the window and wait for Sonny and Ford to join us.

I briefly consider dashing to my room, locking the door and burying my head in the proverbial sand, but by the time I've decided to run, there's a knock at Pink's door.

I groan internally. *Too late, chicken-shit.*

"Come in!" Pink calls out merrily, winking at me. She's loving this.

Kate grimaces. "Want us to stay?"

"Nah, reckon I need to have this conversation on my own. Thanks though," I say.

"Sure thing." Kate nods, grabbing Pink by the arm and dragging her from the room just as Sonny and Ford enter.

"Hey, this is my room, remember?!?" she complains, trying to shake out of Kate's firm grasp.

Kate just yanks harder, pulling her towards the door and into the hallway beyond.

"No getting jiggy with it on my bed, arseholes! I don't need any wet patches!" she shouts from the hallway. I can hear Kate tell her to shut up and the laughter that follows. My cheeks redden at her outburst, but I resolutely ignore the heat prickling my skin and face them both. Now is not the time to be a pussy.

"Have you got me tagged or something? How did you know I'd be in Pink's room and not Kate's or my own?"

"We tried both those places first," Sonny says with a shrug.

"That makes sense," I fumble, not ready to have this conversation. "What do you want?"

Ford shuts the bedroom door behind him and leans against the wood. He crosses his arms and feet, watching me whilst Sonny makes himself comfortable on the bed. I'm currently perched on Pink's desk feeling more and more uncomfortable by the minute. This is a far cry from how I felt falling asleep in their arms not so long ago.

"Want to tell us what's going on?" Ford asks, but it's not phrased as a question. This is a demand. That's just his manner. Demanding, intense, sincere. I glance at Sonny helplessly but he's staring at me just as intently. Looks like he's not going to help my predicament. He seems cool, aloof and far from the jovial kid I've become used to.

"There's nothing much to say. Eastern is joining Oceanside after the Christmas break."

"Why? What did he do?" Sonny asks this time, forcing me to look at him because of the uncertainty in his voice. He's wary, unsure, and the most guarded I've ever seen him. Does he sense the truths I'm hiding, the ones I can't possibly share with him?

"Drug running. Got caught with Mary-J. His lawyer got him a good deal. Now he's here." I respond with quick statements hoping to hide the lie sitting heavy in my chest. Everyone knows if you get caught running Class B drugs you're going to prison. End of discussion. Except he isn't, he's here because we made a deal.

He nods tightly, his gaze penetrating mine until I'm forced to look away.

"He's your best friend?" Another statement from Ford.

"Yes." *And so much more than that.*

He nods, pushing off from the door and striding towards me. He grasps my upper arm in a vice like grip, cupping my cheek gently. The differing holds warring with each other and screwing up my already overwrought emotions. I've just about had enough of today.

"Take your hands off me," I say, trying and failing to sound like I mean it.

"Ford, what are you doing?" Sonny whispers. Out of the corner of my eye I can see him sit up, dragging his arse to the edge of the bed.

"Shut up, Sonny. This is between me and Asia," he retorts.

"Like hell it is!" Sonny stands, but before he can do anything Ford's hand slides around the back of my head and pulls me towards him. He crashes his mouth against mine, forcing my mouth open with his tongue. It's a brutal, soul-searing kiss and as he plunders my mouth with vicious intent all I can do is take it. This is Ford marking what's his and like everything else, he does so with resolve and passion. He doesn't hold back, and he certainly doesn't question whether I want his kiss or not. He just takes, and fuck if I can only respond with whimpers of my own. I'm getting the impression with Ford that it's either all or nothing. He sensed the closeness between Eastern and I… the *love*, and he wants to make himself known.

I want to shout that I hear him loud and clear. That I feel something too, but it doesn't matter how I feel. As soon as I join Camden's crew it's all going to shit anyway.

When he lets me go just as roughly as he grabbed me, I'm left reeling, so much so that I stumble back a few steps. This time it's Sonny who catches me. He holds me against his side, cursing Ford under his breath.

"Eastern isn't the only one who wants you, who has your back. Just so we're clear," Ford says, panting now. He looks from me to Sonny. "If I were in your shoes, Sonny, I'd stake my claim too," Ford growls before turning on his heel, yanking the door open and striding from the room, leaving me speechless and Sonny with his mouth hanging open.

"Well, fuck! Not sure how I follow that display of possessiveness," Sonny eventually says.

Me either, I think.

Not one for giving up, Sonny turns me in his arms and lifts my chin with his finger. "I don't suppose a kiss is on the cards for me?" he asks with a sheepish grin and laughter in his pretty baby blues. He gives me his full, megawatt smile, dimples and all. My mouth pops open and closed as I look up at him helplessly. I can't even form a word, let alone a sentence. Today has been fucking crazy.

"Pretty good kiss then, I take it?" And although he laughs, I can see the hurt shadowing his features.

"Sonny…" I manage to utter.

He stares at me for a long, long time and just when I think he too is going to kiss me, he does something that surprises me. He simply folds me into his arms. "Whoever you choose, Asia, I got you, *regardless*," he reassures me, cupping my head against the firmness of his chest whilst he rubs my back. "And just so you know," he whispers after a beat, "Ford's not the only one who can steal a kiss, but even though I might be a thief, I don't take what isn't freely given. At least not when it comes to you."

My heart stutters at that, and despite everything that's happened today, I allow him to hold me close whilst I gather my thoughts. Eventually he presses a gentle kiss against the top of my head, pushing me away before I can unravel myself from his hold.

"Brick shithouse seems like a good guy," he says with a wry grin. "I'm glad you've got him. Just remember you have us too."

As he leaves the room, I can't help but think for how long.

FIVE

Present day

"Eastern, please, no more!" I laugh hysterically, clutching my stomach. "Seriously, if I go on that rollercoaster one more time I might puke up the three hamburgers, tub of popcorn and that huge bloody candy floss I just ate. I'm not willing to let go of all that junk food goodness."

Eastern grins widely, his face lit up with mirth. "We've only been on it three times, Asia. Where'd your balls go? I thought you were tougher than this."

I punch him on the arm, grinning mercilessly when he winces. "I'm a girl, remember? And this girl's balls are inside her body. They're called *ovaries*. You should've paid more attention in Biology class, you dickhead."

"Come here," he smirks, tugging at my arm and folding me into his chest. His hand slides under my backpack, resting on my lower back, whilst my heart starts jackhammering in my chest after only just recovering from the thrill of the ride.

"Want me to rub your tummy better?" he mutters, the smile evident in his voice as he presses his lips against the top of my head.

"Do I look like a cat?" I respond with a laugh, grinning up at him, then instantly groan when I see the mischievous glint in his eyes. Pretty sure I can see stars in them too, or maybe that's just the reflection of the lights. I wonder if mine look the same. His mouth pops open, a pussy joke right there on the tip of his tongue. I walked right into that one. "On second thoughts don't answer that!"

He cocks his head as though seriously considering whether I am indeed feline, then smiles slowly, like a cat that's got the cream. *Oh, fuck.*

"Follow me," he says, twining his fingers with mine and tugging me away from the rollercoaster and deeper into the funfair.

"This is going to be bad for my health, I can tell," I mutter.

Eastern doesn't respond but I can feel the depth of his chuckle as it vibrates down his arm and disperses between us. He's always been playful; now that playfulness has transformed into full-on flirtation. I like it. I like the way it makes me feel.

As we walk through the crowd, nerves flutter inside my chest. Around us, the air smells of sweet things and smoky meat grilled on barbecues underlined with the distinct briny scent of the sea that I've come to love. Colourful lights sparkle above the stalls and around the rides, so much brighter now that the sky is dark. Children's laughter can be heard above the screams and the chatter, and the tinkly music coming from the rides. Everyone is smiling. This feeling inside my chest, this *happiness* is a natural high I could get used to.

"Where are we going?" I ask, biting on my lip ring. Nerves and excitement battling for attention. I've never been nervous around Eastern until recently. It's a new feeling I don't quite know how to manage. Sarcasm and humour seem to be helping though.

Eastern glances at me, noticing my nervousness. "Somewhere we can be alone of course. Pretty sure my favourite pussy wants privacy when being stroked." He winks, grinning salaciously. I know he's just teasing, but my stomach does a summersault regardless. I bark out a laugh to cover up my sudden lust-filled thoughts, and glance away when I feel his intent stare. Would I stop him if he tried to touch me that way? I'm not sure that I would. Ever since that kiss we shared in Mr Carmichaels office I've wanted more. Circumstance, lack of time and family commitments over these past couple of weeks haven't really allowed for that. Eastern stops suddenly, pulling me between the back of two stalls.

"You *want* me to stroke… I mean touch you?" he asks, a thread of nervousness filtering into his voice, darkening his brown eyes with lust. He bows his head lower, a flop of unruly hair falling forward as he inches closer. I think he's about to kiss me and my body seems to move of its own accord as I step closer to him.

"Your hair is a pretty shade of red in this light," he observes, capturing a few strands between his thumb and forefinger. The gentle tug on my hair has my scalp prickling.

"So is yours, kinda like molten chocolate with golden threads," I muse, laughing lightly at my flowery response as I push back that flop of hair. He chuckles, drawing me closer. Should I really be encouraging him given I still haven't told him about Sonny and Ford, or Camden…? Can't forget him.

"Eastern…" I fumble, my cheeks blushing as the surrounding noise of the fair seems to be drowned out by the thumping of my pulse and the rush of blood beneath my skin.

"Don't worry, I'll be gentle," he murmurs.

"OY! You two get going! This ain't no kissing booth!"

We jump apart, startled out of the moment as a mean looking guy with a cigarette hanging out of his mouth glares at us both from his stall.

"Piss off and find somewhere else to snog!" he continues.

Eastern grabs my hand, laughter bubbling up out of his mouth as he pulls me away. Drawing me into his side once again, we traverse through the crowd.

"That was close," I laugh.

"We should've just given him an eyeful. I should be able to kiss my girl wherever and whenever I want."

My girl? Fuck. I want to be his girl so much but those ugly feelings of guilt creep back in and try to ruin the moment. I push them away. I know I should tell him about Sonny and Ford, but I can't just yet. Instead, I allow him to wrap his arm around my shoulder, settling me into his side. I feel safe there. Happy. My best friend who's always been by my side is now both familiar and alien all at the same time. As we walk in companionable silence, I let this new feeling swell inside my chest. Today, I'm letting the happiness in. Up until this moment, I used to think that happiness was an overrated emotion. I mean, when you spend most of your life miserable and on edge it kinda comes as a shock when you finally feel happy.

Truly happy.

Not the fake smiles on social media kind of happy, where behind the wide toothy grins and pouts are anxiety and false truths. No, right in this moment I feel a kind of happiness that feeds my soul, that makes me feel alive. For the first time in my life I can be the teenager I've always wanted to be, rather than the adult in a teenager's body trying to juggle with life's disappointments. I can honestly say that these past couple of hours have been my happiest yet. Part of that makes me feel a little sad given it's only taken seventeen years to feel this way, the other part is just *grateful*.

Grateful to have my best friend by my side.

Grateful to have this special moment.

Grateful to be happy, even for a short while.

I'm not foolish enough to think this feeling will last, but I appreciate it, nonetheless.

"What's this place?" I ask as Eastern stops outside a red peaked tent, just like a smaller version of a big top that I've seen on TV over the years.

"I've no idea, but I clocked it from the Ferris Wheel. Thought it looked interesting… and deserted," he shrugs with a wry grin.

"No one else seems to think it's interesting," I laugh, looking around us. We seemed to have found ourselves on the outskirts of the funfair. There aren't many people hanging around here, even the lights don't seem to penetrate the ever-growing darkness just beyond the fringes of the stalls. It's only five pm, but the sun has long since gone down. January is a shitty month normally, but at least the rain has held off for now.

"Besides, it's closed, Eastern…"

"When has that stopped us before?" he grins, looking about quickly before crouching down, and unzipping the thick canvas. "You and I both know that it's not breaking and entering if it isn't locked…" He ducks inside, holding his hand out to me from inside the darkness of the tent.

"Tell that to the judge who sent me to Oceanside. Mr Patel's shop wasn't locked either."

Eastern laughs, a bright sound that bursts out of his mouth. I can almost see the colourful bubble floating in the air in amusement. "True, but I really need a moment with you. Pretty sure it's safe…"

"We've only got an hour to get back to Oceanside. The walk through the town centre and up the hill will take at least thirty minutes. We're pushing for time, Eastern." I've no idea why I'm suddenly taking on the parental role. I'm not worried about getting caught or being late. Maybe deep down I'm not ready to explore the next stage in our relationship. Maybe he was joking about stroking my… *pussy*. But even so, stranger things have happened. It's not as though we don't know each other intimately, just not that kind of intimate. First base is one thing, skipping over second base and going for third, quite another. Then again, that didn't stop me with Ford.

Ford… The thought of him has me tingling all over and feeling all kinds of twisted up inside. He's so very different to Eastern, not as open, but someone I feel I can trust despite that; despite Camden's warnings about him. He taught me to fight the right way. He made me feel a part of something that night he looked after me in his room. He stole a kiss, an orgasm and a little spot inside my chest for the trouble. Maybe I'm foolish to trust my gut about him knowing what I know, but it's never done me wrong before now.

And what about Sonny, Ford's newest recruit and the niggle to my consciousness?

Sonny… I can't forget the way he'd danced with me at the Tower and the fire it brewed inside of me. Or the way he stood up for me when he kicked Monk's arse. And what about the way he kissed me on the beach, then a few weeks later the fact he'd refused to steal a kiss like Ford had. Despite his flirting and his tendency to steal, he never took what wasn't offered by me. I'll always appreciate that.

"Come on, Asia. Just a few minutes," Eastern insists, interrupting my wayward thoughts, his crooked smile shining white in the darkness. "I just want a moment alone with you without the world looking on. I get the feeling this might be the last time for a while."

He lets that statement hang in the air between us. I know Eastern, this isn't some ploy to get in my knickers. Well, maybe it is a little bit, but he needs this… this reassurance that all will be okay between us. I guess I need it too when I take his hand and duck inside the tent.

"Just a few minutes," I agree.

SIX

Two weeks earlier

For the rest of the night and the following week after Ford and Sonny ploughed into Pink's room and made their feelings known, they give me space to mull over everything they've said. I remain tight-lipped around Pink and Kate, not trusting myself to withhold why I can't possibly continue my friendship in the new term with the two lads who make my heart skip a beat. In fact, for the most part, I keep to myself and am almost home free without much hiccup until the last day of school.

I'm not sure what possessed me to use my free period to take a walk to the spot that Camden did his 'big reveal', but that's where I end up. Maybe I just wanted to see for myself one last time that I hadn't imagined the brilliance of his tag or the conversation that followed. Maybe I just wanted to admire Bling's artwork one last time. Maybe I just wanted to be alone, and that's the last place I figured anyone else would be.

As soon as my feet hit the pebbles, someone makes themselves known.

That someone is fucking Camden.

"What are you doing here?" Camden asks me as he steps out from behind a large boulder just at the base of the cliff face. He's got his backpack on and two spray cans peeking out of his hoodie pockets.

"Getting some fresh air," I retort lamely. The fact that I'm looking at his tag and ruminating on how fucking amazing it is, really isn't something I wish to share with him right now.

"Things a little intense back at Oceanside?" He cocks his head to the side, watching me closely. Something about his question and his blasé attitude rubs me the wrong way. Especially after *everything* that's happened. Intense is an understatement.

"Did you have something to do with Eastern coming to Oceanside?" I ask before I can stop myself. It wasn't the question I had formed in my head, but it's the one I ask regardless.

Stupid.

Camden frowns. "Why would I have anything to do with that? I'm no judge and jury, at least not one that has any say in a court of law."

"You said to me that you were *giving him back,*" I say, making finger quotes in the air. "And then I step into Mr Carmichael's office and find Eastern. What gives?"

Camden removes his backpack, dropping it to the ground then sits down, his back against the rock. I watch him painstakingly roll a joint, light it and draw in a deep lungful, blowing it out slowly before he decides to answer me.

"I saw Eastern leaving Mr Carmichael's office. Figured he'd got a light sentence like I did…" he shrugs as though that's enough explanation. Besides, I'm not sure I believe him.

"And?" I insist.

"And I owe you for Monk."

"But that's not how it works. Once in a gang, always in a gang, right?"

"I made an exception."

"You can't just make an exception like that."

"Who says? I'm the leader... I can do what I want."

I bark out a laugh. "Yeah, right." If that were true and he has the power to relieve members of their position in the gang, then why not get rid of Monk? Camden knows as well as I do that he hasn't got half the power he claims. He's admitted as much to me already. Then again, he doesn't realise that I know about the King. He was giving me an in when he said that we are all owned. Now I know what he meant by that. Camden is just another kid acting all powerful when really his strings are being manipulated just like the rest of us. Just like me. I'm Crown's puppet. He's the King's. We make a great Punch and Judy.

"I have it under control," he insists, but neither of us believe him.

"You're full of shit," I mutter, something I find myself often saying to him.

Camden curses, then sighs heavily. "Maybe you're right, maybe I am full of shit, Asia. Or maybe I'm just doing the only thing I can for you."

"Why?"

"I told you why. I owe you for Monk."

"You owe me for not chucking him out of your crew because that's one thing you can't do, right?" I press, wanting him to explain why that is. Why he can give up Eastern, but he can't give up Monk. I want to know *why* dammit.

"Yes, that as well, but mainly because he's a sadistic bastard and you deserve someone on your side other than that prick, Ford and his sidekick, Sonny. Eastern will have your back for the *right* reasons."

"What do you mean for the right reasons? You don't trust them?" I ask.

"No, I don't trust Ford, but you know that already."

"Because he beat you in a fight?"

Camden grits his teeth. "Because we have history that cannot be undone."

"Want to elaborate?"

He presses his mouth into a thin line. I roll my eyes. What is it with this guy and his secrets? "And Sonny, what do you have against him?"

"Nothing in particular. Sonny is just a stupid kid who should know better than to believe in Ford. I don't care that they're long lost cousins three times removed or some shit. Blood doesn't make you family."

"You know about the fact Ford and Sonny are related?"

"I know everything, remember?"

You don't know about the deal I made with Crown, I think. Guilt washes over me, just like the waves lapping over the pebbles behind us. The water seeps through the gaps, tiny droplets finding their way to the sand beneath. Just like the guilt that runs through my veins and seeps into my consciousness.

"But aren't we all just stupid kids?" I say, brushing away the guilt I feel. "Isn't that why we're here because we've made bad choices, done stupid things?"

"I'm not stupid. Every choice I've made has been for a reason. Let me ask you this: has Sonny joined No Name crew because he believes that's where you'll end up? Or has he truly made the decision based on his own judgement of Ford?"

"He knows I won't join any gang. He accepts that. Ford does too. Sonny did it because he knows Ford's a good guy. He's a good judge of character. Shame you seem incapable of being the same… Perhaps you're the one who's stupid."

"I'm not, and Ford's still a prick even if your hormones say otherwise," Camden growls, growing angrier by the second. Pretty sure he's acting exactly like a stupid kid right now. A stupid *jealous* kid. His pride was hurt by Ford, his ego by me for turning him down. Today, he's just not *man* enough to admit it. If that doesn't make him a kid, I don't know what does.

"And by the way, this hate you have for Ford, it's pathetic. He beat you in a fight, get over it, Camden."

"You've no idea what you're talking about," he snaps, anger blazing in his topaz eyes.

"Pretty sure I do."

I know I'm playing with fire, that this is probably a stupid idea to poke the beast, but for some reason seeing Camden's tag high above us, so bright, so brilliant, just irritates me. Bling was someone I once looked up to, admired. He was like an urban fucking legend not so long ago. Now all I see when I look at Camden is wasted talent, opportunities missed, and an arsehole. It pisses me off.

"You really don't know when to shut it, do you?" He gets up to his feet quickly, stumbling slightly on the pebbles as they move beneath his feet when he stands. "You think you know the score, but you don't. I don't know how else to spell it out for you. Ford is dangerous and Sonny's a *fool* to join his crew."

"You're wrong. *Monk* is dangerous. *You* are dangerous…" I almost, almost said the King is dangerous, but I bite down on that remark before I make a huge fucking mistake.

"No, I'm not!"

I laugh bitterly. "You're an idiot if you believe otherwise. Like you told me before, you can't be Bling anymore, you can only be Camden. You're the leader of Hackney's Hackers, the most feared gang in London. Your words, not mine."

"This is who I am!" he suddenly shouts, striding over to me and gripping my arm. He points to his tag. "That's me. *Bling*. A kid who dreamed of better things. A kid who thought his art meant something. A kid who had hope! *I'm not this*!" he says, crashing his fist against his chest. Pounding on it not once, not twice, but three times, hammering his point home.

For a moment we're both too shocked to move. Then he lets go of my arm and steps away.

"Those diamonds surrounding my tag, everyone on the street thinks they represent wealth. That this unknown graffiti artist *Bling* either craves money and riches or has it in abundance…"

"I know what they represent because you told me. They represent the girls in your crew." I think of the pretty twins Jade and Opal back in Hackney. I think of Emerald and Diamond here at the Academy. I dislike all of them and not just because they're first class bitches, but because they're his.

"That might be why my girls have those nicknames now," he says, and I wince, not liking the ownership of that statement. "But it's only to remind me of who I once was. Those nicknames were given long after I gave up my tag. There's a different meaning behind those diamonds." He shakes his head, biting on his lip to stop himself from saying more.

"So, tell me what that is then. You can't just open up and share a piece of yourself only to clam up again. You want me to understand you, but you refuse to tell me the truth. You want me to respect you, but you keep Monk in your crew. You want me to be a part of your gang, but you don't give me a good enough reason to want to…" I bite my tongue on the last point knowing that I *need* to join his gang and that I'm not doing a very good job at ingratiating myself with him. I'm royally fucking this up. He's offered me a chance to join twice now. I know he won't be doing that again any time soon. His pride won't let him. How I'm going to get him to ask one last time is beyond me.

Camden looks at me for a long time before finally flicking the half smoked joint into the gentle waves. They're not crashing violently today, even though the air is cracking with untold truths, secrets, and enough tension to cause a storm.

"I'm going to show you something I hope I don't later regret," he says, nodding his head as though convincing himself that's the right thing to do. "Come here." Twisting on his feet he strides back over to the boulder he appeared behind from earlier.

I stay rooted to the spot, not willing to follow him anywhere. Not trusting that behind that boulder isn't his gang ready and waiting to fucking jump me. He stops, glancing over his shoulder.

"There's only me here. Do you honestly think I'd tell my crew about this place, about that?" he asks, pointing to his tag.

"They don't know you're Bling…"

"No, I haven't told them." He looks meaningfully at me, and I nod in understanding. It suddenly dawns on me then that Camden has already trusted me even when I can't trust him. So far I haven't betrayed that trust. I don't want too, not about Bling. Yet here I am knowing full well that I need to get him to open up to me about the King to secure a future for Eastern and me. I need to join his gang, gather all the information I can, then betray him.

Earlier I accused Camden of being dangerous, but in reality I'm the one he should be afraid of because here I am holding his future in my hands. That knowledge makes my stomach curl into a basket of venomous snakes, every one of them having the capability of poisoning my heart, not to mention destroying Camden.

SEVEN

"Do you trust me?" Camden asks, then instantly regrets it. "Stupid question… of course you don't." He thinks for a moment, then looks me dead in the eye. "If you want to know the answer to your question, then you'll find it behind here." He points to a large boulder at the base of the cliff face.

"Are you fucking nuts? I'm not going behind there with you."

"I've already told you that I'm alone, but you don't believe me…"

"Your word isn't something I can trust."

"But," he says, pinning me with his topaz eyes, "If I'm beginning to understand you, Asia, then I think curiosity will trump everything else you're feeling right now. Maybe once you see that there isn't anyone back here wanting to hurt you, you'll be able to trust *me* better? You'll see that I'm not just full of the shit you accuse me of."

I regard him as we stand facing each other in a battle of wills. He seems sincere, but then again he could just be a good actor. He certainly knows how to make me second guess everything I think I know about him. Usually if you're on my shit list, that's where you stay. You don't hover between hate and… well, I can't even say like. Hate and lust then. Alternating between hate and lust isn't something I ever expected to feel. That's not normally how I work. You wrong me, you stay on the other side of the line, you don't walk it like a tightrope. Somehow that's where Camden has found himself.

"Well, what's it to be, Asia? Will you trust my word enough to see what's hidden behind here?" he asks, jerking his thumb towards the boulder behind him, "or walk away without the knowledge."

"I could always just come back at another time…" I say, testing him.

"You could, but it might not be there next time."

"What might not be there?"

"I guess you won't find out unless you trust me."

"Fine," I snap suddenly, not liking how the tables have turned. I'm feeling well and truly played when I should be the one playing him. "You've got my attention, but I swear to God, if you're screwing me, I'll come for you first."

"I don't doubt that." Camden nods tightly, then continues towards the boulder, disappearing behind it. I follow him, tension spreading through my muscles as I ready myself for attack. When I walk around the corner of the huge slab of rock, Camden is leaning against it, alone except for the huge painting of a girl with topaz eyes. Eyes just like his.

"This is Sapphire, my twin sister," he says, resting his fingertips against the rock.

"Fuck, Camden. It's incredible…" and it is. His talent is *insane*. It's a perfect illustration. Wait! I recognise that face.

"She loved gemstones, *diamonds* in particular," he continues. "Not because they were worth anything, but because they're beautiful. I used to call her Gem and she used to call me Bling because according to her I was the one who shone the brightest. But it wasn't true. She was always the one who lit up the world. I just basked in her reflection." His voice cracks on that admission and I can only stare at him and her image in shocked silence.

"I know her," I whisper. This is the girl who appears in almost every piece of Bling's graffiti art that's scattered around London. Always smiling, always happy. Now here she is, emblazoned on the rock, hidden from prying eyes, and only visible to the people who know she's here. Up until a moment ago, that had just been Camden. Now that includes me.

Except this time, she isn't happy.

This time her face is a picture of sadness. Her lips are turned down in a frown. Her eyes are hollow. As hollow as Camden's are now. There's no life in her, nothing but an aching sense of loss. Though it isn't her sadness I'm sensing, but Camden's. His loss, his anguish is all too evident in every painstaking line. I know instantly that she's dead. That this is a memorial for her. That *this* is the truth inside Camden's heart.

"What happened to her?" I ask softly, gently. Expecting a sad story of a life taken too soon by cancer or some other horrid illness. What I get instead shocks me to the core.

"Ford happened."

It takes me a few seconds to absorb that statement. All the while Camden watches me with a heartbroken stare. I know that whatever the truth is surrounding his sister's death, Camden truly believes Ford's responsible. That's a blow I'm finding hard to stomach, to reconcile with the boy I've become fond of.

"What do you mean, Ford happened? What are you saying?" My head snaps to look at him, not wanting to know and needing to at the same time.

"He killed my sister. I can't make it any plainer than that."

"What?!" I stumble back, cold dread rushing over my skin. "You're lying! This is some sick twisted mind game. You're trying to make me hate him. It won't work!" My whole body is trembling with adrenaline as I fight the truth Camden has displayed so well in his artwork, that I can see written all over his face.

"I'm not lying. She loved him and he betrayed her. Her death is *his* fault."

"Wait, what do you mean?"

"I mean what I say. She made a mistake trusting him to keep her safe. I was her twin brother. I was the one who took care of her. Me. Not him. I should never have trusted him." His eyes are wild, intense and the bright shade of topaz I've gotten so used to, dims. In her presence they're void of any colour, drained of it somehow. Where once she might have made him shine, now her ghost only seems to rob him of his happiness, that special kind of sparkle that made him Bling.

"Camden, you're not making any sense. Explain to me what you're saying."

His back slides down the boulder as his feet push out the pebbles making a deep groove for him to sit in. The cocksureness that he always seems to present is no longer there. Stolen by death, grief and pain. His tall frame folds in on itself as he draws his legs up and wraps his thick, muscular arms around them.

"Two years ago, my sister met Ford. She fell in love with him. Spent every moment she could with him. Their relationship was intense. *He* was intense. But I never doubted that he cared for her. I honestly thought he loved her as much as I did… I'd believed that, and I trusted him to look out for her. To look out for *me*."

Oh, God. Were they friends once? It makes sense, the kind of familiarity they have, the kind of deep-rooted hate that can only be born through a history of betrayal and hurt.

"He took her to meet his *family*. The cage fighters of Grim's fight club. He wanted her to understand who he was, and I fucking let her go even though I *knew* it was a dangerous place. Ford wanted Sapphire to see how strong he was. How he could protect her from anything and anyone. She'd believed him. *I'd* believed him. But we were all just stupid kids; fifteen-year-olds who thought we knew how to survive in a grown-up world. I should've trusted my gut, Asia. Instead I went along for the ride, trusting in my friend. I walked into the lion's den with my sister, believing that nothing could touch us." Camden bashes his head back against the rock, his face screwed up in pain and an all-encompassing guilt.

"What happened to her?"

"That night Ford fought against a rival from another club. He lost, but he *should've* won. Everyone knew Ford was the better fighter even at only fifteen. He wasn't as built as some of them, or even as strong, but he'd always had this weird fucking ability to see a rival's weaknesses and exploit them. As unbelievable as it sounds, Asia, if he fought he *won*. There's a streak of unbreakable steel within him. It doesn't bend, and it never breaks. *Never...*"

"Go on," I whisper, needing to hear the rest of the story, needing to understand.

"His boss, the owner of the club, knew that he'd win the fight. So did every single person attending that night. They all backed him to win, even the owner of the other rival club who was there with his people. Everyone except Grim."

Grim?

Camden stops and as he draws in a shaky breath, he turns to look at his sister painted on the rock next to him, then hangs his head. "Fuck," he mutters.

"It's okay, you don't have to say anymore..." I placate, suddenly not wanting to know what happened. A feeling of dread creeps up my spine at the thought that Ford is somehow responsible for Sapphire's death.

"I do. You need to hear this," Camden insists. "After one particular bloody round where Ford's opponent was almost on his knees, my sister managed to get to Ford at the ringside. She didn't like what she saw. She didn't like the complete void that was Ford when he fought. The lack of emotion, the lack of *anything* human. She begged him to stop. She told him that she couldn't stand to see this side of him. She hated it..." He draws in a shaky breath then blows it out again, staring at me.

"What happened?"

"Ford threw the fight. He *lost*. Every single person there, including the rival club owner, lost their money. Ford dropped his guard on purpose knowing his opponent would get a punch in that would knock him out cold. The second his opponent was announced the winner, all hell broke loose. People saw that it was a fix, and they wanted their money back. My sister and I were caught up in the chaos. She was stabbed in the gut trying to get out of the way of two men fighting, whilst Ford was oblivious. I couldn't get to her in time. I wasn't fast enough to reach her. I saw the knife slide into her in slow fucking motion and have wished every day since that it was me who was stabbed. It should've been me... She died in my arms, her fucking blood leaking through my hands. I couldn't save her." He chokes on the words, his head hanging.

My hand flies to my mouth, smothering the apology. "I'm so sorry, Camden. I'm so, so sorry," I mumble.

"So you see, he *is* responsible for her death. He may have taught you to fight, Asia, but there is a coldness within him. A core of steel that's unyielding. He proved it that night. He isn't what you think," he says with conviction, his eyes welling with unshed tears.

My head spins with the revelation, but all I can think of is how Ford has been with me. How he'd looked after me, supported me these past few months. He doesn't do anything without intent. So, if he loved Sapphire as Camden had thought, of course he would throw the fight.

She asked him to, so he did. It wasn't his fault. He couldn't have known what would've happened.

"But if Ford was so callous, so cruel and unbending, he wouldn't have thrown the fight for your sister, right? He did what she asked, you can't blame him for what happened afterward. I'm sorry for what happened to your sister, I am. But Ford isn't this cold-hearted person you speak off."

Camden barks out a painful laugh that somehow seems to lacerate my heart with the grief I hear in it.

"You're a fool, Asia. Ford didn't throw the fight for Sapphire. He threw the fight for Grim."

"Who's Grim?"

"Grim is the owner of the Fight Club. She's Ford's older sister, his half-sister. Same mum, different dad. Grim's father took her from their mother when she was a baby. Brought her up by himself."

"His *sister*? What the fuck?" He never mentioned he had a sister. Why tell me everything he did and not mention that?

"Grim knew everyone had bet on Ford to win. If he lost, she stood to gain a hell of a lot of money. Ford knew shit would go down if he lost the fight, but he did it anyway. So you see, Asia, he threw the fight for *Grim,* for *money.* He sure as fuck didn't do it for my sister."

EIGHT

Present Day

It's pitch black inside and whilst I'm used to heading out into the dark when graffitiing, there's always some light either from the streetlamps or the night sky. In here there's none, and an irrational kind of fear suddenly climbs up my back as I strain to see. Memories of that night when Monk and his wolves tried to hurt me comes hurtling back and I let out a little shriek then slam my mouth shut forcefully. I'm *not* a petrified little girl. I'm tougher than this for fuck sake. *I am.*

"Don't be afraid, Asia," Eastern whispers, the soft feathers of his breath tickling my neck and scattering goosebumps over my skin. He steps so close that I can feel the heat of his body press into mine. The fear that assaulted me quickly disperses when Eastern engulfs me in his embrace, his broad chest against my back. Solid, warm, *safe.*

"Never, not with you," I respond honestly.

Eastern has always known how to make me feel safe. When he's by my side I feel immune to danger. Growing up, we were the superheroes of our childhoods. Nothing could ever touch us. It's probably why we've gotten into so much trouble over the years. Our childish imaginations, naivety, and a strong dose of bravado were a potent mix for attracting trouble. But no matter what we got into, we always got out of it together.

"I've got your back," he says, echoing Ford's words from a few weeks ago. Words, which if I'm being honest, have been haunting me now that I know a little bit more about the history between Ford and Camden. Especially now that I know about Sapphire.

"It's just you and me, Asia. Like it's always been." He presses a kiss against the curve of my neck and though I want to enjoy it, I can't. The fact that I still haven't told Eastern about Ford and Sonny is like having an ice-cold bucket of water thrown over me. I stiffen in his hold for reasons other than just the kiss I'd shared with them both, but from the terrible revelation Camden had seen fit to reveal on the beach that last day of term. Something I've been struggling to comprehend ever since. I need to tell Eastern everything. It's time.

"Asia?" he questions, sensing the sudden change.

"There's something I need to…" I start, but this time it's Eastern's turn to tense up.

"Did you hear that…? He flicks on the torch app on his mobile phone, illuminating the surrounding space. "SHIT!" Eastern barks out as I blink back the sudden light and follow his gaze nearly jumping out of my skin when I see our reflections in a curved row of tall mirrors opposite us.

"What the hell?" I blurt out, willing my overstimulated heart to calm down. It's had far too much excitement for one day already.

"For fuck sake. I nearly had a heart attack!" he exclaims, clutching his chest and blowing out a long breath.

"No shit," I agree, as the arc of light moves about the space, illuminating more mirrors and showing off every angle of our reflections. "Oh my god, you do realise what this place is right?"

Eastern makes a kind of grunting noise. "I'm not a complete fucking moron, Asia."

"It's a hall of mirrors! I've always wanted to go to one of these places." I clap my hands together pushing everything I need to say away and allowing myself a moment of childish glee. The truth can wait another five minutes. Just five more minutes, then I'll tell him.

"A tent of mirrors more like," Eastern grumbles, not nearly as happy about being here as I am.

"This is fucking awesome!" I exclaim, walking towards the run of mirrors and finding a gap in the centre that I hadn't noticed because of the optical illusion. It's both creepy *and* exciting.

"This was *not* what I had in mind," Eastern laughs nervously, trying to hide the fear I recognise so well in his voice. "Pretty sure most carnival horror movies have a hall of mirrors just like this one. Any minute now an axe wielding nutcase is going to barrel in here and chop us up into tiny pieces. I could've sworn I heard something..."

"Shut up. It's just your mind playing tricks on you."

"I *heard* something," he insists.

"Don't tell me *you're* scared?" I laugh loudly, rounding on him. He puffs out his cheeks and chest in response, trying and failing to look untroubled. "You are! Oh my god, Eastern, if I knew your reflection scared you so much I would've ribbed you about it a lot sooner."

"Hey, I am *not* scared of my reflection. This place is just creepy as fuck. Like I said, axe murderer."

"Oh, this is priceless! Eastern who isn't scared of anything, fears his reflection," I gloat, reaching into my coat pocket and pulling out my own mobile phone, thankful that I managed to get it back at the end of term. Camden still has my spare, but I'm not bothered about that one. He can keep it for all I care. Pressing on the torch icon, I give Eastern a mischievous smile of my own and run towards the gap between the run of mirrors.

"Alicia!" Eastern calls, cursing me as I run away from him and into the maze.

"It's Asia, arsehole!" I call out over my shoulder, giggling. He won't be able to resist the chase.

I run; he follows.

It's always been that way, ever since we were kids. If I can count on anything, I can count on that. Always by my side, always protecting my back. I'm not afraid, not like I was back at Oceanside when Monk had tried to screw with me. This is different, because I want to be caught. I want to be caught by Eastern.

"Asia, come back," he yells, following the demand with a long stream of expletives.

His reaction just makes me laugh harder, run faster.

"No way! Catch me, arsehole!"

"Asia, wait!"

But I don't wait, I keep going, running deeper and deeper into the mirrored maze. Turning corners, I feel along the mirrored glass, laughing gleefully with my heart pounding and my skin flushed with joy, I keep running.

You see, the thing with Eastern is that he always loved the chase, loved the challenge, and in my deepest, darkest fears I've often wondered what would happen if he eventually caught up with me. If he gets what he wants will I suddenly lose my allure? Will he cast me aside then?

Sudden overwhelming shame that I'm even questioning his loyalty, and fear that I might be right forces me to stop, to test out that theory. I lean against one of the mirrors, my clammy palms pressed against the glass as I wait for Eastern to catch up.

It doesn't take him long.

Only it isn't Eastern that finds me, it's someone else.

It's Ford.

"What the hell are you doing here?" I hiss. This is not the time nor the place for us to have a discussion. Tonight is about Eastern and me. There's no way I can deal with Ford.

"Come with me?" It comes out as a question, but my choice is taken away when he grabs my wrist and pulls me through a gap in the mirrors that I swear wasn't there a moment ago. My feet move on their own accord even though I know I should protest.

"Alicia! Asia! Where the hell are you?" Eastern calls, amusement mixed with a tiny amount of fear evident in his voice.

"Let me go," I eventually hush out. I try to pull out of Ford's hold, but his grip is vice-like. The motherfucker is strong.

"Ford, let me fucking go."

Like the determined arsehole he is, he ignores me. Traversing through the maze, Ford drags me behind him, as though he's been in here a thousand times before. Perhaps he has. Or maybe his instincts are just more honed than the rest of the population. There's something about Ford that's different to anyone I've ever met before. He's aloof, yes, cold at times even, but underneath I've seen glimpses of warmth. Every other time he's unreadable, just like now.

"Asia! This ain't funny. Where the fuck are you?" Eastern calls.

"I'm here, this fucking arse-"

Ford places his hand over my mouth, backing me up against the nearest mirror, his chest pressed against mine. For the briefest of moments, before my phone crashes to the floor plunging us into darkness, I see the fading yellowy green of a large bruise on his check and a cut through his eyebrow. What the hell has he been up to?

"Quiet. Listen," Ford hisses, pressing his whole body against mine, the tenseness of his body a warning I can't ignore. I can feel the thump of my heart pulsing in my neck. Jesus, what's his fucking problem? Couldn't this wait?

"What the fuck, Asia?" Eastern shouts this time, panic in his voice.

"Stay where you are. I'll find you." He runs, I can hear his feet stomping on the floor, the light from his phone moving frantically, casting shadow and light above us.

"I just need one minute," Ford bites out. "Please," he adds, sensing my anger. He removes his hand from my mouth slowly, tentatively, trusting me not to call out. I don't.

"Were you following us?"

"Yes." He doesn't even try to deny it.

"What's so urgent that it couldn't wait? I'm here with *Eastern*," I hiss.

"I know," his voice flares with sudden jealousy before he shuts it down quickly. "Look, I need you to know that whatever you hear, whatever you think my intentions are, whatever you're told, I have your best interests at heart. I swear to you."

"What the fuck are you talking about?" I wish the light was still on. I wish I could see the truth in his eyes, or the lies he hides behind them.

"There's no time. I need to get back. Trust me, trust *this*…" Ford slams his mouth against mine and kisses me hot and quick before pushing off and running away, leaving me panting, confused and alone in the darkness.

Half a minute later Eastern finds me. "Asia, what the actual fuck?" he grinds out breathing heavily, his cheeks flushed with exertion. "That's not fucking funny!"

"I'm sorry," I fumble, my own body still feeling the heat of Ford's kiss and my head still spinning from his rushed message. What the fuck had he meant? Was he talking about Sapphire? How could he even know Camden told me about her? The two of them are hardly friendly enough to share. I'm so goddamn confused.

"You look freaked out. What happened?" He looks from me to my phone dropped on the floor and picks it up, handing it to me. I grab it with trembling hands. He assumes I'm afraid. I am, but not for the reason he thinks. I should tell him. I should tell him everything, but the words won't come. I owe him the truth. He needs to know about the kisses I've shared, about Camden's revelation, about Ford's rushed request.

"Asia, what is it?" he persists, stepping closer, trapping me against the mirror with his hands either side of my head. "You can tell me. I've got you."

"It's…"

But before I can tell him what I should've hours ago, the air around us charges with electricity. The hairs on my arms stand upright and before I can even form a sentence Eastern's mouth is on mine, replacing Ford's minty taste with candyfloss and promises. I don't push him away. I don't force him to listen. I let him kiss me because right now I'm two things: a chicken-shit and the hormonal mess Camden once accused me of.

Eastern presses the length of his body against mine, successfully pinning me to the cold mirror. "Fuck, Asia," he mutters gently biting my lower lip before spearing my lips with his tongue. I respond in kind, wrapping my arms around his neck and letting him kiss away the memory of Ford's lips, replacing it with his own. And for the second time in just a few short minutes I let another boy's lust and hope seep into my skin and crawl into my bones, settling within the strongest parts of me, only to make them weak.

NINE

I awake in my bed the next morning with sleep still lingering in my body and worry coursing through my veins. Yesterday evening Eastern and I had arrived at Oceanside with just five minutes to spare. Apart from the fact we had to hand over our mobile phones again and Eastern almost getting himself expelled within the first five minutes of entering the academy for refusing to hand over his, it was uneventful. I didn't see Ford again. We didn't come across Sonny or Camden. Pink and Kate were already in the annex when we reached our rooms and after a brief hello, and another awkward introduction with Eastern, we each headed to our separate bedrooms with promises to walk to the dining hall together for breakfast the next morning. I didn't tell him anything.

I fucking should've, but I didn't.

Sighing, I sit up in bed. Given the semi darkness, breakfast is at least another few hours away. It's early still, the sun hasn't risen past the woods beyond the carpark. My room is cast in shadow, the corners still able to hide the monsters that lurk just in the periphery of my vision. Reaching over I flick on the lamp sitting on my desk, feeling minutely better when the shadows disappear and with it my nightmares that still haunt me even after all these years.

They're always the same. Mum dead, a needle in her arm. Eastern next to her, blood seeping from his parted lips. Tracy and Braydon with blank eyes and blue lips. My little brothers curled up into a foetal position, lifeless. All of them, except my mum, are victims of an unseen enemy. I shiver, feeling a strong desire to scream. I've not had this dream for a long, long time. Maybe this is some kind of omen… My subconscious telling me that something disastrous is about to happen.

"Fuck."

Getting out of bed, I walk into the bathroom and turn on the shower. Stripping, I step under the warm water and let it fall over me, washing away my nightmare and the nagging feeling that something isn't right.

Tracy is safe.

Braydon is safe.

Eastern is here with me.

My brothers are fine.

Nothing is wrong.

Then why do I feel like the world is about to be tipped up on its axis? Why do I feel as though the universe is conspiring against me once again? That the storm I've spent my life trying to control is about to come billowing out of my chest, ripping me and everyone I care about to shreds.

"Asia?" a voice calls.

A male voice.

A voice that belongs to Sonny.

What the hell is he doing here? More to the point, how the fuck did he get into my room? I goddamn locked the door. "What the fuck, Sonny? I'm in the shower. Give me a minute," I call out, the beating in my chest drumming in time with the storm that's brewing second by second. Drying myself off quickly, I pull my clothes back on, my skin still prickling with the remnants of my dream and flushed from the heat of the shower. If Sonny's in my room at this ungodly hour it must be urgent, so I ignore that mass of tangles that is my hair. I've got no time to make myself look decent.

"How the hell did you get into my room?" I ask, yanking open the bathroom door.

He holds out his hands, clasped within them are a couple of long, thin, skinny looking tools that look like a larger version of hairpins.

"I'm a thief. I can break into any lock pretty much," he shrugs, looking both apologetic and proud.

"Couldn't it wait?" What is it with these boys and their determination to barge into my life uninvited at the most inappropriate times?

"I wanted to give you the heads up before breakfast. I didn't get here until late last night, otherwise I would have come at a more decent hour. Nice hair by the way. Like the colour," he says, eyeing the red with interest.

I wave his compliment off. He can't distract me that easily. "You do realise that a more decent hour would've been a couple hours from now. It's 6:30am, Sonny." I frown, wiping away a stray bead of water that's sliding down my neck and pooling in the dip above my collarbone.

"Point taken. But I couldn't sleep. I guess I took a chance you'd be awake. Looks like I was right." His gaze lingers a little too long on my chest, before flicking up to my face. He gives me a sheepish grin that's shadowed in lust. I should've at least put my bra on.

Fuck it. I wasn't expecting visitors. He's just going to have to deal.

I huff, sitting down on my bed and drawing up my legs, wrapping my arms around them. "Heads up about what exactly? Does this have something to do with Ford?"

"Yeah, pretty much… Wait, why would you assume it's about Ford?"

"I bumped into him yesterday at the funfair." I don't bother to tell him that Ford found me (and by found I mean stalked), then kissed me, said some weird shit and ran off.

"He was there? Fuck. That was stupid."

"Stupid why?" I frown at Sonny who's pulling a face that I'm not clear headed enough to interpret, and that has nothing to do with the fact he's wearing low slung pyjama bottoms and a grey t-shirt that doesn't quite meet the waistband. That thin strip of bare skin and line of hair disappearing beneath his pyjama bottoms isn't distracting me in the slightest. Nope.

"Ford got into some shit over the break. Real *fucked up* shit with Camden. The pair fought at Grim Fight Club. Things are gonna get bad, Asia. Like apocalyptic, end of the world, zombie bad. Hackney's Hackers are gunning for Ford, and with his own crew down in numbers, he's a walking target."

"Fuck," I exclaim.

"They have history, Ford and Camden. It was bad enough after shit went down before. Now they're at war."

"I know, Camden told me."

"*Wait*, what do you mean Camden told you?" Sonny's eyes darken with distrust. Not for me, no, this distrust is directed at Camden. "What has that motherfucker said?"

I chew on my lip ring, biting on it as I decide what move to make next. Do I tell him? Do I tell Sonny what Camden told me about Sapphire? Maybe he already knows. Maybe it was a lie and Camden had made it up after all, just to get me on his side?

Fuck. No, he didn't.

No one can look the way Camden did without feeling soul-shattering loss. I know because I see the same look written across my face every time I look in the fucking mirror. My mum's death has never left me. Just like Sapphire's death has never left Camden. When you stare death in the face like we both have, it marks you permanently.

"What did he say to you, Asia?" Sonny insists.

"That he fought Ford before, that he lost. I'm guessing he wanted a redo," I respond quickly, schooling my features and trying to decipher whether Sonny knows about Sapphire too, and is covering for Ford and keeping up the pretence that Ford and Camden's history is based on a fight won and lost. Part of me is wondering why I'm even doing the same for Camden, why I feel the need to keep our conversation quiet. I'm not sure I understand it myself, but I keep my mouth shut anyway.

"You bet your arse he lost. Ford wins every fight..." Sonny's voice trails off and the look in his eyes tells me there's way more to this. What isn't he saying?

"So, what's this got to do with me?"

"It has *everything* to do with you, Asia. You were the reason for the fight. Camden challenged Ford for you. To lay claim to *you.*"

"What?!"

Sonny sighs, sitting down on the bed next to me. A flop of dark blonde hair falls into his eyes that he swipes back absentmindedly. He glances at me with his pretty baby blues. "Camden turned up at Grim's, challenged Ford in front of the whole club. A deal was made. The winner gets you. It's that fucking simple. Trouble is, this time Camden fucking won."

I can hear the disbelief in Sonny's voice, but it's nothing to how I'm feeling right now. *Camden won?* Reeling. I'm fucking reeling.

"What?"

"Camden won. Don't ask me how the fuck that happened, but it did. He won. Ford took a pretty nasty blow to the temple and it sent him sprawling. It took me ten minutes to bring him around."

"Wait, what?!" I feel like a goddamn parrot because my brain can't quite understand what my voice keeps repeating.

"Camden won…" Sonny repeats slowly, the words just as confusing for him to say out loud as it is for me to hear.

"I thought you said Ford always wins…" Sonny pulls a face, opening his mouth to speak, but I interrupt him. "Actually, that's not even the fucking point. Who the hell are they to decide who *gets* me? I'm not someone they can fight over as though that entitles them to my fucking loyalty, or whatever the fuck they want. *I'm* the one who damn well chooses!" Anger overrides any feelings of concern I should have given those two arseholes who thought they had a right to take matters into their own hands when it comes to *my* choices in life.

"He knows that. Ford *knows* that Asia, but he couldn't back down. He *couldn't*. That's not how it works, not at the club. You can't turn your back on a challenge. Not ever, not in that place." Sonny sighs heavily, scraping his hand over his face. I notice then he looks tired, haggard even. The guy hasn't been sleeping, that much I know is true from the dark circles under his eyes. "Ford should've won, and then you'd still be free to choose. He doesn't want to own you like Camden does. I swear it."

"It's not for you to swear anything, Sonny. Ford's the one who should be telling me all this. Instead, he interrupts my date yesterday with Eastern and fucking blurts out some confusing message and expects me to get it."

"You had a date with Eastern? Your best friend, who's *more*?" Sonny searches my face for answers, which frankly I don't feel like giving him right now.

"This is all bullshit," I bite out, ignoring Sonny's questions. "I'm *still* free to choose. This is the twenty-first century, for fuck sake. I'm not some toy to barter with. This is *my* life, *my* choice. I get to decide. Me!" But deep down I know that isn't true either. My choice was made back in Mr Carmichael's room. I must choose Camden… And now, I don't have to choose him, seeing as everyone thinks he's won me. I should be glad I've been given an opening to join his crew.

I'm not.

Shit, none of this makes me feel glad. I feel like a pawn in a much bigger game that I don't know the rules of, and I don't like it. Not one fucking bit. Sonny reaches for my hand, but I get up, refusing his touch. This is royally screwed up. I have so many questions, too many questions. Why did Camden even think he could decide about my life and challenge Ford for me? Why does he want me so bad… only because Ford does? Because he wants to get back at him for his sister? And why the fuck did Ford lose when he never loses? The last time he lost Sapphire *died.* Maybe that's it. This has everything to do with Sapphire and nothing to do with me. Maybe Ford feels like he owes Camden and he's using me as a peace offering. He can't really give two shits about me if he's willing to hand me over just like that. Then again his kiss yesterday told me another story altogether. Why seek me out, knowing he's putting himself at risk of being jumped by the HH crew if he wasn't being sincere? Fuck if I know. I'm no closer to working out Ford than I am Camden. The only person I know who actually has my back is Eastern, and I haven't told him about any of this shit because I don't know how to tell him I've kissed three other boys and let one of them finger-fuck me until I came all over his hand.

I let out a groan, holding my head in my hands.

"This is bullshit," I repeat, not having any other words to accurately explain how I feel.

"Ford won't let Camden have you, trust me on this."

"If that's the case, why did the one person who never loses, fucking lose?"

Sonny's mouth slams shut. He doesn't answer because he doesn't understand it either. The only person who can tell me why is Ford, and I can't entertain that conversation right now. Honestly, he's made this easy for me. I have a job to do, futures to secure.

Camden won the fight, so I guess I'm part of his crew now.

TEN

"What's up, Asia?" Pink asks as I slide into my seat next to her in the dining hall a couple hours later.

Eastern is currently piling his plate high with every single item available from the self-service station, a ridiculous look of awe on his face. It should be amusing that he's so happy about filling his stomach. It isn't. It only serves to remind me that until very recently breakfast for Eastern consisted of a cup of cheap tea and smoggy London air. He always gave up whatever portion of breakfast he had for Braydon, knowing his younger brother needed it more.

"You're out of sorts girl, spill," she insists.

"Nah, I'm good," I lie.

Pink makes a snorting noise. "Yup, and my name's Beige. Seriously, you're so shit at covering up your true feelings you know."

"No, I'm not."

"Err, yeah you are. Does this have to do with those four boys fighting over you?"

"I haven't got four boys fighting over me…" *If only it were that fucking simple.*

Opposite us, Kate makes a scoffing noise. She's quiet this morning too, but I don't see Pink grilling her. In fact, she looks distinctly miserable. I'm guessing her Christmas break didn't go too well.

"Not what we heard," Kate snips, her lips pinching together when I glare at her.

"What exactly *have* you heard?" I hiss, very aware that Eastern is making his way over to us. He's giving his best swagger, like he doesn't give a shit all eyes are on him but is also trying not to drop his tray full of food and make a tit of himself. I can't love him anymore in that moment. He lifts his head and catches my eye, winking. My heart swells, then my stomach drops just like it did on the rollercoaster ride last night. Entering the dining hall is Camden followed by fucking *Monk*. The arsehole is looking way too pleased with himself.

I can't believe I'm going to join Camden's crew and will have to put up with that dipshit.

Thank fuck Eastern is oblivious to them both, at least right now as he concentrates on getting his arse into a seat and not dropping his breakfast all over the floor.

"Camden challenged Ford to a fight over you. It's like something out of a fucking movie except they used their fists instead of swords," Pink smirks, finding this all highly amusing.

"At least it wasn't guns," Kate adds. She looks at me with haunted eyes, and for the first time ever gives me a glimmer of the heartache she's shielding.

"Kate?" I question.

She shakes her head minutely as Eastern plops down beside her. *Not now*, her eyes tell me.

"Alright, ladies?" he asks, attempting to be a little more friendly after I told him Pink and Kate had become friends. He knows that I don't have many of them, so he's going to try and not be an arsehole.

"If it isn't the bestie!" Pink exclaims, leaning over the table and nabbing a sausage from Eastern's plate. She takes a large bite out of it, chewing noisily before smacking her lips together. "I do love a nice juicy sausage."

"Not what I heard," Eastern quips, a grin sparkling in his eyes.

Next to him Kate rolls her eyes. She's not impressed by Eastern's charm, but she keeps her mouth shut on the sarcastic remark that I know she's just desperate to unleash on him. Pink laughs loudly, almost choking on the remainder of the sausage. I thump her on the back as tears of mirth spring from her eyes.

"I like you," she says to Eastern.

He grins. "I think I might like you as well, *Pinky*."

"Pinky?" Kate groans, raising an eyebrow.

"What, *Little Miss Sunshine*? Got a problem with that?"

Kate's eyes widen with hurt, then darken with pain. I'm guessing that's a nickname she's heard more than once before now. It's no surprise, given she barely smiles and is about as friendly as a hungry crocodile to those she doesn't deem worthy of her time.

"For a start, do not call me *Little Miss Sunshine*," Kate snaps, eyeballing Eastern, "And her name is Pink, not fucking Pinky. Got it?" Kate pushes her plate away, clearly losing her appetite.

"Shit, I'm just teasing. Sorry, *Kate*," Eastern says, pulling a face before stuffing his mouth full of bacon, scrambled egg and his one remaining sausage. If I didn't love him so much, I'd be calling for a trough, loading all the food in it and suggesting he ate out of that.

"Hey, I don't mind Pinky. It's kinda cute," Pink shrugs, trying her best to diffuse the situation.

"Well, my name's Kate. If I wanted to be called *Little Miss Sunshine* I'd change my name by fucking deed poll." She huffs. But when we all end up laughing, a tiny smirk pulls up her lips and the ice that seems to have re-formed over the Christmas break, cracks a little.

"Okay, so now we've got that settled. What are you going to do about them?" Pink asks, pointing in the direction of Camden and his crew. We all turn to look. Camden is watching us closely, his gaze narrowing on Eastern and me. On the table adjacent to his, Monk is looking more and more smug. Sitting beside him are Bram and Red. Red glares at me and Bram just draws his lips up in a sinister smile. Arseholes, the pair of them.

My gaze flicks around the room until it lands on Sonny and Ford, and the remainder of No Name crew. Ford looks like he's swallowed broken glass, tension rippling off him, and Sonny is giving me a 'shit's about to go down' look.

"What do you mean, what am I going to do about them?" I ask, my own throat suddenly very dry. I glance at Eastern who has stopped eating and is now giving me the stink eye. He thinks I've told them about our plan. I haven't. He's also clocked Monk. Perhaps telling him about the arsehole was a huge fucking mistake. I see retribution glimmering in his eyes.

"Don't, Eastern," I warn, knowing he's two seconds away from launching at Monk and getting his arse sent back to prison. "I dealt with him. It's done."

"Have you seen the look on his face? That prick doesn't think it's done."

"Eastern!" I warn.

"Fuck, Asia. I *know*, you're a badass. I know you served him his arse on a platter, but that doesn't mean to say I can't kick the shit out of him if he keeps looking at you like that. The little prick. He hurt you. He's lucky I don't fucking kill him."

"It's not Monk you need to concern yourself with right now. Camden won the fight, Asia..." Pink mutters, realising too late that Eastern has zero clue what she's talking about. I groan.

"What fucking fight and more to the fucking point what are you insinuating, Pink?" Eastern bites out, the sound of his fork clattering on his plate reverberating around the room. The dining hall descends into a hush, all eyes on us. I can feel Camden's stare, and when I look up Ford and Sonny are watching us too.

Great. Just fucking great.

"You don't know? I thought everyone knew," Kate exclaims, her pretty eyes widening. She glares at Pink. "Way to go big mouth."

"Asia, want to fill me in and tell me what the fuck they're talking about?" Eastern doesn't take his eyes off me. I can feel his dark orbs tracing over my face as I stare at my now cold scrambled eggs on toast. It's time for the truth. I flick my gaze up to meet his.

"Come take a walk with me?" I ask.

He nods his head, his jaw tense.

Every single pair of eyes in the room are on us both as we leave. This time not one food missile is thrown at us. Good. Motherfuckers are learning.

We pass Mr Burnside's office as we head outside. As always his door is wide open. He looks up from his desk and gives us both a warm smile.

"Morning, getting some air?" he asks.

"Something like that," I respond.

"Just make sure you're not late for your first lesson, okay?"

"Sure."

"And, Eastern…"

"Yes?" Eastern pauses, giving Mr Burnside his favourite death stare.

"Don't forgot that your first period is with me. I'm looking forward to getting to know you better." He smiles again completely ignoring Eastern's not so quiet grumble about '*fucking therapy bullshit*'. I must give it to Mr Burnside; he's got thicker skin than a rhino's backside. Most of us would rather poke our own eyes out than talk about our pasts. He's probably got one of the hardest jobs here. Still, I'm beginning to believe he's one of the good ones, so I make a promise of my own.

"I'll make sure he attends, Mr Burnside," I say, before dragging Eastern down the corridor and out the back door before he can say anything else that he might regret later.

"If that guy thinks he's gonna save the world by getting us to talk about our shit, he's fucking deluded."

"Not save the world, just us," I mutter, remembering what he told me about his own shitty past. The guy's been through hell and come out the other side. If anyone is qualified to help kids with fucked-up pasts it's him. I've not told a soul about what he revealed to me, and I won't.

"What was that?"

"Nothing important. Come on, we haven't got long."

Eastern falls into step beside me as we walk to the formal gardens behind the main building. Frost lingers on the grass and crunches underfoot as we head towards a bench tucked beneath a row of conifer trees. I'm glad I'm wearing my thick orange hoodie and my favourite black jeans paired with my combat boots because it's bloody freezing.

"Spit it out, Asia." Eastern says, watching my leg bounce up and down with nerves. "What the fuck was Pink talking about?" Cold air huffs out of his mouth as he watches me.

"I only found out myself this morning. Sonny told me…" I wince realising that as far as Eastern's concerned he was the first person to see me this morning seeing as he knocked on my door ten minutes before we were due to head down to the dining hall for breakfast and kissed me until I had trouble breathing.

"At what point did Sonny come to your room, after we kissed each other goodnight or before we kissed each other this morning?"

"He turned up in my room this morning before you came to meet me for breakfast," I admit.

"What do you mean he turned up?"

"He picked my lock."

"He fucking WHAT?! The little prick!" Eastern jumps up, clouds of warm air releasing from his mouth in puffs.

"Sit down, Eastern," I say, grabbing his arm and forcefully pulling him back down. He's always been protective but being here has made that amplify.

"You don't care that he broke into your room?" he asks. "Who the fuck does he think he is?"

"My *friend…*" I say carefully. "He wanted to warn me about the shit that's gone down over the Christmas break."

"He could've fucking knocked."

"Yeah, he could've." I sigh.

"So what's this shit about? Camden up to his old tricks?" Eastern grinds out, running a hand through his dark hair.

"Camden *and* Ford. Apparently they fought at a place called Grim Fight club…" I look at him waiting for a reaction.

"And what did the winner get?" Eastern asks, his voice veiled in anger.

"Me, apparently."

"MOTHERFUCKING CUNTS!" Eastern roars, slamming his fist against the wood so hard it shakes under the weight of us. "I'm gonna kill them. Who the fuck do they think they are? It's like you get no fucking say in the matter."

"Look, believe me, I had a similar reaction to you. Thing is, this kind of works in our favour." I draw in a deep breath, blowing it out steadily. Eastern is scowling at me, his mouth pressed in an angry line. He knows what I'm about to say but he refuses to acknowledge it.

"This is the in I was looking for, Eastern. Camden fought Ford to have me and *won.* As far as he's concerned, I'm part of his crew no matter how fucked up that sounds."

"You're *not* his," Eastern hisses. "You're not fucking anyone's. No one owns you, Asia. Not me, not Sonny, not Ford or Camden. Not that arsehole Crown or the principal of this school. No-fucking-one."

I grasp hold of Eastern's fist, smoothing my hand over his clenched one. "Of course not, and I appreciate you saying that. It's good to know that I can trust one person not to want to go all caveman on me." I laugh a little at that only to abruptly stop when Eastern suddenly grasps my face in his hands.

"Don't think for one second I don't want to own you, Asia. I want you to be *mine,* but I know you well enough to know that's not how it works for you. I love you enough to keep my caveman tendencies in fucking check. I respect you more than that."

He leans in close and as much as I want to kiss him, I need to come clean. Shifting backwards, I move away from his hold. His hands drop to his lap as he looks at me with hurt in his eyes. In a minute I'm going to hurt him some more.

"There's something I've been meaning to tell you, Eastern…" *Fuck, this is hard.*

"And…?" He waits.

"This isn't easy for me to say…"

"You've never had any problems telling me anything, Asia. What makes this so hard?"

"I don't want to hurt you. That's the last fucking thing I want to do, Eastern."

"Asia, just say it," he warns.

I grip his hand, squeezing hard. "I kissed Sonny…"

He flinches as though I've slapped him. "*What*? This morning?"

"Shit no, not this morning!"

"Fuck man!" He grinds out, his fingers curling into fists.

"Wait, just let me explain."

He's giving me that blank look he's perfected over the years. The one he used to give the teachers at school when they were pissing him off and he was holding his anger inside. Eastern tends to blow raging hot out of nowhere. At least to strangers it seems that way, but his angry outbursts are never a surprise to me, not when I know the tells so well. This mask he's wearing now is the same mask he wears right before losing his shit. But now I've started, I have to tell him the rest. I must.

Of all people, I owe *him* my honesty.

So, that's what I do. I spill everything whilst he sits in stony silence. I tell him about the kiss with Sonny outside the Tower, about how he fought Monk for me. I tell him about the kiss I shared with Ford glossing over the fact that Ford made me come with just his hands. I'm pretty sure that's not something he'll ever want to know about. I explain how they both looked out for me that night of the fight and how, for just a short while, they made me feel safe. I tell him about the kiss Camden stole in the maze, about his sister Sapphire and how Camden isn't the only one owned, but Ford too by his sister. By the time I'm finished we're already ten minutes late for class and Mr Burnside is heading towards us across the frozen grass.

"Aren't you going to say something Eastern?"

He stands up, looking down at me. There's no hiding how he feels. I've hurt him, that's blatantly obvious when you know what to look for.

"Do you want either of them… *both* of them?" he asks me, not even entertaining the idea of Camden even though he appears to be considering the fact I could be with more than one person.

"They were there for me…"

"…when I wasn't, couldn't be there for you, right?" he interjects darkly.

"That's not what I meant…"

"But *I'm* here now. You've got me. You don't need them," he continues on regardless.

I chew on my lip ring remembering how it felt to be held between Ford and Sonny, and the strange pull I still have for Camden. Even though he *is* an arsehole, there's a truth to him that's intriguing. There's more to him than he presents to the world and I'm drawn to that. I want to know more, and it isn't just to save our arse.

"Asia, don't hold out on me now. Do you want them?" he repeats.

Do I want them? I've got no idea. If Eastern had asked if I was attracted to them, then I would've said yes. But do I want them? I've known Eastern my whole life and it's taken me this long to know that I want him, *need* him. How the hell am I supposed to know how I truly feel about Sonny and Ford in such a short amount of time with all this shit going on?

"I don't know." It's a lame answer, but it's the truth.

"Do you want me?"

"Eastern, I told you how I feel about you…"

"You friend zoned me on countless occasions, Asia. I get why you did it. To protect yourself, to protect your heart. Then something shifted between us when we kissed at Mr Patel's shop. Don't tell me you didn't feel that too, that you don't feel this thing between us…"

"I do, Eastern. You know I do. It's just…"

"You feel something for them too." He gives me a look that absolutely guts me, but I nod my head anyway. The truth is always better than a lie, no matter how hard it is to stomach.

"Got it." He turns away from me.

"Wait, Eastern," I grab his arm and his shoulders slump.

"I need to process. Can you give me that at least? It's a lot to take in," he grinds out.

"Yes," I concede. I understand his jealousy. I felt it too when Opal threw herself at Eastern all those weeks ago. It's always just been us. Only us. Now it's way more complicated.

Eastern nods and starts to move away, then stops and looks over his shoulder at me. "Fighting to claim you, Asia, that's *easy*. Any fool can throw a punch, but loving you the right way, the way you deserve, that's the hard part. *I* can do that. Can you say the same for them?"

I watch Eastern walk towards Mr Burnside, somehow feeling I've just lost my best friend all over again. Maybe I have.

ELEVEN

By the time I haul my arse back inside, I'm thirty minutes late for art class. When I step into the studio Miss Moore, or Ros as she prefers to be called, just waves me over to my seat, distracted by Sonny who's showing her something on his sketchpad. He looks up at me as I enter, winking. It's a friendly, *are you okay* kind of wink but I can't even form a smile in response. I'm not okay, and neither is Eastern.

Sitting in my usual spot opposite Sonny, I grab a piece of thick art paper and a pencil from the centre of the desk. On the board, Ros has already written the title of this term's project; *Reject.*

I mean for fuck sake if this isn't the universe's way of giving me the middle finger then I don't know what is. I'm a fucking expert on this subject matter. Looks like I'm heading for an A plus this term or at the very least a day out of Oceanside. Ros cocks her head to look at Sonny's artwork then points out an area he could shade better before looking up at me.

"Okay, Asia?"

"Yeah, sorry I'm late. Just showing the new guy around."

Sonny raises an eyebrow at that. I keep my expression neutral.

Eastern *is* the new guy to Oceanside, he just happens to be my oldest friend too.

"You need me to explain the aim of this term's work?" Her long earrings dangle like sparkly chandeliers from her ears. I like them. I like her. She doesn't see a delinquent or a fucked-up kid with a past splattered with disappointment and pain. She sees the artist in me, the potential. It's a good feeling.

"Sure," I plaster on a smile, focusing on Ros and not Sonny who's pretending to draw when really he's surreptitiously looking at me from beneath his long lashes.

"Well, it's pretty self-explanatory. Take that word, think about what it means to you and then formulate a self-expressive piece of art in any medium you wish. Sonny is choosing to use charcoal, a couple of others are using oil, and one of the group is using acrylic. Our newest class member is going to use clay. He's decided to do a sculpture, which is exciting. All the finished pieces need to be handed in at the end of the school year, by summer break. The marks awarded will be split fifty-fifty between the class work and the final piece. So all the designs, sketches, research, and so forth that goes into the piece is just as important as what you hand in at the end of the term. Does that make sense?" she asks me.

"Yeah, it makes sense." I might be a school dropout, but I can understand the English fucking language. I almost say as much but decide against it. Ros is cool, she doesn't deserve my attitude. It's not her fault my life's a goddamn mess.

"Great. I'll let you think about what you'd like to do. Excuse me, Asia. I just need to help the young man who's started with us this term. He's just getting some more supplies from the store cupboard." She bustles off in a cloud of sweet-smelling perfume, her numerous bracelets chinking, leaving me alone with Sonny.

"Got things sorted?" Sonny asks me the second she's out of

earshot. "You and the brick shit house looked a little tense at breakfast..." His baby blues rake over me, the dimples in his cheek making an appearance. Those goddamn dimples.

"It's none of your business, Sonny," I retort, avoiding his gaze as I write the word *reject* across the centre of the piece of paper, circling around it repeatedly until the pencil line is dark and thick. Fucking *reject*.

My mum rejected me for heroin.

My dad rejected me for a life without responsibility, without me.

Who's next? Will Eastern reject me now after our conversation this morning?

Will Kate and Pink reject me when I join Camden's crew?

Will Sonny turn his back on me?

And Ford? Will he regret ever meeting me, kissing me, touching me?

Fuck.

Sonny grabs my wrist, stopping me from drilling a hole into the table, but much too late to prevent me from ripping the paper.

"Do you want to talk about it?"

"This is between me and Eastern. So, no. I don't want to talk about it."

Sonny nods, squeezing my hand before withdrawing it. "If you change your mind, you know where to find me, yeah? Remember, I got your back."

"Apparently so," I blurt out before I can stop myself.

"Not apparently, *definitely*."

I make a non-committal sound. Let's see what happens when I join Camden's crew. Will he have my back then? Will his actions speak louder than words when I choose a side? No doubt he'll drop me like a sack of mouldy potatoes just like every other arsehole who's let me down in my life. The thought makes me feel sick, but do I have any right to feel this way?

The truth is no. No, I don't. I'm the one who'll be turning my back on him. My actions are going to fuck everything up. Whatever happens next I have to take it on the chin.

"Asia, I can't speak for anyone else, but I meant what I said this morning. Got it?"

We regard each other, and I get a familiar feeling of warmth in my traitorous belly. He seems sincere, he really does, and I so want to believe that he'll have my back no matter what I choose to do. But this is Camden we're talking about. Sonny doesn't like him any more than Ford does. "I want to believe it, but shit is complicated…"

My voice trails off as my eyes bug out as Ros walks out of the art storeroom with the newest member of the class.

"What shit, Asia?" Sonny asks.

"What the hell is *Camden* doing here?" I snap ignoring his question. He's holding a bunch of art equipment in his muscular arms whilst talking to Ros.

"Ah, yeah…" Sonny growls, following my gaze.

"You've got to be kidding me. *He's* the new student?" I hiss.

"Yep, seems that way. The arsehole loves to stir shit up."

"You could've given me a warning, Sonny."

"Yeah, and what difference would that have made? Just ignore him. We talked about this. You ain't his, okay?"

"For fuck sake," I snap loud enough for Camden to hear.

His head whips up, his topaz eyes boring holes into mine as he meets my furious gaze. His expression remains neutral as he assesses Sonny and me. With a determined set of his jaw, Camden quickly says something to Ros then strides over.

"This art shit is a right doss," he says as soon as he reaches us both, immediately inciting a snarky response from Sonny.

"Fuck off, Camden. Some of us happen to take this *art shit* seriously."

"Yeah, right, and my name's *Bling*," he retorts, drawing a shocked intake of breath from me and a scowl from Sonny who's completely oblivious to the inside joke. Well, it's not really a joke given none of us are laughing. Camden *is* Bling and Sonny has no fucking clue.

"Bling has more talent in his little finger than you have in your whole body, Camden. So why don't you give up the fucking ghost and go piss someone else off."

Camden laughs. "I'll be sure to tell him."

I wince, hating that he's baiting Sonny and I'm not doing anything to set him straight. Why is that? I should just call his bluff and tell Sonny right now that he is in fact Bling. Yet, I don't. It's an unwritten rule in the graffiti world. If an artist doesn't want their identity revealed then that must be respected above anything else. Once again, I keep a secret I've no business keeping for a guy who doesn't deserve it.

"You've made your point, now fuck off," Sonny adds, holding his ground. He's not afraid of Camden and I admire him for it. At the same time, I don't want him getting into shit for me. This is a mess already.

Camden scoffs. "No, I won't. Whether I sit at this table with Asia has nothing to do with you."

"Maybe so, but it has *everything* to do with Asia. I'm pretty sure she wants a say in the things that concern her. Right, Asia?"

I look between the two of them. I know Sonny's waiting for me to call Camden out. To give him a piece of my mind over the fact he challenged Ford for me like either one had any fucking claim in the first damn place. But I don't call him out. I've got one goal in mind and I must stick to the plan. No matter what.

I sigh. "Sit down, Camden."

Sonny looks at me in horror. Camden just smirks. "Looks like you've got yourself a new table partner."

"Fucking perfect," Sonny growls, pressing so hard with his pencil that it snaps in half. He chucks the pencil on the table and stalks off to the store cupboard muttering about how much he'd like to snap something else instead.

"I take it you heard then," Camden says, sliding onto the stool next to me and dropping a sketchpad, pencils, some pastels and charcoal onto the table.

"Yeah, I heard. Have you come to claim your prize, is that it?" I look him dead in the eyes, daring him to try. I know I should be offering myself up on a goddamn platter, instead I'm doing what I always do, challenging him. It's second nature for me. Someone pushes, I push back harder.

His gaze flicks from my eyes to my lips and back again. "I should've done that this morning in front of everyone in the dining hall."

"So why didn't you? I'm yours now, right?" The sarcasm drips from my tongue. I can't fucking seem to stop myself.

Camden laughs hollowly. "We both know that isn't true. No one can claim you unless you want them to."

"So, why do it in the first place then? Why challenge Ford for me? You've no right, Camden." The devil on my shoulder is urging me to give him more shit. The sensible part is telling me to shut the fuck up.

"Because I needed to see how much Ford really wants you."

"What?"

"Ford never loses, Asia. He should've won the fight. He let me win you, proving my point."

"And what point is that?" I snap, my stomach turning over with doubt.

"That he never wanted you in the first place…"

TWELVE

I look at Camden, my eyes wide, my jaw clenched. Is he right? Am I a fool to trust Ford?

"This is all just a fucking game to him," Camden continues in a hushed whisper. "He played with my sister's life. He's playing with yours too. He lost the fucking fight, Asia. What does that tell you?"

I look down at the piece of paper in front of me, at the word reject swimming in front of my eyes as I try to get my head straight. I feel physically sick. Has Ford thought better of the promises he made to me last term? Is Camden right?

"The guy looks out for himself. *Only* himself," Camden insists.

No, I refuse to believe it. Ford threw the fight for a reason. I just don't know what that is yet.

"Asia?" Camden says, tapping the piece of paper in front of me and drawing my attention back to him. He rests his hand on the desk, his finger absentmindedly tracing along the thick black line. He has nice hands, long fingers, and wide palms. I'm almost mesmerised by the way they move across the paper… how they'd feel against my skin. *Shit.*

"The guy's messed up in the head," Camden says, pulling me out of my dangerous thoughts. I look up at him, at eyes that are so fucking beautiful, they take my breath away. "He's messing with you. He doesn't have your back, just like he didn't have Sapphire's or mine. You don't need him in your life."

"But I suppose I need you, is that it?" I ask, tucking my hands beneath the table so I don't do something stupid and grab him like some desperate chick. "You won the fight. Aren't you going to claim your prize, make me a member of your crew? Isn't that why you're here?"

"No."

"What?" I whisper, too taken aback to feel angry.

Camden leans close, his fingers reaching up to push a strand of hair behind my ear. The pads of his fingers brushing across my skin. I flinch under his touch not because it sickens me, but because it doesn't. "I'm not a fucking glutton for punishment, Asia. I do have some fucking pride. We've been here before, you and me. So, no I don't want you in my crew." He drops his hand, leaning away from me.

"That was before everything you told me," I rush out, trying not to sound too desperate, trying to claw back the upper hand. "Look, before you told me to be smart, to make the right choice. I'm choosing now."

"And the right choice is to join my crew even though the three people who fucked you over are a part of it, even though you hate me, *can't* forgive me? I don't buy it, Asia."

"Keep your enemies close, right?"

He laughs, moving to stand. I grab his arm.

"I'm not a fool, Camden. I *know* Monk, Red and Bram will be gunning for me this term just like before, but it's harder to shit on your own crew member. I'm a survivor. This is what I need to do to survive." I hold my breath waiting for him to respond. This is as near to the truth as I can get. I'm not going to lie and tell him I've forgiven him because I haven't. But I need to get close to him. He knows how it is on the street; join the gang or be their victim. One way or the other you're fucked over by them. Better the devil you know. Besides, I'm doing this on my terms. Not his.

On the other side of the room I see Sonny walking out of the art store. Ros has cornered him, no doubt asking him about his ideas. She's chatty but Sonny is paying her no attention. He's glaring at Camden. I get the feeling that I'm not going to get another opening like this again. I need to do this right now before I back out altogether.

"Ask me again, Camden. Ask me to join your crew."

"No."

"*No*?"

"You heard me, Asia," he says, gathering up the items on the table, "I think I'll sit over there."

You've got to be fucking shitting me! This is not what I intended. He's rejecting *me* now, how fucking apt. Swallowing my pride and my self-respect I stand, clutching hold of him again. He tenses beneath my touch. "Wait."

He looks down at me. His topaz eyes filled with both an icy distrust and a fiery passion. Two warring emotions. I'm not sure which is winning.

"You've got less than ten seconds to convince me why I should offer you a place. *Again*," he adds.

"What do I need to do?" I sigh, my heart heavy.

"This isn't a game, Asia," he warns. "You know how this works."

"I'm well aware of how it fucking works, Camden." I need to prove my loyalty to him in order to get into his gang. Actions speak louder than words. They always have. "What do I need to do?" I repeat, determined.

His gaze flicks from me to Sonny and back again, an idea forming in his head. He seems to grapple with himself for a moment. Then he grits his teeth and brings his palm up to cup my cheek. The same fire zings across my skin and I feel like Icarus flying too close to the sun. Another story my mum told me as a kid. So many stories, so many warnings hidden within them. I just wish my mum paid more attention to her own sorry tale than spending her time telling me about others.

Camden taps the paper once more. "Reject them…"

"What?" My mouth goes dry, as he pins me with his stare.

"You heard me. Reject them and choose me. *Only* me. That's it."

"That's it?" I parrot back as if it's really that simple. We both know he isn't just talking about me joining his crew given everything he's said to me in the past. This is so much more than turning my back on Sonny and Ford. This dangerous energy between us tells me that better than any words can. My throat closes over, I cough to clear it.

"If I let you in my crew, you have to be *my* girl." he confirms, hammering the point home.

"And Eastern?"

"What about him?" he shrugs, though I see a slice of shame cut across his features.

"You let him go for me, remember, because you *owed* me for Monk. You said I shouldn't trust Sonny and Ford, but that I could trust Eastern. I only just got him back and now you're asking me to give him up?"

"It's the ultimate show of loyalty, cutting him out, *them* out. Are you willing to pay the price?"

Fucking arsehole.

"Well, Asia?"

Am I willing to pay the price? The simple answer is yes, I will do anything to protect the people I love, even if it means hurting them in the short term. I need to stick to the plan and become one of the HH crew. I need information and Camden has it. That's what I came here to do, no matter the cost to me. I need to prove to Camden he can trust me and the only way to do that is to turn my back on everyone who's wronged him, including Eastern.

"Yes or no?" he asks.

"Yes," I agree.

"Good. Then you can start proving your loyalty now by telling Sonny to fuck off."

"What?"

"Tell Sonny to fuck off," he repeats, challenging me. "After that cut all ties with Eastern and Ford."

Camden starts to sketch something on his paper, acting like he's not asked me to cut off my right arm. I want to punch him. Tell *him* to shove his order up his arse. Instead, I grit my teeth and wait for Sonny to return. If this is what it takes to get into Camden's crew, then this is what I'm going to have to do. A few seconds later Sonny pulls his chair out, about to sit down. I hold my hand up.

"Don't," I snap.

"Don't what?" he asks, looking at me with confusion.

"Don't sit. Find somewhere else…"

"You've got to be kidding me? What have you said to her?" Sonny growls, glaring at Camden who looks at him with a smile plastered across his handsome face. He might be handsome but he's also fucking deadly.

"Sonny. Just go!" I growl, giving him a hard stare, willing him to leave. If he pushes, I might break, and I can't afford to break. Too much is at stake.

"Asia. He doesn't own you. Fight back," he insists.

"I need to survive, Sonny." *Please understand.* I look him in the eye, begging him to just go.

For a few seconds he just stares at me, then he picks up his sketchpad, holding it against his chest. "Fine, but remember what I said, Asia. That still stands."

"What the fuck did he mean by that?" Camden asks as Sonny walks away. I watch him take a seat at another table in the corner of the room. He doesn't look at me, but I know he's just pretending to draw. His shoulders are too tense, his jaw too tight.

"That you're not to be trusted, that you're an arsehole of the biggest proportions. The usual," I retort, not willing to tell him the truth that Sonny said he'll have my back regardless… The question is, will he? Does he really mean that?

Camden grunts. "I don't give a shit about what he thinks of me."

"I know that."

"But I do give a shit about what you think of me. I'll prove to you this wasn't a mistake."

I frown, how can this possibly be anything other than a mistake. Camden smiles. It's a brief smile, just a glimpse of the happy go lucky kid I imagine he once was before. Then his expression darkens. He looks at me for a long time. "You're mine now. *Mine.*"

And the thing is, I can't even deny it. I am his. I was his the second I agreed to Crown's proposal.

THIRTEEN

"What the fuck have you done?" Eastern roars, slamming open the door to Mr Burnside's office later that afternoon. Behind him I can see Kate. She looks flushed. Scared. Angry. Eastern has a split lip and a bruise forming under his eye. Blood dribbles down his chin, dripping onto the floor.

"Eastern, what happened?" I immediately say, as if I don't know.

"What's fucking happened? Are you shitting me, Alicia?"

I don't correct him, not in this state. I'm not a complete idiot. Mr Burnside stands, moving around his desk quickly. He gets between Eastern and I. "Eastern, calm down."

"I wouldn't," I warn, only for it to fall on deaf ears.

"Don't fucking tell me to calm down, arsehole. This is between us." He's breathing heavily, his whole body shaking with rage.

"Listen, you're clearly upset but that doesn't give you the right to come barging in here acting like this. You *need* to calm down, Eastern, for your own good. Once you do we can talk," Mr Burnside says, holding his palms up, trying to placate.

"I don't want to fucking talk. I want to fucking kill that bastard, Camden," Eastern shouts.

"I get it, but take that anger out on the punchbag over there first," Mr Burnside insists, pointing to one hanging in the corner of the room. It's a new addition to his office that wasn't there last term.

Eastern's nostrils flare, his angry glare burning a hole right in my heart. "Eastern, the punchbag. Use it," Mr Burnside orders firmly.

He nods, his jaw clenched tightly as he strides over to it and starts punching it with everything he's got. Each smack of his fist hitting the leather makes me wince.

Mr Burnside blows out a breath then looks at Kate. "Can you tell me what's happened?"

She steps into the room a little hesitantly, looking between us all. "Camden and Eastern fought in class over…"

"Over?" Mr Burnside prompts gently.

"Over Asia," she sighs, wincing. She gives me a look that's both worried, confused and pissed off. I guess the cat's out of the bag. "Eastern refused to stay in class. I figured he needed a friend." She shrugs, and for the briefest of moments, Eastern pauses, glancing at her.

"Thank you, Kate. I think it's best you head back to your lesson now."

"But…" She looks at me, at Eastern, wanting answers of her own.

"I'll catch you later, okay?" I ask, sighing heavily.

"Go," Eastern snaps, before smacking the punchbag again.

"Okay," she murmurs, stepping out of the office and closing the door gently behind her.

Eastern is hitting the punchbag so hard it's whacking against the wall with a loud thud each time, practically knocking him over when it swings back.

"Eastern…?" I say hesitantly, moving towards him. I feel like I'm wading through cement.

"Give him a moment, Asia." Mr Burnside perches on the edge of the desk, his arms folded against his chest. He waits for Eastern to tire himself whilst I fiddle with my lip ring.

After ten full minutes Eastern finally calms down enough to look at me without wanting to rip the world to shreds. He's sweating profusely, his dark hair stuck to his head, cradling one fist against his chest.

"Are you hurt?" I ask, stepping towards him.

"Hurt? Am I fucking hurt?" Eastern's voice gets louder with every word. "This," he says, holding up his fist, "Is nothing compared to what I feel in here." He crashes his fist against his chest, and I feel his pain as though it's my own.

"Sit down, Eastern," Mr Burnside orders. "Let's talk about this. Tell me what happened."

"Asia is now officially Camden's. She's his!" he seethes, hurt and anger seeping from every part of him.

Mr Burnside sighs, glancing at me. "You did it then. You went through with it."

I nod, feeling sick. So, fucking sick. "I had too. It was the only way," I implore looking directly at Eastern.

"To secure your future?"

"Exactly that. You were there, Mr Burnside. You heard what Crown said," I reply.

"You agreed to join his crew, not be his fucking *girl*!" Eastern roars.

"He wouldn't accept me into his crew otherwise. I had to do it."

"Did Camden force you into this?" Mr Burnside asks with a frown.

"Are you for real? No! The *situation* did."

"Fuck, Asia. I can't see you be his. I *can't*," Eastern sits down on the armchair, clasping his head in his hands.

"I'm doing this for us. For Braydon and Tracy."

"Are you sure about that? Seems to me you like the fucking variety." He glares at me as he throws everything I told him back in my face. Maybe there's a tiny shred of truth in that. Despite everything, there is an attraction between Camden and me. Of course, I'm indignant. He doesn't get the higher ground on this one. Not this time.

"Don't!" I snap. "Don't you fucking dare. I'm doing this for you, for *us*. We wouldn't be in this position if you hadn't joined his crew in the first damn place."

"I had to do it for mum, for Bray. I thought you understood that?" he bites out, heartache riddled throughout his words.

"Ditto, you fucking arsehole!"

"Enough!" Mr Burnside stands, picks up a heavy paperweight from his desk. He holds it out between us. "This is how it's going to work. When you have this, you get to say whatever you feel. The other person must remain quiet. No interrupting. Let them talk knowing you will get your turn. I will not have a slanging match in my office. Understood?"

I nod tightly, glaring at Eastern. "Got it."

"Eastern?"

"I understand," he snaps.

Mr Burnside hands the paperweight to me first. I hold it in my palms, the glass cool against my skin. I want to throw it at the ground and watch it shatter. I don't. It wouldn't solve anything.

"Go ahead, Asia."

Sitting back down in my seat, I concentrate on the heavy weight I'm holding. "Camden didn't want me in his crew." I swallow deeply, unable to meet Eastern's gaze but I can see his leg bouncing up and down in agitation. "He didn't believe my reasons for wanting to join either. He said I had to prove my loyalty. There was always going to be a price, Eastern. This is it…"

"What, becoming his fucking girl and casting me aside? That's not something I agreed to," Eastern interrupts, rage and bitterness cracking his voice.

"It's just a label. Nothing more." I pause, gritting my teeth and holding back the flood of emotion I feel. "This is only for a short while. I promise."

"And when he tries to kiss you, touch you, *fuck* you? What then, Asia? Or maybe that's what you really want, is that it? Another guy to add to the growing list."

My eyes widen, and I feel the lash of his anger as though I've been flayed by some motherfucking Roman soldier. I know he's hurt. I understand it, but to think that way about me. No. He doesn't fucking get to say that shit. "Don't throw my honesty back in my face, Eastern. Don't you dare do that. Don't make me sound like some fucking whore. I'm not."

"Eastern, you know the rules. Let her talk. Then it's your turn," Mr Burnside interrupts. He's trying to remain neutral, but I can tell he's affected by what's going on. Shocked, even. Well good, he's as complicit in this as Crown and Mr Carmichael are. I didn't see any of them trying to persuade me not to ruin my fucking life.

"Look, I get you hurt. I. Get. It. But I'm doing this for you. For us. Just because we're here at Oceanside, doesn't mean our lives are any different. Not really." I glance at Mr Burnside, who's clutching the edge of the table, his knuckles white. "I love you, Eastern. I always have. That hasn't changed. It *won't* change. I can't help the way I feel about Sonny and Ford, but that's over now. I can't be their friend, and anything more that might've been is just an impossibility…" My voice cracks, my resolve to be strong waning. I hand Mr Burnside the paperweight, not trusting myself to speak without fucking crying. I won't do that. He takes it from me. Holding my gaze for a moment. There's pity in his eyes and pointless words brimming on his tongue. I can see it, almost hear them and it makes me so fucking angry. I don't want pity or words that mean nothing. Neither will help me or Eastern. It won't help any of the kids here. I drag my gaze away and look at my oldest friend. He's staring at me with such despair that I can barely stand it.

"It's your turn, Eastern," Mr Burnside says softly, handing him the glass globe. He takes it, staring into it like it's a crystal ball that can see into our future and let us know it's going to work out okay. For a long time, he just sits in silence. Then he looks at me, brows furrowed, hurt lashing against him like a storm with no end.

"Sorry is such a useless fucking word, isn't it? Sorry doesn't mean anything when all is said and done, but I'm going to say it anyway." Eastern gets up then kneels before me, placing the paperweight on the floor by my feet. He takes my hands in his, his thumbs rubbing over my knuckles. "I'm sorry, Asia. I'm sorry for getting us into this. I'm sorry that somehow you're the one getting us out of this fucking mess. I'm sorry for all the stupid mistakes I've made. I'm sorry that I can't be a better man for you. I'm sorry for making you feel like you're anything less than the most important person in my life. I've had you all to myself all these years and it's hard for me to see you even consider someone else, let alone know you've kissed them…"

"Eastern…"

"Please, let me finish."

"Okay," I murmur. Mr Burnside is staring at us both, but he doesn't interrupt this moment. I frown, not wanting him to hear this conversation any longer. This is private, this is between us. He must pick up on my discomfort because he stands, pushing away from the desk.

"I'll give you two a moment."

Eastern doesn't even acknowledge him as he leaves the room. He shuffles forward on his knees, pushing between my parted legs and sliding his hands up my thighs to embrace my hips.

"I want you to be mine. I've wanted that for years now, but I waited. I was patient because I know you, Asia. I understood that what you needed the most was a friend. That's changed now. We've grown up, you've grown up and you need someone who's worthy of you. You need someone who can protect you, make you smile, make you feel safe and secure, *loved.* You need someone who makes your heart beat faster, and your fingers itch to touch them every time they're near, like mine do when I'm around you. All of that. I want that person to be me, but I also want you to be happy and now I've messed up any chance of that happening by putting you in this position. I'm insanely jealous that you trusted Ford and Sonny enough to let them in, that they got to kiss you too. I won't lie about that." He blows out a long breath of air, his fingers tightening on my hips.

"Eastern, you really don't get it do you? You *do* make my heart beat faster. I want to be with you, kiss you. I want you to be mine too… even when you really piss me off." I laugh sadly, placing my hands on his arms. I know that this is hard for him to hear, for me to say given the circumstances, but I need to say it. I need to make it clear. "But you have to know, Sonny and Ford have made an impression. You're right when you said that I don't let anyone in, yet I let them in. I have to work out what that means even if I can't act on it right now, if ever. You know how hard it is for me to open myself up to disappointment. Please don't make these feelings I have seem ugly. I won't allow that. I *won't.*"

He nods his head in understanding. "I hate that Camden can call you his, it cuts me up inside because I wanted that honour."

"Eastern, it's always been us…"

He gives me a tentative smile, one that shows off his crooked teeth. Then it fades as he regards me. "I do trust you to protect your heart. *I do*, it's just…"

"You're afraid I'll end up somehow falling for Camden's *charms*?"

I sigh heavily. "I don't even like him, Eastern." I don't, but there's no denying that I do feel something. Lust, definitely. But, fuck, I could never love him. No way.

"You admired Bling, even before you knew that was Camden. I remember the way you used to stare at his artwork for hours obsessing over the *mysterious* artist… I can't believe it's him."

"Liking someone's art is very different to liking someone as a person. No one was more surprised than me that Camden is Bling."

"I know that," he admits, then frowns at me. "See, here's the thing, Camden trusts you with his secret and he never trusts anyone. *No one*, Asia. Why would he do that if there wasn't something there…"

"Maybe on his part. Not on mine," I say adamantly.

"If I'm gonna be completely fucking honest here, I lashed out today not just because Camden was being an obnoxious, bragging prick, but because my gut was already telling me that there's something between you. Even if you're not willing to acknowledge that yet. I know you, Asia."

"Eastern, *Jesus*…" My heartrate kicks up a notch because he's fucking right. There is something between Camden and me. This weird fucking hate-lust feeling I can't seem to rid myself of. He shakes his head, cursing under his breath.

"Look, that's none of my fucking business anyway. I don't own you." He grits his jaw and squeezes his eyes closed for a moment. "Fuck, I'm no good at this… Just tell me what I can do to help? I feel so fucking useless letting you carry the weight of this all."

"You need to trust in everything I do. Trust in *me*, okay?"

"I can do that. It might fucking kill me, but I trust you above everyone, Asia. He's not going to make this easy, you know that right?"

"Of course I do. I have to walk away from you, Eastern. From Sonny and Ford. At least you know why I'm doing it. They won't."

"That fucking wanker, he really knows how to twist the knife in. I get that he's lost his sister. I get he's angry at the world, but this, this is fucking wrong."

"And what we're doing isn't?" I remind him. "If he opens up to me, trusts me enough like you believe, I'm going to have to stab him in the back. I've got to live with that, Eastern. Regardless of what we think of him, he is who he is because of circumstance. Just like we are."

"This is so fucked up."

"It is, but this is the world we live in, and this is how we're going to survive it."

"What about Ford, Sonny? If what you say is true about them, they won't give up on you. If I was in their position, I wouldn't either."

"They can't know. You can't tell either of them. Understand?"

"I do." He cups my face in his hands, rising a little so he's level with me. "I want to kiss you. Can I do that? I might not get another chance for a long time. I need something to keep me fucking going." His smile is lopsided, cast in the shadow of his misery.

I don't answer with words. Instead, I lean forward, pressing my mouth against his full, soft lips. He groans, his hands sliding around my hips, grasping the top of my arse and pulling me forward so my legs are pressed either side of his torso. Our tongues tangle, a dance that is unfamiliar in its intensity but feeling like home regardless. We grab hold of one another, kissing like it's the very last time, not the start of many. It hurts, somehow this kiss hurts my heart and that same deep sense of foreboding seeps into my veins. When we eventually part, I press my forehead against his, my fingers digging into his scalp. "We'll get through this. Got it?"

"Got it," he responds, pressing a kiss against my forehead and getting to his feet.

"And Eastern..."

"Yeah?"

"You need to make Camden believe you've given up on us, okay? If he thinks you've turned your back on me then maybe he'll open up more."

"What are you asking, Asia?"

"You know what I'm asking. Let's get this done, okay?"

He looks at me long and hard, fighting with himself then nods. "Catch you later?" he asks, a familiar question I've heard countless times over the years. My answer is always the same.

"Only if you're prepared to chase me."

"Always," he whispers.

When he leaves the room shutting the door softly behind him only then do I allow myself to crumble.

Just for a moment.

Only for a moment.

Others might want to pity me, but I refuse to pity myself.

"Asia, we need to talk," Mr Burnside says, re-entering the room as I swipe at my face.

"No. We're done."

"I don't agree with any of this. Not the deal you made with Crown, nor the way he manipulated you. Mr Carmichael and I have agonised over it. This doesn't sit well with him either, though he understands your situation better than anyone. He knows the rules, the goddamn lines that have been drawn. He won't step in unless you want him too. But I can't see you this way. I want to help. Let me."

"Last term you asked me what you had to do to get me to trust you. Do you remember?"

"Of course."

"Then let *me* do this."

"Alicia…" he protests. I'm not sure if reverting to the name I was given was a mistake or intentional. Either way it's the shove I need to get myself in check.

Standing, I throw my shoulders back, straighten my spine and look him dead in the eye. "My name's Asia and I *own* the storm within me. If there's one thing I know for certain, Mr Burnside, I won't ever let it or them break me."

FOURTEEN

Stripping out of my clothes, I pull on my swimsuit and walk out of the changing room and into the pool area wearing my new two-piece swimsuit courtesy of Libby, my foster carer. It's nothing special, just a black crop top with a zip down the centre and matching black briefs. She bought it for me when she heard that there was a pool here, so I figured I'd take a swim. Why the hell not? I should be able to do what the fuck I want during my free period. Dinner's in a couple hours' time and I need to get my head straight after all the shit that's happened today. I need the silence that only being underwater can provide.

I need to think.

Then I'll deal with the fallout.

Fortunately for me, the pool's empty. Though I'd bet my arse that most kids here aren't swimmers anyway given no one used the pool the whole of last term. Lack of money, and not having any water nearby (apart from the murky River Thames, and no one's swimming in that rat-infested muck) there isn't much opportunity to learn how to swim back home. I suppose one of the only perks of being in foster care for me was that I was taken to swimming lessons from the ages of ten to twelve. It might've been a couple years since I've set foot in a pool, but swimming is like riding a bike, once you've learnt how, you don't forget.

The scent of chlorine and the warm underfloor heating is somehow soothing as I walk along the edge of the pool to the steps leading down into the shallow end. It's a large pool, a full fifty meters in length, deep even at the shallow end. Easing myself into the water which is a cool temperature despite the heat of the room, I try to relax, acclimatising my body. Once the sharp sting of cold ebbs away, I place my goggles over my eyes, hold my breath and dive beneath the surface.

The silence is blissful.

I feel light. Weightless.

Free from all the pressure that's steadily building.

Pressure to secure Eastern's future, *my* future. Pressure to play a role I have no idea how to fulfil without ruining everything. I'm Camden's now. *His*.

I'm no longer my own person. I don't get to choose who I'm friends with, who I want to spend time with. I've got to turn my back on Eastern and hope that by the end of it all we'll still have a friendship left. I have to let go of these feelings I have towards Sonny and Ford, tucking them away and out of sight probably never to be felt again. And what about Pink and Kate? How will they react? Kate was shocked, uncertain, angry even, when I saw her earlier. What does she think of me now? Then, of course, there's Camden. Can I really get him to trust me and then betray him so brutally? Granted, he's not exactly innocent, but does he deserve to be so royally fucked over? Will whatever I tell Crown put him in danger, make his future bleeker?

Probably.

Who am I kidding? It definitely will.

So many people will get hurt, myself included.

As I swim underwater, all these thoughts fill my head. Only the burning of my lungs and the spotting of my vision forces me to break the surface, treading water in the deep end. Tipping backwards, I float, stretching my arms out wide. I stare up at the ceiling, forcing all thoughts out of my head concentrating on the muffled sound of my heart beating as the water fills my ears. Closing my eyes, I steady my breathing and try to relax. I'm not sure how long I float for, long enough for my fingers to wrinkle anyway.

After an indefinable amount of time, I find myself floating near the back wall of the pool. Reaching for the ledge, I grab a hold of the silver bar and press my feet flat against the wall tiles, drawing my knees up and resting my cheek against them.

"There's no escaping now, Asia," I remind myself, squeezing my eyes shut.

"No escaping what?" a gentle voice asks me.

I jerk in the water, dropping my legs. Pink is standing on the side, looking down at me.

"What are you doing here?" I ask her, my voice sharp even though I don't mean it to be.

"Looking for you," she shrugs, sitting down on the edge of the pool and slipping her bare feet into the water. Her baggy jeans are rolled up to her knees, showing off milky white skin, several shades lighter than my own olive tone.

"Why?"

She cocks her head, staring at me as though I've suddenly developed a third eye. "Because you're my friend, that's why. Kate told me what happened."

"What did Kate say exactly?"

"That when Camden claimed you were his in their English lesson earlier, Eastern lost his shit. That they fought. Ford stepped in. Separated them. It was pretty fucked up."

"Ford stepped in?"

"Yep, pulled Eastern off Camden. Got him to back off. She said that Camden punched Ford too, but he just took it. Didn't retaliate."

"I didn't know that. Eastern didn't say."

"Kate said Eastern stormed off to find you. That he was pretty cut up…"

"He was…"

"So it's true then, you are Camden's?"

"Yeah, it's true," I sigh, unable to help myself.

"Want to tell me what's going on? You hate the HH crew, and even though Camden is a real good-looking arsehole, he's still an arsehole. Why, Asia?"

"Survival." It might not be the full truth, but it's the closest I can give her right now.

"Then why not join No Name? Ford and Sonny, they'd have your back. It makes no sense to me." She leans forward, gripping the ledge with her fingers, whilst her feet swish below the surface. The fact that she's unable to look at me churns my stomach.

"But it makes sense to me. It doesn't need to make sense to anyone else."

"You have to give me more than that. I want to understand," she implores.

"This is my business, Pink. Not yours. Don't interfere." *Please,* I think.

Her jaw grits tightly as she looks out over the pool. "Do you know why I steal?" she eventually says. It's a question that is so out of left field that it takes me a while to respond.

"Because you're a Klepto?" I say with a smile that seems unnatural given the conversation.

"Yes, because I'm a Klepto who likes pretty things. But truthfully, it's the high I get when stealing. That rush of adrenaline and endorphins. I don't steal out of necessity, or even because I particularly like the item I've nicked. I steal because it makes me feel *alive…*" She looks at me then, her head cocked to the side. "Do you want to know what I think about all of this?"

"No, but I'm guessing you're going to tell me anyway."

"I think you're joining the HH crew for the exact same thing. You like the danger, Asia, the rush of adrenaline you feel when you're around Camden. I get the allure. But not everything that glitters is worth having. There are some pretty things that are tarnished on the inside no matter how much they shine."

"You're wrong," I protest, but a huge part of me knows she's right. I *am* drawn to Camden. To the external beauty he presents to the world. I'm also acutely aware that whilst he glitters just like the jewels his sister loved so much, he's damaged, *tarnished* just as Pink suggests. His grief, Ford's betrayal, the loss and disappointment he feels have all carved deep cracks in his façade. Bitterness and pain shine through if only you look close enough. He's jaded by a life confined to the rules of the streets. Then again, aren't we all? But that's what I'm drawn to, the broken parts not the parts that shine, not the danger.

"Maybe I *am* wrong. Maybe not. Either way, I guess it's irrelevant. You've made your choice." She shrugs, going back to swishing her feet in the water. "So, Camden, huh?" she muses after a beat.

It's not really a question, more a statement of fact. Only I haven't really chosen him, I haven't chosen anyone. Well, I guess I *have* chosen Eastern… but if things were different and our futures weren't at risk, would I have picked him above the others? Or would I have fallen for someone else… Maybe I'd never have been able to choose given the chance. Maybe I wouldn't have had to choose just like Kate had suggested. I guess I'll never really know now.

"I mean, aside from Camden being freaking hot," Pink continues with a wry grin, "And the whole dangerous thing he's got going on, I'm actually surprised he had any good points on your list."

"He had enough," I mutter.

"And what about Eastern?"

"Eastern will be okay."

"I'm not so sure about that, Asia. I've only known him for five minutes, but he doesn't seem like the kind of guy to watch the girl he loves shack up with the boy he hates."

"No, but he is the kind of guy who respects his best friend's wishes. Will you do the same?"

Pink nods her head, her long, hooped earrings glinting in the soft overhead light. "I can. I know I've taken the piss out of your *love pentagon*." She grins then. "But I mean it when I say who you choose to love makes no difference to me."

"I don't *love* Camden…" I say, disgusted.

She laughs. "Yeah, lust is a pretty potent emotion too."

I feel my cheeks redden, and duck under the water for a moment. When I break through the surface, Pink is grimacing.

"What?" I ask.

"Kate… she's pissed off. She nearly took my head off when I tried to talk to her about you and Camden. She feels betrayed somehow. That girl has a messed-up past. She doesn't trust easily, and she trusted you."

"Why? I never promised her anything." My gut twists, I knew it. From the look she gave me earlier, I knew she'd hate me for this. That hurts so much more than I thought it would.

"No, perhaps not. But she believed you were different. That you were the type of girl to stand up to the bullies. That's what she sees when she looks at the HH crew."

"What do you see when you look at them?"

"I'm not gonna lie, I see quite a few arseholes. I also see kids who are fucked up by their situations and their pasts. Maybe I'm too forgiving, but I always try to see the good in people even when that might be really, really hard. That flaw in my personality is how I'm able to be cool with you now. I *know* you're good, Asia."

"What about Monk?"

"With the exception of Monk. He's a cunt."

I laugh darkly. "Yeah, he's a cunt."

"Bram, Red, and the rest of Monk's wolves are bastards too…." Pink pulls a face, puffing out her cheeks. I know what she's thinking, most of the crew are.

"Better the devil you know, right?" I say lamely.

Pink chews on her lip. "Thing is, Asia. Kate believed you were the type of girl who'd hold your ground when things got tough, when everyone else either keeps their head down or joins the dark side so they're not the next victim."

"This isn't some sci-fi movie, Pink. Besides, that sounds slightly racist."

"You know what I mean. Luke had to choose between the Jedi and the Sith. Anyway," she says, wafting her hand in the air, "You've disappointed her, I guess."

"Looks like I'm doing that a lot lately," I mutter. I can't protest in any way. That's how I would see it too. Could I be as forgiving as Pink, as understanding? I doubt it.

For a while Pink doesn't say anything more and we're left in awkward silence whilst I try to figure out what to do next. Eventually she pulls her feet from the water and stands.

"I'll try and speak with Kate. She might come around to the idea, eventually."

"Thank you… And Pink…"

"Yeah?"

"Will you do me a favour?"

"It depends on what that is," she replies, frowning.

"Look out for Eastern for me. He'll need a friend."

"What about Sonny and Ford?"

"They have each other… They have their crew."

"And what about you? Do you really think Camden has your back?"

"I wouldn't have chosen him if I didn't think that." It's a lie, a blatant one, but it's all I've got.

"Is he worth it?"

"He has to be," I whisper.

"What's that?" she asks.

"Nothing, it was nothing. See you around?" I ask, hopeful when I've no right to be.

She nods. "Yeah, see you around."

I watch Pink walk away, and for the second time in one day my heart fucking cracks that little bit more.

FIFTEEN

A knock at my bedroom door has me chucking my half-smoked cigarette out of the window. I don't bother to try and cover the smell. Getting into trouble for smoking is the least of my concerns right now. The bangs get louder and irritation crawls up my spine. I've got the mother of all headaches and patience that's worn thin hours ago. Whoever is being a demanding dick can do one.

"Hold your fucking horses, I'm coming!" I shout, striding across the room and yanking the door open whilst simultaneously rubbing at my banging head.

"Are you avoiding me, Asia?" Camden asks coolly, stepping into my room and closing the door behind him. The skin on his cheek is swollen and darkening with a bruise. Seems like Eastern got a great punch in. Good. I'd give him one to match on the other cheek if I thought I could get away with it.

"I was taking a shit," I snap back.

He looks momentarily shocked then bursts out laughing. It's so loud and free sounding that now I'm the one who's shocked. "What's so funny?"

"I knew there was a reason I liked you. None of my girls would ever dream of saying something like that to me. Too busy trying to impress me so they can get into my pants."

I cock an eyebrow and place my hand on my hip. "Just because I agreed to be your girl, doesn't mean I'm like one of them. I'm not about to try and get into your pants, Camden. Just so we're clear."

"Challenge accepted," he retorts with an arrogant smirk.

"Whatever," I mutter, dropping onto my bed and rubbing at my temple. I know I should be sucking up to him, be all flirtatious or something. But that wouldn't be me and I'm more than certain he'd see through the act. Better to be my usual snarky self and hope somehow I get him to open up without ruining my chances of getting any information out of him at all.

"What's up?" he asks, taking liberties and sitting down next to me. I can feel the warmth of his body heat between us and that fucking strange pull. I try my hardest to ignore it, which actually isn't too difficult given I feel like someone has stuck a vice around my head and is squeezing tightly with every passing second.

"Headache. This is a bastard one that has me seeing spots. It hurts."

"Sounds like a migraine to me. My mum used to get them occasionally. She had to go lie down in a dark room and sleep them off every time."

"Yeah? I do feel kind of whacked out." I shift on the bed, the slight movement making my head pound and my stomach roil.

"Have you taken something for it?"

"A couple of painkillers…" I glance over at him, trying not to wince as my vision blurs. "Look, I know you've come here to drag me to the dining hall so you can make some grand statement and rub Eastern's face in it *again*, but unless you want me to chuck up all over your Huaraches, I think you're gonna have to leave the chest banging until breakfast. I'm done for today, frankly."

"Fine. Breakfast then," he agrees, surprising me.

"That was easy," I mutter.

He smiles. "I'm not a complete dick."

"You're joking, right?"

He ignores me and continues. "Besides, you look like shit. Can't fake that."

"*Thanks*, arsehole." Mum should've just named me Snarky Bitch and been done with it. Having a migraine clearly doesn't impede my bad attitude any. Not that I owe Camden anything other than snark and bite. Nice Asia won't be coming out to play today. Not that she appears all that often anyway, and most definitely not in the company of Camden.

"Your tongue is as sharp as a whip today. Anything else you'd like to call me? You may as well get it off your chest. Then we can call it quits for now."

"Tosser, dickwad, prick, wanker, pillock, fucktard, douchebag, tit, bellend, twat, motherfucker..." I reel off smiling as sweetly as possible through the haze of pain. He glares at me, but he doesn't bite.

"Great. Looks like you've got most of them."

"Nope, not even started yet… Dickhead, git, knob, minger, numpty, plonker, prat… *cunt*."

"Don't push it."

"You told me to get them off my chest, so that's what I'm doing. Don't ask for it, if you can't take it."

Camden mutters under his breath, then stands and walks over to my window, pulling the curtains shut before switching off the table lamp and plunging us both into semi-darkness. It takes me a few seconds to adjust, a sliver of light seeping beneath my bedroom doors allows me to see just enough.

"You need to sleep this off…"

"What are you referring to; the migraine or the attitude?"

"Both."

"Then you're shit out of luck with the attitude, because this is who I am. Better get used to it because I'm not changing for anyone, especially not you." A sudden sharp stabbing pain has me groaning and clutching my head. "Anything else?" I ask, wanting him to leave so I can get undressed and dive under my covers. Of course, Camden being Camden just sits back down and makes himself comfortable on my bed. With his back against the wall and his legs stretched out, he looks at me.

"Put your head on my lap, Asia."

Squinting in the semi-darkness, I scowl at him. "I'm not giving you a blowjob, Camden!"

He laughs again, a deep chuckle that shakes the bedframe with his mirth. "When you wrap your mouth around my cock, I want you to be fully into it, Asia. Not ready to throw up the contents of your stomach."

"Oh, shut-up." It's a lame comeback, but seriously my head's about to explode. I'm sure if I really concentrated I could come up with a cuss about how small his dick is, but I have the feeling he's the type of guy to prove me wrong by stripping off. I really don't want to see his dick. Nope. Not on my list of wishes today.

"Just lie down, rest your head on my lap. I'm not going to make you do anything but be still."

"No! You can't come in here after goading my best friend and then expect me to curl up in your lap like some… some *lap dog*." God, I'm on fire today. I'd roll my eyes if it didn't hurt.

He sighs. "If it's any consolation, he got a good left hook in. Fucking hurt actually. Didn't know he had it in him, but I'll allow that one. Next time I won't be so lenient."

"And now you're threatening him… *Jesus*. Can you not drop the gang leader act for one minute? I'm tired and my head hurts and I'm done for today, okay?"

"Just lie the hell down and let me help."

"You don't help anyone," I mumble, groaning as my head bangs painfully.

"Asia!"

"Fine." If this is what it takes to get him to shut up so I can deal with this goddamn migraine then so be it. I can feel guilty tomorrow.

Scooting further back on the bed, I curl my legs up onto the mattress and turn on my side then gingerly rest my head on his lap. His thigh muscles are firm, warm, but not very comfortable. I groan.

"What's up now?"

"Hard," is all I can manage to utter. My fucking head is about to explode like some zombie's brain in a bad 80's B-Movie.

"Yep, definitely hard," Camden grinds out under his breath, but I'm in too much pain to come back with anything remotely funny. He leans over, bringing his chest nearer to my head as he reaches for a pillow. He smells good. Not of the cloying cologne that he usually douses himself in but of soap and freshly laundered clothes.

"Here," he says, gently cupping my head with his hand and placing my pillow beneath it. "Better?"

"Better." I shift slightly to get more comfortable and find my hand sliding towards his leg. Thinking better of it, I move to pull it away, but Camden's hand lands on my shoulder.

"It's okay, Asia. I'm not worried about you trying to jump me. Just be comfortable." His voice is low, soothing, and a small part of me is wondering what the fuck is going on. Is he here being… *nice*? Or am I having some twisted, fucked up hallucination because my brain is fried by the migraine. When his fingers slide up and down my bare arm, I know this isn't an hallucination. This is fucking happening.

"Rest. I can stay until curfew."

"You'll miss dinner…" I mumble. Frankly, I'm not sure why I care that he's not going to get any food, but the words slip out anyway.

"I'll survive."

"That's what we do isn't it, survive?"

"Yeah, that's what we do…"

Camden runs his fingers lightly up my arm, gliding them across my shoulder blade leaving a trail of fire over my skin. He begins to gently massage my temple, pressing lightly before stroking his fingers through my hair.

"Camden, what are you doing?" My voice is soft, low, uncertain. I'm so tired. Fucking exhausted, but also weirdly alert. It's a strange feeling. Mix that with a *'I don't know what the fuck is going on'* vibe and we're in unchartered territory.

"When my mum's migraines were so bad that she could barely see straight, I used to do this for her too. It helped a bit… I can stop if it's annoying?" he asks me. His hand stilling.

"I don't understand you," I mutter, turning over onto my back so that I can look up at him. He's swathed in semi-darkness, his expression unclear. "One minute you're acting like the biggest arsehole on the planet and the next like someone who is, well, *alright.* I feel like I'm on a fucking rollercoaster with you not knowing whether I'm going to plummet to my death, or coast along. Either way the ride is rocky and makes my head spin."

"What can I say? I like to keep you on your toes."

"Can you just go back to being a tosser, so I can hate you easier?"

Camden chuckles softly. "Tomorrow. Right now, I'll stick to being alright."

We don't speak again, and after a few minutes of his gentle caresses, I find myself drifting off into sleep. Maybe it's a combination of feeling so shit that my brain has forced my body to shut down, or perhaps it's the soothing feeling of Camden's fingers stroking my hair combined with the painkillers I took. Either way when I wake up a few hours later, Camden has gone and so has my migraine.

SIXTEEN

When I walk into the dining hall the next morning minus a headache and several friends, I'm greeted with stony silence. Eastern gives me a brief, guarded look before continuing to eat his breakfast. Sonny is staring at me as though I've grown an extra limb and he's trying to work out this new version of me. Ford and Kate refuse to acknowledge me, and Pink gives me a small smile before returning to her whispered conversation with Eastern. He grimaces, flashing me another hot stare that is filled with way too much meaning that I can't even begin to unravel in the few short steps to the self-service station. Better that reception from him than any kind of friendly greeting. We're not friends anymore. At least on the surface.

The rest of the cohort are just ignoring me completely. Including the members of the HH and No Name crew. Camden is chatting with Emerald and doesn't even bother to look over though I'd bet my arse he knows I've arrived. Well, whatever. I knew last night was too good to be true anyway. He's back to being a first-class arsehole. No surprises there.

Gathering a tray, plate and some cutlery, I help myself to my usual choice of scrambled egg, toast and a few slices of bacon. Once I've grabbed a cup of tea and some orange juice I automatically walk towards Eastern, Pink and Kate who are sitting together, then stop suddenly as I realise my mistake.

What am I doing?

For a lot longer than is comfortable, I stand with my feet rooted to the spot. My head is telling my feet to fucking turn around and walk towards Camden, but my heart and every other part of me is yelling at me to keep going. To sit with my friends. This is harder than I thought. My skin's fucking crawling knowing I have to sit with that bunch of arseholes.

"Is there a problem with your legs?" A low voice whispers into my ear.

Monk.

"Stay away from me, you fucking prick," I hiss, stiffening as Monk runs his hand down my arm. If I weren't holding the tray I would've turned around and smacked him across that shit ugly face of his. Across the room, Eastern stands. In two strides Ford's at his side, gripping his arm. The exchange is brief, but whatever Ford says, Eastern listens because he sits back down scowling. Guess I'm on my own with this one. That's okay, I can handle Monk.

"That's no way to talk to your fam, Asia."

"You're not my fucking *fam*. Let's get that straight, dickwad," I bite out. The items on my tray slide about as I turn to face him. I don't know how the fuck I don't manage to spill everything on the floor, but apart from a little orange juice spilling over onto the tray, I don't. "Get out of my way," I snap, pushing the edge of the tray into his stomach. I'm pretty sure the whole fucking dining hall is watching our exchange now. I've got to keep my cool, but fuck, this dick needs a kick in the nuts.

"Welcome to the crew, Asia," he says with a sardonic smile. His attitude is less arsehole and more 'creepy fucktard' as Camden approaches us.

"Problem?" he asks Monk but directs his question to me. His face is blank of emotion, but one look in his eyes and you'd be a fool to think he's anything but raging.

"Nah, just welcoming Asia to the crew. We're gonna be great mates now, yeah?" Monk says, grinning.

I make a kind of hissing noise that has Monk smirking again.

"Sit down," Camden orders loudly. When Monk doesn't move immediately, he leans towards him. "I said, sit the fuck down."

Monk smirks. "Yes, *Boss*."

He steps out of the way and I can feel Camden's hand on my lower back as we walk past him. I'm not sure if it's a protective gesture or one of ownership. Either way it doesn't really matter, neither are welcome. One I can look after myself, and two he doesn't own me, not in the way he thinks anyway. Camden steers me towards his crew in their corner of the dining hall. Now they're watching me with varying shades of hate.

"You all know, Asia. She's part of the crew now. Any fucking issues about that you come to me first. Understood?" Camden says, making sure he looks at every single one of them, particularly Monk who's sat back down at the table with another full plate of food.

"You're fucking losing it," one of Monk's wolves mutters. "She'll never be one of us."

"Need I remind you about how I accepted you into the crew, Dagger, even though we were enemies once? You got amnesia or something?" When he doesn't answer, Camden nods his head. "Yeah, didn't think so," he adds.

Dagger grits his jaw, then looks at me. "I don't trust you, but I do trust Camden. Don't fuck this up."

I don't bother to answer. He doesn't deserve my attention.

"Anyone else got something to say?" Camden growls.

They stay silent, but whilst they might not be talking with words, I know exactly what they think of me. Emerald and Diamond are looking me up and down, not even bothering to hide their disgust. Bram and Red are sitting at the far end of the table, glaring. Monk's wolves are sneering. The only person who isn't giving me the stink eye is Ruby, the girl who was lookout when Emerald and Diamond tried to jump me in the toilets last term and who'd smirked when I'd cussed Monk out on the sports field. If ever a person didn't belong here, it's her. I wonder what her story is. She gives me a nod, a small smile pulling up her lip. Monk coughs loudly and she snaps her gaze away. Ah, I see. I get it. Monk rules her with fear. I make a mental note to chat to Ruby at some point. Can't have this dick thinking he's the big 'I am'. I'm certain I've shown everyone he's not.

"Over here," Camden says, taking my tray and moving off to an empty table just to the right of the main one.

"Cosy," I say as he places my tray down and sits.

"I want you to myself," he shrugs as if that's enough explanation. I suppose it is. He told me once he's very possessive of the things that belong to him. I'm guessing that possession is showing now. Sliding into my seat next to him, I pick up my knife and fork and start eating. Every bite tastes like ash in my mouth but I force every mouthful down. I don't want any of these arseholes to think I'm affected in any way. Balls to them. After a few minutes, the rest of the HH crew stop staring at me and start chatting, eating, and generally not paying me anymore attention. For now, at least. Good, the motherfuckers need to get used to me because I'm not going anywhere until I get what I want.

Pushing my plate away, I take a moment to glance over at Eastern. He's talking to Pink and Kate. Despite the tension in the room, all of them seem genuinely at ease with one another. I don't know whether to be happy or gutted. I think I'm a little bit of both.

"Looks like Eastern's made some new friends," Camden remarks, leaning closer to me. He places his hand on the table just centimetres from my own. I pull my hand away, tucking it between my legs so I don't do something stupid like punch him if he tries to get all PDA on me again.

"He's hurt. Can you blame him?"

"I wouldn't let you go so easily…"

"You haven't given him a choice."

"That's where you're wrong. You agreed to my terms. Eastern had nothing to do with the deal we made so why is he following the rules? Like I said, I wouldn't let you go so easy."

"Stop talking," I snap. The thin line of my resolve waning.

"Fine," Camden says, dropping his arm around my shoulder.

"What are you doing?"

"Not talking," he shrugs, pulling me closer against his side at that exact same moment Eastern looks over at us both. The smile he was wearing drops and instead a dark scowl crosses his features. Kate sees the change instantly, and she follows his gaze. Her disappointment cuts me just as deep.

"Camden. Don't make this any more difficult for Eastern than it needs to be," I hush out, forcing myself to look away from my best friend's hurt.

"Maybe this will send a rocket up his arse," Camden responds.

"Don't do that. Don't taunt him." I try to shake him free, but he just holds on to me tighter.

"Besides, what difference does this make now? You didn't complain last night when you fell asleep with your head in my lap."

"I was *sick*."

"And?"

"And I didn't have the fucking strength to argue. Today, I'm asking you to stop rubbing his nose in it. You've got me haven't you? Isn't that enough?"

"Not nearly. Not the way I want…" he whispers, gripping my chin with his fingers and forcing me to face him. I can't distinguish whether he's pissed off or turned on. There always seems to be a very fine line between those two emotions with him.

"Back off…" I hiss.

But that was the exact wrong thing to say. You don't tell the leader of the Hackney's Hackers crew to back off. It's like setting alight a field of sun-dried grass and expecting it not to catch fire.

"No," he says, then brushes his lips against mine, kissing me gently in front of everyone.

Over the whoops and catcalls of the HH crew I can hear the distinct sound of Eastern swearing and Kate and Pink calling his name as he leaves the room.

Inside I'm breaking apart. Breaking apart because I'm hurting the people I care about. Breaking apart because despite it all, his kiss is burning me up even if it is only a gentle caress.

Everything is going to shit, and it's only the first day.

Camden pulls back and gives me a look that dares me to respond. I want to punch him for making Eastern hurt, for making me *feel*. Instead, I pick up my glass of orange juice and knock it back in one go before standing.

"See you in class."

"Where are you going?" Camden frowns, a flicker of remorse in his eyes.

"I've got a date with the principal," I lie before striding off.

Thing is when I get outside the dining hall, Eastern, Kate and Pink are nowhere to be found. So, I end up doing exactly what I lied about and head towards Mr Carmichael's office.

SEVENTEEN

"Asia, come in," Mr Carmichael says when I push open his door and stand on the threshold, not entirely certain I want to enter now that I'm here.

"Actually, I'm good." I move to turn away.

"Asia. You've found yourself at my office for a reason. Come in, *please*?" he adds.

Despite myself and my inherent need to defy authority, I enter his office, shutting the door behind me.

"What's up?" he asks, as I take a seat.

"You don't know?" I cock an eyebrow giving him my most disgusted stare that I can muster. It's not hard, given I feel so pissed off, confused, disappointed, out of sorts.

"I learned about Eastern and Camden's fight from their class teacher. I understand Eastern found himself in Anthony's office whilst you were having your therapy session with him. That's about the sum of it, yes?"

"Mr Burnside didn't tell you more?"

"Anthony may be my partner in life, but he's also a professional.

What happens in your sessions stays private. Of course, if you want to talk about it with me, then that's okay too."

I make a huffing noise, sounding like a petulant child rather than someone who's whole fucking life has been tipped upside down. I don't huff, I don't sulk, and I certainly don't seek out the support of an adult. But here I am doing just that. I glare at Mr Carmichael, fucking furious suddenly.

"Got something to say, Asia?"

"Why didn't you *stop* it? Why didn't you say something to Crown when I agreed to get information from Camden about the King?" I blurt out. That wasn't what I intended to say, but that's what comes out of my mouth regardless.

Mr Carmichael sighs. "If I stepped in at that point, would it have made a difference to your decision?"

"No." I was determined. Certain I could do it, sure of myself, of Eastern, of our friendship and love. I acted on instinct. I did it because I thought I wouldn't have any issue taking Camden down if that's what it took. Now, I'm second guessing everything.

"I knew that, Asia. Listen," he says, shifting forward in his seat and resting his arms on the table in front of him. "You made a deal to secure your futures. You care for Eastern deeply. You love his family as though they're your own. I get that. I know only too well that you protect family at all costs. You avenge them if need be. I *get* it."

"And what about Camden? What about his future? What about him?"

"You care what happens to him?" Mr Carmichael asks, cocking his head to the side.

"No, yes… Look, I don't know. He's a wanker. I don't like him all that much, but what gives me the right to fuck him over to save our arses?"

"Survival, am I right?"

"Yes, but what about *his* survival?" I twist my hands together in my lap. "Do you think I'm doing the right thing…?"

"It isn't about what I think."

"Yes it is. You're the fucking principal of this school. Are you willing to let one kid get screwed over to save two others? I thought you *actually gave a shit not a metaphorical one*," I spit, throwing his words back at him.

He winces, scraping a hand over his face. "I do care. I do give a shit, about all of you."

I laugh bitterly. "Then I'm going to ask you the question again, Mr Carmichael. Why didn't you step in and stop Crown?"

"Because I'm just the principal of this school, Asia. I'm not judge and jury. I'm not the law. My powers exist here in the confines of this academy alone, and even then they're limited. My hands are tied."

"It isn't right."

"Would you rather Eastern went to prison for fourteen years? Would you rather he took the fall for some faceless criminal who doesn't give a shit about the kids he uses to do his dirty work?"

"No, of course not. But this could fuck up Camden's life too."

"You don't know that yet. Crown wants information on the King."

"He also said that he believes Camden is the key to everything. That he's in the King's pocket. If that's true then there's no way Camden won't be fucked."

"From what you know about Camden, do you believe he's worth protecting as much as Eastern?" Mr Carmichael asks me.

"It's different. I've known Eastern since I was a baby. He's *family*."

"I get that, but you're here talking to me about Camden and your concerns for *him*, despite not really knowing whether you even like him or not. You have doubts, so my question still stands. Is Camden worth protecting the same way you're protecting Eastern?"

Is he? He's the leader of Hackney's Hackers, a notorious gang back in London who are famed for causing chaos and ruling the streets with an iron fist. He refuses to get rid of Monk from his crew despite the shit that wanker put me through. He wound up Eastern yesterday then kissed me this morning knowing it would hurt him even more. But not so long ago he was also Bling; a talented artist who once had dreams and aspirations, fucking *hope*. He lost his sister in tragic circumstances, held her when she died in his arms and last night he seemed to care enough about me to ignore his own needs. Maybe that was all a ploy to get me onside, maybe it was genuine. Either way, is there someone inside him that's worth protecting, saving even?

"Asia?"

"I don't know." And I don't. That's why I'm here I guess, looking for answers.

Mr Carmichael nods. "Then I want to give you a piece of advice. Do what you set out to do, find out what you can, but-and this is important-trust your instincts. If he's a decent kid despite his circumstances, then it will become apparent. If he isn't, then that will become clear too."

"So, you're saying *I* should be the judge and jury? That's it's up to me whether I fuck him over or not?"

"Yes, I suppose I am."

"Fucking great."

"Asia, what did you think would happen when you agreed to Crown's terms?"

"I thought I'd find it easy to fuck him over."

"I don't know much, Asia, but I do know this. You're a good kid and you have a conscience. This isn't going to be easy or straightforward."

"So what do I do?"

"You need to see if Camden's worth protecting or if he deserves punishment. I might be the principal of this school with noble ideas of helping you all. But I'm also a man who put another man in a wheelchair. Was it deserved? Yes, I believe it was. I still believe that. But does that make it right? I'll let you consider that. The fact of the matter is, I broke the law and I paid for it, Asia. But am I a bad person? Maybe that's not a question I can answer honestly."

"So you think I should've let Eastern go to prison? Is that what you're saying?"

"No. I'm saying that every action has a reaction. Every decision made, every choice, has a consequence. You know that better than anyone. Eastern did something stupid to try and support his family. Was it the wrong thing to do…? In the eyes of the law, yes it was. But my personal view is that if Eastern and his family got the right support from the beginning he wouldn't have had to do what he did. Now you've agreed to this deal to save them and secure your futures, but at a price. Quite a hefty one. Camden's future is in your hands, and by the looks of it so is your conscience and happiness too. See," he says, holding open his arms, palms upwards like a pair of scales. "Action, reaction. Decision, consequence. Right now, you hold all the cards. I'm not saying it's the easiest position to be in, because it isn't. But you do have a choice about how this can go."

"I don't have a choice…"

"Yes, you do. Crown wants information about the *King*. He believes Camden can provide that and he thinks you're the one who can get him to talk. That doesn't mean to say that whatever you find out, you have to share."

"You want me to lie?"

"No, I want you to be *wise*. I want you to decide on the facts presented to you. I want you to decide whether he's worth protecting or if he isn't. I've said this before, and I'll say it again. It's not brave to protect someone who's wronged you. I don't agree with this shit about loyalty in gangs when that loyalty is wasted on someone who doesn't deserve it. But doing the same for someone who's a good person despite the bad decisions they've made. That's a different thing altogether, in my opinion."

"That's a dangerous opinion to have, Mr Carmichael, especially in your position."

"Maybe so, but it's what I believe. Only you can decide if Camden is worth protecting."

"That's too much responsibility…"

"You're right, it is. But this is where you're at. You're at a crossroads, Asia. You can go one way and lose Eastern or you can go another and possibly seal Camden's fate… or, you can take the route less travelled and do what you think is right, even when that could be wrong in the eyes of the 'law'."

"Fuck."

"My sentiments exactly. I'm sorry this is where you're at, but I will support you in any way I can. Anthony too, if you'll let him. He has a code that he must stick to, an oath that can't be broken. Go to him for advice, just to talk, whatever you need. Let him help."

"I look after myself."

"And yet, here you are…"

Admittedly, he's got a point.

"I should go," I say, getting up. "My new physiotherapy class starts soon."

"Ah, yes. Good choice. Sally is a fine teacher. You'll like her."

I move towards the door, my hand hovering over the handle. "What happened to Bobby?" I suddenly ask, curious that I've not seen him around. He's usually like a fly around shit.

"Bobby is no longer with us." Mr Carmichael frowns. He looks as though he's going to say something further about the matter, then decides against it. "For now, I'm taking up the slack until I can find a suitable replacement."

"You are? I didn't see you last night."

"You were asleep when I did my rounds. Camden said you had a migraine when I caught him leaving your room..."

"Oh." My cheeks flush pink. After everything I've just said, what must he think of me? More to the point, why do I care? Mr Carmichael stares at me with a neutral expression. There's no judgement in his gaze. I appreciate that.

"He seemed genuinely concerned. That much was clear."

"Hmm…"

"You don't think he was?"

"I don't trust him." *I don't trust myself around him*, though I keep that thought to myself.

"Trust is something earned, not something given without thought or care. First you need to trust your own instincts and then make a decision on Camden. Cut yourself some slack. This isn't an easy task, but you have time. Crown won't be back until just before the year ends for summer and you finish your time with us. Use it wisely, okay?"

"That's easier said than done."

"I appreciate the difficult position you're in. That the friendships you made last term might be difficult to maintain now…" He cocks his head to the side. "There might be something I can do to help with that."

"How can you possibly help? Kate hates me. Eastern can't be anywhere near me. Ford and Sonny are keeping their distance and Pink is stuck between wanting to support me and keeping well out of it. Like everything with me, nothing is fucking straightforward or easy."

"I see that." Mr Carmichael's telephone rings, and he gives me an apologetic smile. "Come back any time, okay?"

"Sure," I mutter, leaving him to answer his call.

I lean back against his closed door staring at the exit more than a little tempted to walk out of this building and into a life far less complicated. Of course, I don't. I head back into the storm, holding onto the one within me, hoping it doesn't tear me apart.

EIGHTEEN

My first lesson with Sally goes well. She's a nice woman. Early twenties, blonde, pretty in a neat bun and glasses kind of way. According to the schedule of learning she's given us, for the next month or so we'll be focusing on human anatomy, and by we, I mean myself and Ruby. No one else has taken her class. It's not a full course like you'd learn at university, but Sally is going to teach us the basics that we can build on later if we choose to. I doubt very much that I'd ever get the opportunity to go to university after I leave Oceanside but the thought it could be a possibility, however slim, feels good.

"So, that's it for the first lesson. I'm cutting it short by five minutes as I've got a meeting with Mr Carmichael," she explains, handing both me and Ruby a course book each. "Anatomy and physiology are key to this profession and it's important you do as much study of your own back to support your learning in the classroom. So, why not use this extra few minutes to take a look through before your next class?"

"It's a big book," Ruby mutters, staring at it with wide eyes.

"Yep, and it's a good place to start." Sally grins.

"Start?"

"Yes, start. There's a lot to learn but if you're serious about this, I'm more than willing to teach you what I can in the time allotted."

"Fuck, I wish I'd chosen business studies… At least the teacher is male and fucking hot. No offense, Miss. You're cute and all," Ruby says as an afterthought.

"None taken. Look, it's the first day. It's all a bit overwhelming, but I can tailor the lessons to suit. Don't be put off."

"*I'm* not put off," I say, glaring at Ruby. "I want to learn. I have a friend who's disabled. I'd like to help him if I can. He already has regular physio to keep his muscles from seizing up… but it's not enough."

Ruby is now staring at me with interest. Perhaps I've said too much. It's not often I talk about my private life, especially not Braydon. I'm very protective of him.

"I'm glad, Asia. I can work with enthusiasm, and any life experience you have is helpful too." She smiles warmly. "Now I'd better be off."

"Thanks, Miss," I say, meaning it.

"Call me Sally. Miss is a little formal," she says, as she grabs her bag and heads out of the classroom. "See you Friday."

"Yep," I respond, gathering up my books. Next up is Math which is on the upper floor and my least favourite subject. But bunking the lesson in the first week probably isn't the smartest idea, so I head towards the door.

"You got a minute, Asia?" Ruby asks.

"We've got five apparently," I snap, not feeling particularly friendly this morning.

"I wanted to talk with you…" She grabs hold of my arm, forcing me to stop. I snatch my arm away.

"So talk. I've got a class to get to."

"You need to watch your back. Monk is still gunning for you, Asia."

I bark out a laugh. "Tell me something I don't fucking know."

Ruby looks worried as she peers at the still open classroom door. "Look, bringing you in hasn't gone down well with the rest of the crew. They're not happy."

"I don't think Camden gives a shit."

"He should, Monk won't let this stand. He'll come for you again, Asia. So will the rest of them."

"And what about you, Ruby? Will you come for me too?"

She drops her face. "I hate this bullshit. But…"

"But?"

"But I'm not strong like you." She turns her body to the side, lifting her sweater revealing a multitude of bruises. Some are a dark purple. Some are the mottled yellowish green of an older bruise that's now healing.

"Who the fuck did that to you…?" I growl, anger making my fists clench.

She raises her eyes to look at me. "Who do you think? *Monk*."

"That rotten, dirty bastard!" I shout, unable to help myself. "Does Camden know about this?"

Ruby shakes her head. "Shh, keep your voice down!" she warns me. "Camden doesn't have any idea and I'm not going to tell him."

"Why the fuck not? Are you *insane*? If you can't defend yourself against Monk, then someone needs to do that for you. Camden needs to!"

"Even if he knew he couldn't do anything about it. His hands are tied, Asia."

"That's just an excuse to get away with doing jack shit!" I hiss. Mr Carmichael had said the exact same thing to me earlier and it's quickly becoming my most despised excuse. I'm fed up with all the excuses.

"No. He *really* can't."

"Why?"

Ruby shakes her head. "I've said way too much already."

"Ruby!" I warn, stepping closer. She flinches as though I'm going to hit her.

"Shit, he really has done a number on you. You need to fight back."

"I'm not like you. I don't know how to fight."

"So you just take it?"

"I survive."

A sudden overwhelming urge to scream bubbles up my throat and it takes everything in me to keep it inside. That motherfucker is going to get served his arse a second time and I don't give a flying fuck if it causes problems in the damn crew.

"Look, I appreciate you warning me about Monk. But seriously, I'm sick of hearing that he has immunity. It's bullshit."

"But he does have immunity. Monk *can't* be dropped from the crew, Asia. Camden can't touch him. They've clashed so many times over the last couple years and he's never been able to really fuck him up. A punch here and there, but nothing more than that." She looks at me, blowing out a breath.

"Why?"

"No one in the crew aside from me and Camden know…"

"Know what, Ruby?"

"And I only know because Monk let it slip one time when he was punishing me," she continues.

"Ruby, *fuck*. Punishing you? That motherfucking bastard."

"This didn't come from me, okay," she says, ignoring my outburst.

"Of course not," I say reeling. Monk beats her and she just takes it? I can't even begin to understand that.

"No, you have to promise me."

I grip hold of Ruby's shoulders, squeezing. "I promise you, Ruby. I won't say a word. But I can't promise you I'm not going to kick Monk's arse again."

"You were amazing that night, but that ain't gonna happen again. Not now you're in the crew. No infighting." She pulls a face, rolling her eyes.

"You're shitting me right? Look at your bruises, Ruby! He *beats* you. Regularly, by the looks of it."

"No one knows about that… except now you."

"And you expect me not to do anything about it? For fuck sake."

"I know. But that's just the way it is."

"NO!" I shout. "This isn't just the way it is!"

"Shh!" she says, holding her finger up to her lips. "You can't. You got away with beating Monk at the Tower that night, but Camden didn't. He paid for allowing that to happen."

"What do you mean?"

"Shit went down over Christmas break, Asia."

"The fight between Camden and Ford you mean?"

"No, not the fight."

"What then? Tell me!"

Ruby leans in close, her eyes wide with fear.

"Shit, Ruby, just tell me." Her fear is beginning to freak me out. This is crazy, no one should have to feel this way about some jumped up, arrogant *bully*.

"Monk's the *King's* son, Asia…"

"What the fuck?!" I exclaim, shocked. "You mean that criminal everyone knows about but has never seen. He's like the fucking Loch Ness monster." I mean, I know more about him than most, but Ruby doesn't need to know that.

"Erm no, he's more like Dracula given the amount of blood he likes to spill…" Ruby says, glancing at the door, real honest to God terror in her eyes. "And the King spilt a lot of blood over the holiday. He took out his displeasure on the one person Camden loves above anyone else… his mum."

"His *mum*?" I whisper-shout.

"Yeah, his mum. The King hit Camden where it hurts. He's a sick bastard. Sick. And Monk is exactly like him."

"*Jesus!*" I hiss.

"Not only does the King own Camden, he owns his mum too. He hurt her as penance. So you see there's nothing you can do for me. Nothing Camden can do, not if he wants to see his mum alive."

"No!"

"Yes."

I stumble backwards into the table. My pulse pounding loudly in my ear.

"Camden's mum is the King's *girlfriend.* At least that's what he pretends. Only she's not. He owns her, Asia. Just like he owns us all."

For a few seconds I just stare at Ruby, taken aback. All the anger I feel evaporates into fear. Thick, oppressive, sick-making, body-trembling *fear.*

Fear for Ruby and what Monk is doing to her. Fear for Eastern and the possible repercussions of his talk with Crown. Fear for Bray and Tracy because maybe the King's reach is further than we all thought. Fear for Camden and his mum. Fear for me.

"Do you understand now? Camden might have done bad things but all for his mother, to help *her.* It's fucked up. So, when I tell you to watch your back, I'm not kidding, Asia. Monk is his father's son."

Outside the corridor starts to fill with other pupils leaving their classes. A few members of No Name crew walk past. One of them stops and narrows his eyes at us. If I remember correctly, his name's Lee. I'm tempted to walk over and slam the door in his damn face but getting into another fight when I need Ruby to elaborate right this fucking second wouldn't be wise.

"What the fuck are you two whispering about?" he asks.

"How your dick is no bigger than my pinky, wank stain," I retort automatically, not in the mood to entertain another arsehole with all this shit going on.

"Say that again!" He steps inside the classroom, only to be yanked back by a familiar face.

"Don't. She ain't worth it," Sonny says, giving me an apologetic look that's quickly covered up with a scowl as soon as Lee looks at him. "Let's go."

"She's HH crew now. She's our enemy."

"I said *let's go*!" Sonny snaps, grabbing Lee's shoulder and pulling him backwards.

"What the fuck, Sonny?! Don't tell me you're still hung up on her."

"Nah, I don't give a shit, but I do care if you get hauled into Mr Carmichael's office for getting into a fight. You could do without the hassle right now, Lee."

My stomach rolls over at his words and I feel physically sick, then *angry*. It might be my go-to emotion when I feel the most vulnerable, but really, is he fucking serious?

"Yeah, run away when things get tough," I snap, looking at Lee but aiming my remark at Sonny. I know it's unfair to be angry at him. I *know* that. As far as he's concerned I'm the one who's turned my back on him. I've no right to feel this way. None.

"No one's running anywhere. There's a time and a place for *everything*. That time isn't now," Sonny grinds out. It comes out as a threat, and I would've taken it as one if I hadn't seen the truth in his eyes, the *apology*. He doesn't mean what he said. He hasn't stopped caring. There's a message hidden in his response, one that's aimed very much at me but means something very different to what Lee and Ruby understand. The anger that had quickly flared up, dissolves, leaving me empty and exhausted. Reeling from all the stress.

"I'm not running, just not wasting my time on a turncoat," Lee adds, looking me up and down.

"How can I be a fucking turncoat when I wasn't part of your crew to begin with? Are you thick as shit as well as dickless?"

Lee turns puce whilst Sonny covers a smirk with a cough. Now I know for sure he hasn't given up on me. "Come on Lee, let's go before she self-combusts."

"Yeah you're right. Ain't worth the time." Lee glares at me before walking off.

"Tick-Tock!" I shout at his retreating back.

Sonny gives me one last lingering look before walking away.

"Well, shit. You're one tough bitch, Asia," Ruby says, startling me. I'd almost forgotten she was there.

"Yep, tough as nails and twice as strong," I retort, feeling anything but.

NINETEEN

By the end of the first week my name is mud. Kate hasn't spoken a word to me. Pink has tried to give me her support but with Camden constantly hovering nearby it's impossible to have any kind of conversation with her. Eastern has kept his distance as promised, but all the unspoken words between us are building up so high that I'm not sure we'll ever get back to that easy way we had with each other. Then there's Ford and Sonny. Twice Sonny has tried to approach me to have a conversation, but Ford has prevented him. Cutting in, taking him aside. One time he actually dragged him from the rec room. I heard them arguing outside about it. It's been infuriating not being able to just get up and ask them both what the fucking deal is. I mean I know what my deal is. I've got to keep away from them both, so Ford is doing me a favour really. But what the fuck is his deal? Losing the fight and handing me over to Camden like nothing happened between us last term.

Out of them all, Ford has disappointed me the most.

After that kiss he stole in the mirrored maze almost a week ago, he has completely ignored my existence. In P.E he's kept far away from me. In Math he's sat on the opposite side of the room, not working, but not acknowledging me either. Whenever we're in the dining room he is oblivious to my presence. He simply handed me over to Camden and washed his hands of me. I can't deny that it hurts.

This evening whilst everyone else is either in the rec room chilling out watching crap TV or hanging out with each other before curfew, I'm alone in my room. Camden hasn't even bothered to come check on me. Which is just as well because I'm not sure if I can hold out much longer about how Monk is beating Ruby. She might have begged me not to say a word, but I've certainly not forgotten what she's told me. Nope. I have plans for that waste of life. I may not be able to challenge Monk to a fight so I can kick his arse again, but that doesn't mean to say I can't make his life a misery just like he's done the same to Ruby. I just need to be smart about my vengeance and that's going to take time.

Giving up on reading my anatomy textbook, I grab my swimsuit and towel and head to the pool. It's the only way lately that I've been able to clear my head enough to deal with what's going on. I haven't gone to Mr Burnside with anything, but I'm full up to the brim with fucking worries that my migraines are becoming a regular occurrence now. It's taking its toll.

Maybe on Monday in my therapy session I can offload, just a little bit. I'm beginning to realise that there are some things I just can't hold onto. I'm strong, yes, I've had to be, but I'm not a fool. Keeping this all to myself is slowly killing me and I don't have anyone to talk to about it. Granted I won't be blabbing about everything to Mr Burnside, I'm not stupid, but I can share some stuff. I think.

That thought keeps me going.

Ten minutes later I'm in the pool, which yet again is thankfully empty. This place has become my sanctuary now that I have no one to rely on. I can think and expend all this restless energy in one go. It helps to alleviate the stress a little.

For the next hour, I punish my body, kicking hard with my legs and arms as I swim back and forth savouring the scream of my muscles and the racing beat of my heart until I can't do anymore. I don't really have anywhere else to be, so when I'm done I sit on the top step of the shallow end with my lower body immersed in the water, staring into the depths. I'm not sure how long I stay like that, long enough to feel the warmth of my workout ebb away and the cold of the water to seep in.

"Your muscles will tense up if you stay sitting in the cold for much longer."

I whip my head up to see Ford striding into the pool area. He's wearing a pair of dark swimming trunks slung low on his hips. His body is taught, strong, fucking dangerous to my health. Goddamn him.

"What are you doing here?" I snap, sliding my body lower into the water and backing up against the wall.

He looks down at what he's wearing, which isn't much of anything frankly, and pulls a face.

"To swim, of course," he says before diving into the pool in a perfect arc. He cuts through the water with ease, his shoulder and arm muscles rippling with the exertion of swimming so fast. I hold my breath as he heads straight towards me, then decide I need out of this situation before I do or say something stupid. I move towards the steps with every intention of escaping, but find myself pulled back against a hard chest, Ford's arm wrapped around my waist.

"Don't leave, not yet," he mutters against my ear.

"Ford, you need to let me go." There's panic in my voice as I glance at the entrance to the pool. This is too risky, and it isn't just the fear of someone walking in on us, but the fear of what Ford will do to my heart. He's already managed to crack it just a little this past week. I can't afford a fissure any deeper than the one that's already formed.

"See, here's the thing. I've been trying to do that. Don't much like the feeling."

He grips me tighter against him, walking us backwards until the water laps up over my chest, then twists me in his arms and pushes me up against the tiles.

"I'm Camden's…" I say, lamely. What I want to say is *why have you abandoned me*? but that would show my hand and I'm not willing to lay bare how I really feel. Too much is at stake. Ford's expression is neutral, but there's no denying the fire burning in his eyes.

"You were ours way before he claimed you as his own."

"Ours?" I whisper. My fucking heart is pounding. This is crazy.

"Yes, *ours*. Just because he has you now doesn't mean you don't still belong to us."

"Says the person who's been avoiding me all week, who's been preventing Sonny from getting anywhere near me."

"It's for your own good," he mutters, bringing his hand up to cup my cheek.

"How is any of this good for me?" I whisper, caught by the look of longing in his gaze. "Besides, I'm not yours. I'm not anyone's. In fact, I fit into the role of reject quite well these days. Pretty sure Ros had me in mind when she came up with this term's art project," I add bitterly.

"We haven't rejected you. Sonny and me, we claimed you as our own before Camden did. Eastern way before that. So, yes, that makes you ours."

"I don't belong to…" I start to protest, but he leans forward, brushing his lips against mine, taking both my words and my breath away. My lips and my skin instantly flush with heat. Traitorous, dangerous, scorching heat.

Somewhere inside, I have the sense of mind to push him back. "Don't. Don't do that."

But Ford shakes his head and crushes his mouth against mine, slicing through my resolve.

"I can't stay away," he mutters against my mouth, running his hands up my arms and cupping my head, his fingers tugging on my hair as he nips my lower lip between his teeth. All common sense and any shred of dignity flies out of the window as my own hands find themselves sliding up his chest and around his neck. I push against him, matching his passion with a frenzied, wild abandonment, allowing this kiss.

Just one last kiss.

Ford's hands roam everywhere, they skim over my bikini clad top, and slide beneath the water to my lower belly meeting the undeniable heat that burns within me there. Like with everything when it comes to Ford, it's all or nothing. It's fire and ice. A rash of scorching heat or freezing shallows. I both want to self-combust and drift into sweet serenity.

He does stupid things to my brain, and my body.

Stupid things.

Dangerous things.

Yet still I kiss him knowing how easily we could be caught. Knowing that I'm putting everything on the line just to have his attention. I'm thirsty for it. I hadn't realised how much I've been craving him until now. How much I've missed this electricity between us. Missed him. Missed *all* of them. Ford, Sonny, *Eastern…*

Eastern who I'm trying to protect.

"NO!" I suddenly snap, jerking back and pushing him away, meaning it this time.

He looks slightly dazed, as dazed as I feel.

"No?"

"No! You don't get to do this. You don't get to command my attention, make me drunk with lust and tell me things that make no sense." Meaning the cryptic message back at the funfair. I breathe heavily, panting, every part of me wanting him back in my arms, wanting the fire and the passion that he seems to so easily stoke.

"I make you drunk with lust?" he tips his head to the side, a small smile pulling up his lips. If he smiles fully, really lets me see him I know I'm done for.

"Don't do that. Don't make this into something meaningless. You threw the fight, remember? You lost, and now I'm Camden's. Why?" I ask, suddenly needing to know but also understanding that it wouldn't have made a difference to my decision regardless.

"He needs you. You need him. I did what had to be done."

"What?!" There are so many riddles to be solved in that one statement that my head is spinning with questions. What does he mean, Camden needs me? And me needing Camden? Does he know about Eastern's and my deal with Crown? If so, how? And what does he gain from it by pushing me towards Camden?

Ford sighs. "Camden wasn't always this way. Things are…"

"Complicated? No shit. I know about Sapphire, Ford. I know what you did. Camden told me." The words come out in a rush and I instantly regret them.

"Fuck! He told you about Sapphire?" he grinds out, swiping a hand over his face. He looks genuinely shocked. Then he rights himself, looking resigned but pleased in a weird, messed up kind of way.

"So, forgive me if I can't trust a word that comes out of your mouth or your skewed reasoning for doing anything. You lied to me."

"I didn't lie, Asia. I just didn't tell you the whole story about our pasts."

"She's dead, Ford. Dead because you threw the fight for *money*, for your damn fight club, for your *sister*." I slam my hand against the surface of the water. Droplets splash against my skin, having no effect on cooling me off.

"I can't take back what happened," he implores, holding his hands out. "Don't you think I know that I have Sapphire's blood on my hands. I live with that decision every fucking day. But you must believe me, Asia, I didn't intend for Sapphire to get hurt. I didn't know it would get that violent. I should've, but I was a *kid*. It doesn't excuse anything, but I made a mistake that cost Sapphire her life. I was arrogant and foolish taking her there. Camden has every right to hate me. Every right. Though I hate myself enough for the both of us."

His shoulders slump, the confidence that he carries himself with, gone. It's such a stark contrast to what I'm used to, that for a moment I'm struck dumb. Maybe I should go to him, reassure him, but I don't. It's not my forgiveness he needs, it's Camden's, and that's not going to happen in this lifetime.

"Is that why you threw the fight? You lost so Camden could claim me as his own? Did it ease your conscience, Ford, is that it? Using me like some offering."

"No. I told you I did it for you, for Camden. It's already working."

"What the fuck do you mean?" I shout, then slam my mouth shut.

"He's opening up to you, Asia. Maybe you'll be the one to persuade him to save him from himself."

"It's not even about him saving himself. He's in too deep, there's too much at stake…" I slam my mouth shut before I tell him about Camden's mum and the King's vice like hold over them both.

"Sometimes, all a person needs is someone worth fighting for. I believe that's you, Asia."

I shake my head, not even sure how to take that. "What do I get out of it?"

"Information," he says.

My heart literally stops beating. For a full thirty seconds I'm caught like a deer in headlights. Frozen in time. Only when my heart stutters back to life do I breathe, finally managing to speak. "How…?"

"I saw Crown with Eastern that day they arrived out of the blue before Christmas. I was skipping class, working out in the outhouse and saw the car arrive through the back entrance into the estate."

Fuck.

"You know Crown."

"I know Crown." He confirms, not elaborating further. I don't press the point. I'm too busy panicking about what else he knows. Ford steps towards me, swiping his wet hair back. His eyes are more green than grey today, reflecting the water. "He's been after the King for years now. I'm guessing he gave you a deal?"

I don't answer. Panic seeps into my blood. My fear must show on my face because Ford reaches for me. He takes my hand, squeezing tightly.

"It's okay. Don't answer. The less you tell me the better. Just know I get what you're doing and why. Sonny suspects something big is going on. He's not a fool, Asia."

"So you're keeping him away."

Ford nods. "Yes, because Sonny can't hide his true feelings. He's too passionate, he'll give everything away the moment you give him your time."

"And you can hide your feelings?" I tentatively ask.

"I've spent years hiding how I really feel from the world. It's second nature to me."

"Except here you are…"

"Except here I am."

He stares into my eyes. Not moving, but not leaving either. This is dangerous, stupid. I pull my hand from his but for some stupid reason rather than stepping away, I run my fingers over his crude tattoo.

"Bad Boy…" I murmur. He seems to stiffen as I trace my finger over the damaged skin. When I look up at him, he's staring right through me and into a memory that haunts him far more than my touch. "Can I trust you, Ford?"

"Yes. You'll see." And despite everything that's happened recently, everything I know to be true; I believe him.

"You should go."

He nods. "We'll take care of Eastern, if you take care of Camden."

"I thought you hated Camden?" I murmur.

"I don't hate him. How can I? He was my brother once," he admits, stepping out of the pool.

I watch the water droplets slide down his skin, traversing the peaks and troughs of his ripped muscles before dripping to the tiled floor. My body aches for him to get back in the pool and touch me just the way he did before in the outhouse. But it's way too risky.

"Why would you take care of Eastern?"

"Because he means something to you and because of that, he means something to me."

With that he walks off, leaving me pondering that statement long after he's disappeared through the changing room doors.

TWENTY

"Where've you been?" Camden says as he barges into my room just as I'm rough drying my hair that's still wet from the shower I took after my swim. I'm sitting in my tank top, shorts and fluffy purple socks just about ready to climb into my bed and sleep.

"Evening to you too," I respond, not bothering to turn around to greet him. I remain sitting crossed legged on the floor in front of my mirror.

"That's not an answer."

"Well, that's the only one you're going to get from me." The scowl he gives me is epic. "You know you need to stop pulling that face because you'll have a line deeper than the Grand Canyon between your eyebrows when you're older if you carry on like that."

"I'm not betting I'll see past thirty, so I don't really give a shit," he says grimly, before slamming the door shut and locking it. He leans against the door, making no move towards me.

"That's fucking morbid," I retort.

"But that's the truth, Asia. I'm not going to get to live to the ripe old age of eighty with a family full of kids and grandkids. That's not how it works."

"It could be..."

He barks out a laugh. "No, it really can't."

And given what I know, he's probably right. His mum is owned by the King. *His mum.* One false move and both she and Camden are dead. I've no doubt about it.

It changes everything.

"You've been avoiding me, Asia, and I don't fucking like it," he eventually says, staring at me in the mirror as I continue to deal with my wet, tangled hair or at least try to.

I shrug my shoulders, feigning nonchalance before meeting his gaze. "Avoiding you? I haven't been able to get a moment's peace. You're everywhere I go, Camden."

"You're making me look a fool. You might be with me, but you're not *with* me, with me."

I roll my eyes. "Can you hear yourself? I'm not at your beck and call."

"That's not what we agreed..." he argues, having the audacity to look like he actually believes that.

"We agreed that I would choose you and reject my friends. I've done that." And for the most part I have. He doesn't need to know about the kiss I shared with Ford. *I'm* trying hard not to think about it.

"You've got a short memory, Asia. You *agreed* to be my girl. You're not doing a very good job at it." He moves forward, stopping only when he's standing directly behind me. I remain where I am, then pick up my comb and start combing out the tangles.

"I'm my own damn person. If I don't feel like talking, then I'm not talking. If I don't want you to fucking kiss me, touch me like you *own* me, then I'm going to back the fuck off. I'm fully aware of what I am to you and that is a side piece, a jewel, a *gem* that you can flash about because it strokes your ego to do so. I don't fit into the mould of an adoring girlfriend. I refuse to be someone I'm not." I let out a long sigh and take my frustrations out on my hair, yanking at the strands. The truth is I should be doing exactly what he wants. I should be spending every second of every moment with him trying to get him to open up. I should be acting like his girl. I'm not very good at this undercover bullshit.

"You're fucking impossible, do you know that?" Camden says, as he sits down behind me, his long legs sliding past my own. He takes the comb from me. "Here, let me."

"What do you think you're doing?" I twist around trying to snatch the comb back. He holds it away from me, amusement glinting in his stupidly beautiful eyes. For some reason that just winds me up more. "Give it back, arsehole!"

"Ask me nicely," he retorts as I turn, kneeling in front of him trying to snatch the comb from his hand. The fucker has long arms.

"Well this is fun," he grins darkly, and it takes me a few seconds to realise that my braless tits are practically pressed into his face. No wonder he's smiling. His hands drop and slide around my back. I can feel the hard ridge of the comb digging into my skin as he holds onto me. The air sparks as I hold my breath. My body stiffens, trying to ignore the undeniable attraction between us. Maybe it's the way he's looking at me. Maybe it's the lust gathering in his topaz eyes, swimming there like tropical fish in a warm ocean. Or perhaps it's what lies beneath the shallows, what's hidden in the depths where dangerous creatures swim. Maybe Pink had been right, maybe it is the danger I'm drawn to. But as I stare at him, neither of us moving, neither of us backing down, I see what's beyond the pretty shallows. I see past the depths and right to the core and the solid stone that lines his heart. I see fissures so deep that I'm surprised he isn't drowning.

"Asia..." he mutters, his grip tightening. My body sways, reacting instinctively to his voice and the need I hear there.

What the fuck is happening? I swear to God, I'm about one second away from diving into his depths and never coming up for air. This guy isn't just dangerous to my health, he has the power to end me. I have the sense of mind to rest my hand on his shoulders, pushing him back slightly. He coughs to clear his throat.

"Can I comb your hair?" he asks in a voice so low that somehow it's vulnerable in its gruffness. That vulnerability almost captures me like a damn fish on a hook. I immediately lean back and twist around, facing away from him again. My traitorous cheeks flush a deep pink.

"Do what you want," I snap, ignoring the scattering of goosebumps over my skin and my sudden, very prominent nipples. Fuck sake.

Camden lets out a long breath and begins to gently work out the knots. He takes his time, making sure my hair is free of tangles. "Why did you change the colour?" he asks after a while.

"What's it to you?" I retort.

"I'm just curious."

"Because I want to. Because I can. Because it makes me feel better about myself..." I don't know why I give him that piece of information, but I do.

"I get that, wanting to reinvent yourself. If only life were that simple."

"People do it all the time. You did it after all. You're not Bling anymore, you're Camden, right?"

"I'm still Bling. He's still here," he mutters, avoiding my gaze as I stare at his reflection. Is he? I wonder. Could that kid still be locked away inside just waiting for a chance to escape? Maybe.

"You want me to braid your hair?" he asks after a few minutes.

"You can braid hair?" I stop myself from laughing when I see the look on his face.

"Yeah, I can braid hair. Mum was great at it, but the last few years leading up to Sapphire's death, she stopped doing it for her. Sapphire's hair was as wild as she was. Sometimes it needed taming. I became the man for the job," he explains, his voice a bittersweet mix of happy memories and heartache. The truth of his pain cuts me deep and I almost want to tell him to stop talking, to stop trusting me with his memories like this.

But I don't.

Instead, I ask him why, then hold my breath. Feeling equally ashamed and pleased that he trusts me enough to open up. I daren't look at him in the mirror for fear of giving myself away.

"Mum got involved with someone…" He stalls, one hand on my shoulder, the other placing the comb on the floor. "Someone she thought gave a shit about her, about us…"

"And that person didn't?"

"In the beginning he was the perfect man. He took care of us all. He made promises and stuck to them. That's the one rule he lived by, still lives by; *never back out of a promise… or a threat*."

A threat?

He catches my gaze in the mirror, his eyes darkening with hate. I swallow hard, not daring to breathe unless he changes his mind and stops talking.

"Remember when I said that we're all owned? Well it's true, I wasn't lying to you…"

I know that, but he needs to tell me, and he needs to trust me enough to do that.

"I'm not owned," I reply.

"Yes, you are. Maybe not so obviously, but you are owned by your situation."

"So, who owns you then, Camden?" I ask softly.

He scrapes a hand over his face, and I can see the internal battle going on inside. He catches my gaze in the mirror, then lifts his hands as though placing a crown on his head. "The King. I'm owned by the fucking King. My mum is too and there's not a damn thing I can do about it."

I can see the helplessness written across his face. The absolute belief that he *is* trapped, and it makes me feel sick. So damn sick. When he moves to stand, to leave, I press my palm on his thigh. "Stay, braid my hair, Camden," I say.

That's all I can give him in the moment. I'm not good with words of comfort. Actions are the currency I live by. Words can betray and pretty up lies as though they're truths. I know that better than anyone.

He doesn't thank me or say another word. Instead, he shuffles back slightly and the warmth I felt a moment ago disperses. I shiver, partly from the cold and partly from the tension filling the air. When he begins to section off the top of my hair, that tension rises making my heart beat faster and my throat constrict with confessions that I suddenly want to spill like dirty money and crooked deals.

"You cold?" he asks.

"I'll live."

I watch him in the mirror, watch the concentration on his face as he starts to braid my hair. He takes his time, crossing over the strands with care, treating me with gentle hands. At one point I have to stifle a sigh, this kind of care and attention so foreign to me that when I get it, I react without thinking.

"This okay?" Camden asks.

"Why wouldn't it be?"

"You said earlier you don't like being touched…" His fingers still, as though saying that out loud reminded him of the fact.

"That isn't what I said. I like being touched. I don't like being *owned*. You of all people should be able to understand that."

He flinches, nodding his head. "I fucked up," he says. It's quite an admission, close to an apology and one that I never thought I'd hear coming from his lips.

"Yeah, you did." I sigh heavily, feeling the need to explain how I feel even though that's the last thing I'd ever thought I'd do. Fuck it, I'm not going to pussyfoot around him. "When you kissed me in the canteen the other day it wasn't for my benefit. It was because you wanted to prove to everyone I was yours. That you could do what you wanted regardless of how I felt or anyone else felt for that matter. I don't like that Camden. Don't do it again."

He meets my gaze in the mirror then nods his head. "Okay."

"Okay? I was expecting more of a battle."

"I'm tired of fighting. I'm tired of it all," he mutters, before continuing to braid my hair.

He's so gentle, more so now we've cleared the air a little. It reminds me of how thoughtful Ford and Sonny were that night of the fight all those weeks ago, how Eastern has been with me my whole life. Four guys, so very different but all somehow managing to tear apart my resolve to be an island, a fucking continent, actually. They're like the water lapping at my shoes, breaking down my barriers day by day, bit by bit, turning stone into sand. I've no idea whether that's a good thing or not. But it's happening regardless. Even Camden seems to be taking up that role. Maybe I'm just not as strong as I first thought.

"You may always think the worst of me, Asia. I've done shit things, terrible things in the name of my crew. For *him*," he spits.

"You're trapped…?"

"Like one of those circus bears in a cage with no way to escape…" he confirms bitterly. A couple of minutes later he finishes braiding my hair. His hands fall away as he looks at me in the mirror. "There, done." Camden stands, drawing himself away both physically and emotionally. The shutters are closing. Whatever vulnerability he'd shown is now disappearing behind a façade so thick it'll prove impossible to penetrate if I don't do something.

"Every lock has a key, every cage a way out. You just have to know how to find them," I say, getting up.

"Do you really believe that?" He laughs bitterly, shaking his head. "I've long since stopped trying to look for a way out, Asia. Whilst the King has my mum I'll never be free."

"I get that, but…"

"But nothing. My life is set in stone. No matter which way I look I've no future that doesn't either end with a long prison sentence or death."

And the worst thing is, he's probably right.

"Fuck."

"This is my world. Ours. All I have is my crew. They're my family now, for better or worse."

"You really believe that?" We both know what I mean… Monk. He'd sooner stab Camden in the back than protect it.

"I have to."

"And what about your Mum, doesn't she have your back? Isn't she your family?"

"Mum isn't as strong as she used to be. He's worn her down, taken her beauty, her happiness, her freedom. He's taken everything from her, from us." He sighs heavily. "Your mum was a heroin addict wasn't she?"

"Yeah."

"Well my mum has an addiction of her own. The King has screwed with her head so much that she'd do anything for him, even take the beatings he dishes out and then fucking thank him afterwards for the *pleasure*."

"Camden…" My throat constricts so much with unshed words that I have to take a moment not to spill them. To force them back inside. I have to remind myself why I'm doing this. But he's hurting, and he's doing exactly what Ford had said. He trusts me. I don't even know what to do with that.

He steps back, a muscle ticking in his jaw. "Don't fucking pity me."

"I'm not. I *don't*," I insist. "I know what it's like. I fucking get it."

And I do. Right in that moment I see him for who he really is; a lone figure surrounded by a lot of people who really don't give a shit about him. He's a man trapped by his situation, and just because he has the title of gang leader doesn't mean it's any easier on him. In fact, it's worse.

"Do you know the fucking joke of it all? I had a family once. A *real* one. My mum, my sister, my dad… *Ford,* a few others who're in prison now and will be released back into a world they'll never escape from." He grits his teeth so hard I can hear them grinding over one another. "Gang life took every single one of them from me and here I am taking you from Eastern. I'm a bad person, Asia, but even though I know that, I can't let you go." He reaches into his pocket and pulls out a phone… my phone, the one he took from me last term and never gave back.

"The school has your other one, right?"

I'm not able to fully form a sentence as he hands me it.

"I've programmed in a new number to reach Eastern. I have another phone that I can give to him too. At least you can talk."

"What? Why? After everything you said, why would you do this now…?"

"Because Bling would never *ever* make someone choose, never force someone to do anything against their wishes. He had fucking integrity."

"And what about your crew?"

"They don't need to know." He chews on the inside of his mouth, a flicker of anxiety crossing his features. "I've no right to ask this of you. I've no right to ask you to pretend that you even like me enough to stay, but I'm going to, Asia. If you go now and I do nothing to stop it the news will get back to the King and he'll deem me not worthy. I'll lose the little respect he has for me. But if that was it, I'd do it in a heartbeat. I'd let you go, and I'd walk. But it's not as simple as that. My mum's life could really be fucked. It was bad enough that I let Eastern go, that I allowed you retribution with Monk... I made a decision without the King's specific approval. He didn't like it."

"That wasn't enough for the King to hurt you, your mum?" I'm careful how I phrase this question given that Camden hasn't told me Monk is the King's son, but Ruby, and I know exactly what happened when Camden displeased him.

"Oh, he hurt her alright. He hurt her so bad she was left with five broken ribs, a broken arm and a face that's unrecognisable. He knows how to get to me, through her."

"The bastard," I breathe out.

"So, here's the thing. I do need you. I need you because my mum's life depends on it. I need you because you get how things work in our world. I need you because I can't look at you without knowing you're mine even when that's a lie. I need you because you're the kind of person who's loyal to the bitter end. Maybe I'm grasping for an impossibility. Maybe I'm a fool..." He laughs then, but it's a sad laugh that scores deep into my flesh and marks my bone. "But it's the truth."

"I could hurt you..." I say. Out of everyone, he's putting his trust in me. I'm the one person with the power to ruin him, ruin his mother's life, maybe even be responsible for ending them.

"Yes, but somehow I don't think you will." When I don't answer he takes a step away from me, backing towards the door. "Think about it?" he asks.

Fear pricks the air. Camden's, my own. It crackles and snaps around us with intent.

"I shouldn't have forced you to make a choice. I should never have let you in the crew. I didn't want to, but when you insisted I thought of my own selfish desires and no one else's. If that doesn't make me the worst fucking human alive, I don't know what does."

For a beat I can't move, can't think, can't say a damn word. Then as if on their own accord my feet move towards him. What I do next surprises me. It surprises Camden given he stiffens the second I slide my arms around his waist and press my cheek against his broad chest. The thumping sound of his heart is battle worn and weary. He's fucking tired of all this shit. Goddamn exhausted at battling through the storm. I understand that better than anyone.

Eventually, tentatively, his arms wrap around my back as he pulls me tight against him and although I'm the one who feels engulfed by his sheer size, it's Camden who seems small.

"I'm sorry about your mum," I mutter into his chest, tucking the phone he gave me back into his jean pocket.

"What are you doing?" he asks, surprise evident in his voice.

"Eastern and I are strong enough. We'll survive."

"I don't want you to have to survive, Asia."

"You have a friend, Camden. I'll do what I can," I say cryptically, understanding just as much as he does that he'll never be free. None of us will be so long as the King still holds all the strings.

TWENTY-ONE

For the next week I spend all my free time with Camden. When I'm not in lessons, we're together. Every day I learn something new about him. Small things, little things that other people might not notice or even care about.

He prefers coffee over tea, with cream rather than milk. His favourite colour is grey because it reminds him of his sister's eyes on the dark nights she'd used to carry his spray cans whilst he painted. He's not a big fan of Grime music, preferring R&B. His favourite movie is Lock, Stock and Two Smoking Barrels. His worst Dirty Dancing because he was forced to watch it hundreds of times by his mum and he's sick to death of *Patrick fucking Swayze*. His words, not mine. We might've had a little discussion about that one that led me to believe he actually quite liked it but of course he'll deny that at every opportunity. It's not cool to like a Chick-Flick, after all.

Now, as we sit together during our free period on a bitterly cold Friday afternoon in the formal gardens, I ask him what his favourite food is. They say the way to a man's heart is through his stomach right? Not that I need a way to his heart, just his secrets.

"So, you're telling me the last meal you'd request if you were put on death row is a fucking pepperoni pizza?"

Camden smiles. "What's wrong with that?"

"You're actually saying out of all the millions of different foods you could possibly choose from you'd have that?"

"What can I say? I'm a simple man with simple pleasures."

I roll my eyes at that. "There's nothing simple about you, Camden."

"When it comes to my favourite food, I'm all about the simple things."

"What about pudding?"

"Easy, Tiramisu."

"Are you a secret Italian or something?" I joke, smiling.

"Do I look Italian?" he grins widely, his gold tooth catching the light. "Though, I am built like a stallion, if you know what I mean?"

"Uh-huh, you keep telling yourself that."

"Seriously, have you seen the size of my feet?" he asks, lifting his very considerable sized foot. "Size thirteen. You know what they say about big feet…"

"Oh, Jesus…"

He laughs loudly, winking.

"It's not the size that matters, but what you can do with it," I retort with a smirk.

"Believe me, Asia, I know *exactly* what to do with it. They don't call me Mr Lover Man for nothing." He starts undulating his hips in some weird seated dance. I pull a face, groaning.

"Not impressed?" he asks.

"Nope…"

He bumps me with his shoulder grinning. This is the most relaxed I've ever seen him. Until it isn't…

"Looks like we've got company," he says, his smile fading quickly as he looks off into the distance. I follow his gaze. Leaving the main building are Eastern, Pink and Kate. Monk is following them.

"What the fuck is he up too?" I grind out.

"Nothing good," Camden responds, his demeanour changes from relaxed to stiff.

We both watch, relatively hidden from view given the bench we're sitting on is beneath the arch of a privet hedge that's slightly grown over. Monk approaches the group walking with a swagger that he's no right to feel given I served him his arse last term. I suppose being the King's son gives him a sense of security like nothing else does. God, I want to fucking kill him. He sidles up to Pink, having the audacity to slide his hand down her back and squeeze her arse. She turns abruptly, shoving him in his chest.

"That *motherfucker*!" I snarl, getting to my feet, ready to barrel over there and kick his arse.

"Wait!" Camden says, gripping my arm before I can do something stupid.

"How fucking dare he?!"

"By the looks of it, Pink can handle herself," Camden points out.

We watch as Pink starts shouting at Monk. We're too far away to hear exactly what she's saying, but I'm betting it's colourful. After a beat Kate joins in. Monk argues back aggressively, but Eastern steps in, getting between Monk and the girls. My gut churns and my throat closes over as I watch Monk get in Eastern's face. He's so close I'm pretty sure Eastern can smell his rank breath. I know my best friend can handle himself, but he doesn't realise who Monk is and this could end up so much worse for him if he gets into a fight.

"We should break it up," I say, moving to pull away. Camden draws me back down to his side.

"No, we have no business interfering. I *can't* interfere." We both know why that is… the repercussions on his mum are too great.

"Then I will."

"No, you won't. You go and break it up we'll have a fucking mutiny on our hands. Do you see now, Asia? Do you understand what I'm up against? I'm damned if I do, and damned if I don't." He looks at me imploringly. I do see, I do get it, and it fucking stinks.

Returning my gaze to the group I can see Eastern jabbing his finger in Monk's chest. He's about 2.5 seconds away from hitting him. Part of me wants him to, the other part is fearful given what I know. Fortunately for everyone involved Mr Burnside strides over to the group, no doubt seeing the argument from his office window that looks out onto the gardens. He breaks Monk and Eastern up, gripping hold of Monk's arm and frogmarching him inside. Eastern watches them leave whilst Kate and Pink reassure him. He says something to them and then strides off into the maze. Eventually they walk inside, not understanding that what he needs right now is a friend to talk him down, not let him wallow in his anger. I know him. He'll be fired up and fucking vexed. All that rage will be bubbling inside his chest with no outlet. It's times like these when he needs someone, when he needs *me*.

"Shit," I mutter, wanting to go to him. Itching to run to him, to be there for him. I shift forward in my seat almost without thinking.

"You miss him, don't you?" Camden says after a beat.

"Yeah, I do."

"Are you jealous of his friendship with Pink and Kate?"

"No, I'm not. He needs them right now. I'm glad he has them. Though they really shouldn't have left him alone."

"Is Eastern jealous of us?"

"Us?" I snap my head around to look at Camden.

"Yeah, this thing we've got going on." He points his finger between the two of us.

"This *thing* is called a friendship, Camden. And besides, I wouldn't know how Eastern feels, we don't talk anymore, remember."

"Are we just mates though?"

Whether he does it on purpose or not, his thigh brushes against mine. I don't move my leg away. I need to show him that his closeness doesn't affect me, even when it does. I pat his knee like an aunt would her nephew. It's a completely platonic touch. But he grasps my hand, flattening it against his thigh. His palm practically engulfs the whole of my hand.

"You know I've never told the full story to anyone in the crew about my sister. I don't trust easily, Asia. But I trust you." He runs the pad of his thumb over my knuckles, sliding his fingers beneath the palm of my hand.

"What makes you think that I wouldn't betray that trust, Camden?" I swallow hard, trying to ignore the gentle way he's touching me. I never thought Camden would be the type of guy to be gentle, but more and more he's showing me that he is.

"My gut. It's never wrong."

"What about Monk? I'm not sure your gut was right about him."

"Believe me I know exactly the type of person Monk is." I wait for him to elaborate, to tell me what I already know; that Monk is the King's son, but he doesn't. So, whilst he says he trusts me, he doesn't trust me with that piece of information. Yet.

Our gaze locks as he lifts my hand, pressing a soft, warm kiss against my knuckles. His lips linger on my skin, his eyes blazing with warmth and apology.

"I wanted so badly to be the one who looked after you the night of the fight. It took every ounce of willpower to remain in the Tower whilst Ford and Sonny left with you. It was even harder not to end Monk there and then."

He releases his hold on me. The warmth of his skin quickly

replaced by the cold January air "Eastern's alone right now," he eventually says. We both feel the pull, that attraction between us growing. I'm trying hard to swim against the tide.

"And…?" I say carefully, drawing my hand away and placing it into my coat pocket, holding onto the remnants of Camden's warmth.

"… And you miss him… And he needs talking down. I recognise the look of someone about to go nuclear. I don't need that shit in my life right now. My *mum* doesn't need that shit."

Camden gets up, looking down at me, his topaz eyes flashing with honesty. "I don't own you, Asia so I'm not going to order you to do anything, but I do need to ask you a favour."

"What's that?"

"Go speak with Eastern. Persuade him not to beat the shit out of Monk."

"But…" My forehead creases with a frown.

"Mum is kept by a man I hate, not able to breathe without his fucking permission, Asia. She's in danger all the damn time. One of these days I expect to receive a call telling me she's dead. That he's killed her. I have to make sure that never happens. In the meantime, I'm going to figure out a way to save her. Please, talk to Eastern. Persuade him not to retaliate. He'll get his chance. Just not today."

"What if I'm seen with him?"

"I'll make sure you're not. I'll figure something out. Go now," he retorts before striding away from me without a backward glance. I watch him walk across the frozen grass, his hands tucked into his hoodie pockets, his spine straight, stiff. The second he's disappeared inside the building I run towards the maze, entering by the side entrance.

I FIND Eastern pacing up and down in the centre of the maze. He's so furious that he doesn't notice me entering until I'm standing right in front of him.

"Eastern, I saw what happened…" I start. He snaps his head up. For five agonisingly long seconds he stares at me, his anger buffeting against me. I tip my chin up, taking every last drop of it and wait.

"You shouldn't be here," he finally grinds out. His fists are clenched tightly, so tight that the white of his knuckles are showing.

"Camden wanted me to speak with you. We saw what went down with Monk."

"Camden sent you on an errand, did he?"

"No... yes," I fumble. "I needed to see you. I know you need a friend right now."

"And Camden *allowed* that? The fucking guy has you on some leash, Asia."

"You know the score…" I remind him, taking a step forward. The residual anger from his altercation with Monk lingers as he glares at me. He grits his teeth, nodding tightly.

"Oh, I'm fully aware of the damn score, Asia. You two are as thick as thieves these days."

"Don't Eastern. I don't want to argue. We don't have much time."

"So what have you come to say?"

"You can't challenge Monk to a fight…"

"What?! That dickhead just felt up Pink like she was a piece of fucking meat. He said some pretty sick things to her, and you want me to back off after everything he did to you? She's your friend, Asia. At least she was. Has Monk taken up that role now?"

"Stop being a prick, Eastern. Of course he hasn't," I grind out.

"I'm sorry. That was out of order."

"Yeah, it was."

"I'm just so fucking angry, Asia. That little troll gets away with too much shit and no one is doing anything about it. All I keep thinking about is what he did to you. I know you had retribution. I know it. But you're *my* girl, my fucking heart, and I can't stand how he watches you like he's waiting for the right fucking moment to pounce."

"I get it, Eastern. I know he's gunning for me."

"Then let me beat the fucking shit out of him before he can hurt you again!" he shouts.

"Believe me I want Monk's head on a stick more than anyone, but there are bigger things at stake here."

"What things? What have you found out?"

"We don't have long…"

"Asia, just tell me," he demands.

So, I do. I tell him everything. By the time I've finished explaining Eastern has forgotten about his anger. "Monk's the King's son? What the fuck?!" he exclaims, his face paling.

"Yeah, my thoughts exactly."

"And Camden's *mum*..." Eastern scrapes a hand through his hair, pacing up and down again.

"Yeah, the King beat her because Camden allowed me retribution."

"That isn't on you, Asia."

"Yes, it is. Camden was punished in the worst possible way because he *helped* me, just like he's doing now," I say, as the distinct sound of a fire alarm rings. A minute later we can hear the teachers yelling at the pupils who are making as much noise as the alarm. Camden has caused chaos so I can have this conversation with Eastern.

"This is so fucked up."

"No, it's worse than fucked up. This isn't just about our family anymore. That's the part I'm finding the hardest to deal with, Eastern. We got Tracy and Bray out of immediate danger, but what about Camden's mum? The King beat her to within an inch of her life. She didn't deserve that, Camden didn't. You took the deal to protect your mum and Bray. I took the deal to protect us all. But who's protecting them? *Who*, Eastern?" I press. "None of those arseholes have his back. Not one."

"Are you telling me you've changed your mind, Asia?" Eastern stops pacing, his whole body's trembling. I go to him, cupping his face in my palms. My fingers dig into his skin.

"Not about taking the King down," I say fiercely. "We're both on the same page where the King's concerned."

"I *should* have gone to prison, served my time. This is my fucking fault. All of it."

He tries to turn his face away, but I force him to look at me. "No! We're all trapped by circumstance, by bad decisions made for the right reasons. You taking that deal with Crown has nothing to do with the King beating Camden's mum. That's on *me*. I fought Monk. I forced Camden's hand. I was so desperate to free you from his crew that I didn't see the bigger picture. I refused to see it."

"Asia, you didn't know about Camden's mum when you made the deal."

"You're right. I didn't. But I'm not an idiot, I do know there's always consequences for the actions we take, *always*. Camden warned me his hands were tied, that he couldn't release Monk from his crew, that he wasn't the top of the fucking pecking order. But I didn't want to think too deeply about that. I wanted Tracy and Bray safe and you out of a long prison sentence. I didn't give a shit about Camden when I made that deal with Crown. Now I need to figure this mess out."

I drop my hands wanting to scream at the unfairness of it all. Camden and his mum, the rest of the kids in the HH crew, they're all are just fucking pawns in the King's game. Chess pieces that he moves around to suit his own needs. None of them have any idea whether they're going to be sacrificed for the bigger picture or forced to play on so he can win. It doesn't really matter anyway; the end result is always the same. He wins and the rest of us lose.

"Jesus, Asia. This is such a fucking mess. In fact, this is *my* mess."

"So help me fix it. Lay off Monk for now. Will you do that?"

He rests his hands on my shoulders and nods his head. "Yes. For you I'd do anything."

"Thank you."

"But you have to know that Monk will keep coming for Pink and Kate because he knows you care for them. If I can't retaliate on their behalf they're an easy target. They can't fight like you and me."

"Don't you think I know that…?"

The fire alarm stops ringing and it's our cue to get the fuck away from each other before someone finds us. But despite that, Eastern reaches for me. Grasping my cheeks in his palms, he presses a hot kiss against my mouth. It's quick, brutal, and fucks me up more than I can say. Then he leaves. As I watch him sprint away from me, I realise the tables have turned, but even though I really, really want to, I can't chase him.

TWENTY-TWO

Mr Burnside looks at me with a frown as I sit in his office during my Monday morning therapy session. "So, you're telling me Monk has been abusing Ruby."

"Yes. That fucking prick has been beating her black and blue. She's too afraid to do anything about it. I'm the only one who knows."

"Thank you for telling me." He scribbles something on the pad in front of him. "I'm going to need to take this further."

"What?!" I sit forward in my chair, pressing my hands on the table between us. "You can't fucking do that. She made me promise."

"Asia, she's in danger right now. I have a duty of care…"

"Are you fucking shitting me?! A duty of care? Where was your duty of care when Crown backed Eastern and me into a fucking corner?" I glare at him, suddenly furious.

"That was a different situation. Crown is a member of the Police department. You made a deal. I might not have agreed with it, but he isn't harming you physically."

"That's a matter of opinion," I bite back.

"What do you mean by that?" Mr Burnside asks, placing his pen on the table, watching me carefully.

Of course, I'm not talking about myself, Eastern even. I'm talking about Camden's mum. I wonder whether Crown knows about her relationship with the King. Probably. She's just another casualty of this life we live. Someone not worthy of saving, I guess.

"I don't mean anything. Look, Ruby doesn't want anyone to get involved. She's scared. She trusted me to keep her secret safe."

"Yet, here you are telling me. Why is that?"

"Because your fucking boyfriend told me you couldn't talk about shit that goes on in here. That I could trust you with stuff. If I'd known you'd go blabbing I would've kept my mouth shut."

"Mr Carmichael is right, I can't talk about the things we discuss here with anyone but when someone's life is in physical danger that can be overridden. This isn't a burden you should be carrying, Asia. We both know you have far too many of your own to take on more."

He doesn't even know the half of it. What seemed a simple decision a few weeks back has snowballed into a bloody avalanche and I don't fucking ski.

"What are you going to do?"

"That isn't something you need to concern yourself with, Asia. Rest assured that your name won't be brought up. I've been doing this job for a long time. Ruby comes to me just like you do. If I can get her to talk then the problem isn't yours anymore. Leave it with me, okay?"

I cross my arms over my chest. "Looks like I don't have a fucking choice."

For the rest of the session I clam up, doodling on a piece of paper, barely answering any questions he throws at me. Eventually the alarm clock dings on his desk informing us both that my time is up.

"Anything else you'd like to add before you go to class?" Mr Burnside asks.

"No. Absolutely nothing," I respond ,getting up. I drop the doodle I'd been drawing onto his desk. It's a sketch of a girl sitting in a corner of a room, her head on her knees. The windows are barred like a prison. I hadn't even realised that I'd been drawing me.

I DON'T GO to English. I can't face it today. Instead I find myself wandering towards the part of the main building that students aren't allowed to enter. Standing in front of a set of double doors that says 'Do Not Enter' is like a beacon to someone like me. I'm a rule breaker, a danger seeker. It may as well be lit up in bright red neon saying, 'Trouble This Way' and I'd still ignore it. Pushing against the door, I find that it isn't locked. Well, someone is gonna get fired for that mistake. How fucking stupid.

On the other side of the door the hallway is dimly lit and has a musty smell of not being used in some time. I move along it, pushing against each door I pass. All locked.

"Well, this is fun," I say to myself, leaning against the wall. In the distance I can hear everyone moving about between lessons. A minute or so later, it quietens. No doubt Mr Collins will note my absence and I'll be deducted credits. Not that I care, I don't have fucking time for days out of Oceanside anyway. Time is ticking and I'm no closer to figuring out how to take the King down without taking Camden and his mum down too.

My head's all over the place. Frustration bites at my heels, forcing me to move deeper into this part of the building. When I reach the end of the corridor, I hook a left then stop in my tracks when I hear muffled crying.

Someone is breaking apart. I hear their pain, feel it deep inside.

"Hey, who's there?" I ask tentatively, moving along the corridor. Boxes are piled high, stacked up against the wall. Right at the end of the corridor is a door, slightly ajar. I push it open. "Hello?"

Sitting on the floor, huddled in the corner is Kate.

"Kate?" I whisper.

She looks up at me, clutching something to her chest. Her face is pale, blotchy from crying. When she sees me, she wipes at her eyes and nose, a trail of tears and snot on her cardigan.

"What are you doing here?" she hisses.

"The same thing as you, avoiding class. Wanting to be alone. Sick of today, most days actually," I reel off.

"You made your bed," she bites out, moving to get up.

"Hey, don't go. I've been meaning to talk with you."

"I've got nothing to say to you, Asia."

"Just a minute. Then you can cut me out." I sit down next to her, pulling my legs up. She stays and a spark of hope alights. Maybe I can save our friendship after all.

"You were the one who cut us out. You were the one who joined the HH crew and cast us aside. What were you thinking?" she chokes on the words, but her tears aren't for me or the loss of our friendship. These tears are for someone else.

"Want to tell me what's up?"

"No," she snaps. "You answer my questions first."

"Someone hurt you badly, huh?" I continue, ignoring her.

She eyes me. "Everyone hurts me eventually. I must have a sign that says; '*shit on Kate*' in big neon letters above my head."

"That bad?"

"Worse…" She leans her head back against the wall, a loan tear rolling down her cheek.

"I didn't mean to hurt you, Kate. I did what I had to do…" I say quietly.

"He said something similar before he fucked off and left me."

"Someone you cared about?"

"Someone I *loved.* I loved him, Asia, and he left. The only person who ever truly understood me ran away from what we had. He ran because he was *afraid*."

She looks at me then, her pretty hazel eyes blurred with bitter tears.

"Where is he now, Kate?"

"He's in the army. Some undisclosed location on the other side of the fucking world."

"What happened between you?"

"He left me because he couldn't face up to his true feelings. He left me to face those bitches at Cherrystone Prep on my own. He left me because he couldn't forgive himself. Si was my friend, my protector, the other half to my heart and he fucking ran away when shit got hard."

"Why?"

Kate hands me a photograph. In it is a younger version of Kate, maybe thirteen or fourteen. Two boys are standing either side of her. One is dark haired like Kate with a similar nose and straight white teeth. He has his arm slung around her shoulder, grinning widely. On the other side of her is a blonde kid with the frame of a child, but the beginnings of adulthood in the shape of his jaw and the way he holds himself. Kate is looking up at him, whilst he looks down at her, a secret smile on their lips. I know love when I see it.

"That's Si," she says, pointing to the blonde. "He was my brother's best friend and that's Luke, my brother," she says, tapping the kid who looks like a male version of her. "We all grew up together. Si was one of the family, until the day he became so much more." She swipes at a tear on her face.

"Tell me what happened, Kate."

She looks at me, taking the photo gently from my fingers and placing it back into her rucksack sitting next to her on the floor. After a moment of rummaging around she pulls out a small cellophane bag of marijuana, cigarette papers and a lighter. I watch her in shock as she rolls a joint, puts it in her mouth, lights it then hands it to me whilst she holds the smoke in her lungs.

"What the fuck, Kate? I didn't know you smoked Mary-J." I laugh, shaking my head.

"Sometimes I just need it to get me through. Most nights I smoke a joint… It helps me sleep, stops the nightmares."

"Nightmares?" I ask, drawing on the joint.

"About my brother…"

When I frown, she takes the joint from me, sucking in a deep lungful before blowing it out again. "My brother was shot trying to stick up for me. He died…"

"Fuck, Kate. I'm *sorry,*" I whisper.

She nods tightly, drawing her knees up and wrapping her arms tightly around them. "On this day last year, Luke went to confront the girls bullying me at a party one of them was having at her house. He took a fake gun. He only wanted to scare them off me, to make them stop. It was a stupid thing to do. So fucking stupid, Asia. If I'd known, I would've stopped him."

"What happened at the party?"

"There was a confrontation. One of the girls called the police saying that there was an intruder even though she *knew* it was my brother. The Police arrived, assumed he was a nutjob and shot him dead. Up until then I thought those girls couldn't hurt me anymore than they already had. I was wrong."

"Kate, I don't know what to say…" I want to hug her, but her body language tells me that's not something she wants right now. Instead, I keep her talking.

"Why did Si leave?"

"Because of the guilt he felt. He gave my brother the fake gun and took me out that night so Luke could pay my bullies a visit. Si knew about Luke's plans, and whilst my brother lay dying, I lost my virginity to the person who would eventually break my heart by leaving when I needed him the most."

"Jesus fucking Christ. Kate, I'm sorry. I'm so fucking sorry," I parrot. The words of comfort I know she needs to hear not forming. I'm no good at this.

Kate laughs bitterly. "What for? Because my brother's dead or because you've taken sides with the bullies here?"

"Both…" I say meeting her gaze. I need her to know I'm not one of the arseholes in the HH crew. "I know what it feels like to lose someone you love in tragic circumstances, Kate. You'd be surprised how many others here would too." Of course, I mean Camden, but I can't tell her about Sapphire or his mum. I wish I could, but I can't.

"How can you do it? How can you sit at their table knowing what they did to you?"

"It's difficult to explain…"

Kate passes me back the joint and I take it from her gratefully.

"You chose Camden over your best friend, over Ford and Sonny. *Camden*?"

"He isn't what you think. It's complicated, Kate."

"Yeah, arseholes always are," she says, gathering her bag and getting to her feet. "Goodbye, Asia. Thanks for the chat."

"Wait," I say, scrambling to my feet. "Can we meet here again? Maybe you can bring Pink?"

"Why? Aren't we allowed to speak with you in public or something?"

"You were the one who refused to speak with me," I remind her. When she scowls, I hold my hands up to placate her. "Look, I get why you're avoiding me. I understand. It's just… It'd be good to meet with you girls without all the complications of being seen together."

"So, you do want to hide us away…? What, are you afraid Camden will dump your arse if he catches us together? God, Asia, you fucking disappoint me."

"No. That isn't it at all." How can I tell her that I'm protecting her from Monk and by extension, from the King? Us being seen together will throw up questions and attention that none of us can afford. It will also fuel Monk's fire. If he screws with them any more than he already has then it will lead to all kinds of trouble. Trouble that could lead to worse things than broken friendships and disappointment.

"Then tell me what *it* is. Why don't you tell me the truth?" she presses, grabbing the door handle ready to leave the minute she thinks I'm bullshitting her.

"I miss you, Kate. I miss Pink." It's the only truth I can give her in the moment.

"Then maybe you should have thought of that before you joined Camden's crew."

"Yeah," I agree. "Maybe I should've." But she doesn't hear me because she's already left the room and is halfway down the corridor leaving me acutely aware of the hole in my chest that her absence leaves behind.

TWENTY-THREE

I go to bed Saturday night feeling tired, cold and fucking miserable. The whole week Kate's been avoiding me despite our conversation on Monday. Sonny hasn't attempted to speak to me again, though from the intense way his stare follows me everywhere I go, I know he wants to. Ford and Eastern have become closer, spending time together chatting. I even caught them laughing over a shared joke when I entered the dining hall midweek for lunch. A rumour is going around that Eastern has joined No Name crew and people are pissed. Monk especially. There's no way of knowing whether that's true or not seeing as we haven't talked since the maze. Pink has been the only one who's actually greeted me with any resemblance of friendliness, but conversation has been stilted seeing as I'm being watched by the rest of the HH crew twenty-four fucking seven.

All day today, the rest of the students have been mucking around in the snow that began to fall in earnest yesterday. I could hear their laughter from my room but refused to look out of the window to watch them. Part of me was envious of their ability to kick loose, to be free of their worries and have fun, even if that's just for a little while. So, I kept myself to myself, refusing Camden's offer of company, fighting off another migraine that has been intent on knocking me flat all day.

It's been almost three weeks of going to lessons, building a friendship with Camden and avoiding any form of confrontation whilst I try desperately to figure out how to get Crown the information he needs without hurting anyone in the process. By the time I eventually fall asleep I'm beyond exhausted. So, you can imagine how pissed off I am when a strange tapping noise draws me out of my much-needed sleep.

When I glance at my digital clock, it's just past 2am.

"What the flying fuck?" I grumble.

Tap, Tap, Tap.

Shaking my head, I slide my feet out of bed. It's cold in the room, pitch black bar a shard of moonlight filtering through the gap in my curtains.

Tap, Tap, Tap.

I pad towards the window, the wooden floor cold on my bare feet. I'm not sure what I expected to see when I pull open the curtains, but Sonny wasn't it.

"Oh, my fucking god, Sonny!" I whisper-shout, when I see him grinning at me through the glass, his breath frosting up the window even more. My heart's in my mouth as I lift up the window. "Are you fucking crazy? You're twenty feet up in the air and it's fucking snowing!"

"Can I come in?" he asks, sliding his leg over the window ledge, cool as a fucking cucumber.

"Just get in here. You'll break your damn neck!" I hiss.

"Cheers," he replies, climbing effortlessly through the open window, dropping little snowflakes all over my floor. When he's safely inside I close the window back up and punch him on the arm. "I'd rather you fucking picked my lock! What if you'd lost your footing? You'd be dead!"

"Worried about me, Asia? I thought you'd stopped giving a shit," he says, perching on the edge of the desk, shaking the snow out of his hair. He says it in a friendly manner, but the truth of his hurt is right there hidden beneath the humour.

"What are you doing here?" I say, changing the subject.

"I climbed down from the roof… pretty fucking slippery given the weather."

I wait for him to start laughing. He doesn't. "Are you shitting me?" My mouth drops open in amazement and he leans forward pressing the pad of his finger under my chin, gently encouraging me to close my mouth. A warm smile pulls up his lips, his dimples flashing whilst a shiver rushes down my spine from his cold touch.

"Nope. What can I say? I like climbing things."

"You're crazy."

"So I've been told."

"Jesus, Sonny." I sit down on my bed and look at him, cocking my head to the side. "Seriously though, what are you doing here? More to the point, why were you on the roof?" I ask, a sick kind of churning in my stomach. This can't be good. Ford has been watching him like a hawk, there's no way he'd allow him to come here like this. Then again, Sonny's his own person. Ford can't keep him on lock down twenty-four seven. Though I'm betting he's been giving it a good shot. But the fucking roof?

"Didn't you get the memo? There's a gathering up there…" he says pointing upwards. "A *party*."

"No, I didn't get the fucking memo. What do you mean a party? And why couldn't you take the goddamn stairs?"

"I'm surprised you didn't know. Most of the school's up there *including* Camden, and I told you I like climbing." He grins stupidly then, and I notice how large his pupils are.

"Have you taken something?" I ask.

"Nope. Just high on life, Asia." He laughs. "I like doing things that scare other people. Danger is like a drug to me."

"Yeah, I remember. Sonny the thrill seeker. Is that why you're here now, because of the danger? You have a thing about climbing in and out of girls' bedroom windows, don't you?"

The second time I met Sonny was after he scrambled out of Red's bedroom window after almost getting caught shagging her by Bram. The first time had been a week or so before at the courthouse back in London. I thought he was a player back then. That view has definitely changed now despite what I first thought of him. Though he still very much has the face of an angel and the mind of a sinner given the way he's undressing me with eyes right about now.

He coughs, dragging his gaze slowly upwards to my face. My skin flushes under his scrutiny.

"I thought Max was going to kill me that day," Sonny laughs, shaking his head and the lust from his eyes. "He gave me such shit after."

"I'm not surprised. It's a pretty stupid thing to do. Risking your neck for Red? I could think of more worthy girls to die for." I respond, trying and failing not to show my jealousy. I fold my arms over my chest, only managing to push my braless tits higher up. I don't have big tits, but they're a handful and by the looks on Sonny's face, appreciated.

He snatches his gaze away once more, sitting down on the bed next to me. "She wasn't worth risking my neck for, but *you are*. I'd climb the Shard if it meant seeing you alone for five minutes. What the fuck is happening, Asia?" he asks, reaching for my hand and grasping it in his.

"Sonny," I sigh, pulling my hand from his and absentmindedly fingering a loose strand of hair that's fallen free from my messy bun. "Don't do this."

"You owe me an explanation. Ford won't let me near you. Which, by the way, is pissing me the fuck off, and Kate said you had a fucking list… that you'd made your choice."

"She did, did she?"

"Yeah, well, she actually said a lot more than that. Mostly how you'd stabbed us all in the back. She's pissed. Hurt more than anything."

I flinch, hating that Kate feels so betrayed. "So I've been told."

"Wanna tell me what the fuck's happening then?"

"Nothing's happening. I chose Camden. That's it."

"You really don't trust me enough to tell me the truth do you? I know you're lying, Asia. You do this cute thing where your nose screws up exactly at the moment the lie is coming from your lips."

"I do not…"

"Yeah, yeah you do. I notice. I *see* you," he adds, looking at me in such a way that tells me that he does see me. That he sees right through the lies. "Why don't you trust me?" he asks again.

"It has nothing to do with trust…"

"Has this got something to do with Eastern?" Sonny shifts on the bed, twisting his body to face me. "He's your best friend, right, someone you care about, and yet you're with Camden."

"I am."

"You had *us*."

I meet his gaze, my own hardening and it isn't because I'm angry at him or disappointed, quite the opposite in fact. I'm angry at myself because I'm making a fucking mess of everything. "What did you say to me before we broke up for Christmas, that you had my back regardless of who I choose. I'm guessing that was bullshit?" I say, defensively.

"It wasn't bullshit but you'll forgive me for being fucking shocked that you've sided with Monk and those fucktards who screwed you over. What gives?"

"I haven't sided with *Monk*," I spit.

Sonny raises his eyebrows. "You're a part of Camden's crew so whether you like it or not, you've sided with Monk. At least that's what it seems on the surface."

"No. Never. He's still a wanker."

"Is Camden such a draw that you'll join his crew and put up with that arsehole for the pleasure?"

"Sonny, we're going around in circles. I've made my choice. This is the way it is. Either you have my back, or you don't. Regardless, I won't change my mind."

"Fuck sake, Asia. Why do you think I'm here now? I might not like it, but I *want* to be your friend. Trouble is, I can't have your back because both Camden and Ford are making that pretty fucking difficult right now. Camden because he's obsessed with you and won't leave you alone for five fucking minutes, and Ford for some reason only known to him. This is doing my head in. None of this makes any damn sense to me. So, I can only imagine how Eastern feels. The guy's fucked up over this."

"You want to be my *friend*?" I almost say *only my friend.* I've no right to be pissed off. I've no right giving Sonny these mixed signals. I realise how fucked up it seems to be saying one thing and doing the other. I never thought I'd be one of those girls, but here I am being just that. Flighty. Pathetic. I'm normally a straight shooter. I say what I feel. I have no filter. Yet here I am being a stupid little girl. I need to find those balls Eastern accused me of losing at the funfair.

Sonny leans closer. "Jesus, Asia. I want to be so much more than your friend. If I hadn't made that clear before then I'm going to do that now. I was willing, I *am* willing to share you with people I believe actually give a shit about you but you're not making this easy. I mean Camden, he might not be a complete headcase like Monk but he's still a prick."

"You're willing to *share*...?" My mouth goes dry, and my heart speeds up. This is not what I expected him to say.

"I'm willing to try."

"That's insane. Can you hear yourself?"

"It's not insane. If my foster parents can do it and make it work, then I don't see why we can't give it a try."

"We?"

"Yeah. You, Ford, Eastern and me..."

I laugh. I can't help myself. "Eastern isn't into sharing, and Ford threw a fight so he could hand me over to Camden." Granted Ford did it for non-selfish reasons, but Sonny doesn't know that.

"We could make it work."

"Not happening."

"Bryce-my dad's friend-lives with his partner Louisa and her two other boyfriends Max and Hudson. They're *together* as a family unit. They've got one kid and another on the way. It can work."

"You're fucking insane. Besides, I'm with *Camden*."

Sonny pulls a face, ignoring that remark altogether. "Ford cares about you, I know it. Eastern loves you, that much is fucking crystal clear, and I like you... *a lot*." Sonny shrugs as though what he's said is no big deal. But it is a big deal, a huge fucking deal made worse by the fact it can't happen even if I wanted it too. When I don't respond, he continues. "I thought we were getting somewhere before Christmas. I thought we'd started something. Now you're with the enemy..."

"He isn't all bad..." I mutter. The thing is, up until a few days ago I probably would've agreed with Sonny. Things are beginning to change.

"You're defending him now?"

"You don't understand, Sonny..." I stand and begin pacing up and down, trying to rid myself of this awful fucked-up feeling in my chest. I'm torn in so many directions. I've no idea which way to turn. "Look, I can't be your friend. I can't be anything to you, and you can't be anything to me. None of you can, that's just the way it is now."

"No. I'm not buying it," Sonny says, getting up and grabbing my arm forcing me to face him. "I'm not an idiot, Asia, so don't treat me like one!"

He's angry, and he has every right to be, but I can't deal with this right now.

"You should leave. Get back to the party or whatever the fuck's going on right now. Go take some more pills, get high, because you sure as fuck ain't sober right now, Sonny!"

"I'm *not* high on drugs, Asia. Just fucking high on adrenalin. You're right, I am a thrill seeker. I like the rush of doing something dangerous. It makes me feel alive..."

"Fuck sake. You're an idiot." I'm cross with him. Cross that he could risk his neck doing something so stupid.

"But it's more than that, Asia. I get no bigger high than when I'm with you. You make me feel alive. *You*, Asia. I can't stand this fucking expanse between us. I need to understand."

I snatch my arm away from his hold and step back. He steps forward. "Sonny, don't," I warn.

"Give me something, Asia, so I can at least *try* to understand. Ford knows something. I suspect Eastern does too. Is Camden in on this too? Whatever the fuck this is..."

"Camden isn't in on anything. None of them are," I lie, my back hitting the wall. Sonny boxes me in with his forearms pressed flat against the wall either side of my head.

"Liar!"

"Sonny. I don't owe you a thing. I don't owe anyone anything. Just leave."

"I can't leave. Don't you get it? I want to be around you. I want to help. Whatever this is, whatever shit you've got yourself embroiled in, I want to be there for you."

"There's nothing to help me with. Find someone else to fulfil your *knight in shining armour* fantasy. I'm good."

"Asia, just let me in."

He boxes me in tighter, his hips pressed against my own and it takes all my willpower not to give in, to spill everything. I purse my lips, shaking my head. My chest heaves as I try to maintain control of a situation that is spiralling quickly. How did I ever think I could do this?

"Sonny, back off!"

I almost beg, almost plead, but I don't. I become the girl everyone sees when they look at me, and I harden myself to him. Sonny has only ever been protective, supportive, kind, and yet I'm pushing him away the hardest. I turn cold, abrasive, because I refuse to bring him into this mess too. I won't do that to him. He has a chance of a better life and that will only turn to shit if I accept his help.

"You're shutting me out? *Why*?" he demands, when I push him back roughly.

"This is pointless. Just get out, Sonny."

"No."

"Are you deaf? Just get out. I don't need you. I don't need any of you. I don't!" I jerk forward, about to shove Sonny away again, but he grasps my wrists tightly.

"I'm not deaf, Asia, and I'm not fucking blind or stupid. You might see me as the joker, the kid who's always got a smile on his face, who hasn't got a care in the world, but let me tell you something that you might not realise about me. I'm as stubborn as they come. I don't give up and I *won't* give up on you. I'll have your back even if you don't want me too. Even when you push me away. Got it?"

"Fuck off, Sonny," I say, but there's no conviction behind it. My shoulders sag, my head drops and half a second later I'm wrapped up in his arms trying not to fucking break.

He holds me for a long time, long enough for me to spill every last secret I've been holding onto. Long enough for me to tell him about the deal Eastern and I made with Crown. Long enough for me to tell him everything I've learnt about Camden and his mum, about Ford and Sapphire. I purge myself of it all, only stopping when there's nothing more to say. By the time I've finished, I'm exhausted, fucking weak. But he remains strong. Solid.

"Fuck!" I panic, stumbling backwards when I realise what I've done. "I shouldn't have said anything."

"It's okay, Asia. I swear to you on my life, I'll look out for you…" He looks at me grimly and my gut roils, the perpetual storm within knowing something bad is about to happen.

"What?" I say, forgetting for a moment that I've just blabbed everything. I'll have to figure out what to do about that later.

"Thing is, I reckon shit might get a whole lot worse for everyone if I don't put a stop to what I think is about to happen."

"Stop *what*, Sonny? What do you think is about to happen?"

"You can't blow your cover, Asia. Let me deal with this."

"Deal with what? What are you talking about?"

"Monk has been goading Eastern all night…"

"*What*? Why didn't you say something earlier? He can't fight him, Sonny."

"I get that. Look, leave it with me."

"Sonny…" I warn but my words are snatched away as he cups my face in his hands and presses a hot kiss against my mouth, stealing my breath and any logical thought as his tongue spears my lips and seeks out my own. He backs me up against the wall kissing me as though his life fucking depends on it. I kiss him back just the same, because somehow I need him as much as he needs me. Purging myself of these secrets has proven that.

"I thought you didn't take what isn't freely given?" I say, once my brain has caught up with my lips and Sonny has stepped away from me.

"I haven't. Remember, I *see you,* Asia. I know you wanted me to kiss you, so I did. Besides it might be my last fucking chance. You won't want to do it again after this." He backs away from me then.

"Sonny, what are you talking about?" I say confused, fear unravelling like a dirty coil inside my stomach.

"I'm so fucking sorry," he says, and before I'm able to act he's pulled the key from the lock, opened my bedroom door, stepped out into the hallway and locked it behind him.

"Sonny!" I shout, rushing to the door and yanking at the handle. "SONNY!" I shout, bashing my fist against the door. The arsehole has locked me in.

TWENTY-FOUR

Twenty minutes later, I hear the sound of someone screaming in pain and heavy footsteps pounding along the corridor beyond my locked door. Kids are running, there's a lot of swearing, followed by doors slamming. What the fuck has happened?

"Open the fucking door!" I shout, pounding my fists against the wood.

I yank at the door handle, pulling with all my strength. Nothing. Forcing myself to calm down I stride over to my desk and pull out the drawer, dropping it to the floor so I can search for the hair pins I keep in there. Snatching at the little plastic pot I rip it open and grab a couple opening them up so I can slide them into the lock. For a full minute I try to pick the lock whilst outside the chaos dies down into silence that is even more worrying.

"Motherfucker!" I shout as my attempts to pick the lock fail. Fucking Sonny. Why lock me in? Why ask me to trust him, then do this?

Someone's hurt, someone I care about. I know it deep in my fucking bones.

"Asia, fuck!" My door handle wiggles, a second later the door flies open. Pink is standing in front of me, her face pale, her multicoloured jumper covered in blood.

"Pink, shit! Are you okay?" I rush towards her. She grips me by the shoulders, her eyes filled with unshed tears.

"Not me. *Sonny*. Come quick."

"Sonny?!" I follow Pink as she speeds along the corridor and into Eastern's room. The place is deserted, everyone else is hiding out in their rooms not willing to get into trouble or to fucking help. When I enter Eastern looks at me, his eyes wild with fear.

"The bones fucking sticking through the skin. A fucking plaster isn't going to fix this!"

"Fuck!" I bite out, rushing to his side. "We need to get Sonny help, *now*! This is serious."

Sonny looks up at me, his face pale, fucking ghostly. Eastern's isn't that much better. They've made a rudimentary sling for his broken arm, but blood is weeping through the skin. It's a compound fracture. I remember reading a bit about after care and physiotherapy for such injuries in my coursebook.

"What happened?" I ask, placing my hand on Sonny's unbroken arm and squeezing gently. He gives me a weak smile but says nothing, he's too busy gritting his jaw.

"Monk happened," Ford says. He's holding Kate beneath his arm. She looks dazed, her cheek red and swollen.

That motherfucker! I need to handle this situation quickly.

"Ford," I say, looking directly at him. "Let Pink look after Kate and help us with Sonny. On the way to Carmichael's room you can tell me what the fuck happened."

Ford nods, easing Kate into the chair before striding over to me. "This is gonna hurt, mate," he warns Sonny, before attempting to help him sit up.

"Argh!!" Sonny cries out with the pain of being jostled. He looks about ready to pass out. "It fucking hurts." His teeth begin to chatter and his body shakes.

"Shit! Stop. We can't move him, not without some serious painkillers. Someone needs to go get Carmichael right fucking now," I order.

"I'll go," a familiar voice says from the doorway.

"What the fuck are *you* doing here?" Pink snaps, her usual welcoming self completely disappearing at the sight of Camden standing in the doorway. I've never seen her so angry.

"To *help*," Camden looks at me. "I knocked Monk out. It was the only way to stop him from coming back here and finishing what he started."

"Why?" Kate demands, glaring at him.

"Because… because it was the right thing to do," he simply says.

Kate mutters something under her breath whilst Sonny swears loudly. I know his outburst is as much to do with the fallout of that decision and the impact on Camden's mum as it is the pain.

"He's fucking wasted anyway. I'm betting Monk won't remember half this shit in the morning," Eastern says, looking between me and Camden.

"Let's fucking hope so," I mutter.

Sonny groans again, forcing Camden into action. "I won't be long," he promises, before twisting on his feet and running down the hall.

"Talk to me. Someone tell me what went on," I demand before Pink or Kate can question why Camden is helping and why no one is stopping him from doing so.

"Monk punched Kate when she tried to get between us," Eastern blurts out. "He knocked her to the ground."

"Wait, what? Why would Kate need to get between you and Monk?"

"Because we were fighting," Eastern explains, having the good grace to look guilty. "Sonny hauled me away from Monk in the scuffle and got punched by Monk for the trouble. He lost his footing and slipped on some snow on the roof, falling awkwardly. I heard the fucking bone snap."

"Why were you even fighting, Eastern? You need to learn to walk away!" I yell, angry that he broke his promise to me, angry that he put himself in danger, put everyone in danger. Now look where we are.

"He picked a fight with *me*, Asia. Not the other way around. The kid's a fucking headcase. He was burning for trouble. I walked away so many times, but he kept coming for me. He kept saying all this shit about what he'd do to Kate and Pink, what he'd do to you the second Camden's back is turned. He's a sick fuck."

"You shouldn't have gone up there. None of you should've. What were you all thinking?"

"Who are you to say what we can and can't do, Asia? You lost the right to have an opinion when you chose them over us," Kate snaps, her words having the desired effect.

My nostrils flare in anger, but I refuse to take the bait. "In a couple minutes Carmichael will be here. How are we going to explain this away?" I ask.

"*I'm* fucking responsible. We were messing around, sparring. I caught Sonny on the face, and he fell. Got it?!" Ford says.

"Wait! Why the fuck are you protecting Monk?" Pink snaps.

"I'm not protecting Monk. I'm protecting *us*."

"How do you work that out?" Pink argues as she rubs her hand over Kate's back. She's clearly in shock, her teeth are chattering and her body trembling just as much as Sonny. Her anger for me seems to be the only thing keeping her from passing out most likely.

"We were *all* out of bounds after curfew. We were partying on the damn roof," Ford says, exasperated. "Kate isn't just messed up from the punch Monk threw but because she's fucking *high*. Monk goes down, we all fucking go down. I don't know about you, but I don't want to get chucked out of here to finish my sentence in fucking juvie," Ford says.

"Why does that prick get away with everything though? He starts it all and *nothing* happens," Pink exclaims. She's right of course. He does get away with everything.

"We haven't got time to talk about what that prick Monk does or doesn't deserve. Sonny's our priority right now," Ford counters.

"Monk ain't worth the trouble," Sonny says, catching my eye, a meaningful look hidden within his own. He tries to shift himself on the bed but cries out instead.

"Fuck me sideways, this motherfucking hurts." Half a second later, Sonny pales further. "I think I might pass out…"

"Come on man, you can take the piss out of me all you like so long as you stay awake," Eastern says, kneeling beside him and giving him a half-hearted smile. I look at Eastern and Sonny agog.

"Since when have you two got close enough to rib each other without it leading to a fist fight?"

"Since you've been spending all your time with Camden," Kate butts in, glaring at me.

I frown, biting down on the response I want to say. Instead, I look at Ford. "You could still get chucked back into juvie for this. You're here *because* of your fighting. It breaks the terms of your sentence if you say you and Sonny were fighting, even if it was just messing about."

"Fuck," he mutters, realising I'm right.

"I'll tell them I fell climbing down from the roof," Sonny manages to say through the pain.

"That's fucking ridiculous," Eastern cuts in. "No one's going to believe that. Who willingly climbs down from the roof when they can just take the fucking stairs."

"Sonny does, I've seen him in action," I confirm. "He escaped Red's bedroom and Bram's fists the first day I arrived by climbing out the window and shimmying down the drainpipe. Max, his foster parent, saw him do it." I don't mention the fact that not more than half an hour ago he just did the same. Oh, the fucking irony.

"Exactly. They don't call me *Spidey* for nothing." Sonny attempts a smile, then promptly throws up all over Eastern's feet.

"Fuck man," Eastern says but it isn't because he's concerned about his trainers, more so Sonny. In the midst of all this mess, I'm glad they've become friends.

"Okay, this is what we're going to do." I turn to Pink. "Take Kate to her room. Make sure she's okay. If Carmichael sees her then he'll know this was more than an accident and he'll dig for more information.

Pink nods tightly and helps Kate to her feet. I reach out when they pass me, resting my hand on Kate's arm. "Monk won't get away with this, I *promise*," I say, meaning it. I will get retribution. We all will. Eventually.

"Don't pretend that you actually give a shit," she responds.

Pink winces, but she doesn't correct Kate. I see the look of disappointment in her eyes too, the *rejection*. Blowing out a long breath, I pinch the bridge of my nose forcing my emotions back. If only they knew. I'm doing this all *because* I give a shit, because I care, because I'm looking out for everyone the best way I can.

TWENTY-FIVE

Sitting in Art class two weeks later, I sketch ideas for my project whilst mentally plotting my revenge. After the '*accident*' things appear to have quietened down between the opposing gangs, at least that's the way it must look to Mr Carmichael and the faculty.

Of course, it's all bullshit.

If anything, there's an undercurrent of violence that's just waiting for the opportunity to explode, a ticking time bomb counting down to zero. I'm pretty certain we're nearing that moment. The tension around the school is intense and it's no different today. We all feel it, even if the teachers are oblivious.

Sonny's due back any day now after undergoing an operation and recuperating at a private hospital in London to fix his broken arm. Getting the best medical care money can buy is a bonus of having rich foster parents, I guess.

"That looks great, Asia," Ros says, snapping me out of my thoughts. She peers over my shoulder at the sketch I'm drawing. It's just a rough outline of a graffiti piece I've decided to do for my project, with a selection of different colourways that I may or may not choose.

Ros has somehow managed to persuade Mr Carmichael to let me use one of the garage walls as my canvas. Not sure how she pulled that off given Camden's stunt last term, still I'm grateful to her, nonetheless.

"Thanks," I mutter, distracted by Camden who's sitting opposite me. He's been unusually quiet all morning. In fact, since that night of the fight, he's been completely withdrawn. I've been unable to get him to open up at all. I only know from Ruby that Monk was so high on skunk that night that he can't be certain if he banged his head and knocked himself out like Camden had told him or if he was punched. Either way, no one's talking which is just as well because Camden's mum doesn't need to pay for all our mistakes.

"Make sure you label your sketches with your intentions for colour. I need to understand your thought processes, Asia."

"Sure."

"Okay, good work. I'll let you carry on," she sing-songs, wandering off to another student working on the other side of the room.

"Want to tell me what's up?" I ask Camden the second Ros is out of earshot.

"I'm good," he responds stiffly, not even bothering to look up from his sketchpad.

"Yeah, and I want to shag Monk."

Camden's head snaps up and he narrows his eyes at me. "Ha fucking ha."

I smirk. "Seriously, Camden, there's more chance of me fucking Mr Carmichael and he's married, old, not to mention gay."

He looks at me for a beat, sucking in his plump bottom lip whilst simultaneously tapping his pencil on the table. Brooding, he's brooding.

"Worried about Monk?"

"No."

"So what is?"

He shakes his head, dropping his gaze and starts sketching. I watch him as he concentrates on the image in front of him, blocking me out entirely. He mucks up, throwing his pencil down in frustration. "Fuck sake," he spits, thumping the table with his fist.

"Jesus, Camden, calm the fuck down. No need to take your frustrations out on that beautiful drawing."

His eyes snap up to meet mine. "You think it's beautiful?"

"Yes."

His lips pull up in a half smile as he allows himself a moment to bask in my compliment. Then it fades as he watches me carefully. "I hear Sonny's back tomorrow…"

"And?"

"And… trouble's brewing." He blows out a breath then stands, walking away from me and into the art store cupboard. When he doesn't come back out, I follow him inside. Ros is too busy chatting with another student to even notice we're no longer at our desk.

"Camden?" I say, heading inside the dimly lit room. "You wanna grow some balls and tell me what the fuck is up?"

"I've got plenty of balls, Asia. Blue balls actually," he says, meeting my gaze as he pushes off from the wall, stalking me. I stand my ground. I'm not sure what's brought on this sudden show of dominance, but I'm not about to let him intimidate me.

"Don't expect me to do anything about those," I respond, pointing in the general direction of his crotch.

"Why not?" he insists, getting closer than is comfortable. I can feel the heat of his body through the layers of my clothing as he stands before me. Any closer and those blue balls and his dick between them will be pressed into my damn stomach.

I roll my eyes. "Have you seriously brought me in here to talk about relieving your blue balls? Just have a wank and be done with it."

He laughs. It's a deep, warm sound that makes me grin back at him.

"You've got some front; do you know that?"

I shrug. "Yep."

"No wonder they're crazy about you."

"Who?"

"You damn well know who, Asia."

Camden stares down at me as I look up at him. Neither of us move away, but he doesn't try to touch me like before. He doesn't try to steal a kiss like Ford or just kiss me to prove how much he cares like Eastern and Sonny. No, he waits for permission, acknowledgement from me that there is something growing between us. There is. I can't deny it. Of course, I call his bluff.

"Anything else you'd like to add?" I tease, unable to help the flirtation in my voice whilst keeping my face straight.

A range of emotions flicker through his topaz depths. I can tell he's desperate to kiss me, but he's stubborn and refuses to make the first move. Well, two can play at that game. Besides, kissing him involves more emotions than I'm willing to risk right now. Kissing him takes me one step further over the line. Kissing him means I won't hurt him and though I've already decided as much, thinking I won't hurt him and making sure I don't are two very different things. There's so much at stake, so much to lose.

He raises his hand as though to touch me, but instead he places it flat against his chest, over his heart and gives me an earnest look that's open, willing, *honest.*

"I kissed you in the maze when you weren't ready and I apologise for that, Asia. The next time we kiss I want it to be a mutual decision. I want you to *want* my hands on you, my lips on yours, my fucking tongue caressing your sweet, sassy mouth. There hasn't been a moment when I haven't wanted to make you mine in all the ways I can. Even way back when we first met at the party I've wanted you. You stood up to me like no one has ever done before. You weren't afraid, you still aren't. Nothing scares you. Not me, not Monk, not this place or the life we live…"

"You're wrong, Camden. Everything scares me, I'm just better at hiding it."

He frowns, concern replacing the honesty. "What are you afraid of? Tell me."

Hurting you. Being the reason your mother forfeits her life. Not being able to protect Eastern. Losing my brothers to the care system. Falling for four boys, none of which know how I really, truly feel. The fucking King.

Of course, I don't say any of that out loud. "I'm in an impossible position," I admit instead.

"Because of me…?"

"Partly." *Mostly.*

"Fuck man, knowing that makes everything so much harder because there's nothing that could force me to let you go. I'm a fool for you, Asia." He laughs then, shaking his head in disbelief at his own words then looks at me so intently that I have no choice but to look away. A heavy sigh leaves his mouth. "But I'm not a complete fool. You *love* Eastern. You seem to like Sonny *and* Ford. I might hate that fact, but it's still true. You could destroy me just as easily as I could hurt you. The question is, which one of us will do it first?"

"I don't want to destroy anyone," I mutter.

"Sometimes when it comes to matters of this useless fucking organ, Asia, that's all we ever do," he says, tapping his fingers on his chest.

Camden steps away, leaving me alone whilst I try and fail to get a hold of myself and the warring emotions I'm feeling. One thing I do know for certain; life was simpler when I hated him.

DURING BREAKFAST THE FOLLOWING MORNING, Mr Carmichael walks into the dining hall followed by Mr Burnside and the rest of the faculty.

"Do you think this is about what happened to Sonny?" Camden mutters, as we both watch our school principal walk towards the self-service station.

"Maybe. Though if he wants to give us a lecture about safety, he's two weeks too late." The sarcasm is strong this morning.

He gives me a look, his eyebrow cocked. "I thought you liked Carmichael?"

"He's alright," I shrug. The truth is I do like him. Him and Mr Burnside are about the only two adults bar Tracy that I don't think are complete dickwads.

"Carmichael didn't believe a fucking word we told him about Sonny. He's been shifty these past couple weeks. I've been waiting for something to go down. Looks like that's about to happen."

"Yeah, most likely," I agree. Truth is everyone's been waiting for the fallout of Sonny's *accident.* I guess we're about to find out what that's going to be.

Camden shifts closer to me as we wait, pretending to get a better view of Mr Carmichael. He's trying to be subtle about it, but I know that his thigh pressing against mine beneath the table is no accident. I try to hide my smile.

We're sitting on the fringes of the rest of the HH crew at our own smaller table in the far corner. Monk is watching me with narrowed eyes like he always does, a calculated look on his face. On the other side of the room far away from us both are my friends, or at least I hope they still are. Fuck knows what's going through Kate's head given she's gone even more mega ice queen on me. Pink's sitting with Eastern who's refusing to meet anyone's gaze, in particular mine.

Sonny is watching me closely, his arm in plaster and Ford just gives me a blank look, his mask well and truly down.

"Morning everyone," Mr Carmichael says, standing by the self-service station. He leans against it, folding his arms across his chest. The rest of the faculty find a free table near the kitchen entrance and sit. The room slowly quietens as he waits for everyone to stop talking. He scans the room, his eyes landing on me briefly before moving on. Today he's wearing a sharp tailored black jacket over drainpipe dark blue jeans and his usual Doc Martin's. He's got that smart-casual, punk-business thing going on. The guy's got his shit together in terms of fashion. I admire him for it.

"I apologise I wasn't here to greet you all properly at the start of this term. I've had quite a few things that needed dealing with urgently over the past few weeks that couldn't wait. Now they're sorted, I wanted to fill you in on some changes that are going to happen around here. Most of which you won't like. Though frankly, I don't give a crap."

I smirk. People can say what they want about Mr Carmichael, but he most definitely isn't your standard principal. He swears like we do, and he really *doesn't* give a shit about it.

"What the fuck?" Monk snarls under his breath. He looks over at Camden, who glowers back. Everyone around us starts muttering. A lot more swear words are uttered.

Mr Carmichael holds his hands up. "Quiet," he insists. "When I've finished you can put your complaints in writing, and then I'll ignore them. This is my damn school!"

Motherfucker. Dick. Arsehole. Prick. Wanker. Tosser. Gaylord.

They're just some of the cusses falling like snowflakes out of jaded mouths surrounding me, littering the air and turning it blue. The atmosphere is as frosty inside as it is outside.

"Yes, yes. I've heard it all before," he says, waving his hand in the air and batting off the cusses. "Fact of the matter is, last term things got out of control. This term things are already sliding." He throws a meaningful look at Sonny telling me and everyone else that he knows Sonny's broken arm was no accident, even though he can't prove it. "That ends today. From now on curfew will be nine pm during the week. Anyone caught out of their rooms after this time will be punished appropriately." He looks at Monk then and I can't help but smirk. "Any fighting, there will be severe consequences. Anyone ganging up on another person, there will be severe consequences. Anyone caught taking drugs, there will be severe consequences. Anyone doing one damn thing that I deem inappropriate will be chucked out of this place and sent straight back to juvie before you can even blink. You may have grown up on the streets, you may live by your own set of rules back home, but this is *my* school and *my* rules and if you don't like it you can damn well sit out your sentence in a cell far away from here!"

"Yeah, right. Like that's gonna be enforced." Monk smirks, none too quietly.

Mr Carmichael looks directly at him, his eyes narrowing. "That's where you're wrong. We have a new member of staff I'd like to welcome to the faculty. Like me, like *all* of you he knows what it's like to grow up in an unforgiving environment. He's taking up the role left vacant by Bobby as well as a new position teaching. Come in, Cal," Mr Carmichael says, cutting through the stunned silence like a knife.

The doors to the dining hall open, and in walks a tall, good looking man with honeyed skin and a 'don't take any shit' aura. Across the other side of the room, Sonny stands.

"You've got to be fucking shitting me!" he says.

Ford reaches up and pulls him back down. I'm assuming by his reaction that Sonny knows this man very well.

"Alright, Sonny," Cal says, grinning.

Sonny scowls. I'm no lip reader but I'm pretty sure he just called Cal a *motherfucking interfering bastard.*

Cal saunters in with a confidence that only comes from growing up on the streets. He makes sure to look at as many of us in the eye as he walks past our tables. When he reaches Mr Carmichael, he grips his hand and pulls him for a brief hug. They bump shoulders as Cal slams the flat of his hand against his back. He turns to face us.

"As Mr Carmichael said, my name's Cal. That's what you'll call me. I'm here on a secondment from my usual place of work. I'll be the bastard that makes sure you're all tucked up nicely and in bed by nine… *and stay there*," he adds with a smirk.

"Fuck," Camden grits out.

"And I'm also the man who'll be ensuring all that violent energy that's been bubbling up around here gets put to good use. You want to fight, you want to settle a score, then you do it in *my* ring with *me* in attendance. The way things are, I'm expecting to see all of you at one point or another. Right, Mr Carmichael?"

"Right," he agrees. "Every one of you is going to learn how to box. You will also learn self-defence and discipline. No one gets a free pass. In fact, one of your free periods will be used for this purpose. No arguments."

I hazard a glance at Pink and Kate who are staring at Mr Carmichael as though he's grown another head. I'm betting they're not going to enjoy this new change to the timetable. I, on the other hand, like the idea of punching the shit out of Monk without fear of getting sent to juvie for it. Bring it on.

"Carmichael has gone and lost the plot," Emerald says, catching my eye. There's fear there. Good. Can't wait to see how she holds herself in a ring. I can't help myself; I turn to look at Red, Bram and Monk, then wink. Red's face pales, Bram scowls and Monk's lip curls.

His fists clench as he jerks towards me. Camden reaches over the table and grips his wrist.

"Don't even fucking go there," he grinds out.

Monk snatches his hand free, folding his arms across his chest. I just laugh.

"In addition to this slight change of timetable, I've also made some other adjustments that include the group therapy sessions. I'm fully aware of the divide happening here and even though I'm not stupid enough to believe I can make you all friends, I want to try something radical…"

"Too fucking right. We ain't got time for no fools," one of Monk's wolves pipes up, interrupting him.

"That doesn't mean to say I'm going to sit back and watch you destroy each other," Mr Carmichael continues, silencing him with one look, "Or that I'm not going to try and improve the situation. Mr Burnside has gotten to know you all pretty well by now, and he's put together a new list of therapy groups based on his professional assessment of each of you. From this moment on I expect you to spend your time with your allotted group outside of therapy, *including* social times. That starts today. You can't do that, you're out of Oceanside for good. No exceptions."

"What the fuck? You can't do that!" Monk stands, pushing his chair back. It falls to the floor behind him. I might hate the guy, but his reaction is what everyone else in this room must be feeling. This isn't going to work.

"I can, and I have. You don't like it Monk, you'll be the first sent back to juvie."

"Motherfucker!" Monk grinds out.

"On Saturday night I've extended the curfew to 11pm and I will also allow one group the freedom to leave the site for an overnight stay on a designated weekend. This will alternate over the coming weeks, starting with group one. Mr Burnside will reach out to all of you throughout today and introduce you to your new group. He will also show you the list of trips you can choose from but bear in mind that you will be accompanied by a responsible adult on *every* outing. You'll be babysat until we can trust you all not to fuck up."

"This is more like prison than a fucking prison!" Monk shouts.

"Tell me of any prison that gives you the opportunity to leave the grounds for a night away?" Mr Carmichael challenges.

"We don't need fucking babysitting."

"Like I said. *My* school, *my* rules."

"You can't do this!"

"That's where you're wrong, Monk. I *can* do this, and I *have*," Mr Carmichael says before turning to Cal. "I think we have your first pupil. Want to escort Monk to the gym?"

"Sure thing, Mr Carmichael."

Cal strides over to Monk, stopping before him. The whole dining room hushes as they wait to see what happens next.

"What do you reckon? Will he refuse or will he go?" I whisper to Camden under my breath.

"I want him to refuse, but he won't. He doesn't want to get kicked out of here and into juvie. He'll toe the line with the teachers. Besides, Cal doesn't look like someone you want to fuck with…"

"Yeah, I agree," I say, watching Cal stare at Monk, daring him to disobey.

"What the fuck you gonna do?" Monk snarls, looking Cal up and down.

Cal laughs in his face, leans in close and in a hush voice says, "Your daddy ain't here, son. So, I suggest you fucking walk with me or find out just how committed I am to kicking your arse right here in front of your crew."

Camden and I look at each other in shock. What the fuck? Cal must feel us watching him because he turns to look at me and winks. He fucking winks as though there's some kind of secret going on between us. The guy's nothing more than a stranger to me.

"Come on. Let's go warm up that ring," Cal says, grasping Monk's elbow and frog marching him out of the room.

Camden immediately turns to me. "Want to explain what that was?"

"I've no fucking clue. Never seen him before in my life."

TWENTY-SIX

I find out what group I've been placed in later that day when Mr Burnside collects both me and Ruby from my physiotherapy class last period, just before it's due to finish. We've learned a hell of a lot about human anatomy over the last few weeks from our teacher Sally, who's fast becoming one of my favourites. She's a cool chick, brainy, kind. I like her.

"What's up, Mr Burnside?" I ask, as we follow him along the hallways past classrooms filled with students who I know are just as mind-fucked over this new rule as I am. Since breakfast talk of potential groupings has gone wild.

Kids are angry. Fucking furious, in fact.

It's one thing to be forced to attend Oceanside Academy, quite another to be coerced into groupings not only in therapy but outside of it in our own free time. I'm not entirely sure Mr Carmichael or Mr Burnside know what they're doing. Shit like this could cause a goddamn mutiny. I know better than anyone that the anger everyone feels is covering up their true feelings… *fear*. No one wants to be grouped with someone from an opposing crew.

No. Fucking. One.

"Nothing's up, Asia. Just introducing you to your new group."

"Does that mean I'm in Asia's group too?" Ruby asks, her gaze meeting mine.

Mr Burnside stops outside the gym. "Yes, it does. Are you okay with that?"

"I guess that depends on who else is in the group," she replies nervously.

I know what she's thinking because it's the same thing I'm thinking too. What if he's placed us with Monk? I can handle that dick, but Ruby shouldn't have to deal with him more than she already does.

"Let's meet your new companions," Mr Burnside gives Ruby a genuine smile and me a brief nod. My stomach is turning over with the thought of who I've got to spend the rest of my time here with.

Stepping into the gym, Mr Burnside stands aside allowing us to enter. The first thing I notice is the boxing ring that has replaced all the gym equipment. To the right, sitting in a semicircle with Cal in attendance are Sonny, Ford, Eastern, Pink, Kate and Camden.

Camden?

You can cut the tension with a knife.

Eastern's leg is bouncing up and down. Sonny is glaring at Cal who's ignoring him. Both Ford and Camden are looking at me, the former seems relieved and the latter is gritting his jaw so hard I fear he'll have a mouth full of broken teeth. Pink is puffing out her cheeks and Kate is staring at her hands.

Oh, fuck.

"No fucking way," Ruby says, stepping closer to me as if she expects to be jumped at any moment.

"Take a seat, Asia, Ruby," Mr Burnside says, shutting the door behind us both.

The only seats left available are either side of Camden. I sit on his left, Ruby on his right. Eastern's leg bounces harder.

Mr Burnside stands next to Cal, then clears his throat. "So, I'm guessing this has come as a surprise." He waits, and when no one utters a word, he continues. "You can make this work, or you can choose to take the hard route. Either way, this is what's happening."

Still nothing.

Cal's gaze lands on me and he smiles warmly. "I've managed to extract everyone's names. Want to tell me yours?" he asks.

"Asia," I respond, folding my arms and crossing my legs defensively.

"Nice to meet you, Asia." His gaze flicks to Sonny and a look passes between them. I narrow my eyes. "I've heard a lot about you from *Sunshine* here."

"Don't fucking call me that," Sonny growls, looking far from sunny.

Ford grins but I just raise my eyebrows. "Oh, yeah, and how do you two know each other?"

Everyone looks at Cal, waiting for a response.

"Sonny is family, whether he likes it or not. My best friends look out for him."

Sonny curses under his breath but he doesn't deny it.

"Is that why you're here, to babysit this numpty," Camden says, cocking his thumb at Sonny.

"Nope. I'm here to help the staff keep all you in check."

"You ain't Superman. How the fuck are you gonna manage that all on your own?"

"I'm bringing in two ex-marines. Couple of pretty sound men who will be arriving this afternoon. Between us we'll *manage*."

"Fuck me," Eastern mutters.

"This is bullshit," Camden says, standing. "You think forcing us to play these games is gonna work? We're not the type of kids you can push around. This place will turn to shit by the end of the week."

"That's where you're wrong," Cal retorts, not in the least bit concerned by Camden's outburst, or the clenching of his fists. "Tell me, Mr Burnside, what would happen if Camden broke the new rules we've set?"

Mr Burnside sighs heavily. "Camden will be sent to juvenile prison until he turns eighteen in three months. Then he'll be moved to Wormwood Scrubs where he'll serve the remainder of his sentence."

"That's right, Mr Burnside. Camden here swerved a five-year sentence, didn't he?"

"Yes."

Cal returns his attention to Camden. "Sit down, son. Upsetting your pride and your ego isn't worth losing five years of your life for a few months hanging out with this lot."

"You don't fucking get it. I'm the leader of the HH crew, and these people are my goddamn enemies." He's shaking now with barely repressed rage, but I know it's more to do with the King and how he'll react to this situation than it is because of who we're grouped with.

"Everyone is in the same boat. *Everyone*. You're no good to your *crew* in prison. Sit down," Cal says, his words filled with meaning. I chance a glance at Sonny who's looking more and more uncomfortable. Has he been talking?

Camden hesitates long enough for me to reach up and slide my hand into his. I squeeze gently. "Camden, sit down. *Please*," I add quietly.

Now everyone in the room is looking at us, but I refuse to return their gazes, keeping my eyes locked solely on him. I'm pretty sure I know what I'll see in them anyway; judgement, disappointment, rejection, fear. But if he refuses and I can't get him to stay then he goes to prison and not only will his future be destroyed, but ours too. The room holds its breath. I'm pretty sure I've stopped fucking breathing.

A minute later he nods imperceptibly, his eyes flashing with unspoken words.

He sits, then squeezes my hand and doesn't let go.

"Good choice," Cal says, eventually. He pushes off the desk and walks into the centre of the circle looking at each of us individually. Finally, he points to Eastern. "You, stand."

"What the fuck for?" he retorts.

"No questions. Get up."

Eastern grits his jaw but does as he's told. "I've been watching you, son. Pretty sure you're on the verge of breaking something, or someone. So, we're gonna deal with that right now. Mr Burnside...?" Cal says, giving him a nod. Mr Burnside bends down and picks up a pair of boxing pads and gloves from a gym bag and passes the gloves to Eastern.

"Put them on."

Whilst Eastern's pulling them onto his hands muttering obscenities under his breath, Cal walks over to Camden. "Here, slide these on. Pair up."

Camden's nostrils flare, but he lets go of my hand and takes the pads from him, shoving them over his fists. He stands before Eastern holding the pads up.

"You lads know what to do," Cal says. A beat later Eastern is punching the pads as hard as he can. The sound of leather smacking against leather reverberates around the room.

"Good. Everyone else grab some gloves from Mr Burnside and wait your turn. Camden here is gonna be the punch bag. Big lad like him can take it."

"Dickhead," Camden mutters.

But Cal is right, he takes it.

All of it.

One by one we all have our turn, even Kate seems to enjoy herself when she gets to smack the shit out of the pads Camden's holding. By the time she's finished, panting and red-faced, Camden is grinning.

"Didn't know you had it in you," he says, giving her a backhanded compliment.

"Not many people do," she retorts, ripping off the gloves and chucking them on the floor.

The last person left to face Camden is Ford. For a beat they just stare at each other. Ford's face is impassive, free of any shred of emotion. He isn't wearing gloves. Instead he holds them in his hands offering them to Camden.

"Here," he says.

"Ford, man..." Sonny interrupts, looking between the two then glancing at me. He knows as well as I that this isn't going to go down well.

"Back the fuck off, numpty," Camden growls at Sonny who just shakes his head.

"You're funeral, arsehole," he shrugs, stepping back.

Camden's lip curls up. "Not this time."

He rips off the pads and shoves them into Ford's chest, then snatches the gloves from him. Cal looks as though he's going to say something, but Mr Burnside shakes his head. He backs off, and we all wait for Armageddon.

Two gang leaders going head to head.

Two enemies who were once friends.

Two guys I care about, ready to rip each other apart.

Two broken kids who are growing into broken men, ruled by their pasts.

The second Ford has the pads pulled on Camden lays into him. He hits hard and fast, a rage unlike I've ever witnessed pours from him.

Smack.

Smack.

Smack.

Smack.

Ford takes each blow, adjusting his body to take whatever Camden gives. Over and over again Camden hits the pads. Sweat drips from his brow, sliding down his face. I'm vaguely aware of Sonny and Eastern asking the girls to take a step back. They know as well as I do that this has the potential to get dangerous fast.

Then just like a match to a box of tinder, Ford lights Camden's rage.

"You can do better than that, Cam. Stop being a pussy and *finish* this," Ford taunts, his eyes narrowing.

I see the change in Camden a second before everyone else. If he was livid before, now he's beyond the point of no return.

"You're a motherfucking murdering bastard!" Camden roars, the last shred of his control snapping. Instead of hitting the pad Ford is holding, his glove covered fist smashes into Ford's cheek sending him reeling backwards. But he doesn't stop there. He launches himself at Ford, punching everywhere he can.

And not once does Ford retaliate.

He takes all the punches. His head snapping back. Spittle and blood flying from his mouth. Ford stumbles when Camden's glove meets his face in a neck snapping blow, and when Camden hits his temple he falls to his knees.

"Camden, stop! PLEASE!" I shout.

For a second Camden hesitates, catching my eye. I'm not sure what he sees, but whatever it is only seems to fuel his anger further. If he weren't wearing gloves then I'm pretty certain Ford would be in a much worse state, as it is he's in pretty bad shape.

"Camden stop!" I repeat, ready to throw myself at him when Sonny grips my arms and holds me back.

"This ain't your fight, Asia. There's too much bad blood between these two. It's time the score was settled once and for all."

"He won't stop!" I shout, trying to get out of Sonny's hold.

"Ford can take it."

"That's enough!" Cal grabs Camden's arm but he shoves him away, too lost in his pain and rage. There's too much anger, too much hurt, too much history and heartbreak.

Too much of everything.

Cal moves to grapple him again but is thrown off once more. "Fuck!" he exclaims.

"He's going to kill him. You need to stop this!" Pink shouts, wrapping her arm around Ruby who's cowering.

"Get out!" I shout at Pink, Kate and Ruby. They don't need to see this. Any minute now Camden will break, and I don't want them here to witness when he does. They don't need to see one man fall to his knees so the other can finally break apart. I know what Ford is doing. I *understand*. Camden can't move forward if he keeps holding this rage inside, because this isn't about gang warfare. This is about Sapphire. This is about the death of a girl they both loved.

"I said get the fuck out!" I snap.

They glance at Mr Burnside, who nods, ushering them out of the room. He's about to return, to help Cal get hold of Camden but Cal shakes his head. "Go! Bring back a medical kit. I'll deal with this," he says, gripping Camden's arms, yanking them behind his back. This time he manages to at least pull him off Ford. "Let it go, Camden. Let it go, man," Cal mutters into his ear.

I fall to my knees at Ford's side. He's still conscious, but his eye is already swelling, his lip and eyebrow split.

"Ford," I mutter, brushing his hair off his face. "Can you hear me?"

He groans, opening his eyes. One is swelling so fast that it's hard for him to focus on me. Sonny drops to his knees beside me whilst

Eastern helps Cal pull a still roaring Camden to the other side of the room. It takes the two of them to hold him back.

"Man, what the fuck Ford?" Sonny says, yanking his t-shirt off one handed, and mopping up the trail of blood dribbling from the split in Ford's eyebrow and lip. I glance at Sonny, my cheeks colouring at his ripped muscles and eagle tattoo spread over his chest. The last time I'd seen him half-dressed was on the beach after he fought Monk in the Tower.

Behind us Camden is still struggling against Cal and Eastern's hold, but after a quick glance I can see he's running out of steam, that he's on the cusp of losing himself.

"Fuck," I mutter, my heart torn. Ford is beat up, in pain. But so is Camden. He might not bear the physical marks like Ford does now but that's because his scars are on the inside. They're locked away, festering, fucking killing him slowly.

"Go to him," Ford says, his fingers reaching up to cup my cheek. "I did this for Cam. I will do it every fucking day until he can't throw anymore punches. Until he's purged himself of the pain and I've absorbed it. This is my penance, Asia, for what I did."

"Ford…" I catch Sonny's gaze, the surprise in them reflecting my own.

"Go to him. I've suffered worse. Just go!" he urges.

"Do as he says, Asia. I'll help Ford," Sonny reassures me.

Gripping Ford's hand in my own, I press a kiss against his palm. Then I lean over and kiss Sonny's cheek forgetting who's in the room, forgetting that I'm not supposed to care about either of them, that I should be rejecting them.

Thing is, I'm done pretending.

It's time I face at least one storm head on. Right here. Right now.

TWENTY-SEVEN

"Camden! Calm the fuck down," Eastern says, only prompting a *fuck you* in response.

He's struggling in Cal's hold, his teeth gnashing. When I approach him, he seems to shut down further. His topaz eyes no longer warm and inviting, but shards of ice.

"Let him go, Cal," I say, locking my gaze with Camden. In my peripheral vision I can see Eastern staring at me, concern written across his handsome face.

"Asia. I wouldn't," he warns.

"It's okay, Eastern. I got this."

"Let me help you."

"No."

Eastern gives me a frustrated look, but he knows me better than to try and change my mind when I'm determined. Right now, Camden's living in his past, consumed by it and I need him to come back to the present.

"You sure?" Cal asks.

"I'm sure."

Cal slowly releases Camden's arms, backing away. The second he's free, Camden rips off his gloves and runs from the room. I don't hesitate, I run after him. He sprints out of the building, through the grounds and towards the one place I know he needs to be right now.

"Asia, wait," Eastern calls, catching up with me at the edge of the maze. He grabs hold of my arm, forcing me to stop.

"Asia. You can't fix this."

"He's hurting, Eastern."

"Exactly. Wild things that hurt are the most dangerous. You don't owe him anything."

"That's a matter of opinion. Either way he needs someone." I try to shake Eastern off me, but he refuses to let me go.

"I don't want you hurt. You don't know what he's capable of when he's like this, Asia."

"I know that I can't leave him to his own thoughts. I know that I'm going to see if he's alright regardless of what you say. I know that if you follow me and he sees you then he'll react badly. I don't need to see him beat the shit out of someone else I care about."

"Why do you do this? You can't save everyone."

A wind picks up, buffeting against us both causing my hair to whip around my face. I pull up my hoody, protecting my head from the cold.

"Because it's the right thing to do. Because I couldn't save my mum and I'll be damned if I see someone else lose theirs to this bullshit life we live."

"So you've decided not to go through with it?" Eastern asks, finally releasing his hold on me.

"I've decided not to fuck *Camden* over. I won't do that to him, or his mum. Can you honestly say you'd be happy doing the same?"

He breathes out slowly, his shoulders slumping. "No, I wouldn't, but what are we going to do now?" He frowns then grips me tightly. "I'll take the sentence. I'll go to prison."

"No fucking way, Eastern. That isn't even an option. We'll think of something. Just know I don't have an issue taking the King down. He needs to pay. He's the one responsible for all this shit. Not you, not Camden, but *him*," I spit.

Eastern watches me closely, then nods his head sharply before he cups my face in his palm and kisses me deeply.

"You're the bravest person I know. Be careful, okay?"

"I will. Go check on Ford for me. Keep Cal and Mr Burnside busy. I need time with Camden."

"You got it."

When my feet hit the pebbles on the beach ten minutes later, Camden is by the shore roaring out into the expanse of the ocean. He's standing in the water, oblivious to the rising tide. Nothing appears to penetrate the depths of his hurt. Not the bitterly cold waves. Not the harsh wind that batters against him. Not the icy rain that has begun to fall or the thunder that rolls overhead. He feels nothing other than the raging, burning agony of losing his sister, and I feel every single bit of it as though it's my own. It breaks my last resolve to keep myself emotionally separated from him.

When I move towards him, I step over the line I drew in the sand all those months ago.

In this moment I choose to be more for him. I vow to save him from the King, from Crown, from his fucking crew, from himself. I walk towards him making a promise to protect him, just like I'm trying to do for everyone else.

"Camden…" I begin.

He doesn't hear, or at least if he does he doesn't acknowledge me. Still he roars. The hoarseness of his voice pitted with tears and years of fucking pain. So, I wait.

I wait whilst he breaks.

I wait whilst he strips himself down to the core, until he's nothing but an organ bleeding his pain into the ocean that crashes at his feet.

When his shoulders drop and his head slumps, I go to him.

"Camden..." I murmur, touching him with hesitant fingers expecting him to lash out. When he doesn't move, I step closer resting my palm on his back. The freezing water seeps into my trainers, covering my ankles, but I remain where I am.

"I can't do it anymore," he mutters, his voice full of anguish.

"Do what, Camden?"

"*Fight.*"

"Then don't. Let it go."

I press myself against his back and slide my arms around his waist, resting my head between his shoulder blades. It's an impulsive move, one that surprises me. But I don't let him go. I hold him close as the thumping of his heart beats wildly in my ear loud enough to block out the thunder rumbling in the distance.

"I can't be weak, Asia. I'll be crucified. My mum will suffer."

"Letting it out, letting everything go every now and then isn't being weak. How can you find the strength to keep fighting if you're filled to the brim with this kind of pain? You're not a fucking machine, Camden."

"Why are you doing this? I'm not worth the trouble, Asia."

"Everyone needs someone. That someone you need is me..."

Camden's hands cover my own, gripping tightly. "And what do you *need*, Asia? I know you being with me isn't just about keeping your enemies close. I believed your story because it was easier than facing the truth, easier to make you mine. At least on the surface I could pretend that was true. I know now for certain that you're not. I saw the fear in your eyes when you thought I was going to kill Ford. I glimpsed the real feelings you have for him. There's so much more to all of this. So, what the fuck do you want from me? What is this really all about?"

"So many things, Camden. *Everything*." I sigh, drawing my hands away. He turns around to face me, rivulets of rain running down his face, or maybe they're tears. I can't tell.

"I saw the fear on your face when I hit Ford and it made me so fucking mad, Asia. I knew you cared about him, but I didn't realise just how much until now. I *saw* it. How can you want him? He killed my sister."

"He didn't stab her with the knife. He didn't do that, Camden."

He tries to shrug himself out of my hold, but I grip onto his arms tighter, my fingers digging into his skin.

"Don't do that, don't make excuses for him."

"I'm not. But he was a *kid*, bound by loyalty and controlled by an adult just like you are. How many things have you done because the King forced you, coerced you? How many times have you turned your back on the boy you were, on Bling, because the King threatened your mother's life over and over again?"

"It's not the same. He loves his sister. He'd do anything for her. I hate the fucking King. I hate what he makes me do."

"Love is just as powerful a motivation as hate, Camden. Maybe more so. We do stupid things for the ones we love."

"Are you talking from experience…?"

"Yes."

"What has love motivated you to do?" He watches me closely, waiting.

This is it. This is the moment where I can choose to do the right thing. I remember what Mr Carmichael said; to trust my instincts and see whether Camden is a good person worth saving. I believe he is.

"Well?"

Camden's question is drowned out by a loud clap of thunder as the heavens open in earnest. The rain becomes a downpour. The wind roars around us and the waves crash a few feet away trying to claw back the sand and stone beneath our feet.

"I made a deal. I made a deal to protect my best friend and his family."

"What deal, Asia?" he bites out.

Above us lightning streaks through the sky, illuminating his face that's now twisted with confusion, with doubt and distrust.

"I'm not going through with it, at least not in the way he expects. I *can't*."

"What fucking deal, Asia?" he insists, gripping my arms tightly. He practically lifts me off my feet, hauling me upwards and away from the incoming tide.

"A deal that would give the police information about the King. A deal that meant you would be the informant without even knowing it. A deal that would put both you and your mum in danger…"

His grip tightens, his fingers biting painfully into my skin. Disappointment and hurt rips up the air between us, making it hard for me to breathe.

"That's why you agreed to join my crew so you could fucking betray me?" he spits, laughing loudly before shoving me away from him.

"Yes. In the beginning, yes it was…"

He sways on his feet from the impact of my honesty. "Why?" he bites out.

"Why do any of us do these things…? Because I needed to protect the ones I love, just like you're trying to protect your mum. Just like Eastern tried to protect his family from a life of fucking poverty by joining your crew and running drugs for the King. Just like Ford threw the fight for his sister and Sonny lied about how he broke his arm to protect us."

"I thought you were fucking different! I thought, finally, I found someone who had my back. Who gave a shit about *me*! I trusted you, Asia. I fucking trusted you!" he screams in my face, and this time there's no mistaking the tears. I'm pretty sure he doesn't even realise he's crying. But he is, and I'm the cause of all his pain. *Me.*

"Camden…" I begin, reaching for him.

"No! Don't!" he snaps, batting my hands away. "Don't you fucking dare touch me."

Rain pours over us, sticking my hair to my scalp and my jumper to my skin. I'm drenched, but none of that matters. I could die tomorrow from fucking hypothermia and I wouldn't care. I need to set this right. I need to make him see.

"Camden. Listen to me!"

"Give me one good reason why I should!" He stalks me, his body overshadowing mine physically as I backpedal over the pebbles. I can feel his hurt as though it's a fucking living entity battering against my strength.

"Because I don't want to hurt you or your mum. I don't want to ruin your lives."

"Tell me why I should believe anything that comes out of your fucking mouth. You were willing to throw me under a bus. You were willing to see my mother DEAD!"

"No. I made the deal with Crown before I knew about your mum. It's different now."

The thing is, it isn't just about his Mum, it's about Camden too. I don't want to betray *him*.

He laughs bitterly. "Stop fucking lying. Nothing's changed. You said yourself that you made the deal to protect the ones you love. You won't betray them. Me and Mum are your fucking sacrifice. I. Get. It."

There's so much I could say to try and convince him to believe me. So many words I could feed him. But those words have no meaning. Not really. Not to him, not to me. They don't change what I've done. I can't undo that now. I can only try to fix this.

"You *lied* to me."

"Yes."

I've lied to everyone, including myself. Now it's time for the truth.

"Camden I was wrong. I took the deal without thinking about you. I *didn't* fucking care about anything other than the safety of my family. You *hurt* me. You allowed Monk to hurt me and when I took the deal, I didn't give a shit if I hurt you back."

"So what's fucking changed?"

"This. *Us.*" I say, pointing between us.

"Us?" he spits. "There is no us, there never fucking was."

He storms away from me, striding across the beach. He stumbles a few times, the pebbles beneath his feet slippery from the rain. I run to catch up, getting in front of him and pressing the flat of my palms against his chest. He stiffens, his fists clenching.

"Get the fuck out of my way," he seethes.

"No."

There's only one way to make him see. Actions speak louder than words. They always have.

In one step I push myself up against his body, grasp his face between my palms and kiss him. Pushing my tongue between his lips, I draw him closer to me, grasping the back of his head

and for a few bliss filled minutes, he kisses me back.

He kisses me with gentle violence.

He kisses me with soft lips and harsh fingers. With tentative strokes of his tongue and a hand fisted in my hair. He's the fucking storm raging around us and the gentle hum of warmth building in my chest. He's the chaos of crashing waves, and the calmness of a gentle sea. He overpowers me with passion, want and *need* as his hands slide down my back and he lifts me off my feet. A deep rumble builds in his throat when I wrap my legs around his waist. We don't stop kissing as he walks with me over to the boulder that his sister's image is painted upon. We don't break apart as he presses me against the rock and his hand works its way up and under my jumper. We don't stop clawing at each other as he bites my bottom lip and squeezes my breast, or when he grinds his hips against mine, the long shaft of his dick, thick through his trousers. And when his fingers undo the buttons of my jeans and he slides his hand beneath the elastic of my knickers, I don't push him away. Instead, I groan into his mouth, needing to feel his finger knuckle deep inside of me. When he pushes two fingers inside, the pad of his thumb rubbing against my clit, I lose my mind a little. A rush of heat pools low in my stomach as he draws out an orgasm that is going to ruin me. I feel it, the building pressure within that's waiting for the moment to detonate just like the clap of thunder overhead. Camden pulls back, watching me, his fingers working magic between my legs. I close my eyes, but he barks out a demand.

"Look at me."

My eyes snap open and I'm captured in his gaze, drawn so deep into his depths that I'm struggling for air. Struggling to maintain control. My body is hot, so fucking hot for him that if it weren't for the freezing rain and the wind I know this would go so much further. There's too much attraction between us. There's an all-consuming kind of lust that I've been fighting ever since I first met him. This feeling inside is similar to the way I feel about Ford, like I'm out of control, like I'm on a train that is going too fast. It makes sense I suppose, they're both so intense.

"You feel just as good as I imagined," he utters, his lips trailing against the length of my neck, leaving scorch marks that not even the freezing rain can soothe. I grind against his hand, gripping onto his shoulders to steady me.

"Camden…"

"Come for me, Asia. Let me see you," he murmurs.

And I let him. I let him see me at my most vulnerable. I break apart in his arms, drowning in his eyes, panting for breath, devastated by the orgasm he's so effortlessly drawing from me. It laps at me slowly, starting from that tiny spot between my legs and winding outwards, warming my stomach and curling my toes. When he presses his thumb firmly against my twitching clit and curls his thick long fingers inside of me I break apart and not the freezing rain, nor the howling wind can dampen the fire burning bright between us. When I finally suck in the air I so desperately need, Camden leans over and presses a soft, heartfelt kiss against my mouth before taking a step back and devastating me with his words.

"Fuck me over once, shame on you. Fuck me over twice, shame on me. Fuck with my life, my *mum's* life, you'd better goddam run," he grinds out, all tenderness gone.

I stare at him in shock, my skin still zinging under his touch. "Camden, I thought..."

"No, Asia," his mouth twists in a sneer as he becomes the boy everyone fears. "You don't get to tell me how you were willing to ruin my life then kiss me and think the slate is fucking clean. You're lucky I don't fucking kill you with my bare hands right now."

"You wouldn't do that."

He leans in close, his hands slamming against the wet rock. "You don't fucking know me well enough to know what the fuck I'd do," he spits.

"Yes, I do. You won't hurt me. I just came all over your hands, Camden. If you wanted to hurt me you wouldn't have given me the best damn orgasm of my fucking life. "

"You don't know shit."

"I know that you kissed me like a boy willing and ready to trust in his heart. I know that you touched me like a man ready to fight for the people he loves. I know that deep within you is Bling, that kid who had ambition and dreams and a fucking future. I know you hate Ford as much as you do because you love him, and he hurt you."

"Stop fucking talking!"

"No, I won't. Ford made a mistake that cost you both dearly. He'll never be free of that but he's willing to try and make amends. Eastern made a mistake joining your crew. I made a mistake agreeing to the Crown's deal. I. Made. A. Mistake," I repeat, pleading with him as he backs away from me.

"You're no different from everyone else who's screwed me over. You're no different from the people who've come into my life and made me trust them only to walk all over me, chucking me away, rejecting me like I'm a worthless piece of scum."

"I'm *not* like everyone else and I'm not your enemy, Camden. *We* are not your enemies. The King is, and together we can take him down. We can save your mum. Just let me help you to do that. Let me *fix* this."

"And how can you possibly do that?"

"By trusting in the people I've come to care about. By *you* trusting *me*." When he moves to walk away, I grab his wrist forcing him to stop. "I won't give up on you."

"It's too fucking late!"

"Someone told me recently that trust is earned, not something given without thought or care and I'm trusting you. Who's to say you won't just tell the King about all of this. Maybe it'd earn you some brownie points. Maybe he'd give up your mum in exchange for ratting me and Eastern out. I've just as much to lose as you do, the only difference is I'm brave enough to take the risk."

"I'm not a fucking coward."

"No?" I retort. I know I'm pressing his buttons, but I can't seem to help myself. "Seems to me you're afraid."

"Fuck you, Asia. I'm not afraid."

"Then prove it. Prove it to me now."

"I don't have to do shit."

"Don't do that, don't walk away. I will fix this," I say, jogging to catch up with him.

"And what if you can't? What if this blows up in our faces and the King kills my mum anyway? What then, Asia? How the fuck are you going to help me then?"

"We'll destroy him before that ever happens," I promise vehemently.

TWENTY-EIGHT

The walk back to Oceanside is silent, both of us lost to our thoughts. Now that the adrenaline has worn off, the chill has set in and I'm fucking freezing. Wrapping my arms tightly around me I jog to keep up with Camden's long strides. We've missed dinner and there's only a couple hours to curfew but I'm not ready to give up just yet.

"Will you come back to my room, Camden, so we can talk some more?" I say through chattering teeth.

"What's the point?"

"Please?"

He nods his head in agreement but says nothing more. Ten minutes later we're back at the annex, standing outside my bedroom door. I slide my key into the lock, and he follows me inside, shutting the door behind him. As soon as the warmth of the room hits me, my body decides to go into full on teeth chattering, body trembling shock. I mean I don't think I have hypothermia, but I'm fucking cold.

"Fuck, Asia, your lips are blue. You're freezing."

"Just a bit," I respond.

"You need to get those wet clothes off…"

"You trying to get me naked, Camden?" My smile drops when I see the expression on his face.

"Don't flirt with me Asia. *Don't*," he growls.

"Got it." I study his face. He's trembling too. I'm pretty sure he's just as freezing as I am. "You need to get out of those wet clothes as well."

"I'll be fine. I'm not staying long. Sort yourself out first," he says stiffly.

"Okay, give me a second." I grab my soft pyjama bottoms and a t-shirt from my wardrobe and head into the bathroom. It takes me a while to peel off my clothes and put on the clean dry ones. I realise too late that I didn't grab any underwear. Not that it matters. Camden won't touch me again, not now, and especially not since I'm wearing fluffy Supergirl patterned pyjama bottoms. Towel drying my hair roughly, I look at myself in the mirror, stifling a laugh. I'm being fucking ridiculous. I've just told Camden *everything* and I'm worrying about what I'm wearing and how I look? Christ, the cold must have addled my brain. I'm fucking losing it. Tomorrow, Eastern and I could find ourselves at the mercy of the King if Camden decides to talk. I laugh almost hysterically. *Mercy*? Who am I fucking kidding?

When I walk out of the bathroom Camden is sitting on my chair, his teeth chattering. "You need to take some of your own advice and take off those wet clothes, Camden. I can wait for you to go back to your room."

He shakes his head, stands, then rips off his jumper and t-shirt in one go, revealing his broad shoulders and tattooed stomach. The roaring lion's head peeking up over the waistband of his jeans.

"What are you doing?" I ask.

"Taking my wet clothes off. Got a problem with that?" he challenges me.

"Nope," I pop the p, sitting down on my bed and pretending that him getting fucking naked doesn't bother me in the slightest.

"I'm going to take a shower," he states, rolling down his jeans and underwear at the same time. He's already kicked off his trainers and peeled off his socks whilst I was in the bathroom. Why the fuck am I thinking about his socks when his very naked, very large dick is on full view?

"Alright, Asia?" he asks me, locking his gaze with mine.

"I'm pretty sure showering when you've got hypothermia can kill you."

"I haven't got hypothermia."

"Well, if you're sure," I shrug, keeping my eyes up, focussed on his face and not his broad shoulders or his strong muscular arms. I'm certainly not looking at his firm pecs or defined abs. Nor am I looking at his lion tattoo or the shit-hot v muscle sliding towards his groin. And I'm definitely not looking at his ten-inch dick wondering whether he's a grower or a shower.

He smirks, evilly. "So, I'm gonna take that shower then."

"Sure," I mutter, reaching for my desk drawer and reaching for the cigarettes stashed inside. I light one, desperately wishing I had a cup of tea to warm me and having to make do with the smoke filling my lungs instead.

After a piss-taking amount of time, Camden eventually walks out of the bathroom with a towel wrapped around his waist. He smells of my body wash. Something about that lights a fire inside me.

"Better?" I ask.

He grunts, not deigning to answer me with words. Instead he sits next to me on the bed, not giving a shit that the towel is barely covering his dick. He's trying to intimidate me. It won't work.

"If you want to get your own back, showing me your dick won't really do it. I'm not a child, Camden. I've seen a cock before. You can sit here naked for all I care, so long as you listen to what I have to say."

"Good, because I'm not planning on leaving the room starkers, and I'm not putting those wet clothes back on. Can I have a cigarette," he responds, leaning over me and grabbing the pack and the lighter that's sitting next to me on the bed before I've even had time to respond. The towel slides off his lap and he doesn't bother to cover himself up again. Maybe I should've had a shower too, perhaps I wouldn't feel so fucking cold still.

"Help yourself," I sigh. He's being a dick and *showing* his dick. Granted he's got a reason to be a wanker, but still. I watch him light a cigarette and wait. He smokes it in silence, taking deep pulls and savouring the smoke filling his lungs. When he's smoked it down to the butt, the ash collected in the palm of his hand, he gets off the bed and saunters to the window, opening it and throwing the butt and ash out. A blast of cold air rushes into the room, making me shiver. Camden closes the window quickly then turns to face me, naked as the day he was born.

"You should wrap that towel back around your waist, Camden, it might shrivel up left out in the air too long…" I jerk my chin towards his dick, raising my eyebrows. I know full well I'm pushing my damn luck but do it anyway.

"Aren't you afraid, Asia?"

"I'm not frightened of a naked body Camden, if that's what you're getting at."

"Good."

He stalks towards me, nudges my feet apart and kneels on the bed between my parted legs. My skin rushes with heat, partly because he's fucking beautiful but also partly because he's pushing this too far. Yet, I refuse to show fear. I know what this is. This is about dominance. I ripped his away the second I told him the truth, now he's trying to reclaim it back. I keep my gaze fixed firmly on his face and when his hand reaches to cup the back of my head, my heart begins to hammer like a dozen kids pounding the pavement with their feet.

"I could hurt you so bad, Asia. I could hurt you like you hurt me," he says, his voice low and penetrating.

"But you won't," I reply, certain, sure of my faith in him.

"You really believe that whilst I'm naked before you, my cock in one hand, your head in the other?"

"You won't hurt me," I repeat, gritting my jaw. I refuse to show fear, even though a tiny thread pierces my heart.

"You're shaking...."

He's right, the shivering is starting in earnest now and I can't tell whether it's because he's threatening me, I really am suffering from hypothermia or because I want his damn cock in my mouth. Perhaps all three.

"You won't hurt me."

"But *you* hurt *me*. I'm fucking bleeding, Asia. I'm fucking torn up. What you see now is an illusion. My chest is torn open, my fucking heart shredded to bits. You did that. You did that to me."

"I have hurt you, and you've hurt me too. Now we're even. But don't for one second think I won't bite your dick in half if you try and shove it in my mouth unwanted," I snarl, my frantic heart beating a rhythm that I don't understand.

Excitement, fear, *lust*.

All of it churns inside of me now, a heady mix that's intoxicating. His fingers tighten in my hair as he regards me. For one achingly terrifying, panty-melting moment I think he's going to do it.

"Good girl," he mutters, releasing his hold, smoothing my hair back down. "I needed to be sure."

"Sure of what?" I ask, breathing out heavily as he gets off the bed, grabs the towel and wraps it around his waist.

"That you're strong enough to face what's coming. When we go up against the King you need to be ready."

"What are you saying?"

He picks his wet clothes up off the floor and heads towards the door. "I'm saying let's do this. Let's take down the fucking King and be free of him once and for all. Maybe then I can be the man you deserve, not the fucked-up kid he made."

"You want to do this?"

His hand stills on the door handle. "I want to fight back. I want to save my mum. I want more than this shitty existence I live. I want *you*."

"You have me, Camden. I promise," I reply gently.

"No I haven't, not yet. I'm not fucking worthy of your promise, but I will be. I'll prove my worth. I'll never ever give you a reason to hate me again."

"And the others? Eastern, Sonny... *Ford*. I can't do this without them."

He nods tightly. "I know. I'll tolerate them for you."

"Even Ford?" I press.

"Even him," Camden grits his jaw, determined.

My heart swells with hope. "You can stay... until curfew, at least," I blurt out, my gaze tracing over his naked chest and the towel slung low on his hips. I'm not sure why I ask him to stay, only that I don't want him to leave just yet. He hesitates.

"I *want* you to stay," I murmur, shifting on the bed and sliding beneath the covers, making room for him. I'm shivering in earnest now. Cold right down to my bones.

He lets go of the door handle and walks towards me. "I'm naked."

"Talk about stating the obvious. Get in, Camden. I'm not about to fuck you."

He cocks his head to the side, hooking his finger under the towel and pushing it loose. "No?" he asks, as it drops to the floor in a puddle at his feet.

"No," I confirm, biting on the inside of my cheek to stop myself from giggling like a little girl. A minute ago, he was threatening to stick his cock in my mouth and here I am inviting him into my bed butt naked. If nothing else, that tells me just how much I truly trust him. He slides under the covers, stretching his length out beside me.

"I've never had a girl invite me into her bed and not want to fuck me," he whispers, his gaze flicking from my lips to my eyes and back again.

"Well this girl is different."

"You ain't wrong there," he agrees, drawing me against his body and holding me against his warmth. My cheek is pressed against his chest, his hand cupping my head.

"Wrap your arms around me, Asia. Get warm."

I do as he instructs, pressing myself close against him. To be held like this is not something I'm used to. It's hard for me to relax. Most of my childhood I'd cuddle my pillow or teddy, desperate for human touch, human warmth, comfort. There were so many nights when my mum just wasn't around, and I lay awake crying for her when she was either out getting high or at home passed out with a needle stuck in her arm. Only when my brothers arrived, could I finally experience that basic human need, to be held, to be loved unconditionally.

Sighing, I breath out a long slow breath.

"What is it?" Camden asks, murmuring gently. He has his chin pressed against the top of my head with his arms folded around me. I feel cared for, which is crazy given the events of tonight and the fact that he's completely frigging naked.

"Just shit from my past," I say, not able to express myself further. That pain isn't something I can share just yet.

"I get it. I fucking get it, Asia."

He doesn't say one more word, he simply holds me, and I realise that despite the persona he presents to the world underneath it all he's just a broken kid like the rest of us. We're the legacy of fucked up parents in a fucked-up world. We're the broken and the bruised. We're the battered and the torn. But maybe, just maybe we're the stitch to each other's wound. Maybe we can help each other to heal.

After a few minutes my teeth stop chattering and I begin to warm up, his heat penetrating through my clothing settling beneath my skin and seeping deep into muscle and bone. Eventually, I find myself relaxing into Camden's arms as he holds me tightly against him with a boner that could slay an army. I'm pretty sure I'm grinning as I fall into a dreamless sleep.

TWENTY-NINE

A loud pounding on the door has Camden cursing and me sitting up in bed.

"Asia, goddamn it, you better be in here!"

Fuck, Eastern.

"Goddamn that fucker," Camden complains, groaning as he throws back the covers and strides over to the door.

"What are you doing?" I screech, my cheeks flushing traitorously as my gaze lands on his semi-boner. Fuck me, he's a shower *and* a grower.

"Opening the door," he responds, looking at me as though I've lost a few brain cells whilst I've been asleep. Then starts grinning when he notices my gaze drag up from his pretty dick, over his tattoo and ripped chest, finally resting on his topaz eyes.

"You're naked!" I hiss, pointing out the obvious.

"And?"

"And you have a semi going on," I say, waving my hand in the general direction of his dick. When he grins with intent, I shake my head. "I don't want a repeat of earlier and you getting into a fight, especially not like that."

"Like what?"

"*Naked* with a *semi*, for fuck sake. You could injure it," I blurt out, scrambling out of bed

and yanking my wardrobe doors open. I've still got the black tracksuit bottoms and grey t-shirt Ford lent me when I stayed in his room last term. I chuck them at Camden. "Put those on."

He catches them and smirks, stalking me. "We could just ignore him, Asia," he mutters, pressing me up against the wall. He rests his forearm against the wall by my head, and a sudden rash of heat rushes over my skin.

"Camden," I say, though it comes out more of a plea than a warning.

"Yes, Asia?" he asks, leaning down and brushing his lips against my own sending firebolts of electricity right to my clit. Jesus.

Eastern calls my name again, just as Camden slides his tongue over the seam of my lips. I groan into his mouth and he growls, swearing under his breath. "Better let the fucker in," he says, stepping back.

I cough, scraping a hand through my hair, trying to get a hold of myself and nod to the clothes he's got bundled in his hand. "Not until you're dressed."

"You've had these all along…?" he asks, holding them up.

I know what he's getting at and I roll my eyes. "I forgot. Just put the damn things on."

He laughs but does what I ask, then makes himself comfortable on my bed, grinning at me mercilessly.

"Open the door then," he smirks, as he adjusts his considerably sized dick.

"Fuck sake," I mutter under my breath, pulling the door open, hoping I don't look like how I feel; a girl who is wound up and needing to be fucked.

I'm surprised to find Sonny stumbling forward, almost falling headfirst into my chest.

"Sonny, what the fuck? I exclaim. "You're picking my locks again… with one arm?"

He rights himself and gives me a sheepish look. "I'm the resident lock picker, and you weren't answering. What was I supposed to do?"

"Wait?" I retort, rolling my eyes and glancing at Eastern and Ford behind him. From his position on the bed, Camden won't be able to see Ford. I'm not sure it's wise that he's here, honestly.

"None of us are particularly patient, are you okay?" he asks me, flicking his gaze to Camden who's still lying on my bed.

"Of course, she is. What the fuck do you take me for?" Camden smirks from his spot on my bed, looking like the cat that's got the cream. Back to the arrogance then. I shake my head. How the hell am I going to manage these four?

"I'll choose not to answer that," Sonny replies as Eastern enters the room behind him. He takes one look at my dishevelled hair, crumpled clothes and Camden's salacious grin and swears loudly.

"Eastern, this isn't what it looks like," I begin.

For a moment he looks as though he's about to lash out, and I'm fully prepared to deal with his insecurities and his temper, but what he says next surprises me.

"You don't need to explain a damn thing to me, Alicia. I know you. Come here," he says, opening his arms to me. I walk straight into the broad warmth of his chest and hold onto him tightly.

"It's Asia, dickwad," I say, grinning into his chest.

He laughs. "I know. You okay?"

"I'm okay."

"Then that's all that matters." He lets me go and grins. When he glances over my shoulder at Camden, his smile drops. There's dislike there still, but despite that, a growing acceptance.

"I'd tell you both to get a room if we weren't already in one," Ford says as he steps into my room and shuts the door behind him.

Behind me, the bed creaks as Camden shifts to his feet. "What the fuck are *you* doing here? Back for more, eh?" he growls.

I step in front of Camden blocking him from moving towards Ford. I can feel his harsh breaths against the bare skin of my neck. He grasps my hips as though to anchor himself. I'm not even sure he's aware of doing it, but I am. I'm hyper aware. So are the rest of them.

"We're checking on Asia. Making sure you've not hurt her," Eastern says matter-of-factly.

"He hasn't hurt me," I confirm, swiping my still damp hair back off my face.

"Good, because I won't tolerate it. You hurt her, I'll kill you," Eastern warns.

Camden's fingers tighten on my hips. "Noted," he says.

For a while not one of us moves, talks, or fucking breathes if me holding my breath is anything to go by. Eventually Ford breaks the silence. He looks at me, his gaze trailing to Camden's hands on my hips, to the clothes he's wearing. *His* clothes. A range of emotions flood across his features.

"We're here because the three of us have come to a decision," Ford begins, then winces. His right cheek and eye are bruised and swollen, and his lip and eyebrow split. He has a butterfly plaster pulling together the skin on his brow. It looks like it needs stitches but if I know Ford as well as I think I do, then he's refused a trip to the hospital to get it sorted so that he can be here instead.

"What decision?" I ask, looking between the three of them.

Ford dabs at his mouth, his tongue sliding across the split, licking at the blood. "That we're willing to do what it takes to fix things. That *I'm* willing to do what it takes to fix things," he says, looking at Camden.

"That's big of you, fucktard," Camden growls, tensing.

"Look, Camden, Asia gives a shit about what happens to you and we give a shit about Asia. That means whatever the fuck we feel for each other gets put aside for her. That's the agreement the three of us have come to, and now we need to know you're on board," Eastern says, refusing to break eye contact with Camden.

"What are you saying exactly?" I press, wanting to understand what this means, really means. Are we our own crew now? Or is this more than that?

"I'm saying… No, *we're* saying," Ford corrects himself, "That we're willing to be a unit, Asia, if you're willing to have us, that is? As friends... as *more* than friends." He locks eyes with me, unafraid and certain of himself. I can feel a flush of heat warming me from the inside out. Sonny is smiling, and Eastern has a determined look on his face, one that is filled with respect and love. It must be hard for him to concede like this. I daren't look over my shoulder at Camden. Things are so new between us, if there even is an us. I'm still not one hundred percent sure he's forgiven me despite the last few hours curled up in bed with him.

Swallowing hard, I look at Eastern. He's the one I'm most concerned about. Ford and Sonny didn't seem to have issues about me being interested in both of them last term, but Eastern and I have a lifelong history that makes this trickier to manage. I know he always hoped that it'd only ever be us.

"Eastern?" I ask gently.

His beautiful brown eyes fill with determination. "I'd tear up the world to be with you, Asia. I'll accept these arseholes if that's what you need. I want you any way I can have you. If this is truly what you want then I'm with you. *Is it*?"

"I think so," I say.

"You think so?" he questions, regarding me.

I frown, biting on my lip ring. "I don't trust easily, and I don't do relationships, Eastern. You know that better than anyone. Despite all of that, I do trust you all."

"Good, we can work on the rest," Ford says.

"But I don't know how to be with one guy, let alone *four*. Not to mention that you all hate each other, so that kind of complicates things wouldn't you say?"

"We'll figure this out, *together*," Sonny says, his eyes darkening with lust, promise and determination.

"Damn straight," Ford adds.

"These guys might not be my favourite people in the world," Eastern explains, keeping his gaze fixed firmly on me. "But *you* are, Asia. I'll do whatever it takes to make you happy."

"Ditto, arsehole," Camden says, his fingers digging deeper into my hips as he holds onto me possessively. He senses in that moment that I want to go to Eastern, but he doesn't let me go. He still clings on to me when Eastern strides over. In fact, his arms tighten around my waist as he pulls me back against his chest, but he doesn't try to stop Eastern and that in itself tells me a lot.

"One day, you'll love me as much as you love Eastern, Asia. I'll prove my worth," he says before loosening his fingers a little.

"I've fucking missed you," Eastern growls, glaring at Camden but taking another step closer regardless. He cups my face in his hands, forcing my head back against Camden's chest then kisses me. His tongue spears my lips as his fingers slide into my hair. I'm acutely aware of Camden's heavy breathing and deep rumbling growl that penetrates through my back, but Eastern ignores it and claims what's his, what's always been his. My hands slide into the back pockets of his jeans as I hold him against me. He groans, clearly turned on as his tongue plunders my mouth, seeking out my own and twining with it. Heat pervades my front and my back as

I'm encased between the two. Both of their cocks are hard, hard for me and I can't help but move my hips grinding against them both.

"Fuck me, Asia," Eastern utters, the sound guttural and raw as he steps back reluctantly. My cheeks flush with more heat as he stares at me with unbridled lust. I grin and he chuckles, flashing a pleased look at Camden. Behind him Sonny is biting down on his knuckles and Ford is gritting his jaw.

Well, shit. For a moment I'm left speechless.

"Was about time you manned the fuck up," Camden says, then points at Ford. "But if *he* does the same in front of me I might just rip his head off."

Eastern shakes his head. "I know how you feel, Camden. You've got your arms around the only girl I've ever loved but here's the thing; it's about time you realised that Asia is just as much theirs as she is yours or mine, and she'll *only* be yours if you accept *us*. So, *you* need to suck it the fuck up," Eastern retorts, backing off and giving me space.

He knows me well enough to understand that I need a moment to breathe. To absorb what's just happened. Camden on the other hand is still learning. I grip his wrist, and peel his arm gently off me.

"This isn't going to work if every time you're faced with Ford you want to kill him, and I want this to work. We *need* each other," I laugh a little at that, still not quite sure how the fuck we got here, "Besides, we all have a common goal. Remember that."

"*We* have a common goal," Camden responds, pointing between us and Eastern. "But Sonny and Ford, what the fuck do they get out of this?"

"We get Asia," Sonny says, grinning at me, giving me his best megawatt dimpled smile. He doesn't give two shits that Camden is giving him evils, and I admire him for it.

"And we get to take down that cunt who has your mother," Ford adds, staring directly at Camden.

"How the fuck do you know about my mum?"

"I walk in the same circles as you, remember? There isn't much Grim doesn't know about."

"That bitch better stay out of my business," Camden snarls.

Ford tenses, his fingers curling into fists, but he doesn't take the bait. Instead his gaze flicks to mine. He's covering for me already, but I won't have secrets between us, not now. It's time to clear the air whilst I have them all in the same room not killing each other.

"I told them everything," I admit.

Camden's mouth drops open then slams shut on the curse words I know are brimming. All four of us are watching him closely. Eastern steps forward, sliding his arm around my waist and drawing me into his side, reassuring me with his touch.

"Weren't you supposed to be undercover, Asia? You make a shit informant for the police," he says after a while, a tentative smile in his voice covered only by the reality of the situation. I breathe out a steady breath.

"Yeah, I'd agree with that," I say.

"So, you all know I'm the King's fucking pawn. How about Sapphire, do you know how this prick threw a fight to help his sister and that my twin was killed because of it?"

When neither Eastern nor Sonny respond, I do. "Yes, they know about Sapphire too."

Camden turns his back on us and slams his fist into the wall. Better that, I guess, than someone's face. Things are improving.

"Now everything's out in the open. How are we going to get past this and sort out the real issue here?" Sonny asks not in the least bit bothered by Camden's outburst.

"Fuck knows," Eastern mutters. "The King's untouchable."

"Not quite. There's Monk…"

"Monk?" Ford frowns.

"Yeah, Monk." I glance at Camden who narrows his eyes at me. "He's the King's son, isn't that right, Camden?"

Camden nods tightly. "How did you know?"

"Ruby," I explain.

"Ruby?" Camden frowns.

"Yeah, she told me. She warned me about Monk. He beats her you know…"

My voice trails off as all four of them stiffen with anger.

"That motherfucker!" Camden growls, heading towards the door as though he's going to kick the shit out of Monk right this second. Not a good idea.

"Don't!" I grab Camden's arm, pulling out of Eastern's hold. "She's afraid, and you are not going to do anything that will put your mum in danger, or her. We need to be clever, Camden."

"That nasty piece of shit!" Ford exclaims.

"He's been beating Ruby for some time and she's scared for her life. I have a feeling Mr Burnside and Mr Carmichael have put us into these new groups in part to help me, but also to help her."

"They know about all this too?"

"Not everything. Not about Monk being the King's son. But they were there when Crown offered Eastern and me the deal. They know about that."

"And they were willing to let you screw me over? Fuck man." Camden sits heavily onto the chair, dropping his head into his hands. I go to him, kneeling before him and grasp his wrists. He looks at me despairingly.

"They don't like this anymore than I do. I think we need to go to them for help."

"We don't need their help," Ford says. "This isn't their fight. *Grim* will help us. She fucking hates the King just as much as we do."

Camden stands, pushing against my hand that's holding him back. "No, she ain't getting involved!"

"Listen, Cam, I know what you feel about her. I understand that you blame her as much for Sapphire's death as you do me, but you don't know everything about what happened that night or why. It's not as cut and dried as you think. You never gave me a chance to explain."

"I don't need no fucking explanation, no excuses. It's pretty fucking cut and dry to me. She went there to watch you fight. She died because you threw the fight for your damn sister, for *money* to line Grim's pockets."

"No, Cam. It's not as simple as that."

"This is bullshit!" Camden exclaims, moving towards Ford threateningly.

Eastern steps up blocking him, but it's Sonny who manages to extinguish the tension that's about to erupt into another fight.

"It isn't bullshit, Camden. I know the truth, but I think you need to hear it from the horse's mouth. Saturday we're meeting Grim and she's going to tell you the full story. You're going to want to hear it."

"Fuck you all, and your damn lies. I ain't going near that bitch."

Behind us the door opens, and in steps Cal. He looks at us all gravely. "You haven't got a say in the matter, Camden, because you're meeting her, whether you want to or not. Mr Carmichael has signed off on the trip. You're going to speak with Grim and you, my friend, are going to purge your demons once and for all."

THIRTY

"The fuck I am!" Camden exclaims, his body tensing.

"Were you listening at the fucking door?" Eastern mutters looking as confused as I feel.

What the hell has Cal got to do with this? More to the point, why the fuck is he helping us? Sonny puffs out his cheeks then blows out a heavy breath.

"Blame me for this. I might've shared a few things with my foster family. They want to help. Carmichael's hands are tied. He can't do what he wants as principal of this school, but they can. They will. I *trust* them," Sonny says, looking at Cal and nodding his head as though only just realising that fact.

"And we're going to sort this shit out. The King has no right to use kids for his own gain or threaten the people you care about to get what he wants. Besides we have a vested interest in taking the King down," Cal says, looking at Camden who's so furious he's barely holding the rage in.

"We?" Ford asks, folding his arms across his chest.

"Yes, the Freed brothers and me."

Eastern whistles low and Camden narrows his eyes at Cal.

"Start talking," Camden orders, taking my hand in his.

Cal nods. "You all better make yourself comfortable. This may take a while."

Each of us takes a spot around the room. I sit on the bed between Eastern and Sonny. Ford is sitting on the floor at my feet and Camden is sitting stiffly on the chair by my desk. We're all looking at Cal, waiting.

"As you know I was brought in by Mr Carmichael after he decided to get rid of that complacent, good for nothing piece of shit, Bobby Rusk. In fact, he was going to hire someone else, but Hud asked a favour, and I was brought in."

"Bobby could be a dick at times, sure, but he was alright," Camden says, shrugging.

He wasn't alright at all. He was a fucking pervert. Then again, Bobby was totally in Camden's pocket, turning a blind eye when we all fucked off to the Tower. None of us have been back since the start of the new term.

"He was alright because he let you run amok," Cal says, glancing at Camden. A look passes between them, one that I'm not able to interpret.

"As you're probably aware Max, Bryce, Hud, and their partner Louisa, foster Sonny. He came into our lives when his father passed. The Freeds kept in touch with many of the kids who were in the care home they grew up in. Quite a few work for them and a whole lot more remained friends. Including Sonny's dad. We care about the little shit." Cal winks and Sonny grumbles something unintelligible under his breath.

Camden sucks his teeth, unimpressed, or at least that's the impression he's trying to give because I'm pretty sure I've just seen a little jealousy flash across his face.

"Alright, we get it, you're the fucking Brady bunch. What's the deal with you guys and the King?"

"Camden, shut the fuck up and let the man speak," Sonny snaps. It's unlike him to be short-tempered, but he's more tense than usual.

"Cheers, sunshine," Cal grins, not giving a crap that he's pissing Sonny off more.

"S'alright, *tosser*," Sonny retorts, raising his eyebrows in defiance. Cal flips him the finger. They both laugh.

"When Sonny was being taken care of at hospital he told us about you, Asia…" He looks at Sonny giving him a devious glare. "Actually, he wouldn't shut up about how he met this *fiery, sarcastic, beautiful girl* with blue hair who rocked his whole world… Though I can see you changed the colour now."

"Fuck, Cal, could you just get to the point and stop embarrassing me, please," Sonny groans, tipping his head back and squeezing his eyes shut.

"He did, did he?" I respond, unable to hide the grin in my voice. Sonny peeks at me from behind his fingers. I give him a warm smile. He shows me his dimples and when he lowers his hand, he takes mine in his.

"Yes. He was worried about you. We couldn't get him to talk at first, when he eventually told us the story we were pissed off. The King has been a thorn in our side for some years now."

"What do you mean?" Camden asks. "You guys are clean, right? Apparently the sun shines out of those Freed brothers' arses. Pretty sure they eclipse the sun when they bend over."

Eastern laughs and even Ford smirks. I, on the other hand, am holding my breath because Sonny has his thumb pressed into my palm and he's swirling it around and around making my skin prickle with sensation. When I glance at him, he's looking directly at Cal, but I can't help but notice the amusement playing around his lips. I'm still wound up from Camden's naked hotness and Eastern's kiss. Now this. I might implode soon.

"Yes, we're clean, but that doesn't mean to say we haven't come across some dark bastards in the past. There's a Cuban businessman called Santiago Garcia who Hudson had a run in with a few years ago. He hurt someone Hud cared about. Her name was Beth…"

"Was?" I whisper.

"Yes, was. She died a year ago. Hud's anger has escalated since then. He needs retribution. Just like you all do."

"What happened to her?" Eastern asks.

"After a business deal went south and Hud refused to work with Santiago, he sent his minions to beat Beth so badly that she was paralysed from the waist down. She was in a care home until she passed. Her life was taken by that bastard and Hud feels responsible."

Camden shifts uncomfortably on the chair. "So what's this Santiago prick got to do with the King?"

"He's in business with him selling cocaine and heroin to the vast majority of the south coast."

"Holy fuck!" Eastern exclaims. He grips my hand, his fingers twining with mine tightly. I know what he's thinking, that this is bigger than any of us ever thought. I glance at him frowning.

"Your mum and Bray are safe, Eastern. We made sure of it," I say, trying to reassure him, hoping I'm right.

Cal glances between us. "As soon as Sonny told us what's been happening, we sent someone to watch over your mum just in case. He's a good man. Ex SAS, *he'll* keep her safe."

Eastern grips my hand tighter. "You don't trust the police to look after her?"

"Honestly, no."

"Fuck me!" Eastern swears.

"And what about my mum? What about her? The only person

who's looking out for her is me, and now I'm about to put her in even more danger if what you're saying is true!" Camden exclaims. He stands, scraping a hand over his face. "I need to go. This was a stupid fucking idea." He looks at me. "I'm sorry, Asia. But the risk is too high. It's too fucking high."

"Wait," Cal says, holding his hands up. "As long as the King still believes you're on his side, then she'll remain safe."

"She's not safe. She's never been safe with him."

"No, I hear that, but he won't kill her so long as he thinks he has you under orders. We'll figure this out, okay?" Cal says.

"No, it's not fucking okay. Monk is suspicious as it is. Who's to say he's not fucking listening in on this conversation right now?"

"He isn't. Buddy is working with Monk and Frank has his little sheep, or should I say *wolves*. They're both trying to knock some fucking sense into them. A couple of them might be turned around, but Monk… he's a lost cause. He's his father's son, I'm afraid."

"No shit," I mumble.

"So, what do we do?" Eastern asks.

"We need to get away from Oceanside to work out how to move forward. Like I said, Mr Carmichael signed off on your trip out of here this Saturday. In five days, we'll meet with the Freeds, with Grim, and we'll make a plan."

"What the fuck has Grim got to do with this?" Camden asks, glaring at Cal. "What has Ford told you about her?"

"Let's just say, she has a vested interest of her own and let's leave it at that, okay? It ain't my place to tell her story. You'll find out soon enough."

"Yeah, a vested interest in *money*. The Freed brothers might not be dodgy, but she fucking is. You can't trust her."

"I trust Hud and he trusts her. That's all I need to know."

"You're a fool," Camden mutters.

"But what about Crown. Why don't we just tell him all of this? Surely, everything you know about this Santiago dude and the King will be enough to appease him, get Eastern off the hook and Camden out of trouble? I don't get why we don't just do that," I say.

"Because we need *proof*. The words on the street, the whispers, aren't enough. Every decision Crown has made so far is all to get to the King, to Santiago. If he had proof then Eastern would be locked up in juvie already. The fact of the matter is, Camden was going to be the sacrifice, the *proof*. Crown is using you both to get to Camden, what he hadn't counted on was you having a conscience, Asia."

"Jesus," I whisper, glancing at Camden. He's putting on a brave face, but I can tell this is getting to him.

"Crown isn't interested if you go down Camden, and after everything we've learned there's no way we're going to let that happen."

"This is just fucking perfect," Camden mutters.

"Look, I know this is a lot to take in. That this is bigger than any of you understood and I'm not going to pretend that there isn't a possibility that this won't go tits up, but if we pull together then maybe you don't have to end up as a statistic, Camden. Another kid lost to the system; another woman hurt by a sadistic bastard who has no fucking morals. We can help. Let us," Cal urges.

"What do we need to do?" Ford asks, sitting forward.

"You need to keep up the pretence of disliking each other…"

"Shouldn't be hard," Camden interrupts, glaring at Ford.

"Mr Burnside has put you in these groups to give you a reason to be in each other's company, but Monk needs to believe you are still enemies to keep Camden's mum safe. We keep everything on the downlow until there's a plan in place," Cal continues. "As far as the rest of the school is concerned you guys are getting a social trip this weekend as part of this new scheme Mr Burnside has put together. You get it first because of the fight that broke out today. It's already all over the school, so we're taking advantage of that. We're taking you to an undisclosed location for *therapy* as far as everyone else is concerned. We leave first thing Saturday morning. We meet with the Freed brothers and Grim and we make a plan. We sort this shit out."

"What about Ruby, Pink, Kate?" I ask.

"Pink will be cool, Kate too once she knows about everything, though right now she's angry," Sonny says, pulling a face.

"No shit," I respond.

"I'm not sure about Ruby, though. She's so shit scared of Monk that she might rat us all out to protect herself," Sonny says, unafraid to speak the truth. He's right, beaten women often side with the men who hurt them for fear of repercussions if they don't and that makes her a dangerous ally.

Cal rubs a hand over his face. "Ruby will be taken off- sight this weekend under Mr Burnside's recommendations. She's already shown signs of wanting to commit suicide because of everything that little arsehole has put her through. So, he's taking her out of the equation for her own mental health and to keep her away from Monk. She's being placed in a home for kids with emotional issues. She'll be taken good care of, I promise."

"She wanted to commit suicide?" I ask, choking on the words.

Camden smashes his fist against the desk, making me jump. "That little prick Monk. I swear to you I didn't know about what he was doing to her."

"And if you had, what could you have done?" Cal says. When Camden scowls he holds his hands up to placate. "I'm not having a dig at you, but really, what could you've done, eh? Monk's his father's son, and his father has your mother. You beat the shit out of Monk, your mother pays. It's a no-win situation for you. I can see that even if others in the past haven't been able to."

"She's so broken." I mumble. Eastern squeezes my hand tightly and Sonny curls his fingers around mine.

"Yeah, she is. The kid's in a bad way, but this care facility she's going to is full of people who will help her to heal. I'm only sorry we couldn't get to her sooner." Cal sighs.

"I've been so wrapped up in my own shit that I haven't been there for her like I should've."

"Asia, you're one person. You aren't responsible for the wellbeing of every kid in this school," Ford says, turning to face me. He rests his hand on my leg, squeezing gently.

"I can try," I mutter.

"Ruby isn't your responsibility, she's mine. I'm the one who let her down," Camden says, rage and a deep-seated pain flashing in his eyes. We all fall silent. No one has any words of comfort for Camden, because we all know deep down he's right even if that is fucked up.

"This whole thing is risky. Monk might be a prick, but he's no fool," Sonny says, breaking the silence that has descended like an oppressive fog. "He'll know shit is up if we all start giving each other the time of day."

"Then we just have to convince him. Make him believe we're still enemies," Ford says.

"We *are* still enemies," Camden snaps. "I'm tolerating you for Asia. Don't think for one second this makes us friends, arsehole."

Ford nods. "Got it."

Cal looks at his watch, then frowns. "It's almost curfew so we need to wrap this up, but whilst I agree that this is risky, I'm also going to be honest with you Camden," he says regarding him. "We might be the only chance you have. I see no other way of getting you out of this shit you're in and if that means relying on Ford, on the rest of these guys, then you're going to have to trust us."

Camden squeezes his eyes shut, pressing his fingers against them.

He takes a long, steadying breath then straightens his shoulders. "Then I guess I'm doing this."

"Good," Cal nods, looking at each of us in turn. "Let me give you all a piece of advice. I was once a kid who trusted no one. I fought my corner to survive. I was thrown from one foster home to another until I ended up in a group care home for kids who were difficult to place anywhere else. That's where I met the Freed brothers. That's where I found *my* family. We hated each other at first but now I'd lay my life down for Hud, Bryce and Max and they'd do the same for me."

"And your point is?" Camden asks.

"Look, I know there's history and distrust between you and Ford, between all of you in some way, but believe me when I say that once you find true friends, a *family* who has your back they're the only ones worth a shit in this world. Let Ford prove his worth, let him make amends and then decide whether you want to remain enemies. Either way he's got your back and that has to count for something."

"Unless he can bring back the dead, Ford *can't* make amends. So, forgive me if I think you're talking shit, Cal."

"Camden," I start, but he shakes his head.

"No, Asia. I've got *no* choice but to bring down the King, but I do get to choose who I make my family. Ford lost that right the night my sister died. I'll tolerate him for you but that's it, that's the only promise I can make."

"Then I'll make a promise of my own, Camden, I'll look out for you regardless. No matter what."

THIRTY-ONE

The next day during English class, I'm called to Mr Carmichael's office. When I arrive, Mr Burnside and Ruby are sitting in the room. The atmosphere is heavy, stilted.

"Is everything okay?" I ask, glancing between them.

"Come in and close the door behind you," Mr Carmichael says, looking at me grimly.

"What's up?"

"Take a seat, Asia," Mr Burnside urges. He's sitting beside Ruby whose whole demeanour is broken. Her face is downcast, her shoulders rounded as though she's barely able to hold her own body upright. In her lap her hands are clasped together, nails bitten down to the quick. The door clicks shut, and Ruby jumps as though a gunshot has just gone off.

"Can someone tell me what's going on? Ruby, are you okay? We didn't see you at breakfast this morning," I ask gently, knowing full well that she's far from okay. I know a scared, broken girl when I see one. She looks up at me with watery eyes but doesn't say a word. It's only then I notice the deep purple mark around her throat.

"What happened to you?" I hush out, knowing in my heart what she's done, but not wanting to believe it.

She shakes her head, stifling a sob with her hand, dropping her head once more. Shame sits heavy on her shoulders. It wracks her body, making her feel even more worthless. I choke back the words of pity, knowing she doesn't need to hear them now. She needs strength.

"Ruby is being transferred to another unit today. She was due to leave at the weekend but she's in crisis, Asia," Mr Burnside explains gently, his voice full of remorse. I know what unit he's referring to, but I don't let on for Ruby's sake. I'd hate her to think that I was betraying her by knowing her business and not being upfront about it.

"Crisis? What do you mean?"

Mr Burnside gives me a sad smile. His gaze flicks to Mr Carmichael who sits stoically, hiding how he really feels. That's the street kid in him. We all have the ability to hide away our true feelings, we know how to bury them deep down inside. When there's no one to comfort you, to chase the pain away, when you have to grow up too fast protecting the ones you love, you learn to bury the hurt and pain. It becomes second nature. Thing is, I know only too well that those feelings erupt eventually, and god help anyone who is there to witness it.

"Ruby, you wanted to see Asia before you left," Mr Burnside reminds her. "Are you okay with me telling her what's happened, or would you rather do that yourself?"

She blows out a long shaky breath, lifting her head enough only to glance at me. "I'd like to speak with Asia alone, if that's okay?" she asks quietly beneath the curtain of her hair. Her voice is merely a whisper, but I can hear the pain in it loud and clear. It rings like a fucking bell.

"Sure thing. We'll wait outside," Mr Burnside says, getting up. When he passes by, he briefly squeezes my shoulder. The moment the door closes, I move to sit beside Ruby. I want to hug her, but she kind of shifts away from me, wrapping her arms around herself.

"Talk to me, Ruby. Tell me what's going on," I urge her.

For a while she just picks at the skin surrounding her nails, her body shaking violently. "I tried to kill myself last night," she whispers eventually, and I swear the world stops spinning. I gulp, swallowing down the wave of nausea and the burn of bile rising up my throat.

"Ruby…" I breathe out slowly, a wave of shock and sadness spilling from my lips. "Why?" It's a stupid question, and one I wish I could take back the second it leaves my mouth. But it's out there in the open now floating in the air about us. I have no right to ask her why. She doesn't need to explain herself to me, to anyone. I want to open the window and set the question free, let it disperse. I certainly don't expect Ruby to answer me.

"Because I'm not strong enough to fight like you are. I'm not strong enough, Asia…" she whimpers, her voice breaking on another sob. This time I put my arm around her shoulders and hug her close to my side.

"It's okay," I hush out. "It's okay. You're not to blame. This isn't your fault."

"I *wanted* to die. When I put that rope around my neck, I wanted the pain to go away. I wanted it to end."

"Oh, Ruby. I'm so, so sorry."

"It's not your fault… it *his*," she hisses.

I hear the hate split her words into jagged shards, making them sharp. They give me hope. She's not given up, not yet. Hate is a powerful emotion, one that keeps you alive when nothing else can. I hated my mother for loving heroin more than she loved me. I hated her for choosing to shoot up over being my mum. I hated her addiction. I hated the person who supplied her with the drug. I hated the man she was in love with, my father. I hated him for abandoning us. I hated myself for never being enough to make her change.

"I want Monk to pay. I want him to understand what he did to me. But I don't have the strength to fight back. I'm *weak*," she wails, her voice pitted with heartbreak and despair.

"You're not weak. You're here aren't you? Don't discount how fucking hard it is to have the strength to *survive*," I say fiercely.

"I hate him so damn much… He made me like this. He made me feel worthless. He beat the strength out of me. He made me feel like I was no better than a doormat, that I deserved every punch, every kick, every unkind word. I just couldn't take it anymore."

"Is he still hurting you?"

"No, he hasn't touched me since the last time I showed you my bruises. But even though the marks have faded, the pain never goes away. It's been eating me up inside. Last night, I got to the point where I couldn't live with it anymore."

"Ruby, I'm so fucking sorry."

"Me too. The thing is, I'm worried, Asia. So, fucking scared."

"You'll be safe now. He'll *never* hurt you again."

"That's not what I mean. I think he has his sights set on someone else. The last time he beat me he said that it would be the last time I'd feel his hands on me, that he has plans for someone else. I should've told you earlier, but I was too fucked up. Someone here is in danger… I think that someone might be you," she hushes out, covering her mouth with a shaking hand.

I laugh. I can't help it. It bursts from my lips before I can stop it. It slashes at Ruby's fear, belittling it, making it a mockery and I immediately feel guilty. My cheeks flush with shame.

"Ruby, I shouldn't have laughed. I'm sorry." I lift her chin, forcing her to look at me. "Listen. I'm not scared of that little prick. He won't hurt me, and I swear to fucking God, if he tries I'll kill him."

"I believe you." She grips my hand in hers, squeezing it tightly as a sudden tremulous smile fights through the darkness shadowing her features.

"Do you know what I thought when the air was leaving my lungs?" she chokes out, tears spilling down her cheeks despite the smile. It's a rhetorical question, so I don't respond. Instead, I wait for her to find the courage to continue.

"I thought of *you*. I remembered how you stood fearless before Monk. I remembered how you took every punch then hit him back twice as hard. I remembered the sound your fist made when it met his body. I remembered how that made me feel strong even though it was you, not me, hitting him back. You made me remember what it felt like to *fight*, to be *strong*. You laughed in the face of his evil. Just like now. Don't be sorry for it."

"Ruby. I don't know what to say." My throat constricts with tears a moment away from falling. I lock them down for her. I need to show the same strength she presents to me now.

"In the beginning I was just like you. I was *fearless*. I wasn't so very different from you once upon a time. Slowly he took that from me, but somehow at my lowest moment that strength you showed pierced through the pain and the self-destruction I felt. You made me want to live, you made me want to fight. *You*, Asia."

"I didn't do *anything*… I should've. I should've done something about Monk the second you told me about how he was hurting you," I say, a sudden rush of anger bubbling in my veins.

Ruby shakes her head violently. "Don't take the blame. Don't do that." She grips my hand tightly. "But promise me something."

"I will, whatever you need…"

"Don't let Monk hurt you like he hurt me."

"There's no way he'll get close enough to even try."

"And find a way to stop the King from hurting Camden's mum. Set her free, then you can set Camden free."

I squeeze her hand back tightly. "We'll deal with the King, but I want *you* to make *me* a promise, right here, right now…"

"What's that?"

"That you'll get strong again and then *you'll* make Monk pay," I say, fiercely. "Retribution, payback, that belongs to you and you alone."

She grits her jaw, swipes away at the tears and nods her head. "I'll make him pay. I *swear*."

And when I look in her eyes I know she means to keep her promise, and that strength, *that* is just as powerful as anything I hold inside.

THIRTY-TWO

Two days after Ruby's attempted suicide, we sit in the dining hall for breakfast, separated into our designated groups.

The atmosphere is toxic and that's just around our table. The boys might have called a truce, but Kate's anger is enough to mar the delicate equilibrium I've fought so hard to create. This bad feeling was only compounded last night at dinner when Mr Carmichael announced Ruby's departure from Oceanside. He might've been vague about the reasons why she was being placed elsewhere, but when Monk had reacted the way he did it didn't take much to figure out who was responsible. He'd laughed. He'd fucking laughed then looked directly at me and *winked.* It took every cell of willpower not to pick up my dinner knife and stab it in his eye.

The bastard has no heart. None.

Kate had seen the exchange and had glared at Camden and me as though we were just as responsible as Monk, and honestly, I wouldn't blame her. Ruby had suffered alone and neither Camden nor I were able to do a damn thing about it. I'm just glad she's got away from this place, away from Monk. I really hope she finds the strength to fight for her survival, to become the woman I know she can be. I won't lie, I'm gutted that she never got the chance to face Monk in the ring before she left. Beating the shit out of him, in my opinion, would've been the best form of therapy. It certainly made me feel a whole lot better when I got to serve Monk his arse. All I know is that he will rue the day he ever decided to fuck with Ruby. Him and his bastard father have got it coming.

Glancing around the room I spot the twisted shit, Monk, sitting with Red and Bram. They've been placed with a couple of his wolves and three kids from No Name crew, none of whom seem at all bothered to be grouped with that arsehole. Ford notices too and if he could narrow his eyes he would, but right now, one eye is swollen shut and the other is bloodshot.

Cal and the two ex-marines, Frank and Buddy, are watching over us all from their table in the corner of the hall. Both are big, burly men with large muscles and broad shoulders, but their appearance isn't what makes them fierce. Nope, it's their take no shit attitude they seem to have. I'm pretty sure they'd wipe the floor with any of these arseholes if they were ever foolish enough to try and take them on. But I'm steering clear, it's obvious that those two men have seen and done shit that would rival any kid in this room and lived to tell the tale. They're not to be messed with.

"Well, this fucking stinks," Sonny says.

"You're telling me, someone stinks to high heaven," Kate mutters, glaring at me from across the table. Beside me, Camden stiffens, gritting his jaw.

"Leave it, Kate," Pink says, giving Camden a wary look.

"Yeah, I'd take Pink's advice if I were you" Camden snaps.

"Stop," I murmur, placing my hand on his thigh beneath the table. "Don't do that, don't threaten my friend. She's hurt, leave her be."

"And let her speak to you like that?"

"This is between us. Don't interfere."

Camden mutters something indistinguishable under his breath, but he doesn't press the point further. Kate is hurt. Yes, she's being a bitch, but this is something that Kate and I need to settle. I don't need him sticking his size thirteen foot into the mix.

For a few minutes we all fall into a tense silence and eat our breakfast. After a while, I make small talk with Camden whilst everyone else has their own conversations. When I feel the heat of Kate's gaze burning a hole in my cheek, I place my knife and fork on my plate and give up trying to finish eating my scrambled eggs. I'm suddenly not very hungry. I know I have a lot of explaining to do, but over the last couple days I haven't found the right moment to pull her or Pink aside. I need to rectify that today.

"Kate, Pink, will you come to my room later after the last period? I want to talk to you both."

Kate looks at Pink before resting her gaze on me. "Why? There's really nothing to say," she hisses, keeping her angry voice low so as not to draw attention from unwanted ears.

"There's *plenty* to say, and you need to stop being such a whiny little bitch and give Asia a chance to explain," Camden pipes up.

"Explain what? How she became *your* little bitch?"

"Kate!" Pink exclaims.

Camden snarls, his top lip curling. "Say one more bad word about Asia and I'll…"

"What, you'll set Monk on me like you did Asia?" she seethes under her breath. "I'm used to dealing with bullies, Camden, what's one more to add to a very long list?"

I flinch, her retort cutting deep. "This isn't what you think Kate, and Camden isn't like those girls who hurt you. If you come to my room later, I'll explain everything."

Ford looks up and frowns, giving me a questioning look but I shake my head. Sonny and Eastern are too busy talking to pay any attention to our own muted conversation and I'm glad. I don't need this to get out of control. It's bad enough to hear such hate spill from Kate's lips. She still believes I turned my back on her and I have to make her understand that I didn't do it without good reason.

"You sold us out for Camden and his nasty little crew of bastards. What can you possibly say to change that?"

"Kate, you're being completely unreasonable. At least let Asia explain," Pink interjects, trying to make her see sense.

"No." She stands, pushing back her chair but Pink grabs hold of her wrist.

"Let go of me," Kate hisses, her eyes welling with bitter tears.

I reach out to touch Pink's arm. "It's okay, let her go. Now's not the time."

"No, it isn't okay, Asia," she says, before returning her attention to Kate. "As much as I hate to admit it, Camden's right, you *are* being a bitch."

Kate shakes her head, giving us all a disgusted look. "I'm not staying here a second fucking longer," she snaps, snatching her arm back and striding from the canteen. Over the other side of the room I hear Monk's laughter and I know it's aimed at us. The little prick is loving this.

"I should go, make sure she's okay," Pink says apologetically. "We'll see you later. I'll make sure she comes."

"Thanks, Pink." I smile weakly, feeling suddenly exhausted. I can take a lot of things, I *have* taken a lot of things in my life, but harsh words from friends I care about cut far deeper than wicked comments from arseholes I don't.

After period six, I head back to my room and wait for Kate and Pink. There's a couple hours of downtime before we need to be back in the canteen for dinner. Not that I'm very hungry.

After ten minutes of waiting, I hear a soft knock at the door. Drawing in a steadying breath, I let Kate and Pink in.

"Thanks for coming," I say, urging them inside.

"You can thank Pink for dragging me here," Kate says, folding her arms across her chest defensively. "Let's get this over with."

"Jesus, Kate. Just let Asia speak," Pink huffs, yanking her arm and pulling her to the bed. They both sit as I pace up and down in front of them. "I'm not sure where to start…"

"How about at the beginning," Pink says, smiling kindly.

"Yeah, from the beginning…" I grab a cigarette from my drawer and light it. When I've taken a deep lungful and blown it out, I tell them everything. Kate and Pink sit in stunned silence as I give them every detail. I even tell them about the kisses I've shared with each of the boys, including how Camden and I made out on the beach in the pouring rain that day after the fight. Lastly I tell them about Ruby and how Monk had abused her so badly she tried to take her own life. By the time I've finished, I've smoked three cigarettes and am feeling lighter than I have in weeks.

"Fuck, poor Ruby…" Kate hushes out.

"Yeah, it's fucked up."

"Jesus, Asia. You really know how to make life difficult for yourself, don't you?" Pink exclaims. "I need a stiff drink."

"Right now, I could do with a drink, *several* actually."

"I can't believe you've kept this to yourself. That's some heavy shit, right there."

"I know. I'm not gonna lie, it's been a mindfuck."

"I bet," Pink agrees. "So, let me get this straight. We're going off-sight Saturday to meet the guys who own this place, as well as Ford's sister Grim- who Camden fucking hates- to try and figure out how to get you all out of this mess?"

"That about sums it up, yeah…" A heavy throb begins to pound in my head with the stress and the worry that I haven't allowed myself to acknowledge until now. "I'd never admit this to the boys, but I'm fucking terrified. What if the King finds out and hurts Tracy and Braydon, Camden's mum? What if he comes after *us*?"

Kate stands, her eyes trained on my face. "No. That won't happen. We won't allow it."

After a beat her face crumples. Tears slide down her cheeks as she strides over to me and pulls me into her arms. "I'm so sorry, for everything," she mumbles, squeezing me tightly.

"I know. I'm sorry too, about all of this. But most of all, for dragging you both into this mess."

"You've had to deal with this shit all on your own. You've had to hold yourself together for everyone. Now, we're going to be there for you," Kate adds vehemently, pulling back and wiping her hand over her face.

"Kate, I swear I didn't want to hurt you, but I had to protect my family. There was no other way. Then after I found out about Camden's mum and I began to get to know the person he hides from the world. I knew I couldn't fuck him over. I *couldn't* do it."

"I get that. I understand now. I only wish I wasn't such a bitch to you, Asia. I jumped to the worst possible conclusion based on my past experiences. It was wrong."

"You weren't that bad. I knew you were hurting."

Pink snorts, getting up to join us. "Oh, come on. She *was* a first-class bitch, let her own it. We're just lucky you ain't the typical girl on the block who'd rather stab us with a knife than protect us from our enemies. Fortunately for those boys, for us, you've got that big heart hidden inside of you coupled with a core of steel. You're a badass, Asia, do you know that?"

I laugh, shaking my head. I've bloody missed this girl. Missed them both.

"Seriously, I'm not fucking joking. *Four* men. How the fuck are you going to figure that out?" she asks, pulling a funny face. "Is that even physically possible, you've only got three holes…"

"And two hands," Kate deadpans, before bursting out with laughter.

"Oh, my fucking God. Remind me why I wanted to fix this friendship, again?"

Pink grins. "Because you love the shit out of us, just like you love every single one of those misfits of yours."

"I don't love them *all*…" I protest.

"Yeah, say that to me again in a church with the Pope looking on. Pretty sure the lie won't be as easily told whilst God's right-hand man is listening in."

"Oh, shut-up," I retort, giving her a friendly punch.

"Now let's hug this shit out and get fucked on Kate's stash of weed, yeah?"

I can't help but laugh. "We can totally hug it out, but smoking weed probably isn't the best idea you've ever had. Mr Carmichael is cracking down."

"Are you shitting me? Mr Carmichael owes you one. I'm pretty sure *if* he caught us smoking a zoot he'd let us off given all the crap you're going through right now."

"Exactly," Kate agrees, putting her hand down her top and pulling a bag of weed and some papers from her bra. Pink bursts out laughing.

"You're carrying around Mary-J in your *bra*? Jesus, Kate."

"Well, it's not as if I'm letting anyone feel my tits, is it? Seems as good a place as any."

"Come on," I say, "Let's get out of here."

"Where to?" Pink grins, pulling open my bedroom door.

Kate nudges in front of us both. "I know the perfect place. Follow me," she says.

The three of us sneak into the west wing of the main building and into the room I found Kate in that day she told me about her past. As we enter the room and sit down waiting for Kate to roll a joint, I feel stupidly giddy about having my friends back. I didn't realise quite how much I missed them until today. Part of me knows this is a stupid idea, but a bigger part is done with playing by the rules. It's been a stressful few weeks and I need a moment to just let loose.

"Here," Kate says, passing me the joint after taking a drag. She closes her eyes, leaning her head back as she blows a steady stream of smoke out of her lungs.

"You know, Kate, you're an anomaly. You gave me and Pink such a hard time for smoking and here you are doing just that."

She pops her eye open, and grins. "Marijuana is *medicinal.* Everyone knows it, but the government won't make it legal because the big pharmaceutical corporations don't want to go out of business. It's better to fill everyone with synthetic crap than actually use something natural to help ease symptoms of pain…"

I look at Pink and we both burst out laughing.

"What, it's true!" she complains. "Plus, this spliff is pure Mary-J, no tobacco at all. I refuse to fill my lungs with that shit."

"Fair enough," I retort, taking a deep toke on the spliff before passing it to Pink.

"So who's the best kisser?" Pink suddenly blurts out. She looks at me with glassy eyes, and a mischievous look on her face. I groan.

"Don't ask her that!" Kate says, elbowing Pink in the side.

"What? Don't tell me you're not just a tiny bit intrigued…"

Kate pulls a face. "Alright, maybe just a little."

They both giggle, the Mary-J well and truly in their blood stream now.

"So, who's the one who rocks your socks the most?" Pink insists.

Clearly neither are going to let this go until I tell them. I puff out my cheeks then exhale a long breath. "They're all so different. I can't really say," I start.

"Okay, but one of them *must* pip the post and make your fanny flutter just that little bit more," Pink says, covering another burst of laughter.

"Fanny flutter?" My mouth drops open in mock horror, but I join in on the hysterics with the both of them until tears of mirth are running down my face.

"Yeah, you know, when that area down there starts pulsing and you have a desperate need to get off to appease Queen Clit," Pink adds.

"*Queen Clit*? You're making your clit royalty now?"

"Of course, I am, that area of the body deserves to be worshipped. Why the fuck shouldn't it be crowned Queen?"

"Oh, my god, Pink. You fucking kill me," I giggle.

"Stop stalling, Asia and spit it out. Who's the best kisser?" Kate presses, forcing her facial muscles into a more serious expression. That makes me laugh harder.

"Okay, okay!" I respond, holding my hands up. "I can see you're not going to let this go."

"Damn straight," Pink says.

"They're all amazing actually."

"Seriously?" Pink grouses, rolling her eyes in mock disgust. "No wonder the girl has problems choosing."

Kate shoves Pink on the arm. "Shut up and let Asia speak."

"*Seriously*. When I kiss Eastern it's like I've come home. It feels right, you know. Like we were always meant to be together. He knows all the bad parts of me and accepts them, like I do his. He might not be perfect, but he's the perfect fit for me. I can't ever see myself living a life without him in it."

Kate shifts on her arse, making herself more comfortable. She draws on the spliff, the bright red tip sizzling and crackling. "So, what about the others?"

"Sonny is passionate, but he's also caring, considerate. I know that might come as a surprise to you both since he's such a flirt, but it's true. He kisses me like I'm the only girl in the world for him and when I'm in his arms I feel adored."

"I know what you mean," Kate says, her gaze looking wistful.

"You've kissed Sonny too?!" Pink screeches.

"No! Shit no! I just meant that I know what it feels to be kissed like that…"

"Si?" I question.

"Yeah," she confirms. Pink leans over and squeezes her arm in solidarity. I'm guessing Kate told her all about Si and the tragedy surrounding her brother's death.

"And Ford… *Camden*?" Pink asks, wiggling her eyebrows.

I chew on my lip ring for a moment, trying to find the words to describe Ford's kiss and the way he makes me feel. "Ford's a mystery. He's dominant, overbearing almost, but hot as hell. He kisses like he wants to sink beneath my skin and not come up for air. He's fucking intense, sure of himself. He certainly knows what to do with his hands… Queen Clit would agree." My cheeks flush at the memory of him making me come so hard I saw fucking stars.

"Shiiiittt!" Pink exclaims whistling low.

"He made you come?" Kate adds, grinning mercilessly.

"Yep, they both did."

"Wait, are we talking about Camden? You told us that you kissed but failed to mention *that* important detail!" When I nod her mouth pops open in shock as she glances at Kate then back at me. "Did this happen the day he beat the shit out of Ford?"

"Yeah."

"And how was it?" Pink ask, her eyes sparkling.

I chew on my lip ring for a moment. "He's intense too, but a different kind of intensity to Ford. He was angry with me and yet he touched me in a way that made all the hurt between us go away."

"No kidding seeing as Queen Clit had a party in your knickers." Pink smirks, coughing on the smoke she's just inhaled.

"No. It was more than Camden just getting me off. I can't explain it. When we kissed it was a need, not a want. Do you know what I mean?" I ask frowning. "Jeez, I really must be high. I'm not making any sense."

"It doesn't have to make any sense. What you feel often doesn't," Kate muses.

"When we got back to my room, he just held me like I was his… *lifeline*."

"Knowing everything we do now, I get it. You see beyond what he presents to the world; the hard-nosed gang leader…" Kate says, her voice trailing off as she loses her train of thought. She closes her eyes and for a minute I think she's fallen asleep. A beat later she bursts out laughing.

"What's so funny?" I grin.

"Everything…" More belly deep laughter follows. It's the kind of laughter that treads the line between happiness and hysteria. One minute happy, the next sobbing. I think we're all feeling the stress of the last few weeks.

"This shit is good," Pink chimes in, finishing the last of the joint.

After we've shared another joint, I get a bad case of the munchies. "We should go eat," I say, looking at my watch. "Dinner starts in half an hour. You guys should go first. I know we're supposed to be together given this new rule of Mr Carmichael's, but I don't want Monk to get suspicious. It's better that he thinks we still hate each other. I'll catch up in a few."

"You've got a point. We'll head there now. See you in a bit?" Pink says, hauling Kate onto her feet.

"Yep," I respond, stifling another giggle that bursts from my lips.

I wait another ten minutes, then get up on unsteady legs. My body feels heavy, languid. But my heart is lighter than it has been in weeks. By the time the weekend rolls around that lightness evaporates and the storm settles inside once more.

THIRTY-THREE

For the rest of the week we play our roles well. For anyone who bothers to look, we are still a divided group, a bunch of angry kids forced together because of this new rule. I go through the motions in class, not really paying attention. I can't even summon up enough energy to draw, let alone study human anatomy. My mind is elsewhere.

Time alone with any of the boys has been non-existent. We've kept ourselves apart outside of the time we're supposed to be in each other's company and even then we're playing enemies which is proving more difficult than I'd imagined it would be. Still, it's better that way, especially since I'm finding it harder and harder to ignore the growing feelings within me and not act on them. It's too risky.

By the time I head down to the car park early Saturday morning, I'm coiled up tight. I'm tense, apprehensive, *scared*. All of that. I've no idea what today is going to bring.

Waiting outside for me to arrive are the rest of the gang. The lads are already in the minibus, and Kate is standing beside it with Cal who keeps checking his watch. I've made them late.

"Where's Pink?" I ask.

"Sick. She's been throwing up all night. The girl can't even get out of bed," Kate explains.

"Fuck. Maybe we should put this off?"

Cal shakes his head. "We can't. Things are in place. We need to go today."

"But…"

"No buts, Asia. We've got to do this."

"I don't like leaving her alone. Not with that arsehole Monk prowling."

"It's okay," Kate reassures me. "It's only one night. You'll be back tomorrow afternoon, and Frank and Buddy are here. That little prick won't do anything whilst they're watching him."

"You're not coming?"

"Pink needs a friend and you need to spend time with those boys. We both know Queenie needs to be worshipped and I sure don't want to be the spare part getting in the way." Kate grins, winking.

My cheeks flame. "It's not that kind of weekend…"

"The guys are all ready to go," she says, pointing to the minibus where they're patiently waiting. "You need to do this. It's more important you're there. You can fill us in when you return. We'll be okay."

"Kate…" I start, but she's already giving me her back and walking towards the annex.

When I climb in the minibus, there's a free space next to each of the lads. They all watch me silently as I try and decide who to sit next too. In the end, I walk up the aisle and sit right at the back of the bus, choosing them all by not favouring any of them.

An hour and a half later we arrive at a farmhouse that sits at the end of a long winding lane. It's a large brick building with a red roof, surrounded by rolling green fields and sheep. In the drive is a black Land Rover Discovery with tinted windows and the latest number plate.

Ford whistles low. "That's a 60k car right there…"

"Yeah, my foster parents have expensive tastes," Sonny agrees, not in the least bit impressed by the slick, top of the range car.

Cal pulls up besides the Land Rover. "Let's get this show on the road," he says, putting the minibus in park before hopping out and sliding open the side door. We all pile out.

"This should be fun," Camden grumbles.

Just as I'm about to enter the front door, I feel a warm hand slide into mine. Eastern smiles down at me. "We've got this, okay? I've got your back. No matter what."

"No matter what," I repeat, squeezing his hand tightly.

Inside, the farmhouse is warm and cosy. The smell of coffee and freshly baked bread has my mouth watering and my stomach grumbling in protest. None of us have had breakfast so I'm guessing the lads are just as hungry as I am.

"Ah man, that smells so good. I could eat a horse," Eastern says.

"Or a sheep… there seem to be plenty of them out in the fields."

"Are you suggesting I go and slaughter a sheep?"

"You're kidding, right? You hate blood, you'd faint like a big sissy."

"I didn't with Sonny," he shrugs, winking. "I guess it's just as well breakfast is being made for us, I wouldn't want you to splatter your hoodie with sheep's blood."

"Ha ha!"

We follow the sound of talking and the delicious aroma of sizzling bacon and walk into the kitchen. On one side of the large, open plan kitchen-diner is Bryce, the handsome, bearded man I saw Sonny with at the courthouse back in London. He looks over his shoulder at me and winks. Eastern puts his arm around me tighter, hauling me into his side.

"Who does he think he's winking at?" he grumbles.

"That would be me," a female voice says from behind us. "I'm Louisa by the way, that handsome boy's foster mum." A woman in her mid-twenties walks into the kitchen grinning. She's beautiful, stunning actually, with long blonde hair and pretty blue eyes. She walks over to Sonny who rolls his eyes in mock disgust at her compliment, but he doesn't bat her away when she hugs him tight. In fact, he folds his arms around her and gives me a tentative smile from over her shoulder.

"Hey, Lou. How's the tummy grub?" he asks her when she pulls away.

She grins, patting her stomach. "Little grub is doing just dandy."

Louisa is sporting a pair of ripped black jeans and a t-shirt that only seems to accentuate her small bump rather than hide it. I remember Sonny telling me that the Freed's already have one child. I'm guessing by the size of her bump she's a few months into her pregnancy. Maybe four at a guess.

"And the crotch goblin, how's he doing? Is he here?"

"Ollie's good, and no he's not here. Nisha is watching him back home. We thought you'd need our undivided attention this weekend, so that's what you've got," she explains.

Beside Sonny, Ford watches their exchange with a guarded expression. Anyone looking at him would assume he isn't bothered by their interaction, but I know him well enough now to see how it affects him. Affection isn't something he ever received from his own mother. He's as starved of it as I am. Abuse, harsh words and cruelty are the only things he associates with family. Their whole exchange is alien to him, and in some ways to me too, given my own mum was less and less affectionate the older I grew and the more addicted to heroin she became. Ford catches me staring at him, and he seems to shut down further as he stares into his coffee cup, his fingers gripping it tightly. I have a sudden urge to go to him, but I don't. Maybe later we can talk.

After briefly introducing herself to Ford and Camden, Louisa makes a beeline for Bryce, passing Max, who I met the first day I started Oceanside. She gives him a peck on the cheek and he gently pats her bump.

"Tea?" he asks her.

"I'd rather have a coffee," she sighs, but takes the proffered mug. "Thanks, Max," she murmurs.

I watch as she kisses Bryce on the lips before prising the spatula out of his hand and nudging him aside with her hip. "Go sit, talk. I got this," she orders.

"Thanks, baby," he says, grabbing a cup of coffee from the table and taking a sip. He looks at Eastern and I over the rim of the cup. "Are you going to take a seat?"

"Sure," I mutter, a little bit overwhelmed by the sense of family and love I feel between the three of them. For some reason that makes it difficult for me to enter the room.

Eastern squeezes my hand tighter. "It's okay, Asia. I'm here for you," he says.

"We all are," Camden growls none too quietly, his eyes flicking from our joined hands back to my face.

"Jealous, mate?" Bryce asks, passing Camden a cup of coffee.

"Ain't got nothing to do with you," he bites back.

Bryce grins widely at me. "You got your work cut out with this lot, Asia."

"Leave the girl be, Bryce," Louisa warns him before fixing her gaze on me. "Come on in. There's no judgement here. If you hadn't guessed already, these two grown arse men are my husbands and they're *always* arguing. It takes a strong woman to keep all the testosterone in check, I certainly have fun doing so, and I can already tell you're fit for the job. These lads are all here for you, aren't they?"

I nod, giving her a tiny smile. She grins knowingly, and I immediately warm to her.

"These two are your *husbands*? Why haven't you been arrested for bigamy?" Ford asks, more curious than anything.

"Three actually, Hud will be here a little later. In answer to your question, they're my husbands all but legally. We made a promise and a vow to one another a few years back. I don't need a slip of paper to confirm what I already know. They are my husbands and I am their wife, and now we're a family. I know what it's like to juggle." She winks at me, then returns her attention to the stove as though this is just a normal day for her.

Pulling out a stool from beneath the large kitchen island, I plonk myself upon it, my short denim skirt riding up and showing off my barbed wire tattoo around my upper thigh. I generally don't wear tights. Not something I can be bothered with normally or can afford to waste my money on. Camden, who's to the right of me, notices the expanse of flesh and slides his hand under the table, his fingers warming the bare skin of my leg as his finger traces over the tattoo.

"Didn't realise you had this," he mumbles, his fingers pressing into the sensitive skin of my inner thigh. I place my hand over his, enjoying his touch but knowing it's not appropriate whilst we're here sitting at the table making small talk with the men who are going to help save his arse. He releases me, but not before giving me a look that heats my skin further.

Once Louisa has served up a round of bacon sandwiches that we each inhale in 2.5 seconds flat, Cal enters the room flipping his phone off.

"All set?" Max asks him, reaching for the last bacon sandwich. Cal smacks his hand, hard.

"Hands off, that has my name on it," he says, grabbing the sandwich and the last mug of coffee from the table. "And yes. They'll be here in an hour or so."

"Good. I think these guys here could use some time to get their heads straight before Hud arrives with Grim."

Camden stiffens beside me, but rather than act out he simply gets up and walks from the room. I watch him leave, worry coursing through my veins.

"Are we going to need security when she arrives?" Max asks, glancing at Camden's retreating back. He pushes off the table and gathers Louisa into his side, pressing a kiss against the top of her head. She kind of relaxes into his hold, so certain of her place there.

"Camden will behave just as soon as he hears what she has to say," Cal says, around a mouthful of bacon sandwich.

"And before that?" Bryce asks, as he gathers up the plates and empty mugs and puts them in the sink. "I'm not having him lose his shit whilst Louisa's around. I don't care what trouble he has with Grim."

"We'll make sure he doesn't. I promise," I say, standing.

"Where are you going, Asia?" Sonny asks, reaching for me.

"To see if Camden's alright, of course."

"I'll come too." Sonny gets up and places his hand on the small of my back.

"And me…" Eastern begins, but Cal rests his hand on his shoulder.

"You and Ford can stay put and wash up the dishes."

"No way, man," Eastern grumbles.

Ford stands and heads towards the sink. "Let them deal with Camden. Sonny seems to piss him off the least anyway. You and I aren't at the top of his best buddy list."

Eastern swears under his breath but he stays put. "Fine, I'll dry, you can wash. Catch you later?" he says to me.

"Only if you're prepared to chase me."

"Always," he whispers.

"See, you've got them in hand already. Behind every man is a strong woman," Louisa remarks, smiling at me knowingly.

"You got that right, baby," Bryce agrees, kissing her adoringly.

"Come on, I'm gonna puke if this lot carry on the way they are. Let's find Camden," Sonny says, grabbing my hand and pulling me out of the kitchen as laughter follows us down the hall.

"Are they always like that?"

"So loved up and touchy-feely? Yeah, all the damn time," Sonny confirms.

I nod. "It must be nice to be loved so fiercely."

"Yeah, it must be," Sonny agrees, squeezing my hand that little bit tighter.

THIRTY-FOUR

Sonny and I find Camden outside leaning against the fence that separates the back garden of the farmhouse and the surrounding field. He's smoking a cigarette, the blue-grey cloud billowing out of his mouth in the cold February air.

I don't ask him if he's okay, because it's obvious he's not. Instead, I stand next to him and place my forearms against the wood, lifting my foot against the lower slat. Sonny settles beside me and we all just look out at the view whilst Camden finishes off his cigarette, understanding that he needs a moment to regroup. When a sheep waddles over to us, I grab a handful of grass and offer it to the creature. It looks up at me with big mournful eyes, ignores the grass I'm holding and does a big shit right in front of us. Camden barks out a laugh whilst Sonny makes a gagging noise from the smell.

"Well, I guess that just about sums up this shitshow. Even the sheep wants to crap on us," Camden says, flicking his butt into the field. I have a moment of panic that it's going to set the grass alight before I realise the grass is wet from all the frost and the cherry has already sizzled out.

"Talking of shit, they're worried you're going to lose it when Grim arrives," I say, glancing at him.

"They'd be right to worry. Even though I fought Ford back at her club over Christmas break, I haven't seen Grim since the night Sapphire died. There are quite a few things I'd like to say to the bitch actually."

"Hudson and Grim are tight, Camden. You need to keep your emotions in check around him. Don't piss him off. Find a way to put a lid on whatever you feel and let her speak. He won't tolerate anything less," Sonny warns.

"I don't see why I have to listen to her giving me excuses as to why it was okay that my sister died. She's responsible for her death just as much as Ford is."

"There won't be any excuses, just facts…" Sonny starts, then slams his mouth shut.

Camden turns to the side, leaning against the wood. He looks over my head and directly at Sonny.

"Wanna tell me what you know?"

"It's not my place."

Camden jerks forward, reaching over me and grabs Sonny by the collar. "I'm fucking sick of hearing that. Just. Tell. Me. What. You. Know!"

"Jesus, Camden. Lay off him. If it weren't for Sonny, none of this would be possible. He's done nothing but try to help us!" I exclaim, placing the flat of my hands against Camden's chest and shoving him backwards. It's enough to off balance him and he lets Sonny go with a curse.

"Help *you* maybe. He sure as fuck ain't doing this for me!"

"You're right I *am* doing this for Asia. I give a shit about her, and because she cares about what happens to you that means I happen to give a shit about you too. So, stop being a prick and man the fuck up."

For a second I think Camden is going to shove me aside and lay into Sonny. He doesn't, instead he looks down at me and cups my face in his large hands. He doesn't say a word as he steps closer pressing his length against mine, nor does he care that Sonny is still standing beside us. Camden looks deep into my eyes until my heart is pounding and my clit is throbbing, then leans over and presses his lips against mine.

Behind me I hear Sonny groan, like he's enjoying this as much as I am.

"I'd tell you to get a room if I didn't want to join you."

That remark has Camden smiling into my mouth as his fingers slide into my hair. I welcome the heat of his tongue and softness of his lips. When we finally break apart, Sonny is watching me with hungry eyes as Camden turns me in his arms and wraps his arm around my waist. It's cold out, but I don't feel it given Camden's warmth is seeping into my back.

"If you want Asia, why don't you come get her," Camden challenges.

Sonny smiles leisurely, his dimples showing. "I don't need to get Asia. I'm not in competition with you, Camden. None of us are."

"Oh, yeah?"

"Yeah. Now, shall we go inside? My nuts are turning blue."

Camden smirks. "You little prick," he says, but there's a warmth behind the cuss. He's not being a dick, this is banter. I never thought I'd see the day.

"There's nothing little about it," he retorts, grinning mercilessly. "Perhaps one day, you'll get to see it."

"I ain't into men."

"I wasn't talking about me fucking you, Camden. I was talking about a threesome. What do you say, Asia?" Sonny grins mercilessly as we head back into the house.

"I say you two need to calm the fuck down. Let's take this one step at a time, okay?"

"You can't hurt a man for trying," Sonny quips.

"But, I can," Camden says, punching Sonny on the arm.

"Ow, you fuckwit, that hurt."

"It was supposed to."

With that we start laughing, even Camden, and that in itself is a miracle.

BACK INSIDE THE kitchen is empty, *and* spotless. Looks like Bryce set the boys to work. Cal is in a side room talking on his phone. When he sees us, he covers the mouthpiece.

"Ford and Eastern are in the den. Hook left at the end of the corridor and follow the hallway right to the end."

"Where's Louisa, Bryce and Max?" Sonny asks.

"Gone for a walk. You know how Louisa likes the great outdoors," Cal explains.

"Yep. I've heard all the stories about their time in the French Alps. Pretty sure they've gone to shag in the woods," Sonny mutters, as we head towards the den.

"Shag in the woods? Louisa's *pregnant*."

"Hasn't stopped them before…" Sonny makes a gagging face.

Camden raises an eyebrow. "You're foster parents ain't normal."

"Define normal," Sonny bites back. It's clear from the sound of his voice that whilst he's more than happy to take the piss out of their unusual relationship, he's not so happy about anyone else doing the same.

"I just meant that they're happy. Most people I know come from broken homes with their parents at each other's throats."

"Yeah, they're happy. It's sickening." But Sonny smiles, telling me he actually quite likes it.

When we enter the den, Eastern and Ford are sitting in front of an open fire playing chess. My mouth drops open in shock. They're being very civilised.

"What the fuck is this?" Camden says, plonking himself down on the sofa. He pats the space next to him, but I ignore the request and perch on the arm of Eastern's chair. Sonny takes up the space instead, winking at Camden who frowns.

"Everything alright?" Eastern asks me.

"We're good. You?" I ask, looking at Ford.

"Yeah, good. We're just playing some chess to pass the time."

"I didn't know either of you played."

"Eastern didn't until about half an hour ago. I'm teaching him. He's picking the game up quick," Ford explains. "Though I'm about to beat his arse… *Checkmate*," he says.

"Well, shit. Let's go again."

"Nah. I reckon we should play something we can all take part in." Ford looks at me then and there's intent in his gaze. The kind of intent that should worry me, but instead makes my insides turn to mush.

"Like what?" Sonny asks, a note of caution in his voice.

"Truth or dare," Ford responds, placing the chess pieces and the board back into the box.

"What are we, fucking twelve?" Camden sucks his teeth, unimpressed.

Ford leans back in his seat and rests his foot on the coffee table. "Afraid to speak the truth, or not man enough to take the dare?"

"Neither."

"Then let's play. Who's first?" Ford asks, looking between us all. His gaze lands on me, and a spark of challenge alights in his grey-green eyes.

"I'll go."

"Okay, truth or dare?"

"Truth," I respond immediately.

Ford nods his head, his hay blonde hair flopping into his eyes. "Okay, who's got something they want to ask Asia?"

"Yeah, I got a question. What do you see in that prick?" Camden grunts, narrowing his eyes at Ford.

"Fuck sake," Sonny mutters, but Ford just shrugs and looks to me for my response. I'm guessing I'm not going to get away with saying he's got nice eyes because although they're pretty, they're not the reason I'm so drawn to him. Taking a deep breath, I look at Ford and tell him.

"I see a kid who's been scarred by the very people who should've loved him. I see a guy who wants to do right by the person he hurt the most and I see a man who will fight to the death for the ones he loves. I believe he's a good person, Camden. That's what I see even when you refuse to do the same." Ford's nostrils flare as my gaze flits from his to Camden's.

"Well, fuck, that told you, Camden. Don't ask the question if you don't want to hear the answer," Sonny exclaims.

"Whatever man."

Sonny chuckles, loving this. "Okay, my turn." He looks between us all until his gaze lands on Eastern's arm that's currently wrapped around my waist. "This one's for you Eastern. Truth or dare?"

"Truth," he responds immediately.

"Okay, truth it is. Is falling in love with Asia really as easy as it seems?"

Eastern's fingers tighten on my thigh as my breath hitches. Did Sonny just confess that he loves me?

"I need to know the truth, man. I've not been in love before and I don't know whether what I feel for Asia is love or lust. Either way it's screwing with my head."

"Sonny…" I begin, not really knowing what to say.

"Falling in love with Asia was the easiest, most natural thing I've ever done," Eastern admits. "I've loved her since I understood what the word meant, and probably long before that too. Love should never be difficult, and it should never hurt. Lust is superficial. It's the heat and passion of a moment in time. Do I want to rip Asia's clothes off and make love to her until we both go blind? Yeah, of course I do. But will I wait until she's ready to give herself to me? Abso-fucking-lutely. Will I allow her the space to be with each of you despite how fucking envious I am? Yes, yes I will because that's what she needs. And will I admit when I'm wrong, when I've overstepped the mark? Every damn time."

"Eastern…" I mutter, my cheeks flushing with warmth.

"I'm not done yet," he says, a determined look on his face. "Will I do everything in my power to make Asia happy because she's the one I love? Of course, I will. And will I chase her every time she runs from my love because she doesn't know how to accept it? *Always*," he says fiercely, locking his gaze with mine. "That's love, Sonny. That's how I understand it. If you feel that way about Asia, then I've no doubt that you love her too."

"Fuck, man. It's like you've just carved me open and pulled out all my internal organs. Who knew you were a fucking poet," Sonny mutters, looking more pained by Eastern's response than relieved by it.

My mouth pops open then closes. I really don't have any words to describe how I feel right now. So, I keep quiet, and try to accept the honesty Eastern has shown and the possibility that he's not the only one who loves me. Ford and Camden remain quiet, thoughtful, though I just feel more uncomfortable by the minute. Not by Eastern's words but by the heavy tension that fills the air and all the unspoken words that seem to be brimming on everybody's lips.

"Well, that's me done," Eastern says, breaking the silence. He looks at Ford. "Your turn. Truth or dare."

"Seeing as everyone else is on the truth train, I'll take a dare."

"Fair enough. I dare you to do something that scares you."

"That's not very specific," he retorts, frowning.

"That's the dare, do something that scares you. Crack the façade a little and show us what's underneath."

"Fine." Ford looks directly at me as though considering something, then stands pulling off his jumper.

"This ain't a strip tease, Ford," Camden mutters, disgusted.

"Shut the hell up, Camden," Sonny interjects.

I exchange looks with him. We both know about Ford's past and the scars he can't escape. By the look on Camden's face when Ford rips off his shirt and throws it on the floor revealing his scarred chest, he doesn't.

"Until I met Asia, I kept these scars hidden. If she hadn't walked in on me that day I was training in the outhouse, I may never have had the courage to let her see. When I fought at the club I always wore a top. When I was with Sapphire not once did I show her these scars, and it wasn't because I thought she'd be disgusted by them but because I was *ashamed*. I was ashamed by the fact that I allowed my parents to burn me with their cigarettes. I was ashamed to admit that they beat me, that they saw fit to tattoo this into my chest," he says, pointing at the crude tattoo on his collarbone. "I'm showing you them now because these scars, this tattoo are the evidence of my weakness."

"Ford, you were just a child," I say, gently. "You weren't weak because you didn't fight back. How could you? What you did was survive, that shows a great deal of strength. Maybe more strength than any of us could claim we have."

"Jesus. I'm sorry, Ford. You don't need to go on, man," Eastern mutters, releasing me as I stand. I want to go to Ford. I need to, but he holds his hand up, halting me in my tracks.

"I need to finish," he says to me, there's an edge to his voice, a vulnerability I've never heard before.

"Okay," I nod, waiting.

"I joined Grim Fight Club when I was twelve, looking for some way to fight back, against my past, against that weakness that I believed lived within me. I wanted to be strong. I wanted to be like the men who fought there. Grim welcomed me in, not knowing who I was. She saw something in me no one else did. She saw that strength you mentioned, Asia. She saw the man I could become and so she allowed me to train with her fighters, with her. A few weeks in we found out that we shared the same mum. Grim's father took her a few weeks after she was born and never allowed her to return into the arms of that bitch. I'm glad she wasn't damaged by my mum like I was."

"How fucking lucky for you. At least you still have your sister. Mine was fucking ripped away from me," Camden stands, his hands balled into fists.

"You're right. I *am* lucky. Lucky to have found her, to have found a family with a bunch of men broken by their pasts and put back together again with blood, sweat and tears. We have a bond us fighters and I won't apologise for it."

"And who's going to apologise for my sister?"

"*I am.* I. AM," he repeats, bashing his fist against his chest. "I'm sorry. I'm so fucking sorry, Camden. I will regret bringing Sapphire to the club every day for the rest of my life. It was no place for her, and I know it's not an excuse, but I wanted her to see that I was strong enough. I wanted to prove to her that I wasn't that scared kid who let his parents beat him, burn him, terrify him. I *loved* Sapphire and I'm so fucking sorry I wasn't able to protect her." He hangs his head, his body trembling with the effort of holding himself together.

"So, why the fuck didn't you? Why didn't you *win*?"

"Because the man I was fighting was the Beast…"

"AND?" Camden roars.

"And if I didn't throw the fight the King would've killed him. I *had* to let him win to save his life."

"Why? Why the fuck would you save some stranger's life?" Camden yells.

"Because I asked him to, because Beast is the man *I* love, and I couldn't see him die just to satisfy the whim of a man I loathe. It was never about the money, Camden. It was always about love."

We all turn to face the open doorway. Stepping into the room is an attractive woman with long brown hair, shaved on one side. An intricate rose tattoo snakes up her neck and over her collarbone. She's in her mid-twenties, but her eyes hold a lifetime of experience that only a woman twice her age should have experienced. Behind her is an attractive man I don't recognise with dark hair and deep blue eyes that assess me quickly. He nods, acknowledging me. I'm guessing he must be the illusive Hudson.

"Now you know, Cam. I threw the fight to save the Beast so that my sister didn't have to see the man she loved killed by the man we all fucking hate. I did it for Grim because she took in a broken kid and taught me how to be strong. I owed her and now I owe you. Sapphire's death is the biggest wound I endure. I deserve its existence. I can't bring Sapphire back, but I can have your back for the rest of my shitty life. It's all I have to offer. It's all I have."

Camden pushes past Grim and Hudson. This time I don't follow, this time I walk into Ford's open arms and give him the kind of affection he's been starved of his whole life.

Gripping hold of him tightly, I press a kiss against the tattoo on his collarbone. "You've never been, nor will you *ever* be a bad boy. You're the complete opposite, you're *good.* Don't let anyone ever tell you otherwise," I whisper against his skin.

He just holds me tighter.

THIRTY-FIVE

We gather in the living room, another huge space that's more than big enough to seat all of us comfortably. Louisa sits between Hudson and Max, with Bryce at her feet. Her leg is hooked over his shoulder and he's massaging her foot. She's leaning her head against Max's shoulder, relaxed, comfortable. Hudson has his hand on her thigh. They look perfect together and something about their ease with each other makes me feel envious. Louisa notices me staring and smiles. My cheeks blush and I look away.

To the right of us, Cal is sitting on the smaller two-seater, Grim is sitting beside him smoking a cigarette. The five of us are all piled on the long L-shaped sofa opposite. Camden sits at one end, Ford the other just about as far apart as they can be. I'm sandwiched between Sonny and Eastern even though there's plenty of room. On the coffee table between us is a bottle of whisky and enough glasses for the adults. We've got Cola and tumblers, which grates my last nerve. They're talking to us like adults but treating us like children, fucking hypocrites. I could use a damn drink.

"Well, who wants to start?" Cal asks, leaning forward and perching his elbows on his knees. He grabs his drink and takes a large gulp.

"I will," Hudson's states, looking at the five of us. He looks tired, worn. Dark circles sit heavy under his eyes, and his chin is covered in a week-old stubble. The guy looks like he could do with a good night's sleep.

"As you know, I'm Hudson, the oldest Freed brother and the smartest by a long shot," he grins.

Max reaches behind Louisa, clipping Hudson on the back of his head. "But not the best looking, arsewipe," he says, smirking.

"Shut the fuck up both of you, we all know I'm the beauty *and* the brains of this family," Bryce says, from his position on the floor.

"Be serious," Louisa admonishes. They listen.

"The truth is, *together* we're going to get you out of this mess you've got yourselves into," Hudson says, including Grim in his sweeping statement. They exchange looks and she tips her head in acknowledgement, saluting him. "But we can't do that unless you trust us. We need to know that you won't do anything rash. That you'll come to us if anything happens. Do I have your word?" He looks directly at Camden then as the one with the most to lose in the circumstances given his mum is the King's property.

Camden crosses his arms over his chest defensively. "Well, that all depends. Cal told us about your issue with Santiago. So, don't bullshit us into thinking you're doing this solely for us. Can I trust *you* not to fuck any of *us* over to get what you want?"

Hudson regards Camden, respect filling his gaze. "I appreciate your frankness and I can assure you that I'm not trying to bullshit anyone. But you're correct, I do have a vested interest in taking down the King because it will lead to Santiago and he's the one *I* want. Cal has already filled you in about my friend. I need payback but I refuse to do it at the cost of putting you kids in danger. You must trust us."

"You do realise that none of us trust easily. Trust is earned not promised. I don't know you, any of you," Camden points out.

"Sonny," Bryce says, pointing at him. "Are we trustworthy?"

Sonny locks eyes with him and nods. "More than my own father," he admits, quietly, his fingers brushing against mine as he reaches for my hand. "I loved my dad, but was he trustworthy…? When it suited him, I guess? But mostly he was just a criminal with his own agenda. I was lucky these guys took me in. They might all get on my last fucking nerve with their happy family shit, but I trust them."

"Your dad loved you, Sonny. He might not have won any father of the year awards, but I know you were his heart. Don't forget that," Bryce says gently.

"Yeah…" Sonny mutters, his head dropping. I squeeze his hand tighter.

"We'll help you deal with the King, Camden," Hudson continues. "But we have to know you're not going to talk. I need your word. The success of this all depends on you keeping your head. I know he has your mum, and we're working on finding a way to help her too, but I'm going to be straight up with you, she's at the most risk. I know this isn't easy. In fact, the easy choice for you would be to tell the King everything you know."

"He won't do that," I say with absolute certainty.

"I believe you, Asia. Camden's a smart kid. He wouldn't be here otherwise. So, I'm going to ask you one more time, son. Do we have your word?"

Camden grits his jaw, then nods his head once. "You have my word," he says.

I'm pretty sure the whole room lets out a collective breath. I eye the whisky on the table suddenly wishing I could have a shot. Instead, I lean forward and grab a tumbler of coke, making do.

"And what about this Santiago dude?" Sonny asks.

"Santiago is for us to deal with. He has nothing to do with any of you, and that's the way it's going to stay," Hudson says, picking up his own glass of whisky and knocking it back in one go.

"So what's the plan then? How in the fuck are you going to take down the King when no one before has ever managed to do it?" Camden asks, swiping a hand over his face.

Eastern shifts in his seat. "Camden's got a point, what makes this attempt any different?"

"Well, that's where I come in," Grim says, locking her gaze with Camden. "Over the last couple years, the King has been investing in his own underground fight club fronted as a high-end spa hotel. On the surface it's just like any above-board business. Wives of the crime underbelly go there to get pampered whilst their husbands meet to do business and to bet on fights behind closed doors. We believe that a great portion of the drugs Santiago ships in are distributed from there also, though we have no proof of that… yet."

"Where is this place?" Ford asks.

"Not far from Oceanside, actually. The spa hotel is in Rye, about half an hour away from Hastings."

Eastern rests his hand on my leg, squeezing my thigh, trying to steady my jittering leg. It hasn't stopped jumping up and down since I sat down on the sofa. I really need a drink, or a joint. Both would be good. "Okay, so where do you come in?" I manage to ask, despite my growing anxiety.

"For the last six months I've had three women working at the resort posing as beauty therapists and masseuses. They tell me *everything* that goes on there. In the beginning I sent them to keep an eye on the competition."

"Frightened he'd take your business?" Camden growls.

"In the beginning, yes. Look, Camden, everyone in this room knows that I'm no saint. Men come to my club to fight without all the rules and regulations you'll find in a normal ring. They do it to earn money, and I host the fights to do the same. It's a business, one my father built, but it's also my home. The men are my family and I protect my family and any threat to their existence. You can discuss the morals of me running such a place another time. What I will say is that I don't have any interest in drugs and the shady deals that surround such criminality. As hard as that might be to believe, it's the truth. My girls were sent in to find out what he was up to. They're loyal, and they keep me well informed. I know a great deal."

"Don't tell me the King is stupid enough to allow a couple beauty therapists into his business meetings?" Camden shakes his head in disbelief.

"Of course, he isn't. But he *is* foolish enough to discount the frivolous wives of his business associates. He hadn't counted on how much they *talk*. They know a lot more about what their shady husbands get up to than they'd ever let on and when they're being plied with champagne and in a relaxed enough state they sing without even being forced too. They might talk in code, but my girls know exactly what they're saying. All that information comes back to me."

Hudson grimaces, glancing over at her. "Grim has found out some worrying information surrounding a new business venture the King and Santiago have recently invested in. In part, that's why we've been forced to step in and deal with the bastard now. We were biding our time, waiting for the right moment to make our move on Santiago. That's been brought forward considerably, in part because of your predicament but also because of this new business venture of theirs."

"What new business venture?" I ask.

"Human trafficking. Specifically, underage girls being sold into the sex trade."

"You've got to be fucking kidding me!" Sonny shoots forward in his seat as though he's been jabbed with a cattle prod.

"I'm afraid not. What's more, we found out that Bobby Rusk, the guy Cal replaced at Oceanside was under the King's payroll solely for that purpose."

"What?!" I exclaim.

"He was sent to Oceanside to sniff out the most vulnerable girls who come through the doors. He was after the ones with no family or at least a family who'd given up on them, knowing that when they served their time they'd need a job, *security*. He would tell them about the Spa resort in Rye, get them an *interview*. Fortunately for all of us, he never got a chance to send anyone there given he was only brought in at the end of last year. There was one girl who almost took the bait, thankfully she smelt a rat and didn't. That's how we found out what he'd been tasked to do. If she'd taken his advice and gone for an interview at the resort she would've become another statistic, just like all the other girls drawn into the sex trade."

"The fuck man?!" Sonny shouts, looking at me nervously.

"We caught it early. Mr Carmichael became suspicious of Bobby at the end of last term, not because he knew about his real role but because he knew you kids were up to something. After he told us about his concerns we took an interest in Bobby and did some digging. Low and behold we found this shit out," Bryce explains, his eyes growing dark with anger. "Believe me when we found out, we all saw red. That son-of-a-bitch Bobby was first on our list to deal with."

"I knew he was a dirty, rotten bastard. What happened to the fucker?" I growl, incensed.

"Disappeared. The arsehole did a runner the moment he realised someone was asking around for information about him," Cal says.

Camden glances at me. He looks pained, troubled. "Shit!"

I turn to look at him. "What Camden?"

"I figured he was on the King's payroll, not because of this sex trafficking shit, but because he covered for me so much. He turned a blind eye every time we snuck out of Oceanside. I thought he was there for that reason. *Motherfucker*."

"We thought as much. We're also more than positive that he was the person informing the King about everything that's been happening at Oceanside," Cal explains.

"No way, that little shit Monk would do anything to get on the right side of his father. Of course he'd talk," Camden says.

"Wrong. His father gave leadership of the HH crew to you, not to Monk. Why? Because he knew Monk wasn't capable of leading them. Monk is a bully, yes, but a leader? No. You're level-headed, clever. Monk is vicious but he's a wild card. The King can't trust him to do what needs to be done without fucking it up. That's why Monk hates you as much as he does."

"Maybe."

"I think Cal has a point," Eastern says. "It would explain why he went after Asia. She challenged you at the party and instead of dealing with her how everyone expected, how I expected, you warned her and let her go. You saw something in Asia that you liked, and he wanted to destroy that as payback for his father favouring you."

"The King never favoured me. The man fucking made my life hell by beating on my mum. Monk fucking new that."

"Precisely. The King knew you'd do anything to protect your mum, what better way to keep you in check by using his kid to taunt you, push you to your limits so you'd react and he'd have the excuse to beat on her and keep you in check," Grim says, meeting Camden's gaze. "The King is as powerful and as untouchable as he is because he uses the people we love as weapons against us. The King despised my growing business and wanted to put me in my place, so he forced my hand that night your sister died. He threatened Beast's life knowing that I'd ask Ford to throw the fight to save him. He knew when that happened everyone in the club would lose their bet and all hell would break loose. He was right. Sapphire got caught in the crossfire, and for that I am sorry." Grim places her hand over her heart and bows her head, then meets Camden's piercing gaze. "I'm here in part to set things straight. When Hudson told me about the predicament you're in, I knew this was my chance to make amends. I want the King's head as much as you do. So, I'm going to help you bring that motherfucker down."

"I still don't see how we're going to do that? Crown needs information, he wanted Camden to talk so he could use him as proof of the King's criminal activities. That isn't going to happen now, and you said that your word isn't enough. So, what do we do?" I ask, chewing on my lip ring.

"You are not going to do anything. *I am*, or at least my girls are. They're going to gather the evidence needed to hang the King and you'll give that to Crown, Asia. Eastern swerves his sentence because you've supplied Crown with what he needs, and Camden is off the hook too."

Ford leans forward, reaching for the bottle of whisky and a glass from the table. He pours himself a generous helping and knocks it back before any of the adults in the room can say anything to stop him. He stands, grabbing the bottle and turns to face us.

"I don't know about you four, but I'm done for tonight. They have a solid plan and we need to get shitfaced. Why waste a perfectly good evening drinking fucking cola like a bunch of ten-year olds?"

"Ford, put the whisky back down," Cal demands.

"What, you gonna tell us we're not old enough to drink?" he scoffs.

"You're not old enough to drink."

"And I don't give a shit. Who's coming?"

Eastern gets up, pulling me with him. "Damn straight. It's been a long fucking few weeks. Are you in Asia?

"Hell, yes," I say.

"Sonny?"

Sonny looks between Ford and his foster parents, then shrugs. "There's no more than a couple of shots each left in that bottle and most of us are almost eighteen anyway. Where's the harm? "

"Fuck sake. Goddamn teenagers," I hear Bryce grumble, but he doesn't try to stop us.

Ford heads towards the door. He stops at the threshold looking over his shoulder at Camden. "You coming?"

"Yeah, I guess I am," he replies.

A look passes between them. A look that isn't filled with hate and distrust and whilst they're a long way from being friends, it's a step in the right direction.

THIRTY-SIX

Instead of heading to the kitchen or the den like I expected, Ford hooks a left and climbs the stairs. We all follow, piling into one of the bedrooms. The room's practically the size of the downstairs kitchen and even though it has a double bed and two singles there's still enough room for a three-seater sofa. I can already see their overnight bags thrown on the beds. I'm guessing this is the room they're staying in tonight, and I realise I've no idea where mine is. Not that I'm particularly bothered right now, sleep is the last thing on my mind.

I'm wired, and I need a fucking drink.

"This place is ridiculous," I say, flopping down onto the sofa. "What kind of people actually live like this?"

"The rich kind. This is their house in the country," Sonny answers, kicking off his shoes and lying down on the double bed. "You should see their home in London, it's off the scale impressive. You can talk to the room and the fucking lights go on and off, the blinds up and down, and whatever music you want plays in these state-of-the-art surround sound speakers."

"Alright for some. Most of us are lucky enough to put food on the table," Camden mutters, perching on one of the single beds.

"They worked hard for it, so why not?" Sonny replies a little defensively.

"I'm not dissing them, just stating a fact. If I manage to get out of this fucking mess, I won't have a home to return too. Maybe prison's the better option after all?"

"No fucking way," I say vehemently. "I refuse to see any of you put away. After this is over, we have a chance to start again. All of us." I almost say *together* but lose my nerve and instead take the bottle Ford offers. The whiskey burns my throat the whole way down but after a second its warmth fills my belly. "What?" I ask, as all four boys stare at me.

"You're doing that thing again…" Sonny mutters.

"What thing?"

"That fierce thing you do…" Eastern adds, grinning.

"I don't know what you mean?"

"Yeah, you do. That fierce, sexy-as-fuck, hot-as-hell thing you do," Camden says, casually, his topaz eyes drilling into me until I'm flushing with heat. Or maybe that's the whiskey?

Sexy-as-fuck, hot-as-hell?

"I have to agree with Cam," Ford says, swiping a hand through his hair. He takes the bottle from me and chugs back another generous mouthful, his grey-green eyes flashing with undeniable lust.

"Pass me the bottle, Ford," Sonny says after a beat. "I need a drink to warm my blue balls."

"No shit," Camden agrees. They all chuckle.

Ford passes the bottle to Sonny, then sits down next to me on the sofa. "You alright with everything?" he asks, a frown forming between his brows. Serious once more.

"I guess. We have to trust them, what other choice do we have?"

"If it's any reassurance at all, Grim won't fuck about. She'll get this done," Ford says, picking up my hand and drawing circles in my palm.

"Yeah, and the Freeds will make sure she does," Sonny chimes in, getting up off the bed and plonking himself on the other side of me. He rests his hand on my bare thigh, the warmth of his palm sending goosebumps flashing over my skin.

"I hope you're right, because if this goes tits up, we're all fucked. The King won't show any mercy…" Camden says, jumping up and grabbing the bottle of whiskey from Eastern who took it from Sonny a moment ago.

"It's going to work. It *has* too," I mutter, staring at the floor, trying to keep my shit together. We all fall silent. It isn't easy for any of us to sit here together in relative peace let alone trust these people to help us. I've spent my whole life looking after number one, and aside from Tracy, Braydon and Eastern, I've never really had anyone to rely on. As much as Tracy has supported me, her priority has always been her own children and I understand that. I do.

The truth is, I *should* feel secure in the knowledge that this will work out, but I only feel uncertain. Yes, these boys are with me now. Yes, they've agreed to put aside their differences to bring down the King, but how long will it really last? Can Eastern keep to his word and give me the space to explore these feelings I have for them all? Will Ford and Camden overcome their past hurt and lay it aside? Will Sonny really stick with us knowing he already has a family unit that will give him so many more opportunities than any of us could ever possibly hope to do? Is it too much to hope we have a future after all is said and done? I don't know. My heart wants to believe there's something special between us, but my head is telling me to be cautious.

Screw that.

Today, I'm following my bruised and battered heart. It's about fucking time.

When I finally raise my head to face them, I know what I need to do in the moment. Words mean very little to me. Actions speak the truth, always. It's time I really see if these boys are willing to put their differences aside and become a unit. I want to know if there really is an *us* and I need to know now.

"We never got to finish our game of truth or dare," I say, getting to my feet, swallowing hard when they give me their full attention. I school my emotions as much as possible but around these guys it's harder for me to hide my true feelings. Over the last few months each one of them has chipped away at that protective wall I've built around my heart but today I need to break through it once and for all. I need to cement this thing we have into something solid, something we can all hold onto. Taking another glug of whiskey for Dutch courage, I straighten my spine and become the strong girl I know I am.

"This is my truth... I want you all." I laugh at that, at how it sounds. But I continue on regardless. "I don't know how this will go and I'm terrified, more scared than I've ever been in my fucking life. But I do know that whatever the future has in store for me, I want… no, I *need* you all to be in it. Watching Louisa with her men has shown me that *this* is possible."

"You've got us," Sonny says, solemnly.

"Always," Eastern adds.

"I'd ride through hell and back to make this work," Ford exclaims sincerely, his fierce gaze moving between me and Camden.

For a beat, the air is thick and heavy as we all wait to see if Camden is with us too. When he stands and moves towards the bedroom door, my heart plummets, but he doesn't leave like I expect him to. Instead, he flicks the lock then turns to face me.

"Words aren't enough, Asia. Empty promises damage us all in the end. I understand that better than anyone. We both do. So, I'm not going to make any promises. What I will do is spend every moment from this point onwards *proving* my loyalty to you."

He walks towards me, pulls me into his arms and kisses me long and hard. When he's finished ravaging my mouth, he presses a gentle kiss against my forehead then turns to Sonny.

"You're actually an alright guy. Thanks for speaking up, thanks for having Asia's back, and for having mine." They grip each other's hand and bump shoulders. Sonny grins, his dimples showing.

"You're a miracle worker, Asia," Sonny mumbles. He's shocked but I'm not. I knew this person was always inside Camden.

Next he approaches Eastern who gives him a wary look. "I'm not gonna lie, I'm envious of you, Eastern. I have been ever since I met Asia at that party. She stood up for you no matter the cost to her and I realised that I wanted that kind of unflinching loyalty, that kind of love. You've had Asia so much longer than any of us, and there's a bit of me that can't help but worry that no matter what I do, you'll always take up more space in her heart because of it. But you know what, I *can* live with that because I get the feeling that owning just a tiny piece of Asia's heart is just as good as owning it all. If she loves you like I know she does, then you've got to be a good guy. *Friends*?" Camden asks, holding his hand out for Eastern to shake.

"Yeah, friends," Eastern agrees, a smile pulling up his lips. He takes Camden's hand and pulls him in for a hug. Inside my poor beating heart squeezes tight. When Camden turns to face Ford, it stops altogether. He holds his gaze for a long time, then finally, breathes out slowly.

"I don't hate you, Ford. I did for a very long fucking time because it was easier to blame you about Sapphire's death than it was taking responsibility in the part I had to play. I was there at the club with her. At any point during that night I could have made her leave, but I didn't. I. Fucking. Didn't. I'm owning that shit now. Maybe one day we'll get back to how we were, maybe we won't, but like you I care about Asia and whatever shit we have between us will be put aside for her. From this point onwards we're a team. Shake on it?"

Ford takes his hand. "You got it, bro," he says.

"Well, shit! If that ain't worth celebrating, I don't know what is?" Sonny exclaims, grabbing the whiskey bottle from me and downing another mouthful. He offers it back to me, but I shake my head. Camden grabs it from him and finishes it off with a loud smack of his lips.

"So, what now?" Eastern asks, shifting on his feet. He's giving me that look I recognise, the kind of look that makes me want to run knowing he's going to catch me.

But I don't run. Instead, I plant my hands firmly on my hips and grin mischievously.

Sonny tips his head to the side and narrows his eyes at me. "Why do you look like you've got something wicked planned?"

I snatch the empty whiskey bottle from Camden and bite down on my lower lip. "It's been a while since I've played spin the bottle… you in?" I ask them all.

THIRTY-SEVEN

"How's this gonna work? I ain't kissing none of these arseholes," Camden remarks, his arms crossed across his chest.

"What, are you afraid you might like it?" Sonny grins mercilessly.

"Shut the fuck up, dude. That's the second time you've propositioned me."

Sonny roars with laughter, high-fiving Eastern's hand. "Jesus, Camden. Lighten the fuck up!"

I roll my eyes. "Sonny, stop winding Camden up and listen."

"Okay, shutting the fuck up and listening."

Like the rest of the boys, Sonny watches me with interest. Taking the bottle, I move to the centre of the room, kick off my shoes and sit down on the wooden floor. "Sit in a circle around me. I'm the one spinning the bottle, so you don't have to worry about kissing one another. Though if the whim takes you, I won't be upset about it." I try hard not to giggle when I see the look on their faces. Though Sonny doesn't seem the least bit bothered, which makes me grin stupidly. I may or may not have a slight thing for two guys snogging. Just saying.

"Think of this as a social experiment. If this is going to work, then you all need to stop getting all caveman and shit and accept each other as my…"

"Boyfriends?" Sonny offers helpfully, dropping down opposite me.

"I… *guess*?"

Sonny grins, flashing me his best dimpled smile. "I'm down with that."

"I never thought I'd hear you say the words." Eastern says, sitting to my left, blatantly undressing me with his eyes.

"Ford, Camden?" I ask, biting on my lip ring.

Camden settles behind me, so I have to twist around to face him.

"I'm in. I'm sick of the fake arse bitches. I want the real deal. I *want* you…"

My gaze flits to Camden's crotch and the way he's adjusting his dick to get comfortable, a rueful smile on his face. The fact we're about to play a game that could get out of control fast has heat gathering between my thighs. "Ford?" I catch his gaze and see the answer in his eyes before he even opens his mouth to speak.

"I don't need any labels to know you're mine. You got me, however the fuck you want me."

"That's settled then," I respond, a little awkwardly. "But don't blame me if I'm a shit girlfriend. I've never done this with one person before, let alone four."

"And I've done it with too many girls to count and I already know you'll be better than all of them," Camden says, perusing me with his gaze. I'm pretty sure he's talking about fucking and not relationships.

Feeling suddenly very hot, I pull off my hoodie and fling it onto the bed. Underneath I'm wearing a bright yellow singlet vest top and a pink bra. The material of the vest top is thin, and I know my lacey bra is showing clearly beneath it.

"Fuck me, Asia," Sonny groans, dragging his eyes up from my breasts to my face.

I bite down on a laugh. This is going to be so much fun. Kneeling, I grab the bottle and give it a spin. After a few agonisingly long seconds, the bottle finally comes to a halt, pointing directly at Ford. My heart stutters in my chest.

"I guess you're up first?" I say.

"Guess so," he responds, tipping his head as he regards me. Heat spreads outwards from my belly at the lust and longing in his gaze. "But I think we need to up the ante a little." He grins, giving me a taste of his beautiful, panty melting smile. God, that smile makes me want to do wicked, wicked things. I swallow hard.

"What are you suggesting?"

He reaches behind his back, and in half a second has pulled off his top, leaving his chest bare. "Your turn," he challenges.

I think he expects me to back down. I won't, but not before I get what I want. Two can play that game. "I'll remove this top, if the rest of you take off yours too."

"Fuck, yeah," Sonny exclaims, ripping his top off and chucking it over his shoulder, showing me his beautiful eagle tattoo. Eastern and Camden follow suit, and I have to bite down on the inside of my cheek to stop myself from giggling like a girl who's never seen a man's naked chest before. But, shit… these guys. Correction. *My* guys are H.O.T.

Smiling seductively, I reach for the hem of my tank top, and lift it over my head leaving me in just my denim skirt, bra, and knee-high socks. A round of groans fill the air, making my nipples peak and my pussy clench.

"Let's have that kiss then, Asia," Ford mutters, his tongue wetting his lips as I crawl towards him on my hands and knees, eliciting another round of groans. Eastern must be getting an eyeful given I'm wearing a thong and my skirt has ridden up around my arse. Honestly, I don't know what has possessed me to be so seductive, possibly the whiskey, or maybe it's just my need to scratch that itch that's been bugging me for weeks now. Either way, I'm going to get these boys to worship Queen Clit tonight, one way or the other. Pink will be proud. I grab hold of Ford's shoulders and slide my legs around his waist. When my skirt makes it difficult for me to get closer, I yank up the hem letting it bunch up around my hips. Camden makes a familiar growling noise as the temperature in the room goes up about fifty degrees.

"Hey," Ford says, his voice dark, dangerous as he grabs my arse, forcing my crotch against his. My damp knickers meet the hard granite of his cock and sensation zings from my clit up my spine. I can't help myself. I rock my damp core against his dick. Once, twice, three times, loving the friction.

"*Asia*. Don't, I might lose control," he grinds out.

I lean forward and press my mouth against his ear. "So, lose it."

In that moment, the usually calm, clear headed Ford does exactly that.

One minute I'm straddling him, the next I'm pinned beneath his firm, muscular body like all those weeks ago on the field. Except this time, I'm practically naked and his tongue is unapologetically plundering my mouth. His kiss is hot as fuck. So hot, that I find myself losing all my inhibitions and widening my legs, wrapping my calves around his arse. He kisses me with deep strokes of his tongue, cupping my head and tangling his fingers in my hair as he rides against me, the soft material of his jogging pants providing just the perfect amount of friction. Ford kisses me to prove a point; that he turns me the fuck on. And he does. He really, *really* does.

I reach down, my fingers seeking out the waistband of his joggers as I lose all sense of my own self-control. Above the frantic beating of my heart, and the rushing pulse of blood in my ear, I hear the others groan. But when my fingers stroke against the tip of his velvety cock, feeling the warmth of pre cum beading there, he rears back, pulling me up with him.

"Believe me I want to… I really, *really* want to but the first time I fuck you it won't be with anyone watching. That pleasure will solely be mine."

Queen Clit nearly calls for his head.

"Holy Jesus, fuck," Sonny exclaims, swiping a hand through his hair. "Please, God, let me be next," he says, putting his palms together in a prayer as I crawl back into the centre of the circle.

Everyone laughs, relieving some of the tension.

Pulling my skirt back over my hips, I spin the bottle for the second time. It stops equal distance between Eastern and Camden. I tap my finger on my chin, looking between them both. "So, who's it to be?"

"Well, this arsehole here has had you his whole damn life. I got to make up time. Come here, bae," Camden says, his voice low, sexy.

Eastern rolls his eyes, then grins wickedly. "Go for it mate, the best things come to those who wait."

Camden laughs softly, drawing my attention back to him. I bite on my lip and he groans again, his pupils enlarging with lust. Crawling forward I give Sonny the same view of my arse that Eastern had a moment before and his groan has me laughing as I climb into Camden's lap, straddling him the same way as I did Ford. Camden regards me, his topaz depths swirling with the promises he refused to say out loud.

"You've got me in chains," he grinds out, pulling me closer and kissing me deep and hard. His tongue sweeps into my mouth, his hands circling my back. One dips low, his fingers searching beneath the waistband of my skirt clutching my arse. The other finds it way around the front of my body, cupping my breast gently, his thumb circling my nipple. I grip hold of him, my nails digging into his wide shoulders. I hold on tight and let him guide me knowing he'll keep me above water.

Knowing he won't let me drown. We kiss long and hard, neither one of us coming up for air, until eventually, reluctantly, Camden pulls back.

"Fuck, Asia. If I don't stop now, I won't let the rest of these motherfuckers get their turn."

I laugh softly, giving him one last gentle kiss, then untangle myself from his hold.

"Is it getting hot in here?" Sonny complains, wafting his hand in front of his face as I return to the centre of the circle on wobbly legs.

"It's about to get hotter," Eastern mutters as I trail my finger down the neck of the bottle. I've never felt more adored or more lusted after. It's a powerful feeling, knowing all four of these guys want me as much as I want them. Without hesitation, I spin the bottle for a third time.

It points to Sonny.

"At last!" he exclaims, locking his gaze with mine, a dirty grin on his face.

Without waiting for an invitation, I climb into his lap, not expecting the violence of his kiss. It's brutal, filled with passion and abandonment that has me gasping. He kisses me to wipe away the two kisses I've already received. He kisses me with intent, marking me. Our teeth clash, as his fingers find my hair and pull sharply. My scalp prickles, my body shudders as he reaches between my legs and finds my soaking wet panties.

"You're so fucking wet," he growls.

All I can do is groan in response, needing his touch, needing to find release.

"Asia, I can't fucking take this," Eastern mutters from behind us, and if weren't for the obvious heat and heady lust in his voice I would've assumed he couldn't stand me seeing me in someone else's arms. This time I know it isn't jealousy he feels but desire. Deep, hot, bone melting desire. I know, because I feel it too.

Sonny doesn't stop, his finger slides the thin material of my panties aside as he finds the spot I've wanted him to touch for months now. His thumb circles my clit with just the right amount of pressure, and I lose it. Tipping back my head, I let out a deep, toe-curling moan.

I don't care that Ford, Camden and Eastern look on. I don't care that I'm letting all my inhibitions go. I need release. I need to feel adored. I need to forget the shit we're in and just *feel.*

And boy does Sonny make me feel.

His lips score a trail of heat down my throat as he gently guides me back. Not even a broken arm can prevent him from giving me pleasure as his mouth closes over my lace covered nipple. The cry I let out must do something to Eastern because before I know what's happening he's cupping my head and kissing me like a drowning man. He groans into my mouth and I hear Sonny's chuckle as he allows Eastern to lay me on the floor. Only pulling back a moment so I can get comfortable.

"So, you're the one who's up for a threesome, yeah?" Sonny laughs before he pulls my breast free from its lace confines and leans over taking my nipple between his teeth gently.

Eastern grins. "Whatever Asia wants, I want."

Sonny sucks my breast, pulling and tugging on the tender flesh, his hand between my legs, his fingers drawing in and out of me at a rhythm that has me writhing beneath them. Eastern fucks my mouth with his tongue making sure I'm reminded of the way it felt to be in his arms that night in Mr Patel's shop. Between them I'm brought to the edge of nirvana, ready to dive right into these overwhelming feelings, ready to let the hell go. I'm vaguely aware of Ford and Camden shifting closer, neither willing to sit back and watch anymore.

Two boys become three, then four as Camden and Ford settle around me.

My boys. *Mine.*

Hands are everywhere, moving over bare flesh. I reach out and touch, desperately needing to find some purchase, to give back what I'm feeling. To show them I want this, I need this as much as they do. My fingers find the smooth plain of Eastern's pecs, only to be replaced with Ford's rippling stomach.

It's chaotic, and blissful and overwhelming in a really, really good way.

I'm the eye of the storm, the centre of everything. And as they kiss and lick, suck and touch, knead and stroke, we become more than separate parts, we become a unit. We become one.

"Bae, I'm so fucking hot for you," Camden's guttural voice rasps. I reach for him blindly through the fog of my lust until his lips replace Eastern's and his tongue plunders my mouth.

I feel my skirt being pushed upwards and my knickers pulled down whilst another warm mouth covers my aching core, a firm tongue sliding up and down my slit. My back arches off the ground, as my eyes roll back in my head.

"Oh-oh," I cry out as that same warm mouth latches onto my pussy and sucks hard.

"You taste so sweet, Asia."

It's Ford. Ford with his hot mouth against my aching, wet pussy. His teeth graze against my clit, ravaging me as though I am an opponent in the ring. But he's not here to win a fight, he's here to make me see stars. They begin to sparkle at the edge of my consciousness, building, growing brighter every second. And just when I think I can't take anymore because there's too much feeling and I might just break apart with the intensity of it all, two other mouths find my nipples and encourage them into hard points. Eastern and Sonny tease me with their expert tongues, giving me so much pleasure. Too much. Not enough. I twine my fingers in their hair, pulling them closer, riding the impending wave, wanting more.

More, more, more.

I'm greedy, needy. So fucking needy. And I don't care. I own my desires, my wants, and I *want* this. I don't care what the world might think. Screw everyone who'd frown upon what we're doing. Screw them. I want this. Now, tomorrow, for the rest of my life.

My breathless moans burst into the air around us, making it thick and pulsating. Their answering groans only heighten the intensity.

"Bae, we got you," Camden growls, answering my silent pleas. Understanding what I can't express with words. He hauls me upwards slightly and unclasps my bra with skillful fingers. Eastern and Sonny take a strap each and haul the thin piece of material from my body. Somewhere deep inside, my head is telling me to slow down. But my heart and Queen Clit flip the finger.

I trust these boys.

I trust them with my body and my heart. *With my life.*

Because this isn't about sex, not really. This is about finding a place with each other. This is about five people needing to forget for a moment, needing to cement this bond we share. This is about the possibility of a future forged in friendship and love. This is about a place we could someday call home. And throughout it all, not one of them removes the rest of their clothes. This is about my pleasure, not theirs. I'm their focus. Me.

And I feel like a fucking Queen.

Their lips find tender, swollen flesh.

Their hands grasp and tug, smooth and soothe. They worship.

Tongues flick and taste every inch of my hot skin until I'm a quivering hot mess beneath them. Until I'm nothing but a swirling mass of feeling. Inside, those walls I built are cracking, falling, crumbling under their ministrations and all thoughts of the danger we're in go out of my head as I let these boys have their wicked way with me. It feels right. More right than anything has before. This is four boys adoring one girl, all with a single-minded determination to mark me as theirs.

And I am.

I belong to them all.

I belong to Eastern; the boy who held my hand through every sadness I ever bore witness too. The boy who first stole my heart and who'll guard it with his forever more.

I belong to Sonny; the dimpled, happy-go-lucky thief with a heart of gold and a dirty, sinful mouth that sets me on fire.

I belong to Ford; the brooding, broken, mysterious fighter who'd rage against the world for the ones he cares about, for *me*. Who makes me see stars.

I belong to Camden; the gang leader, the talented artist, the kid who's grown into a man under the worst possible circumstances and still has room in his heart to trust. The man who kisses with an intensity that matches my own.

In this moment, four boys come together to give me the best damn orgasm of my entire existence, and as I fall off the precipice, entangled within their arms I know one thing for certain…

I am *theirs*, and they are *mine*.

THIRTY-EIGHT

Early the next morning, a frantic knock on our bedroom door has me sitting up sharply. It takes me a moment to slide out between Eastern and Sonny, the memory of last night making my cheeks flush with heat. I'm not sure who I became, but I like her. I plan on becoming her again very soon.

"Who's that fucking banging on the door?" Ford groans, grasping his head.

It must be pounding given we carried on drinking late into the night after our little thief Sonny stole another bottle of whiskey from the kitchen. I know the alcohol was needed, mainly because the guys were all so wound up from our moment together. Not one of them made me feel like I needed to return the favour, and that told me all I needed to know about them. Yes, they might be horny teenagers, but every single one has the heart and soul of a man. A man who's okay to wait until I'm ready to take that next step with each of them. And boy am I ready.

Eastern pops an eye open, his hair ruffled with sleep. "What goddamn time is it?" he grumbles, then groans as Sonny rolls over and smacks him in the mouth with his arm.

"Get off me, dickwad," he jibes, but grins when Sonny lifts his head and blows him a kiss.

"Sorry, arsehole."

When the banging gets more insistent, Camden jerks awake. The duvet falls from his chest giving me the perfect view of his muscular torso and lion tattoo.

"Who do I need to punch," he snarls, clearly not a morning person.

My own head is pounding too. I should've stopped after the third shot, of course I didn't.

"This better be a bloody emergency!" I call out, hauling myself to my feet, quickly pulling on my jeans. I slept in my t-shirt and knickers and even though both boys had a hard on all night, they were respectful and didn't try to initiate sex, keeping their boxer shorts on. I'm not sure I can say the same for Camden and Ford, however. They slept in the single beds, so it wasn't as if they needed to protect their junk.

The banging gets more insistent, and I grumble under my breath, yanking the door open just as I'm repeating my grumble that this is in fact an emergency. Half a second later, I wish I could take that statement back because standing before me is Kate, her face a swollen mess of tears.

"Kate! What the fuck are you doing here?"

The second the guys see who's at the door and the state she's in, they're up and out of bed grabbing their clothes. Behind Kate is Frank, one of the ex-marines Cal left in charge at Oceanside, and Hudson. I can hear a commotion downstairs, and the distinct sound of Mr Carmichael's voice.

"What the fuck is going on?" I ask, as she falls into my arms, sobbing.

I look between Frank and Hudson who for some fucking reason aren't speaking. Hudson clears his throat when Cal comes sprinting up the stairs and rushes into our room.

"Get dressed. NOW!" he barks out.

"Woah! Calm the fuck down, man! We *are* getting dressed," Sonny shouts, disoriented from lack of sleep and a hangover. He stumbles, pulling on his clothes.

Kate grips hold of me, crying in earnest now. She's mumbling something that I can't make out, but the fact she's here isn't good.

"Kate, tell me what's happened!" I grip her shoulders, pushing her back. Fear makes me harsh.

But she can't respond as her knees suddenly give way, heart-wrenching sobs wracking her body. Ford is at my side immediately swooping her up into his arms. He carries her to the sofa and sits with her, hauling her into his side. He gives me a look that shatters my heart.

Something is terribly, terribly wrong.

"Someone better tell us what the fuck is going on!" Camden growls, stepping up beside me and wrapping his arm around my waist. I lean into his hold, gripping him tightly needing to find something steady, someone solid to anchor myself to because I know something life-altering is coming. I see it in the way Hudson looks at me as he steps into the room, a heavy sigh leaving his lips.

"This is for you, Asia," he says gently, holding out a folded piece of paper. I take it from him with shaking fingers.

"What's this?"

"I'm so sorry. This isn't something I could've predicted. We had no idea."

Eastern is beside me in a second. "Sorry for *what*?" he snaps.

"Is it Tracy? Braydon?" I ask, my hands shaking as awful thoughts rush through my head.

"No, they're safe," Hudson reassures me, fiercely.

"Then what the fuck is it? Why is Kate here? Is that Mr

Carmichael's voice I can hear downstairs?" Sonny asks, the questions he fires at Hudson and Cal are sharp and relentless.

"He's here because there was an incident at school this morning," Frank says, solemnly.

"What fucking incident?!" I scream this time, because it suddenly dawns on me that there's one very important person missing...

Pink.

"Where is she?" I snap. "Where the fuck is Pink?"

"She's gone, Asia. She's fucking gone!" Kate wails, verging on hysterical.

"Gone?! What do you mean, gone?" My knees sag, and this time it's Eastern who holds me up because Camden has released me to grab hold of Frank's shirt.

"Speak right fucking now!" he roars into his face, not giving a shit that this man is twice his size and could probably knock him out with one well-placed punch.

"Kate raised the alarm this morning when she went to check in on Pink. She wasn't in her room, but that note was..." he says, pointing to the slip of paper in my hand.

"What do you mean? She ran away?" Sonny asks, there's hope in voice, but we all know that isn't what Frank's insinuating. Deep down, so does Sonny.

"No. She was taken..."

"*Taken*? What do you fucking mean, taken?" I scream, repeating myself. If I had any strength left I'd scratch Frank's eyes out for being so fucking vague.

"Pink was kidnapped," he explains, guilt making him look away when I lock eyes with his. He feels responsible. He should. Frank's an ex-marine for fuck sake. How can she be taken?

"Taken by who?" Camden asks for me when I can't form the words.

"By your brother, Asia," he responds, looking directly at me.

"What?! Sebastian and George are just kids. What the fuck are you talking about?" I cry out, my head shaking furiously.

"Not them. You've got an older brother," Hudson explains, pointing at the note crumpled in my fist.

The room falls silent, or perhaps I've suddenly lost the ability to hear. My attention zeros in on the note clasped tightly in my shaking hands. Unfolding it, I read…

ASIA,

If you want to see Pink alive again you better do what Daddy Dearest says.

Welcome to the fam, little sister.

Monk.

TO BE CONTINUED IN *FAMILY*, the final book in the Academy of Misfits grab it here

AUTHOR NOTE

Thank you for reading *Reject* and sticking with Asia and her bad boys of Oceanside Academy! This story has been one hell of a journey and I'll be truthful, these characters totally lived up to their delinquent ways! Many a late night was had trying to get Asia and her boys in hand. Honestly, all their voices were so loud it was tricky to give them the time they each so desperately wanted. I hope, however, I've done their story justice!

I must admit, I had so much fun bringing in Cal, Louisa and the Freed brothers into this story. Those characters were my first contemporary loves and I haven't quite yet gotten over them not being in my life every day. I've loved weaving them into this story, and they will appear more in the final book *Family*.

If you've not read the Brothers Freed trilogy you might want to check it out here.

And now for the thanks...

This book wouldn't have happened if it weren't for the support of some amazing people. Special thanks to Courtney, my incredible PA, alpha reader, organiser, shoulder to cry on and most of all, friend. NONE of this would be possible without your support and belief in me. I count my lucky stars every day that you stalked me, lol! I adore you woman!

Thanks to Lisa and Gina who are my amazing BETA readers who crack me up with their comments and tell me that I'm doing an okay job at this authoring lark! You keep me going ladies, thank you!

Huge thanks to Janet who isn't afraid to tell me where I'm going wrong (and she's always right by the way) and is my eagle-eyed proofreader. You push me to be a better writer, and for that I'm eternally grateful!

To my close author buddies, Skye, Ari, Laura, and Ivy. I love you all. Thanks for being there when I've lost my nerve or am so goddamn exhausted that I can't write another word. You keep me going. Our convos bring me up when I feel down. Make me believe I can do this, even when it's hard. Thank you for all the virtual shoulders to cry on!

To my family, for all the hours I've not been the best mum, the best daughter or wife because I'm trying to be the best writer I can be. To you, I owe the most. All I do, *all* of it is for you.

And finally, to my readers, to the members of the Hive. Without you, I wouldn't even be sitting here writing this. You've made my dreams come true. From the bottom of my heart, thank you for reading these words of mine.

Much love, Bea xxx

ABOUT BEA PAIGE

Bea Paige lives a very secretive life in London... She likes red wine and Haribo sweets (preferably together) and occasionally swings around poles when the mood takes her.

Bea loves to write about love and all the different facets of such a powerful emotion. When she's not writing about love and passion, you'll find her reading about it and ugly crying.

Bea is always writing, and new ideas seem to appear at the most unlikely time, like in the shower or when driving her car.

She has lots more books planned,
so be sure to subscribe to her newsletter:
beapaige.co.uk/newsletter-sign-up

Check Be a out on TikTok:
https://www.tiktok.com/@beapaigeauthor

facebook.com/BeaPaigeAuthor
instagram.com/beapaigeauthor
pinterest.com/beapaigeauthor
bookbub.com/authors/bea-paige

ALSO BY BEA PAIGE

Their Obsession Duet

The Dancer and The Masks

The Masks and The Dancer

Academy of Stardom

(academy reverse harem romance)

#1 Freestyle

#2 Lyrical

#3 Breakers

#4 Finale

Academy of Misfits

(academy reverse harem romance)

#1 Delinquent

#2 Reject

#3 Family

Finding Their Muse

(dark contemporary romance / reverse harem)

#1 Steps

#2 Strokes

#3 Strings

#4 Symphony

#5 Finding Their Muse boxset

The Brothers Freed Series

(contemporary romance / reverse harem)

#1 Avalanche of Desire

#2 Storm of Seduction

#3 Dawn of Love

#4 Brothers Freed Boxset

Contemporary Standalones

Beyond the Horizon

The Infernal Descent trilogy

(co-written with Skye MacKinnon)

#1 Hell's Calling

#2 Hell's Weeping

#3 Hell's Burning

#4 Infernal Descent boxset

Printed in Great Britain
by Amazon

80811999R00197